Hold on to Your Heart

Malika Nekhla

This is a work of fiction. Names, characters, places, and incidents either are the product of the author's imagination or are used fictitiously. Any resemblance to actual persons, living or dead, events, or locales is entirely coincidental.

Copyright © 2025 by Malika Nekhla

All rights reserved. No part of this book may be reproduced or used in any manner without written permission of the copyright owner except for the use of quotations in a book review.
For more information www.malikanekhla.com.

First paperback edition May 2025

Book cover design by Malika Nekhla
ISBN 978-9-0904-0036-5 (paperback)

For my mother. For everything.

And for the fools who dream. Never give up.

1

Midlife will be easier than your twenties, they said. It'll be fun, they said.

Bloody liars, Olivia thinks as she faces the pastel green door of her parents' West-London Victorian terrace, heart pounding in her throat. She puts down the cardboard box she's carried from the rental car and rings the bell while letting herself in with her key, announcing herself as per her mother's instructions.

'Mum? Dad?' Her voice echoes in the black-and-white tiled hallway. But instead of waiting for an answer, she uses the box as a doorstop and returns to the car to get the rest. Before she reaches it, her mother's low voice startles her. 'What's in the box?'

When Olivia turns, her mum is standing in the doorway with a frown so deep you'd think she was Brad Pitt at the end of *Seven*. And she doesn't even know yet what Olivia is about to tell her. This should be fun. Olivia's waited as long as possible to break the news, and judging by her mother's posture and expression, she concludes it was the right decision. No need to be around disgruntled parents longer than ten days, is there?

'I'll explain in a minute.' Olivia sags under the weight of a stack of photography books. 'Can you give me a hand?'

With a reluctant sigh, her mother slips her feet into a pair of slippers. 'Are you moving?'

Nobody ever accused the woman of being dumb. Olivia ignores the question and juts her chin in the direction of a box of pictures.

'You're not doing anything stupid, are you?'

As she suppresses an eye-roll, Olivia wonders if she can just get in the car and drive off, avoid the inevitably agonising confrontation she's barrelling towards. Would that be so bad?

But then she remembers who she is, and instead, takes the last blue IKEA bag from the car, following her mother inside. 'Where's Dad?'

'Upstairs. On a call.'

'A work call?'

'Yes, Olivia, a work call.' The look she gets from her mother is one she'd expected to see at some point today, but not nearly this early on. Off to a swell start.

Olivia sets down the bag, and heads for the kitchen while pondering whether to wait for her dad and tell them both simultaneously, or focus on her mum and rely on her to deliver the blow. If only Graham were here. Not that her parents like him, but they do hold back when he's there. He's like Captain America's shield, but for passive-aggressive attacks instead of actual ones. Unfortunately, Graham is at the paper, trying to meet his final deadlines, leaving her unshielded today.

With arms folded across her chest, her mother stands by the kitchen island, the porcelain surface gleaming with cleanliness. 'Well?'

'Tea?' Olivia asks. Without waiting for her mother's answer, she flicks the switch on the kettle, buying herself a few more seconds. From the cupboard she takes her favourite mug – the one her sister gave her for her tenth birthday, with a large handle and a faded picture of Take That, the rim chipped from nearly three decades of usage. The fact her mother has kept it all these years warms her heart a little. Perhaps there's a sentimental bone in the woman's body after all? Encouraged by this, Olivia takes a deep breath. 'Graham and I are moving to Vancouver.'

The kettle clicks and then there's nothing but silence. Very loud silence.

'We're starting a non-profit for underprivileged teens to get into the arts.'

The blank stare her mother gives her could be one of confusion or bewilderment. Olivia isn't sure. It's probably both.

'How on earth are you going to afford that?'

Ah. Money. Her mum's go-to concern. For someone who has so much of it, she sure spends a lot of time thinking about not having it. Any other mother would be sad to see their child move across the world, but hers is thinking of money.

'We'll both still be working our current jobs.'

This elicits a scoff. Olivia's job has always been a joke to her. After all, photography is a hobby, not a profession.

'When are you going to stop playing around, Olivia? You're thirty-eight and Graham's what, forty-four?'

'Forty-two.'

Olivia and Graham have been together for over five years. Five birthday parties have gone by, at which point her mother could've easily remembered his age. But let's be honest. She's never cared for Graham and his less-than-conventional ideas. He's not someone who abides by societal rules and expectations. Perhaps it's because he was raised by a single mother, perhaps it's his Canadian nature. Either way, her mother doesn't care for his rule-averse attitude. She was probably hoping the boxes meant they'd split up and Olivia needed to move home again for a while. Chills run down her spine at the thought of it.

'When are you two going to get married? Have children? Buy a house? Time is running out, Olivia.'

Olivia turns all her focus to lifting the teabag from the mug and pouring the milk in slowly. She's learned to wait before she says anything she'll regret. Especially around her mother. The impulse to let the child inside her take over and shout whatever it wants is strong, though.

'We've been over this. Graham and I don't want that kind of life.'

'Oh, please. You don't know what you want. That's him and you're just going along with it. You always were easily influenced.'

Olivia's cheeks flush. There are very few people in the world who can make her feel as small as her mother does, who can make her question everything about herself even when she thinks she's doing well.

'Can we store some boxes here for a while? We'll have a moving company come and pick them up in a few weeks once we've settled over there.'

Her mother's eyebrows shoot up. 'I'm sorry, when are you leaving?'

'In ten days.'

'Ten days.' She repeats it, not as a question but a confirmation to herself that she has not misheard her daughter. A slow nod is followed by a short, humourless laugh. 'Honestly, you and your sister. I don't know what we did to deserve this.' Behind the bitterness, her eyes are sad, her usual proud posture slightly slumped in defeat, as though every decision Olivia and Anna have ever made is a reflection of her failed parenting.

'Mum…' Olivia starts, but her mother is already halfway out the door, heading for the stairs. The reaction triggers Olivia's dormant guilt for not being the daughter her parents want her to be. It's taken her the better part of her adult life to figure out who she is and what she wants, and most times she still isn't certain. Like her mother, she once thought she'd have children of her own, a house, a husband. But were those her own desires? Or just what she thought her life was supposed to look like?

Olivia goes after her mother, ready to apologise for not living up to her expectations, but on the last step before she disappears out of sight, her mother pauses and faces her again. 'At least your sister gave me a grandchild.'

Game. Set. Match.

As soon as Olivia's in the car, she types out a message to Graham.

How many years do you think I'll get for matricide?

Unsure whether to laugh or cry, she leans her head against the backrest, waiting for Graham's answer. She closes her eyes, tears burning behind her eyelids.

Is she making a huge mistake? Should she be thinking about a secure future instead of taking this risk? Her phone buzzes before she can spiral any further.

G: Depends. I'm assuming it was self-defence?
O: Of course.
G: I'll ask my buddy at court reporting and I'll get back to you.
O: Will you visit me in prison?
G: I'll get a back tattoo and have myself committed to help break you out.
O: You might want to consider a sex change then.
G: Anything for you.

Olivia smiles, feeling some of the doubt her mother instilled in her fade. There are many things in life she's unsure about, but Graham is not on that list.

Before she drives off, Olivia clicks her phone into the wireless set and rings the one person who understands exactly what she just went through.

'It's me,' she says, her voice a little shaky.

'What's wrong?' Anna immediately picks up on her little sister's distress.

'I told Mum about Canada.'

'Oh, fuck. Just now?'

'Yeah.'

'I'm assuming it went really well?'

Olivia leans her head on the steering wheel. 'If by really well you mean, did she end the conversation with *at least your sister gave me a grandchild*, then yes, it went fabulously.'

'She didn't!' Anna shouts in surprise. 'I came out on top?!'
'Believe it or not.'

An evil laugh travels through the phone. 'I'm really sorry for you, but wow, I should ring her now and ask for a favour. It might work. I've never been the good daughter.'

'We're both on the blacklist. Don't kid yourself.' Putting the keys in the ignition, Olivia starts the car, ready to get away from there.

'Are you driving?'

'Yeah, we had a few things we wanted to store at Mum and Dad's, so I rented a car for the day. I'm still in front of the house.'

'What did Dad say?'

'He was on a call. I didn't stick around in case they'd set up a firing squad.'

'So you'll talk to him about it at the party?'

Olivia's heart drops into her stomach. Their dad is celebrating his seventieth birthday next Friday and with all the anxiety coursing through her, she'd forgotten all about it. 'Fuck!'

'Don't worry. You won't be alone then. You'll have Graham and me – and Charlie, the world's greatest grandchild. He'll distract Mum and Dad for you.'

'Get him prepped. Tell him he owes me from the million times I changed his nappy.'

'Yes, I'm sure that will motivate a sixteen-year-old.'

Olivia gives a short laugh and sets off in the direction of the nearest Hertz facility. Along the way they chat about what Charlie's up to during the summer – gaming – who Anna is dating – some IT guy who came to fix her modem recently – and Olivia and Graham's upcoming move.

'Do you think Mum's right?' Olivia asks, turning onto the busiest road in the history of time and cursing her temporary need for a car in London.

'What do you mean? Of course not.'

'But shouldn't I have my shit together by now? What if I get no more assignments? I've been lucky so far, but she's right, photography is not a proper job. I don't have a steady income. What if we're still renting ten years from now and something happens and people don't like my photos anymore – how will we pay the bills?'

'Olivia, calm down. Don't let her get into your head like this again. First of all, there's no such thing as having your shit together. Nobody knows what that means. And secondly, you didn't get lucky. You're a fucking great photographer, and aside from that, you have a billion other talents. Don't make me pull you back to Ireland to make you realise that again. Charlie's too old for a nanny now, and I'm too young for a carer.'

Images of that six-month sabbatical flash before Olivia's eyes. Even though she'd been reluctant to go and help her sister out, her life changed during that spring and summer in 2009. There's an Olivia before Ireland, and one after. And frankly, she prefers the one after. Her sister did that for her. And so perhaps taking her word for it might not be the worst idea.

'I just worry,' she adds.

'I know. But if worst comes to worst, you can always move in with us, okay?'

Olivia smiles, eased by her sister's promise. 'Thanks, Anna.'

'So? What's the plan for the rest of the day?'

'Graham's at work, so I'm gonna drop the car off and then head to the bookshop. I think I've earned a book after a morning like this.'

'You always think that.'

'I always deserve it though.'

'I won't argue with that. I got the new David Nicholls just because I did the washing up when the dishwasher broke down.'

At the mention of Olivia's favourite author, she pounds the steering wheel in exhilaration. 'Ooooh I finished it yesterday! I love Marnie!'

'Me too! We'll chat about it at the party. I'll see you then, yeah?'

'Alright, bye, Anna.'

'Bye, Livvie.'

When she arrives at her favourite bookshop, *Pages & Leaves*, Olivia finds a chalkboard outside announcing a signing at three p.m. and immediately excitement bubbles up. She loves meeting authors and if Sam and Suze, the owners, invited them, they must be good. One day, about ten years ago, she stumbled upon the place as she was avoiding tourists on Camden Road. It's small, situated in the middle of a narrow alley, with a café next door to it. From the outside it looks like two separate places, but if you walk to the back of the bookshop, the two merge into one, opening everything up; glass windows bring the leaves and trees from the adjacent park into it, as though the books grow directly from the branches. The two sisters quickly became Olivia's friends and she trusts their taste blindly.

Suze is not behind the till when she enters the shop, but at the back a handful of people are seated, facing the café. Olivia can hear Sam's voice addressing them. 'Hi everyone, and thank you all for coming. We have a bit of a surprise for you: not only will there be a book signing today, but we've been able to persuade the author to do a short reading followed by a Q&A. Not an easy feat, mind you.' She laughs and the audience faithfully joins in.

'Thank you for doing this,' Sam says to the author. Olivia can't see them yet from where she's standing, but assumes they have set up a small stage-like area in the café as they usually do. Eager to get a spot, she heads for the chairs in the back where Suze is waving her over.

'Yeah, no worries. Thanks for having me.' The author's voice is deep and grainy and so horribly familiar Olivia's chest compresses at the sound of it, robbing her of breath. She freezes. It can't be. She's imagining things. It's just the stress of the move and her mother that are getting to her.

Get a grip, Olivia.

She's about to round the corner so she can see the stage when Sam speaks again: 'We're absolutely delighted, Eamonn. Suze and I read the book and have been …'

Eamonn. The mention of his name throws her off balance. Everything Sam says next is muted by the rush of blood in her ears. Olivia's world spins and spins and spins until she's so dizzy she has to steady herself by leaning on a stack of books on the table in front of her.

It can't be. *Please, don't let it be.*

With sweaty palms and a dramatically high heart rate, she looks around for a copy of the book to dispel her fears, only to realise there's a stack of them under her palm. Her eyes land on the author's name, Eamonn Murphy, and nausea swells up as an image from the last time she saw him clouds her vision. Bare, freckled shoulders. Brown hair falling over dark blue eyes. His forehead pressed against hers.

She's tried so hard to forget about him all these years, tried to let go of all the questions he left her with. But it's been nearly impossible. Only an hour ago, Anna had reminded her of him with her talk of Ireland. Has she somehow summoned him here? Or is this just one of life's little cruelties, adding to the complexity of her situation, as though it isn't complicated enough yet?

'Olivia.' A loud whisper from a few feet away brings her back into the present. Suze is pointing to an empty chair. 'Sit.'

Olivia, clutching the book to her chest, fails to find the words to protest and does as she's told without looking up. It's been nearly fourteen years since she last saw him. She doesn't even have to do the maths. She's imagined this moment so many times in the past years, it's become entirely abstract. Like saying a word over and over until it loses all its meaning. If she looks up now, he'll be real again, and that's not something her heart can take.

2

Eamonn takes a sip of water, clears his throat. At the back of the room a woman joins the audience. She's facing away from him but Suze seems to know her. There's something about the interaction that holds his attention. He watches intently, unsure of why he's doing so. But then he remembers he's on a stage and someone's talking to him.

'Eamonn, are you ready to start reading?'

'Sorry, yeah.'

There's a copy of his novel on the coffee table in between him and Sam, a bookmark stuck between its pages, telling him where he'll find the prologue. This is the first reading he's ever done – something he'd always hoped would not be a part of his publishing journey. Talking to big groups of people has never been his preferred manner of communicating, let alone reading aloud his very personal words. From the moment his editor-slash-publisher-slash-ex-girlfriend, Ruby, convinced him to publish, he's been trying to come to terms with the fact anyone would read them at all. This is not a story he had meant to send out into the world.

Tiny beads of sweat coat his forehead and he takes another sip of water. As he does, he faces the small audience, his eyes drifting to the newcomer, and that's when something clicks into place. It's like his heart knows before his brain does: it picks up speed, sending blood rushing upwards, flushing his cheeks. There's only one person in the world who's ever had that effect on him, and even though he hasn't seen her in a very long time, he's certain it's her. Her hair is shorter, but the way she moves is still the same. Even from afar, he feels it's her, no matter how unbelievable it seems. Olivia Clarke, the woman he wrote a book about. Its pages tremble in his hands.

In a way he's always known that publishing his book would reunite them, one way or another, but he had not expected it to happen so soon. Did she purposely come to the reading?

He tries to meet her eye, but she's keeping her gaze down. It takes a world of effort not to call out her name, to force her to face him. Perhaps even to ask why he hasn't heard from her in fourteen years.

'Eamonn?' Sam looks at him expectantly.

'Sorry, yeah,' he says again. 'Not used to being on a stage,' he explains, giving her a sheepish smile. He adjusts the book in his hands and clears his throat. If reading aloud from his novel was unnerving before, now it seems downright impossible. But there's no way around it. All eyes are on him. All eyes, except hers.

✢

Wild Waves
Prologue - July 6, 2009

'Where do you think we'll be, five years from now?' Ava asked. 'Do you think we'll still be friends?'

They were the only ones left on the beach, even though it was early July. An old Arctic Monkeys album played in their ears, the white chord of her headphones dangling between them. He turned away from her and fixed his gaze on the horizon.

'Friends…' he repeated, visibly dissecting the word before he answered. 'Yeah, sure.'

The deflation in his voice filled her with dread.

Perhaps it was wrong of Ava to reduce their relationship to a mere friendship after all these months together, sharing all the parts of themselves they tended to keep hidden. But what else was she to do? The world just didn't work that way.

Ava pushed on. 'I think we should make a pact.'

'A pact?' His dark blue eyes scanned her face, their intensity weighing on her heart. She swallowed the unease away. 'Yeah, I think five years from today we should meet. No matter what happens in the meantime. It's the only way to make sure.'

For a while he didn't speak, as though trying to imagine every possible scenario, considering each outcome and the likelihood their pact would stand. Looking at him, the thought of leaving him behind nearly broke her. If she could get him to agree to meet her again, perhaps not all would be lost. The world could be a different place, five years on.

'No matter what?' he asked.

'No matter what.'

❊

As he turns the page, Eamonn looks up to find her eyes on him, disbelief contorting her features. He has his answer. She did not come here intentionally and she had no idea what the book is about. It's not how he'd imagined their eventual reunion. He'd hoped he'd at least have time to talk to her before she found out about the book. But maybe it was supposed to happen like this. Maybe now he'll finally find out why he never heard from her again.

Eamonn glances at Sam and she gives him a little nod, encouraging him to continue. He turns the page to the first chapter.

❊

Wild Waves
Chapter 1 - March 2009

The waves were wild that morning as the tide came in. Conor hadn't been in the water long when he noticed the dark clouds gathering overhead. A storm was heading their way, and even though he loved swimming in the rain, he was expected at the grocery shop soon for his Sunday shift, and wanted to do one last check of the barn before that. Apart from the roaring wind and crashing waves, the town was quiet. All the people of Ballybridge were hiding inside their houses, attuned to the weather without having to check the forecast. Conor grabbed his bicycle from where he'd dropped it in the dunes, and with his swim shorts still dripping wet, cycled back to the farm.

At home he changed into a pair of jeans and a charcoal jumper, before helping his dad get all the sheep inside. They bolted the barn doors, and when Conor was reassured everything was secure, he grabbed his rucksack and headed for the shop.

As was to be expected, there were no customers. Conor kept himself busy for a while labelling cans and sweeping floors, but when that was done, he got his pen and notebook from his bag and went to work. Even though he'd quit uni years earlier, he hadn't stopped writing stories. It was as though he had no choice in the matter. Somehow his thoughts always found their way onto a piece of paper. There were times he'd find something in his own handwriting without even remembering having written it down. For Conor, writing was like breathing: instinctive and sustaining.

He'd jotted down a few ideas when the doorbell chimed for the first time that day. Placing his pen in the fold of his notebook, he looked up to see Mrs O'Leary closing the door behind her. He glanced at the clock, confirming the time. Every single Sunday, for as long as Conor had been working at Paddy's grocery shop, Mrs O'Leary had come in at 11.30 a.m. sharp to buy ingredients for her Sunday bakes. People were creatures of habit, Conor understood that, but her impeccable timing never ceased to astonish him. The fact he'd seen her come and go every weekend of the past five years unfortunately also reminded him of his own predictable life. Would it ever change?

'Howya pet, alright?' Mrs O'Leary asked, giving her umbrella a shake and dropping it in the designated bin.

'Ah, not too bad. Calm day with the storm and all,' Conor said.

'Aye, you wouldn't put the dog out in it, would ya?'

'Why are you out then?' he asked.

'Ach, you know me, son, tough as nails.'

Conor gave a short laugh. 'So, what's on the menu today?'

'Well, I was thinking I would make me buttermilk scones. What do you reckon?'

Conor's mouth watered at the thought. 'Ah well, you know I think they're class.'

'They are class. I'll bring you some when they're done.'

He loved buttermilk scones, especially those baked by Edna O'Leary – she was a master baker. But to ask her to walk through the storm again just felt wrong.

'No, you're alright.'

'Ah, don't be daft, Conor, I'm not going to melt or break. I'm bringing you a couple when I'm done.'

There was no point in arguing – he'd known her long enough to not make that mistake.

'Alright so.'

With a smug smile on her face, she gathered her ingredients and brought them over to the till. While Conor carefully put the eggs in her shopping trolley, she rummaged through her purse for the exact change and paid him what he was owed. She patted his hand and smiled. 'Thanks, love. I'll see you in a bit.'

The doorbell chimed again as she left, and Conor returned to his notebook. Before he could finish the first sentence, a rustling sound made him look up. There was another customer by the entrance. She must have come in when Mrs O'Leary left.

With her back turned to him, Conor tried to make out who it was, but he didn't recognise her. Someone he'd never seen before in Ballybridge? Improbable if not impossible. And yet...

The girl was wearing a bright yellow poncho and struggling to take it off. Somehow it had caught on her rucksack. She twisted her arm in a way that looked unnatural and painful. Conor flinched at the sight. When she finally managed to free herself, she grabbed a basket by the entrance and tossed the wet poncho in it with a sigh of relief. Without the hood, he could see her face more clearly. She looked to be a similar age to him, somewhere in her early to mid-twenties. Her cheeks were red from the cold and plastered with a few strands of hair that had escaped the cover of her hood.

'Hello,' she said, noticing Conor's presence, her smile bright and warm.

'Hiya,' he replied.

Perhaps it was the colour of her poncho, perhaps it was the English accent he thought he'd recognised, but despite the storm raging outside, there was something sunny about her.

She browsed the shelves, clearly not in a hurry, scanning the displays as though strolling through a museum, appraising her surroundings. Conor tried to continue writing but her presence made it incredibly difficult, his attention drifting back to her every few seconds. It wasn't every day there was a stranger in his shop, let alone one that looked like her.

When she approached the till and placed her basket in front of him, he put his pen behind his ear, closed the notebook and grabbed the scanner.

'Busy day?' She glanced around.

Conor couldn't help but smile. 'Opening the second till any moment now.'

'Good. Can't keep the customers waiting.'

'Customer *is* king,' he said.

She smiled too now, and something unfamiliar stirred inside his chest.

One by one, he scanned the items while observing her from the corner of his eye. What was an English girl doing at Paddy's?

'Did you find everything you needed?' Conor asked.

'Actually, I didn't. Do you have dried apricots?'

'Yeah, sure.'

'Ah, I must have missed them.'

Stepping out from behind the counter, Conor was suddenly very aware of his own arms. Not sure what to do with them, he buried his hands in his pockets and headed for the aisle with the dried fruits.

'Last two packs,' he said, holding them up in the air so she could see.

'Lovely, I'll take 'em both. I'm surprised you have so many exotic products in stock.'

'Yes, well, if anything, we are quite exotic around here.' He threw a look out the window where the trees were fighting to hold on to their branches.

She gave a soft chuckle and again, that strange sensation stirred in his chest. He scanned the two packs of apricots and watched her put them away.

'What are you writing?' she asked, her gaze drifting to the notebook lying on the table beside him.

Cheeky and nosy... Interesting.

'Everything and nothing.'

'Your journal?'

Her eyes homed in on his, the glint in them suggesting she was messing with him.

'Manifesto,' he said. He might as well play along.

'Like the Unabomber?'

'Exactly like that.'

'Intriguing. Is it almost finished?'

'Oh, I haven't got far yet. Busy day, you know.'

She let out a short laugh. 'I'll leave you to it then. Maybe I can read it next time.'

Next time? So she was staying around, and not just passing through?

She lifted her rucksack onto her back and pulled the poncho over her head. As she contorted her arm once again to make sure the rucksack was covered, Conor stepped in.

'Do you need help?' he asked.

'Would you mind?'

Moving closer, he could feel the heat radiating off her body. He had not expected that. His heart picked up speed as he untangled her poncho and draped it over the stuffed backpack.

'There you go, now,' he said.

When she turned on her heels, she was standing so close, Conor could see the freckles on the bridge of her nose and the tiny piercing on the left side. For a second, he imagined her with a small nose ring.

'Cheers!' she said.

She smelled of rain and something familiar, something sweet. A bright smile lit up her entire face, and that's when he noticed the golden glow in her warm, brown eyes. It was mesmerising, hypnotic even, leaving him completely flustered.

'Yeah. No worries,' he said, taking a step back, nearly stumbling over a box of canned beans.

'Good luck today. Hope it calms down a little.'

She gave him an exaggerated wink and as she reached for the door handle with one hand, she used the other to pull the bright yellow hood over her auburn hair.

'Bye, Ted!' she said.

It took Conor a second to get the reference but when he did, he laughed. 'See ya.'

A strong gust of wind flew in when she opened the door, carrying her sweet scent all the way down to where he stood. And then it hit him. Coconut. She smelled of rain and coconut.

3

Olivia doesn't move as the audience applauds. On the stage, the first man she ever really loved puts the book down on the oval coffee table beside him.

'That was beautiful, Eamonn. Thank you,' Sam says.

'Cheers.' His eyes drift to the last row and she quickly looks away. The walls close in on her, the atmosphere thick with years of unanswered questions. Beside her, Suze says something, her lips moving, eyebrows raised, waiting for Olivia to reply. But Olivia can't hear any of it.

'Sorry, I need to get this,' Olivia whispers, lifting her phone to her ear and heading for the exit. Her heavy legs make it difficult to walk as fast as she would like. Thankfully, the shop is small, and she's outside soon enough. She crouches, leaning against the wall, gulping fresh air as though she's been under water for hours. There's a drizzle and she lifts her face to the sky and closes her eyes, welcoming the tiny, cool drops on her flushed cheeks. Memories of a time in Ireland swim across her vision, memories she's tried hard to forget. In her mind, a broken record of words plays: *He wrote a book about us. He wrote a book about us. He wrote a book about us.*

No matter how many times she repeats these words, they don't make sense. Why would he do that when she was the one left broken-hearted? He promised her he'd be there the day of the pact, but she waited on the beach for hours, starting out hopeful and then slowly, as time went on, feeling more and more foolish. The painful memory reverberates throughout her entire body, making her bones ache, pushing her to get away from the bookshop, from him.

The rain intensifies when she rounds the corner, making her aware of the book she's clutching to her chest, like a life raft in an endless sea. A book she hasn't paid for.

'Fuck.'

She stops at the first Pret A Manger she sees, orders a coffee and types out a message for Suze while she waits for her drink.

Had to leave and forgot to pay. Sorry! I'll be in tomorrow to settle. Xx

There's no way she's going back in there today.

'Oat flat white,' the barista calls out, faster than she'd expected. Olivia takes the drink from the counter and turns to leave, but suddenly going home seems equally as impossible as returning to the bookshop. Either decision could change everything. It's one of those moments in time where the tiniest choice can have a life-altering ripple effect. For a second she imagines having gone to Waterstones today, or Foyles. Would she have noticed the book then? To think her decision to go to *Pages & Leaves* could be more determining for the rest of her life than her move to Canada seems outrageous, and yet, here she is. Stuck in limbo, afraid to move.

She finds an empty, crumb-free table by the window and places the book in front of her. There's a black-and-white picture on the ochre cover of four people facing the ocean, their backs to the camera. She doesn't have to read the book to know who they are: Ben, Erin, Eamonn and her. Olivia's trembling fingers trace the image's contours while her mind drifts to the road trip the four of them went on in 2009. She can still smell the ocean air, feel the grains of sand, rough on her skin. Her fingers turn the pages until she reaches the dedication.

To E & B, for being my buoys.

To O, for being the sea.

The words travel straight to her core, and salty tears roll down her cheeks as she reads them over and over. Everything she thought she knew is turned upside down. Not only did he write about them, about the pact – he also dedicated his book to her. Clearly she meant something to him. But then why did he leave her behind? Is this book his way of explaining and apologising?

She sips her coffee, acutely aware that this might be the worst moment in time to revisit her past.

And yet, the urge to know where they went wrong pushes her to turn the page.

Wild Waves
Chapter 2

Kate frantically moved around the house, gathering her laptop, phone and keys. 'I left a list of phone numbers on the fridge in case of an emergency. I should be back shortly after six. George takes a nap around noon, so if you could give him his lunch around half eleven, that'd be great.' She stuffed everything inside her leather bag and checked her makeup in the mirror once again. The doorbell rang.

'Ava, can you get that please?'

Ava was on the floor, pretending to be asleep as George crawled over her, trying to wake her up. 'Boo!' she said, suddenly opening her eyes and lifting him up in the air. George squealed with delight, and this in turn made Ava's heart swell. With no babysitting experience whatsoever, looking after a one-year-old full time was daunting, even if she was the boy's aunt. It had kept her awake more than once in the days before she arrived. But seeing his bright brown eyes twinkle back at her eased her anxiety considerably. She headed for the door, balancing him on her hip. When she opened it, a girl about her age with a big bunch of blonde curls and a beaming smile stood in front of her. 'Howya!'

'Hello!'

'Orla, is that you?' Kate shouted from inside the house.

'Yep! I just wanted to see you off on your first day back in work! How are ya feelin'?' Orla stepped inside and pinched

George's nose. 'Hello there, Georgio. Jam this morning, was it?'

He kicked his chubby legs with excitement at the sight of her.

'Ava, this is Orla – my neighbour and friend, and the greatest babysitter in town,' Kate said when they joined her in the living room. She was still in front of the mirror, combing through her long ginger locks.

Orla curtsied. 'The one and only.' She reached out to shake Ava's hand. 'Good to finally meet ya, Ava. So, you're here to take my babysitter title, are ya?'

'Hardly! I'll be happy enough if we all get out of this alive.'

'Ah, you'll be great, Ave. George loves you already. Look at him,' Kate said.

George was gazing at Ava adoringly, one of his doughy arms draped around her neck, her plait clenched in his fist.

'Anyway, I should be off. I don't want to arrive late on my first day. How do I look?'

'Gorgeous!' they chimed in unison.

Kate laughed and turned to Orla. 'You can stay if you want. I've a feeling you two will get on very well. There's fresh coffee and pastries in the kitchen.'

'I actually have to get to work myself,' Orla said, checking the clock behind her. 'However, wasting food is against my principles, so…' She trailed off and disappeared into the kitchen as Kate gave George one more kiss. 'Ok, I'm off. Bye now! Bye, sweetie.'

'Bye, Mummy.' Ava took hold of George's hand, waving goodbye to Kate as she closed the door.

'Mamma?' George said, his voice on the verge of cracking.

'Mummy's gone to work. She'll be back soon.' Stroking his black curls for comfort, Ava walked him into the kitchen, where Orla was halfway through a croissant.

'So, how come I've never seen you around here?' she asked, mouth full of pastry.

Ava, resting George on her hip, pulled back a chair. 'I don't know. I've been here a few times since Kate moved. I guess we must've always just missed each other? And it's mostly Kate coming to London anyway, to see Mum and Dad.'

'Makes sense. I'd go to London too if it were up to me. Give me the money and I'll move there tomorrow.'

'Really?'

Orla nodded. 'London has it all: theatre, gigs, musicals, museums… For creatives, all the opportunities are there, like.'

'Hmm, I guess that's true. It can be an exhausting place to live, though.'

George reached for the fork on the table, but Ava got to it first, pushing it out of his reach.

'So what do you do there?' Orla asked.

'I'm in between jobs at the moment, but I have a sales assistant role waiting for me at my uncle's firm when I return. What about you? What do you do?'

'I'm a musician and a music teacher.' Orla got up to find a mug in the cupboard, filled it halfway with coffee and then topped it up with milk.

'Aha! Hence the desire to move to London.'

'Exactly. The teaching helps pay the bills and it's not too bad, but I'd rather just be making music. Maybe one day, who knows…'

'I'd love to hear you play some time.'

'We're looking for a new drummer at the moment, but I'll let you know once we've found someone.'

Ava liked Orla. She felt familiar in a way, so full of energy. In her lap, George wriggled, trying to set himself free. 'What is it? You want to play?' Ava asked. She put him down on the floor, giving him a small chunk of croissant to munch on.

Checking the clock on the microwave, Orla jumped up. 'Fuck… Oh, sorry, George… *Fudge*, I really have to get to work now. Ava, we should talk more. Do you wanna come to the pub on Friday night? A few of us are going and there's live music and all that. Should be fun, like.'

'Yes! Definitely.' Making a few friends was an enticing prospect. Spending six months in a small town with only Kate and George for company could become very lonely, very quickly, especially with Kate full time at work.

'Perfect. I'll drop by around eight to pick you up.' Orla tried to high-five George but he just stared at her hand and grinned. 'Next time maybe, huh Georgio? Bye bye then!'

The moment the door closed behind Orla, George put up his hand and squeezed his tiny fingers into a fist, attempting a wave. Ava looked at him and took a deep breath. She could do this.

'Just you and me now, hey, boyo? What do you want to do? Want to go for a walk?' She kneeled down beside him, studying his chubby face covered in pink jam. In response, he reached for her, still clenching a chunk of croissant. 'First things first, though,' she said. 'Let's get you less sticky.'

Half a pack of baby wipes later, Ava strapped him in the buggy and put on her sandals. Overnight, the storm had subsided and given way to very mild temperatures and a clear blue sky. The beach seemed like the perfect option to spend their first morning alone together. She packed a pink plastic shovel and green bucket, along with the nappy bag and an old quilt Kate had said they could use for picnics.

The ten-minute walk took them past the hairdresser's, fish monger's and local pub, where she assumed Orla was taking her that Friday. As they passed the grocery shop, she could see an older man behind the till talking to a customer. Where was Mr Manifesto from the day before?

'Who's that, George?' she asked, as she peered through the window to see if the other guy was there too. With no answer from the one-year-old, she continued along the road, singing 'Wheels on the Bus', until they arrived at the seafront. Leaving the buggy behind, she grabbed the toys and carried George onto the beach. The grains of sand immediately found their way into her sandals, making it more difficult to walk with each step. With the tide coming in, she found them a place just out of the water's reach. George squealed and giggled, clearly pleased to be there.

As was to be expected on a Monday morning in March, there weren't many people around. An older man walked along the shoreline, his German Shepherd following closely behind, and to her left, near the dunes, a young couple sat, the girl reading, the boy lying down, staring up at the sky, his head in her lap. A little to her right, Ava spotted a towel and rucksack, but when she glanced around, the owner was nowhere to be found.

While George used the shovel to cover the blanket in sand, Ava closed her eyes for a split second to breathe it all in. The fresh air was intoxicating and she felt the tension in her body dissolve. She'd been reluctant to come to Ireland for such a long time. If Kate hadn't been so desperate, she wouldn't have come. This was the moment to build a career, to get a head start on her future. Taking a six-month break was not part of the plan.

But a week into her stay, Ireland was growing on her.

As Ava watched the waves crash onto the beach, mesmerised by the ebb and flow, she almost didn't spot the lone swimmer in the ocean, slowly approaching the shore. When he got closer, it finally registered and Ava figured it was his towel lying in wait on the beach. It was a lovely spring day, but to be swimming in the ocean was a bit of a stretch, she thought. To be fair, swimming in the ocean on any given day in the year was unthinkable for Ava. The maverick got out of the water and when he was finally close enough, she recognised him. With his back turned to her, he picked up his towel, rubbed his hair dry and wrapped it around his shoulders.

'If it isn't Mr Kaczynski himself!' she shouted, competing with the white noise of the waves. He jerked his head up, clearly taken by surprise. When he recognised her, he laughed.

'Morning,' he said, walking over to where they were sitting. 'We meet again.' Water dripped from his hair onto his face, his cheeks scarlet from what must have been freezing cold water.

'What are the odds?' Ava said.

'Well, in a town with a population of eight hundred or so, I'd say it was bound to happen.'

'Fair point.'

When he spoke, his voice was gravelly and deep, almost like Tom Waits. She'd been surprised by it the day before too, so much so that later at home, she'd listened to 'Martha' just to see if the comparison stood. It did.

He looked over to George and then to her, lifting an eyebrow.

'Oh, this is George, my nephew. Kate Kingston's my sister.'

'Ah, I thought I recognised him.' He kneeled and ran his hand through his curls. 'Hiya George.'

He was so gentle with him, Ava briefly stumbled over her words. 'Yeah, uhm, she's returned to work today and the au pair couldn't start until September, so…'

'Right. So you're staying until September?'

'That's the plan, yeah.'

Was that a smile? Before Ava could be sure, he used the corner of his towel to wipe away the water trickling from his forehead, hiding part of his face as he did so.

'Can I ask you something?' she said, and without waiting for his answer continued, 'What were you doing swimming in the ocean? It must be freezing.'

'I swim every day,' he replied, as though that was a satisfactory answer. Instead, it only brought up more questions.

'Every day? Why?'

'I don't know, I guess it helps clear my mind.'

'Why? What's on your mind?'

For a moment he was silent. He wiped at some drops trickling down his temples and scanned her face, his expression inscrutable. 'You ask a lot of questions for someone I just met, you know?'

Ava laughed. 'Sorry. I just don't see the attraction of swimming in the ocean, that's all.'

'And why is that?'

'Sea creatures.' She nodded, convinced no further explanation was needed.

'Sea creatures?' His raised eyebrows made his forehead wrinkle.

'Yes, like sharks and jellyfish and just plain fish – you know, creatures that live in the sea.'

'Sharks? You do know we're in Ireland, right?'

Ava rolled her eyes. 'Sharks swim, don't they?'

'Is that a rhetorical question?'

'You're cheeky for a guy I've just met. And yes, it is. But can you just acknowledge that sharks swim and therefore have the ability to move around in the ocean and the ocean basically has no barriers, so sharks can go wherever they want, whenever they want, including Ireland?'

A soft chuckle escaped his lips, triggering something inside her. Not wanting to examine what had just happened, she continued: 'And if I'm not mistaken, it was you who said you were quite exotic around here… so… I rest my case.' She raised both hands to support her statement. Opposite her, the boy from the shop failed to suppress an enormous grin.

Sitting there half naked, ocean water glistening on his pale, freckle-covered skin, he was not your typical good-looking guy. His upper lip was slightly too thin and one of his bottom front teeth crooked, but the longer she looked, the more beauty she saw in him. The day before, she hadn't noticed the scar in his left eyebrow, asymmetrically slicing it in two. She'd been distracted by those dark blue eyes that now homed in on her, their depth intensified by the reflection of the cloudless sky. Ava often struggled with eye contact. Every time someone looked at her, she felt the urge to avert her gaze. But this time it was different. She couldn't look away. It unsettled her and she wasn't sure what to do next. Fortunately, George started crying as if he knew she needed saving. He'd shovelled a bit too enthusiastically and got sand all over his face, including in his mouth and eyes. She picked him up and comforted him, brushing the dirt off him with the tips of her fingers.

'How's that manifesto coming along?' she asked, keeping her eyes fixed on George.

'It's more of a rant than anything else at the moment, to be fair.'

'Aren't all manifestos just madmen's rants?'

'I don't think so. There's a lot of interesting subject matter in the Unabomber's manifesto, for example. Perhaps he could've chosen a different way to get it out there—'

'Perhaps?'

'Okay, fine, definitely. But essentially, his take on the industrial revolution and the effects it had on society was spot on.'

Ava's eyes widened. 'You're really into this, aren't you?'

'I'm not an expert or anything.'

The look on his face told her he had a lot more to say about the subject, but was holding back.

'So is that really what you're writing?'

He shook his head. 'Not really, no, I'm working on a story. But I'm mostly gathering my thoughts at the moment, putting down some ideas.'

'What's it about?'

He shook his head and smiled, holding her gaze for a few seconds before he spoke. 'It's about this guy who meets an incredibly nosy girl with a big mouth and an odd shark obsession.'

Ava couldn't help but laugh. She'd been accused of being nosy and mouthy before, but somehow, he made it sound like a compliment.

'Sounds like a wonderful girl. The guy must feel really lucky.'

'He's not complaining or anything,' he said.

Ava's stomach flipped, and for once, she was speechless. In the background, the church bells sounded and the guy from the shop pushed himself up to stand. 'Here, I should be off,' he said.

She covered her eyes with her hand to shield them from the sun as she looked up at him. 'So, uhm, Ted?'

He smiled. 'Conor.' A lock of wet hair fell over his forehead and he pushed it back with the palm of his hand.

'Aha. So Conor, I guess I'll be seeing you around then.'

'Inevitably.'

'I'm Ava by the way, in case you were wondering.'

He nodded. Had he been wondering, or was he just acknowledging her name?

'See ya around, Ava. Bye, George.'

He retrieved a T-shirt from his bag and pulled it over his head as he walked off towards the dunes, the fabric clinging to his broad shoulders. Ava watched him go, but just before he was out of earshot, she couldn't help but shout: 'That is, if the sharks don't get to you first!'

He turned around, shook his head and laughed, baring his crooked teeth. She liked that. She liked that a lot. Even though she knew she shouldn't.

Wild Waves
Chapter 3

On his way home, Conor was so preoccupied with his conversation with Ava, he forgot to buy the paper. It wasn't until his dad pointed it out that he noticed. To avoid further questioning, he immediately got on his bike and made his way to town. Outside the news agent's a car slowed down and honked, its driver calling his name. Conor didn't have to look to put a face to the voice.

'What are you doing here?' he asked when the car had come to a full stop.

'Warm welcome, mate. No hiya bestie, I've missed ya, it's good to see ya?'

'I saw you Friday, Matt. It's Monday.'

'Still.'

Conor rested his arms on the roof of the car and leaned in through the window. 'Aren't you supposed to be working?'

'I have the day off. Promised Ma to come over and help her with a few things. Why are you here, anyway?'

'Getting the paper.'

Matt checked his watch. 'A bit late, no?'

'What are you? The time Garda?' He raised his eyebrows in defiance and then shrugged. 'I forgot so I had to come back.'

'You forgot? You never forget.'

Matt was right. Conor's morning routine was so solid he could do it in his sleep. In all those years he'd been back home, he hadn't forgotten to buy the paper once after his morning swim. And Matt knew Conor through and through. Having someone in his life who knew him better than he knew himself was mostly a blessing, but sometimes it was extremely inconvenient. Like now.

'Well, first time for everything,' Conor said, keeping it light.

Matt narrowed his eyes and studied him. 'What's up?'

'Nothing. Monday morning, I suppose.' He shook his head, hoping to come off as nonchalant as possible.

'Hmm.' Matthew wasn't convinced. And knowing him, he would keep going unless Conor found a way out.

'I should get back. Dad's waiting,' he said, hoping that would do it.

'Right. Better hurry. The way you're going at it, the news won't be news anymore by the time you get home.'

Conor rolled his eyes. Always the funny guy, Matt. 'See ya Friday?'

'If you don't forget.'

'That is extremely clever,' Conor said matter-of-factly, tapping the roof of the car to send Matt off. With a big grin Matt closed the window, and Conor went on his way.

His dad had already put on the kettle when he entered the kitchen. Conor dropped the *Irish Times* on the old wooden table and got two mugs from the press.

'Alright, son?' Jim asked.

'Yeah, sure, why?'

'I don't think you've ever forgotten the paper.'

'You too?' Conor sighed.

Confusion was written all over his dad's face, making Conor instantly regret his reaction. 'I ran into Matt in town. He was on to me about it too,' he explained, trying to make up for his tone.

His dad smiled. 'Well, I suppose he knows you about as well as I do.'

Thankfully, the click of the kettle relieved Conor from more questioning. Like every morning, they had their tea in silence while his dad read the paper and Conor continued scribbling in his notebook. For about fifteen minutes it was quiet in the Delaneys' kitchen. From across the table, Conor glanced at his father. He looked tired, his skin dry and rough, with deep wrinkles on his forehead and around his mouth. The face of an Irish farmer, hardened by the weather, but mostly by life. His dad had aged noticeably in the last couple of months and Conor couldn't help but think time was somehow moving faster. He often found himself worrying about things like time, ageing and death. It terrified him but he couldn't stop either, as if by doing so, he could somehow prepare himself for the death of the people around him.

When his dad left to tend to the farm, Conor returned to his chores inside the house: cooking, cleaning, doing the shopping… It had all fallen to him when he'd quit uni. It was never discussed, but it worked fine for both of them. It allowed Conor to write in between chores, and it gave his dad the time to focus on his sheep and the maintenance of the farm.

But that day, Conor struggled to continue with his story. His mind kept wandering back to Ava. Why was he so intrigued by this girl he'd only met briefly? What was it about her that made him smile every time he remembered their conversation? Perhaps it was the fact she was so open and unabashed, and he'd never really met anyone like her before. Perhaps it was that golden glow in her eyes, perhaps that deep chuckle travelling all the way from her stomach whenever he'd said something that amused her. It could be one of those things, it could be a combination. It didn't matter which. He was intrigued, and that hadn't happened since university, and the night he met Niamh.

4

The Q&A takes longer than he'd hoped. Or maybe it just feels longer because he knows she's here. The problem is, he hasn't seen her since he finished reading. Keeping his focus on the questions, while simultaneously worrying about where she went, is proving to be difficult.

'If they turn *Wild Waves* into a film or series, who would you want to play the main characters?' a tall woman with short, grey hair asks.

'Ooh, good question!' Sam's eyes are wide with expectation.

Eamonn takes a sip of water as he considers his answer. It's something he's never really thought about. Ava and Conor are sort of the actors playing him and Olivia, so there was never a need to imagine anyone else in the roles.

'Uhm, that's a tough one. I really love the actress who plays Esme in *Peaky Blinders*.'

'Aimee-Ffion Edwards,' Sam nods, clearly agreeing with him, judging by the intensity of her nod.

'And uhm, for Conor, I don't know, there are a lot of very talented Irish actors out there. It's not so much about looks, as it is personality, I suppose.'

The grey-haired woman nods, pleased with his answer, and about ten minutes and a handful of questions later, Sam announces the Q&A is over. Eamonn smiles and takes in another applause. With a Sharpie in hand, Sam guides him to a table where a stack of his own books is waiting to be signed.

When he takes his seat, he scans the room again, but it seems Olivia's gone. Relief and disappointment pull him in opposite directions. On the one hand, he wants to talk to her again. But on the other hand, he has no idea what he would say.

'I loved the reading. I'm excited to get to the rest of it,' a short woman with thick black curls at the front of the queue says, her large teeth exposed in a big grin.

'Thanks,' Eamonn replies. 'What's your name?'

She tells him it's Jane and below the dedication, he writes one of the lines he prepared the day before: *To Jane, Do what you love. No matter what..* And then he signs his autograph. It goes on like that until the last shopper has left and he's alone with Sam and Suze again.

'Thanks for doing this,' Sam says. 'It was such a great afternoon.'

'I should be thanking you.'

Suze waves his comment away. 'We love your book so much. It was a pleasure.'

'And we sold quite a few, so win-win, right?' Sam adds.

'Well, yeah, I suppose.'

'One of them loved it so much she left without paying for it.' Suze is laughing but her sister frowns. 'What?'

'Not really, though. Liv came in and had to run home just after the reading. She forgot to pay, but she said she'd be in tomorrow.'

'Really? I didn't see her come in,' Sam says.

'Yeah, she wasn't here long though.'

The mention of her name has made the hairs at the back of his neck stand, and Eamonn knows this is his cue. He's not much of a believer in fate, but her showing up here at that exact moment has to mean something. It would be a monumental waste of an opportunity if he stayed silent now.

'That's not Olivia Clarke by any chance, is it?'

The sisters gape at him open-mouthed. 'You know Olivia?' Suze asks.

'Yeah, uhm, we used to be friends.'

'Really? How odd. She didn't say anything.'

Sam cocks an eyebrow and looks him right in the eye, like she's just figured something out. 'Yeah, odd.'

'You don't have her number, do you?' he asks, before they can dig deeper. The moment he gave up on ever hearing from her again, he erased her contact details from his phone, knowing the temptation to call her would otherwise always be there. On several occasions, he'd proven himself right. Every time something good or bad had happened, he'd wanted to call her. His father's wedding, the day he got a puppy, the time he lost his job at a literary magazine and then a few months later, when he found a new job teaching English in a secondary school near Ballybridge. No matter how big or small the event, Olivia was always the one he wanted to tell.

'Yeah, just a sec.' Suze takes her phone from her jeans pocket, swipes at it until she's found Olivia's number and dictates it to him. Eamonn thanks them again, and promises to return when his next book is published, before the sisters send him on his way with a freshly brewed cup of coffee.

Usually, when Eamonn is in London, he stays with Ben and Erin. But things have been off ever since he announced his book was going to be published. Erin hasn't really said so explicitly, blaming the children for not having Eamonn over, but Eamonn knows it's because of the book. And the worst thing is, he understands. Erin told him Olivia's side of the story, thinking it was all just for him, so he would finally be able to let go, get over everything that happened. And initially that had been his intention. He wrote the book from a dual point of view so he could try and put himself in Olivia's shoes, using the stories Erin had told him. He never intended to publish the book, but encouraged by his editor, he did anyway. He's been meaning to apologise to Erin, but every time he brings it up, she changes the subject.

So now, instead of staying over at their place, Eamonn is meeting Ben for dinner in a pub in Primrose Hill. Instead of getting public transport, Eamonn takes his time strolling along Regent's Canal while he processes what just happened. It's raining, but he doesn't care. All he can think about is Olivia. He wonders how well Sam and Suze know her, and if they're texting her now, questioning her about him, telling her he asked for her number. He's not sure he'll text her. What would he say? *Great seeing you at my book event, even though you bolted as soon as you found out the book's about you and how you broke my heart?*

Not the soundest of plans.

He could return to the bookshop tomorrow, wait for her to come in. But that could be a long and awkward wait, and seeing as Sam was already catching on, not an option either.

But he has to talk to her. Even after writing the book, he's never entirely got over the heartache. It doesn't matter how much Erin has told him, or how much he thinks he knows her. Her part of the story is still an enigma to him, and he needs answers if he ever really wants to move on.

Under one of the bridges over the canal, he stops, takes out his phone and stares at her number. His thumb hovers over the keys. He types and deletes and types and deletes. A jogger rushes past but he hardly notices. All his energy is going towards finding the right words. After about nine attempts, he shakes his head in frustration and pockets his phone again. *What a writer.*

5

At Pret, Olivia is surrounded by tourists sipping from paper cups while she stares at the pages in front of her, unsure of how long she's been sitting like that. When she was at the reading, she hadn't given much thought to the point of view in Eamonn's book. She'd been so overwhelmed just by the sight of him that the details of it all had not caught on her radar. But now, she's riddled with questions. If half of the book is written from Ava's perspective, does that mean he made it up? It's impossible for him to know her half of the story, and yet he got almost everything right, even her thoughts and feelings. How did he do that? Someone had to have told him, and there are only two people who know Olivia well enough to have acted as his source. One of them who also happens to be his best friend. Erin.

A surge of anger has her reaching for her phone.

'Hiya, Livvie!'

The cheerful greeting of her best friend goes unrequited.

'Did you know?' Olivia asks instead. Around her, people turn their heads to look at her. Clearly her tone is conveying her agitation.

'Oh, so we're not doing hello then?' Erin jokes.

'Erin, did you know?'

'Did I know what?' In the background, a baby howls.

'Did you know about Eamonn?'

'Jayzus, Liv, can you be more specific? I don't have the energy for guessing games. Miles has been crying since four this morning.'

On any other day, Olivia would sympathise with her friend. Erin and Ben have been struggling with Miles' sleeping pattern, and with another toddler in the house wreaking havoc, they haven't had much rest in the past couple of weeks. But today, she doesn't care. There's not a single universe where Erin didn't know about the book. And why she would've kept it from her is beyond Olivia's comprehension.

'Don't play dumb, Er. I just ran into him at *Pages & Leaves*. He was reading from his book. You know, the one he wrote about me?'

On the other end of the line, Erin is quiet. Only Miles' wails break the silence.

'Did you know he's here?'

'Liv…'

Erin's pleading tone tells her everything she needs to know, but still she presses on for an answer. 'Did you?'

Before Erin can answer, Miles' crying stops and a tiny voice shouts: 'Look, Mammy, Mawes has a hat!'

'Alex, no! You can't put the strainer on your baby brother's head.' Nearly instantly, Miles kicks off again, joined by his sister. The sound is painful, even through the phone.

'Olivia, look, I have to go. Can we talk about this later?'

Blood rushes to her cheeks. 'He wrote a book about me, Erin. What am I supposed to do with that?'

Erin lets out an audible sigh. 'Nothing. Okay? You let it go. It's been years and years and nothing good can come of it. Go to Canada, forget about Eamonn. Move on.'

Olivia is speechless. Did Erin just tell her to move on?

'I—' she starts, but Erin cuts her off.

'I have to go. Bye, Olivia.' Erin hangs up, leaving Olivia with her jaw to the floor. 'What the fuck?' she says out loud, staring at the dark screen in her hand. A group of teens, whispering and giggling, clearly about her, catch her attention. Her anger towards Erin transfers to them and she throws a deadly glare their way. 'Wankers.'

They laugh even louder. Olivia turns away from them and for a while she stares out the window, trying to make sense of Erin's reaction. How could she tell her to just let it go? She made it sound as though Olivia was blowing it all out of proportion. When clearly, this is not the case. If anything, she's underreacting. He wrote a fucking book about her. Indignation has her clenching her teeth, and then, just to defy Erin, she picks up the book again and turns to the next chapter.

Wild Waves
Chapter 4

'So, how's the first week on your own been?' Orla asked as Ava stepped outside.

'Well, I only dropped him once, so all things considered, I think I nailed it.'

'And the award for Auntie of the Year goes to…' Orla said in a dramatic voice, mimicking a drum roll on her thighs. Ava gave a small bow and they both laughed.

'And what about Ballybridge? Is it growing on ya?'

It had only been a little over a week, but to her own surprise, Ava hadn't regretted her decision once. 'Actually, yeah. Everyone's so nice. How is that possible?'

'It's all the Guinness – we're just perpetually drunk,' Orla said.

'Ha! That bodes well for tonight. I can't wait to discover Ballybridge's nightlife. Having spent most of my days with George, it'll be nice to talk to people who don't throw food when they disagree with me.'

Orla wrapped her arm around Ava's shoulders. 'Oh no, love, we all do that. It's a cultural thing.'

The warmth of Orla's gesture went straight to Ava's heart and, not for the first time that week, she felt she was where she was supposed to be.

Outside the pub, a few people were having animated conversations, cigarettes dangling from their lips, their pints resting on the windowsill behind them.

'Conor and Matt are probably already inside,' Orla said, scanning the crowd. At the mention of Conor, Ava froze and her stomach lurched. Was Orla talking about the guy from the shop? Conor is a common Irish name, but the twenty-something population of Ballybridge probably didn't have too many Conors walking around. Ava quickly pushed a loose strand of hair behind her left ear and wished she'd gone for a different look. Maybe she could pop into the loo and put some lipstick on? Ugh, of course not. Why was she acting like that? *Twat!* She gave Orla what she hoped was a reassuring smile, and followed her in.

Inside, there was a large TV hanging from the ceiling over the bar, broadcasting some sort of sports game. Ava couldn't tell if it was football, rugby or something very similar. Not that she cared. She'd never been interested in sports – playing or watching them. A few men at the bar shouted at the screen as though it could magically change the outcome of the game, and she suppressed a laugh. She'd never understand.

As they waited to get served, Ava's phone vibrated in her handbag. She was expecting a call from James and when she checked, his name lit up on the screen. She tapped Orla on the shoulder. 'I have to get this. I'll come and find you after.'

'Sure. What are you having?'

'A pint's fine,' Ava said.

'Grand. I think the lads are over there.' Orla pointed to the back of the pub.

When Ava looked over, she caught a glimpse of Conor sitting opposite a dark-haired guy in a chequered shirt; Matt, she presumed. Before Conor could see her, she walked out onto the street to answer her phone while ignoring the jittery feeling in her stomach.

'Just a sec!' she half shouted, making her way through the crowd outside the pub.

'Where are you? What's all that noise?' James asked.

'I'm at the pub.'

'The pub? With your sister?'

'No, with Orla, Kate's neighbour. She invited me to meet a few people.'

'Oh, that's nice of her.'

Ava crossed the road to keep the noise to a minimum. 'Yeah, she's great. We haven't had much time to chat, but I already love her.'

'Good. I'm glad you're not alone. How's the baby? Still alive?'

'Oi! I'm an excellent babysitter, I'll have you know.'

'Really? I seem to remember a reverse nappy situation at my sister's.'

Ava couldn't help but laugh. When she and James had offered to babysit one night for his sister, she'd accidentally put on little Cleo's nappy backwards and if James hadn't pointed it out, she wouldn't have been any the wiser. 'I was testing you, obviously,' she said.

'Sure you were.'

'My nappy game is fine now. Better than fine, even. Top notch, some might say.'

On the other end of the line, James let out a short laugh and Ava knew exactly what he looked like in that moment, his chin jutting forwards, his nose crinkled, his eyes half closed. When she first met him at uni, she'd immediately been attracted to him. Not only was he good-looking – he was also a dependable guy. Not a single red flag in sight; just a kind, solid man.

'Whatever you say, love.'

'No, honestly, it's been fine.' Ava continued to tell him about her first week and how, even to her own surprise, she'd settled in quite quickly. James in turn explained his new position at work, and even though she couldn't imagine what it was he loved so much about it, it was soothing to hear his voice, to know he was content living his life selling insurance. And he was good at it. If anyone was going to sell people a sense of security, James was the one to do it.

'I miss you,' James said at the end of his story.

'I miss you too,' she replied.

'I'll come visit soon. When things calm down at work.'

'I'd like that.'

When Kate had begged her to come help out, her relationship with James had been one of the reasons she'd been reluctant to consent. She and James had just agreed to move in together after the summer, and so spending six months apart seemed ludicrous. But Kate had been desperate, and Ava loved her sister too much to leave her hanging.

A small van pulled up in front of the pub and, one by one, musicians emerged from the back, carrying gear and instruments.

'I have to go now, they're waiting for me inside,' Ava said, already turning to cross the street.

'Okay. I'll call you Sunday, yeah?'

'Great. Bye, love.'

'Bye, muppet.'

She pocketed her phone and smiled before heading back inside, glad to have been reminded of how much she missed her boyfriend.

Wild Waves
Chapter 5

When Orla joined them at their table, carrying two beers, Matt lifted an eyebrow. 'Are you okay? Do you need help?' he asked.

Orla shook her head but before she could say anything, Matt continued, 'As in, professional help?'

'You're hilarious. But no, there's one for me and one for my new friend, like.'

Matt searched the crowd and turned back to Orla. 'Lovely to meet you,' he said, addressing the void next to her.

'Oh, fuck off. She's outside taking a call. She'll be here in a couple of minutes,' Orla said, throwing Matt a look of faux despair.

'Who's this new friend, then?' Conor asked.

'Kate's sister, Ava.'

Conor swallowed. The glimpse he'd caught of her earlier had not been a figment of his imagination after all, then. Wiping his suddenly sweaty palms on his trousers, he straightened his back, readying himself for her arrival. When she appeared moments later, Conor took a swig of his beer, just for something to do with his hands. She was wearing a long, camel coat over a pair of jeans and a dark green jumper, but it was her bright smile Conor noticed first. It was mesmerising, just as he remembered it.

Orla introduced them, pointing at each person. 'Ava, Matt, Conor.'

'So you're still alive, then?' Ava said to Conor.

'It's a miracle,' he replied, the corner of his mouth lifting.

'I'm sorry, you two know each other?' Orla threw a questioning look in Conor's direction.

'Oh yes, we go way back,' Ava said.

Conor tried to keep a straight face, feeling Matt's eyes on him. When he met his gaze, Matt bared all his teeth in the biggest knowing grin Conor had ever seen.

'Nice to meet you,' Ava said to Matt, before giving Orla an explanation. 'We met at Paddy's.'

'Oh?' Now Orla's eyes were boring down on him. He pretended not to notice. Instead, he focused on Ava. Once again, her openness charmed him.

'Have a seat,' Matt said, kicking back the chair next to Conor's. Orla handed Ava her pint and raised her own in a toast. 'To old and new friends. Sláinte!'

They all joined in, raising their glasses. 'Sláinte!'

The booth they were in was small for four people. Ava's knee occasionally brushed up against Conor's thigh, making it incredibly difficult for him to focus on anything else. Every time she moved, a whiff of coconut reached him and his mind drifted to that Sunday at Paddy's. A warmth settled in his chest. What was happening?

'So, Ava, do you like Arctic Monkeys?' Matt asked.

'That's a rhetorical question, right?' she replied.

'Fair point. We were just talking about going to see them when they tour their new album. You should join us.'

'I'd love to! Alex Turner is a genius. "Do Me a Favour" is the best song ever written, hands down.'

'Oh my God, yes, although I would go for "A Certain Romance". The lyrics that man produces? Mental!' Orla jumped in.

'Nope, definitely "505",' Conor said.

Ava met his eye. 'A romantic,' she said, and nodded as though his answer had pleased her. Around the table, Matt and Orla went quiet for a second, and Conor knew without looking at them that they were fixated on him and Ava. Ava must've picked up on it too, because she quickly continued.

'I saw them at Glasto,' she said. 'Best gig ever. I mean, Alex doesn't say much, but when he does… God, that man has a way with words.'

'You were there too?' Orla's eyes were big with wonderment. 'This, you and me, it was always meant to be… I knew it.'

Matt made a face behind Orla's back, and even though she couldn't possibly have seen it, she poked him in the ribs with her elbow.

'Ouch! I didn't say anything!' He put his empty glass down and raised his hands, palms facing forwards to prove his innocence.

Grateful for the distraction, Conor got up. 'Who wants another drink?' he asked.

They all raised their hands.

'I'll help you out,' Matt said, that big smirk back on his face.

On their way to the bar, Conor nearly ran into a very short man carrying a bass drum. He was part of the band who'd begun setting up their equipment on the small stage in the back. Conor had seen them perform once before, and remembered being impressed by their energy. He was looking forward to seeing them play again, if only to distract Matt and Orla.

'The Monday paper mystery has been solved.' Matt threw his arm around Conor while they waited their turn.

'Huh?'

'Don't *huh* me, Conor. You got distracted by Ava! That's why you forgot the paper.'

Conor shook his head. 'Don't be ridiculous.'

But Matt ignored him. 'I knew it! Something had to be up. Your routine is so set, you'd never simply forget.'

'How would you know? You're not always here.'

'Oh, I know you, my friend. And I know what I'm seeing at the moment.'

'And what's that?'

'You're into her.'

'I've literally met her twice before now.'

'Twice? At Paddy's?'

Hmm, he shouldn't have said that. 'No, once at the beach.'

Matt let out the loudest laugh, slapping Conor on the back as he did. 'Let me guess: Monday morning?'

'Fuck off, Matt.'

'Mate, this is great. Finally a reason for you to stop all that dreaming and actually do something again.'

'Excuse me?' Conor said.

Matt turned away from Conor and leaned over the bar to order their pints and some crisps. When he turned around, his expression was serious. 'Here, look, you know as well as I do that fuck all goes on in this town, okay? This could be the most exciting thing that's happened to you in years. You're always talking about following your dreams and not doing what everyone else is doing. But you never *do* anything. You've been here five years now, living with your dad and working at Paddy's. Do something for once, Conor! Get that girl!'

He shoved two pints in Conor's hands and when he registered the shock on his friend's face, he added: 'I'm sorry mate. But think about it.'

Matt had always been an honest guy. But he was also a joker, never passing on the opportunity to make the people around him laugh. It was easy to forget sometimes how honest he could be. In the twenty years they'd been friends, they'd had some heated conversations, but never on a personal level. They agreed as often as they disagreed, but they'd never fallen out, and even though Conor knew Matt had his best interests at heart, he was still shocked by this level of frankness.

Was he right, though?

Orla was laughing at something Ava said when Matt approached them, and Ava got up to take the beers from him. Conor lingered a little, watching them all. It looked surreal. On the one hand, it was disorienting seeing Matt and Orla with someone else in their booth, and on the other hand, it was as if she'd always been there, as if she was supposed to be there. When she noticed him, she smiled and that thing in his chest stirred once again.

'Crisps?' he asked, handing Orla her pint and tossing the bags onto the table.

'Ava's a musician, too!' Orla said, clearly enamoured with her new friend.

'Not really, though. I mean it's nothing professional or anything.'

'What do you play?' Conor asked.

'I mostly sing, and I play the guitar a little. Nothing spectacular.'

'Don't you think we should be the judge of that?' Matt asked.

Ava laughed and shook her head. 'No, you can trust me on that. Really.'

She had the kind of smile that made it impossible not to smile too. It was radiant, and every time her face lit up, the corners of Conor's mouth involuntarily tugged upwards. Orla glanced at Conor from across the table. Not wanting to catch her eye, he looked away, but she kicked him in the shin, forcing him to face her. She was communicating with him by frantically wiggling her eyebrows, and although he had an idea of what they were trying to say, he pretended not to understand. Her eyes went from him to Ava and back and he almost laughed out loud. She looked ridiculous.

'I might be looking for a new guitarist, actually,' Orla said, giving her eyebrows a rest when she realised Conor wasn't going to engage.

'Oh no, really, I'm not that good. Strictly campfire songs – "Country Roads" and what not,' Ava said.

'Really? I find that hard to believe.'

'Me too,' Conor said, meeting Ava's gaze.

She held onto it and tilted her head to the right. 'Are you calling me a liar?'

'I would never.'

'Hmm.'

The room around them seemed to disappear for a moment, and all he could see was the golden glow in her defiant eyes. Fuck, she was beautiful.

'If you change your mind, let me know, though,' Orla said.

'Don't hold your breath.'

'So, what brings you to Ballybridge, then? Orla says you're staying with Kate?' Matt asked.

'Uh-huh, she's back at work but couldn't find an au pair before September, so she basically forced me to come help out.'

'She can be quite convincing, can't she?' Orla said.

'Oh, she's the worst.'

'Did you take time off work then?' Matt asked.

'I'd just finished a temp contract and didn't really have anything lined up immediately. I'm starting a job at my uncle's firm in September though.'

'What's the new job?'

'Sales assistant. My uncle manages the sales team of a software company.'

'Really?' Conor leaned back in his chair, giving her a quizzical look. She did not seem like a sales assistant at all.

'Yes, really.'

'Huh.'

'Huh, what?'

'Nothing.'

'You said, *huh*. It clearly meant something.'

Conor shook his head. 'Just didn't peg you for a corporate girl.'

'What's that supposed to mean?' Her brow furrowed with indignation.

'Oh no, it's a compliment,' he said.

'A compliment? What's wrong with corporate?'

Conor laughed. 'Are you serious?'

'Yes, please enlighten me.' Ava folded her arms across her chest.

'Everything,' Conor said.

'Oh, here we go again,' Matt chimed in, reminding Conor he was not alone with Ava. He'd temporarily forgotten. Again.

'Conor thinks everyone who works a nine-to-five corporate job is a sell-out.'

'Do you, now?' Ava said.

He did, but he didn't want to put her off any more, and so he needed to give this a spin.

'Matt is pulling it out of context. I just think a lot of people are very unhappy, but they don't do anything about it because they're stuck in their golden cage.'

Maybe not the best spin he could've given it, but he wasn't going to lie either.

'Elaborate,' Ava said.

'People always want more. A bigger house, more cars, fancier cars, a massive garden, kids… but all of those things cost money. And in order to get that money, they need a higher paying job with lots of benefits. They don't care if they love their jobs, they just desperately need the pay. And so they become unhappy, but there's no way out. They're stuck.'

'Is this your manifesto?' Ava smiled. 'Or just a madman's rant?'

'Ah, see, I knew you thought I was a madman.'

'I saw you swimming in the ocean. It was only going to go downhill from there on out, to be honest.'

Their eyes locked again, but Matt broke the spell. 'How is your sister, by the way? Is she still single, then?'

His question was followed by a loud, short laugh from Orla. 'Ha! In your dreams, like.' She turned to Ava. 'Matt here has a thing for older women, but the problem is, they don't have a thing for him. Isn't that right, Matthew?'

He narrowed his eyes at her at the mention of his full name, but then recovered quickly.

'Is that jealousy?' Matt asked. Conor could've sworn he heard a hint of hope in Matt's tone. The three of them had been friends for the majority of their lives, but lately he'd noticed something had shifted between Matt and Orla. He felt a tension that hadn't been there before. Maybe something had happened, he wasn't sure. It wouldn't have surprised him though. Conor didn't believe in friendships between straight men and women, especially ones this close. It was the whole *When Harry Met Sally* thing. If the friendship was profound enough, eventually at least one of the two would fall – the balance was too delicate.

'Yes, obviously, my burning desire for you is turning me into a monster.' Orla picked up her pint and took a big swig, her eyes still on Matt, who grinned back at her.

Conor made a mental note to check in with Matt the next day, and then turned his attention back to Ava, not willing to let her off the hook just yet. 'What job would you do if you could choose anything?'

'Why are you assuming I wouldn't be a sales assistant?'

'Would you?'

At that exact moment, the band wrapped up the sound check, introduced themselves as The Weeping Willows and invited everyone to join in if they knew the words. Ava shrugged as though it was no longer possible to reply now that the band had started playing. But she didn't have to answer his question. From the look on her face, he knew he was right. This girl was not a corporate sell-out.

The band played Irish folk songs with a modern twist, perfectly catering to their audience. Ava looked delighted as people joined in and when Matt asked her to dance, she didn't hesitate. Conor was not much of a dancer himself, although with a couple more beers he could probably be persuaded. For now, he just sat there and watched her move, her plait bouncing up and down on her shoulder to the rhythm of the music. She laughed as Matt held her hand and twirled her around, nearly tripping over his feet. Conor reminded himself not to get carried away – she was only here for a few months. But it was harder than he'd hoped. The energy she brought with her lifted him up somehow. It was like that feeling at the very end of winter, when you first realise the light is coming back in and you hear a couple of birds singing in the morning and you know better days are just around the corner.

Beside him, Orla nudged him gently with her shoulder. He turned to face her, and she gave him a sweet smile. 'You like her, don't you?'

Conor looked over to Ava and at the same time she looked at him. 'Maybe,' he said, not breaking eye contact.

Orla grabbed his hand under the table and squeezed it. 'I think you'll be fine,' she said.

The rest of the evening they danced, sang and laughed until they were too tired to do anything else. Orla left first. She had to get up early in the morning to teach and hoped to give her voice enough time to recover by then. When Matt announced he was leaving too, Conor and Ava got up and joined him. Matt unlocked his bike and, moments later, they watched him zigzag home.

'I'm heading that way.' Ava pointed towards her left.

'Me too.'

They walked in silence for a while.

'So, are you glad you came?'

She turned her head sideways to face him. 'To Ireland, or to the pub?'

'Both.'

It took her a beat longer to answer than he'd hoped.

'I am,' she said then.

Even though she was still walking beside him, he already longed to see her again. Would it be strange if he asked her to go for a drink with him alone? And how would he ask? He hadn't done this in years.

'Orla and Matt are lovely,' she said. 'Have you been friends long?'

'Most of our lives, yeah.'

'Wow. I've only got friends I met at uni.'

'It's a small town thing, I suppose.'.

'Sometimes I wish I lived in a small town. It's rather comforting to know everyone, isn't it?'

'It can be. But it also means there's no escape.'

'Escape from what?'

'I don't know – people's ideas, opinions… They've known you all your life, and because of that, they have their assumptions about who you are now. They can never forget what they've always known about you. No clean slates here.'

'Hmm, I see that.'

Her fingers brushed up against his, but instead of reaching out, he pulled back and buried his hands in his pockets, immediately regretting it.

When they arrived at Kate's, Ava ruffled through her bag for the key. 'Thanks for walking me home.' She leaned in to kiss him on the cheek, the touch of her soft lips burning his skin.

'Ah, no bother. It's on my way,' he said, cocking his head in the direction of his house. He wasn't sure if it was wishful thinking, or if she really looked disappointed by his answer. Still, he gathered his courage. 'Do you maybe want to get a drink sometime next week?'

There it was – those were the best words he could come up with. Ava seemed to hesitate. He was already thinking of something to say to take it back, when she broke the agonising silence. 'Yeah, I'd like that.'

They exchanged phone numbers and, encouraged by her answer – and probably also by the alcohol in his system – he leaned in and kissed her on the cheek again, inhaling some of that coconut scent. 'Goodnight, Ava.'

'Night.'

He watched her close the door behind her and then headed home. When he got there, he found himself still smiling.

6

When Olivia pulls herself from the pages, the rain has stopped. The evil teens are gone and have been replaced by a group of tourists from Belgium, a tiny flag sticking out of the guide's backpack. But still, she has no idea where to go. She's so worked up, going home seems like an even worse idea than before. Graham will immediately catch on and ask her what's wrong, and she does not want to lie to him. But how can she explain it all? How do you tell the man you love that you've just run into another man, the one you loved before him, who broke your heart? And you clearly never got over him because seeing him made your body crumble. Oh, and also, he wrote a book about you, and your best friend is telling you to get over it, because you're a thirty-eight-year old woman who should get a bloody grip.

Yeah, there's no procedure for that. Walking around aimlessly it is, then.

She dumps her empty paper cup in one of the bins and makes her way outside. The book weighs heavy in her handbag as she paces through the wet London streets. A part of her wants to hide out somewhere and read the thing from start to finish in one go, but another terrified part is stopping her. The part that still loves Eamonn. Even though she wants to shout at him, slam her fists into his chest and call him out for his hypocrisy, she can't deny it. The moment she heard his voice, even before she'd seen him, she'd felt it. His voice is

Pavlov's bell and she's just a stupid, drooling dog. How is that fair? What has she done to deserve this? She's been nothing but a decent human being. Sure, sometimes she can be moody, short-fused and a bit judgmental, but that's no reason for karma to make her life so complicated, is it? She has a good thing going with Graham. Why send Eamonn to her now? Is this a test? And if so, what are the requirements for a passing grade?

Perhaps Erin is right – although she could've been nicer about getting her point across. Reading his book is only going to make things worse. Even after a few chapters, it's clear it'll only bring back more memories and ignite old feelings, and for what? She and Eamonn have proven more than enough times they're wrong for each other. And she loves Graham. They've worked so hard on their project, put everything they have into it, and if it works, it'll be the greatest thing they've ever done together. And they've already done so many fantastic things. Graham has pushed her to think bigger ever since she met him. From the moment he got her to go to the US with him for an exposé on Black women's mortality rates during childbirth, she's been in awe of him and his talents. He's adventurous, wild and just the most wonderful human being. What is she even doing, putting any of that at risk for someone who broke her heart more than once?

Stupid, stupid dog.

With renewed clarity, she stops in the middle of the road to figure out the fastest way home. The nonsense has to end. She will pass this test. When she looks around, she finds she's walked all the way to Regent's Park, which means the closest Northern Line stop is the Chalk Farm one. As she crosses the small bridge near London Zoo that takes her to the main road, she makes a list of things she's excited about. Getting far away from her mum and dad is the first thing that comes to mind. Having an entire ocean between them will automatically lead to fewer interactions, and that in itself is a dream come true.

Then she remembers the old Vancouver warehouse they're renting. The loft upstairs with its exposed brick walls and massive industrial windows. The view of the ocean and the mountains. The open space downstairs that will serve as their workshop. She can already imagine Graham, standing amongst the teens, inspiring them with his passionate speeches about ethics and morals in journalism, as she catches him in just the right lighting with her camera. Her heart swells at the thought and she picks up her pace, desperate to get home to him now, to fall into his arms and tell him she loves him.

Her phone buzzes in her back pocket as she crosses the park towards the tube station. On autopilot, she takes it out and finds a message from Graham. As though he was reading her mind.

When are you home?

She quickly types out her reply.

On my way. Half hour tops.

His status indicates he's typing again and, as she walks on, she keeps one eye on her screen.

'Olivia.' A voice coming from behind her. Her stomach drops for the second time that day at the sound of it and she freezes.

No. No. No. No. No. She closes her eyes, willing it to go away.

But then he calls out again. 'Liv?'

And she turns around.

Damn you, Pavlov.

7

She turns, looks at him and shakes her head. 'Go away, Eamonn.'

Before he can say anything, she stalks off again. It takes him a second to recalibrate. When he saw her crossing the park from the hill, he ran after her. An accidental run-in with her twice in one day had to mean something. But Olivia wants nothing to do with him.

'Olivia, could you please stop for a second?'

'No.' She trudges on, leaving him behind.

The legging-clad mothers of Primrose Hill, with their buggies and labradoodles, stare at their interaction. Eamonn ignores them and catches up to Olivia. She's trying to out-walk him without running, but his legs are longer and now they're side by side. At the park's exit, they have to stop to cross the road.

'Let me buy you a coffee,' Eamonn tries.

'I don't drink coffee anymore.'

Eamonn lets out a short laugh. 'Really?'

She turns sideways to look at him, anger emanating from her narrowed eyes. 'People change.'

The unveiled stab at their history hits its mark. For a second Eamonn has nothing to say. Has she changed so much that he doesn't know her at all anymore? Or is she trying to hurt him so he'll walk away? 'You can drink something else, you know. I'm sure they have tea as well.'

She doesn't react. Her focus is on the traffic.

'Five minutes, that's all I'm asking.'

A car stops to let them cross and, as she steps out ahead of him, he can see his book poking out of her bag.

'I never pegged you for a book thief.'

She halts on the footpath, her cheeks flushed with what he hopes is shame for stealing and not anger. But then he sees her balled-up fists, pointing towards the least favourable outcome. Maybe calling her a criminal was not the best way of easing the tension between them.

'Don't worry about that,' she snaps. 'I'm returning it tomorrow. Apparently, I already know how it ends.'

Bewildered, Eamonn stammers. 'What?'

People push past them and they take a step aside, Olivia's eyes still boring down on him.

'You want to talk?' she says. 'Fine.' She adjusts her bag on her shoulder and buries her hands in her pockets. 'What is wrong with you, Eamonn? I haven't seen you in ages and all of a sudden you show up at *my* bookshop with a book about *me* which I knew nothing about. What did you think was going to happen? Did you expect me to welcome you with open arms and ask for your bloody autograph?'

Even if she broke his heart, he knows she's got a point. If it had been the other way around, he'd have been shaken up too. He softly shakes his head and meets her eye. 'I'm sorry.'

Olivia shrugs. 'It's too late for that. Just go home, Eamonn.'

Before he can say another word, she turns again and stalks off.

'Livvie, please!' he shouts, a last attempt at holding on to her, even though he hates making a scene in public. If he could see himself now, he'd crumble in shame. But it works. Olivia stops and slowly turns around.

'Why did you write the book?'

Her eyes are pleading for an explanation, making him desperately want to give her one. But the problem is, he can't.

Why did he do it? Was it really just a way of processing what happened? If that's the case, he could've just written it and never showed anyone. Both their lives would've just gone on as they were. He would probably never have seen her again. The thought of it floods him with grief. Maybe that's why he did it? To make sure he'd get to see her face again? Even the angry version of it.

'Can we just sit down somewhere and talk?'

Olivia opens her mouth to answer, and she looks like she's about to agree when her phone lights up in her hand. She reads the message on her screen and briefly closes her eyes before looking back up at him. 'I can't do this now, Eamonn. I have to go.'

With one last disappointed look, she turns and walks away. Eamonn doesn't follow. He's only seen her look like that a couple of times, and on each occasion broken hearts had been involved. It's a look he'd hoped never to have to see again.

When Ben arrives at the Queens pub, Eamonn is already at a table in the corner, cradling a pint in his hands, the cold glass cooling his warm skin. Ben smiles, but when he sees Eamonn's expression, it turns into a frown. 'What happened? Did you get heckled?'

'Something like that.'

He throws his coat over the chair opposite Eamonn and turns to the bar. 'Give me a sec.' When he returns with a Guinness in hand, they clink their glasses. 'Go on, what happened?'

'Olivia was there.'

The sip Ben has just taken nearly comes flying back out again. 'Fecking hell.'

'Yeah.'

'Was this the first time since—'

'Uh-huh.'

'What happened?'

Eamonn tells him what little there is to report and as usual, Ben listens until he's certain Eamonn is done talking. 'I'm sorry, mate. But can I ask something?'

'If I say no, will that stop you?'

Ben smiles and then he delivers. 'Why didn't you just tell her why you wrote the book?'

There's a long pause in which Eamonn considers the question and the answer. Then he shrugs. 'Because I don't know.'

'Feck off.'

'I don't.'

'Eamonn…'

'Ben…'

Ben's eyes widen with frustration. 'You're really going to sit there and tell me you don't know why you spent years writing a book about her and then decided to publish it?'

Another shrug from Eamonn while he sips his pint.

'You're such an eejit sometimes, you know?'

'Thanks. Have you considered cheerleading?'

'I have, actually. Just not a pyramid kind of guy.' Ben brings his pint to his lips and then wipes his mouth with the back of his hand. 'Why don't you just tell her you still love her?'

'I don't. I haven't seen her in over a decade.'

'Sure. I also write eighty-thousand-word love letters to women I don't love.'

'More like fifty. It's a novella,' Eamonn retorts.

'Yeah, that's the essence of the argument here.'

Eamonn shrugs. Does he still love her? Is that really why he wrote the book?

'Actually,' Ben says, 'I think you've nailed the problem here.' He picks up the beermat and twirls it between his fingers. 'You're afraid to admit to yourself you still love her. You've always been afraid to admit it, even back then. That's why it didn't work out.'

Ben's blatant honesty catches Eamonn off guard once again. Throughout their friendship it hasn't happened all that often, but when it does, it always knocks him sideways. The worst thing is, in hindsight, Ben is always right. It's just hard to process in the moment. But he can't be right this time. Because if he is, the past fifteen years of Eamonn's life need some serious revaluation.

'So, what's your answer then, Dr Phil? Why did I write it?'

Ben shrugs as though it's blatantly obvious. 'Because that way, you don't actually have to tell her. You think she'll get the message this way and if she doesn't, you're safe. No risk taken. Again.'

Eamonn shakes his head, but Ben's words nestle inside his brain.

Opposite him, Ben opens the menu on the table, giving Eamonn a moment to process what he said.

'Burger?' he asks then.

'Yeah, alright.'

In mere seconds, Ben makes his way to the bar to order their meals while Eamonn watches his best friend, now a married man and father of two. He always thought he'd be a dad too, by now. And he still wants that. As a man, time is biologically less of the essence, but he definitely doesn't aspire to Mick Jagger status. With his fortieth birthday a few months behind him, and his love life barely existing, he can't help but wonder if his friend is right.

When Ben returns with new drinks, Eamonn asks: 'Is she still taking photos?'

'Yeah, she's a pro now.'

This makes Eamonn smile. He always knew she had it in her.

'But mate, there's something you probably need to know.'

The tone of his voice makes Eamonn push his fingertips in his eye sockets in anticipation. 'Go on.'

'She's moving to Canada… next week.'

His hands fall to the table and he looks up to see if Ben is messing. 'What?'

'You sure you want to hear more?'

No, he's not sure. But it seems that if he ever wants to get the resolution he's been looking for for years, now is the time, and that means taking his head out of the sand. He waves a hand at Ben, suggesting he can go on.

'She has a boyfriend – Graham, a journalist – and they're setting up this project together in Vancouver.'

Nausea swells in his stomach. How did he not see this coming? Of course she has a boyfriend. Of course she's happy without him. She was the one who left him behind.

'I'm sorry, mate,' Ben says.

Eamonn cradles his face in his hands, elbows resting on the table, and grunts. If Ben is right and he still loves Olivia, it doesn't matter anymore. There's no way he's telling her now.

'Fecking hell.'

'Just... Eamonn, can I say something else?'

With his eyes closed, he grunts again. It's apparently the only sound he remembers to make.

'I still think you should tell her.'

Eamonn's head snaps up at this. 'What?'

'I think you two need to talk. It's been years, but clearly neither of you have let it go. If you want to move on, and give her a chance of moving on, I think you should finally talk about what happened.'

'I'm not going to mess up her life again. And anyway, she doesn't want to talk to me.'

'She literally just found out you wrote a book about her and then saw you reading from it, after not having seen you in over a decade. The girl's in shock. Give her a moment, will ya?'

Behind Ben, the waiter appears with two plates stacked with food, food that Eamonn suddenly doesn't have the stomach for anymore. They both thank him and wait until he's gone.

'Do you really think she'll talk to me?' Eamonn asks while Ben dips a large chip in some ketchup.

'I do. But tell her the truth, yeah? All of it.'
Eamonn nods, even though he's still unsure it's a good idea.

8

When Olivia arrives home, Graham is in the kitchen with two frozen pizzas ready to go into the oven. 'You were gone longer than I thought. I was beginning to think you went ahead with that matricide.'

Olivia smiles the best smile she can manage. 'Nah, I'm saving that for the party.'

'So, it went well?'

'She basically scolded me for not giving her grandchildren and insinuated my job was just a hobby, so... smooth sailing.'

Graham slides the pizzas into the oven and walks over to where she's leaning against the fridge. He wraps his arms around her shoulders and pulls her close. 'I'm sorry I made you go alone.'

Focusing all her attention on his embrace, she closes her eyes. His solidity and warmth wrap around her like a weighted blanket. 'You're going in first on Friday. I'm using you as my armour.'

'About that...' He pulls away and when she looks up at him, his expression morphs into something ominous, making Olivia's heart plummet into her stomach. She can't handle any more bad news today.

'I got a call from the plumbing company in Vancouver. There's been a double booking apparently, and if we want all our plumbing done before September, they have to do it on Monday.'

'Monday? This Monday coming?'

'Yeah.'

'But we won't be there yet. We only leave on Wednesday.'

'That's the thing. One of us will have to be there.'

Olivia's chest tightens with anxiety. Did she wake up in hell this morning?

'But I promised Amira I'd manage the centre until the ninth. And my dad's party. Anna's coming over for that with Charlie. Can't your mum go?'

'No, she's working and can't get the time off.' Graham places his hands on her cheeks and steadies her. 'I'll go. It's okay. I think I can still change my flight, and when you join me the week after, you'll have a toilet and a shower.'

The entire day catches up with her and tears burst from her eyes. 'We were going to do this together,' she says in a broken voice.

'Hey, we still are. Why are you so upset?' He pulls her close again and firmly kisses her forehead. 'It's only a few days.'

For a split second she considers telling him everything, but she's tired and everything is falling apart, and the last thing she needs is to make Graham upset too.

'I'm just knackered. My mum wore me down.'

Graham brushes away her tears and smiles. 'Remember when we first met, and I pretended not to know you were the famous photographer Olivia Clarke?'

Of course she remembers. It was her second solo exhibition, a series about women living in poverty in London, and it had gone really well. People were interested in her photos, the stories behind them. Someone had even put in an offer to buy the whole series. By the final day, Olivia had been over the moon and unaware it could get even better. But that day, just before closing time, she'd found a ridiculously attractive man staring at one of her works. When she approached him, he didn't take his eyes off the photo in front of him, but started telling her how much he loved it, how it portrayed something he had been trying to put into words but had never managed. He'd asked her what she thought, and then she'd told him who she was. An hour later, they were in a bar somewhere in East London, making their first plan to work together.

A soft smile shines through her tears. 'Of course I remember.'

'I knew even before we started talking I wanted to work with you on whatever project you had in mind. And I still do, five years later. You're amazing at what you do, and I'm not just saying that because I wanna get in your pants.'

A snort escapes her. 'Graham.'

'I mean it. Don't listen to your mom. It's not a hobby and you don't owe her grandkids either. Nobody owes anyone children, okay?'

Olivia nods against his chest, her tears staining his dark green T-shirt.

'Now, what do you say we eat these pizzas and drink some wine, and I try to get in your pants anyway?'

His fingers rake through her hair as she looks up at him. 'Don't you have plans with Turner?'

'Oh, fuck! I forgot. Maybe I can reschedule?'

'You're leaving this weekend, remember?'

Graham throws his head back in exasperation. 'Fine. Let's skip the pizza then.'

A genuine laugh takes her by surprise. Give it to Graham to make her laugh after a day like today.

The moment Graham leaves the flat, she heads into the bathroom to change into her pyjamas, her entire body aching with exhaustion. In the mirror, her face looks drawn, her eyes have dark circles under them and her wrinkles seem deeper than usual. All clear signs of what went down today. She can still hardly believe it. If someone would've told her yesterday that this would happen, she would've never stopped laughing. The ridiculousness of it. Yet, here she is. Definitely not laughing.

Worn down by a full day of riding emotional rollercoasters. And Olivia hates rollercoasters.

She pulls her hair back in a bun and leaves the mirror behind. All she wants to do is get into bed and watch some episodes of *New Girl*. A hefty dose of Winston Bishop is exactly what she needs right now. She makes herself a cup of tea, takes her laptop and phone from the kitchen table and grabs a packet of digestives to take with her into the bedroom. As it's the end of June, and not yet eight p.m., she draws the curtains to darken the room and keep all evidence of the outside world where it belongs. Outside. She knows most of the episodes by heart, but still laughs every time Furguson makes an appearance. Halfway through her favourite episode, 'Background Check', Olivia's phone buzzes on the bedside table. Without giving it much thought, she unlocks the screen, taking her straight to her messages. An unknown number appears, but it doesn't take her long to put a name to it.

I wrote the book because it was the only way I could keep you.

Olivia sits up, heart racing, a lump stuck in her throat.

What is he talking about? If he wanted to keep her, then why didn't he just meet her as he'd promised? The words make no sense to her at all. Is there a possibility she's got it wrong? Olivia's stomach turns as the idea takes form in her mind. It would explain why he wrote the story. It would also explain why he'd hoped she'd talk to him today. But it wouldn't explain why he wasn't there ten years ago. Or why he's never tried to get in touch with her since. Does his book hold all the answers?

She sits frozen for a long time, an image of Jessica Day stuffing her bra with aquarium rocks locked on her laptop screen. This is the part that always makes her laugh the most. Not now, though.

Before she knows it, she's pushing the duvet to the side and heading over to the living room, where her bag is hanging off a chair, *Wild Waves* sticking out from the top. She understands the danger of what she's about to do, but like a recovering addict, she's unable to resist the source of her addiction when it's within reach.

Back in bed, Olivia inhales deeply before she takes another hit.

Wild Waves
Chapter 6

When Ava woke the next morning, George and Kate were in the living room – George playing with a baby doll on the rug; Kate stretched out on the sofa, laptop balanced on her thighs.

'Morning,' Kate said.

'Morning.' Ava kissed the top of George's head, disappeared into the kitchen and came back a few moments later, a cup of coffee in one hand, a slice of buttered toast in the other.

She sat down in the chair opposite the sofa and folded her legs underneath her.

'How long have you been up?'

'Since six.' Kate yawned, making Ava do the same. She was feeling a little dehydrated from the night before but other than that, she felt fine. The only hangover symptoms she was feeling had nothing to do with the alcohol she'd consumed. She'd spent half the night trying to convince herself that there was nothing wrong with accepting Conor's offer for a drink. They could become friends. After all, she would go for a drink with *Orla* alone. Did it make that much of a difference that he was a man? Theoretically it didn't, but she couldn't ignore the fact he'd occupied her thoughts more than once since she met him in the shop. From the moment she'd first seen him, there had been something about him that pulled her in, and it was that exact same thing that made her slightly nauseous now.

'How was it?' Kate asked, closing her laptop and sliding it onto the coffee table.

'It was fun, yeah. We talked, we laughed, we danced, we drank… a lot.'

'That sounds about right. Anything exciting happen?'

'Yeah, Matt wanted to know if you were still single actually.'

'Really?' Kate said, more flattered than surprised.

Ava hadn't expected that. 'Yes. Why? Are you interested?'

'Do I want him to be my baby daddy, you mean? No. Definitely not. Would I enjoy a different sort of "relationship" with him? Maybe…'

The look on Kate's face betrayed the options she had in mind.

'Are you serious? Also, please never say baby daddy again.'

'I know you haven't been here long, Ave, but he's about the finest specimen to roam this wee town, so yeah, I'm dead serious. Mummy has needs too, you know.'

Kate had a point. Matt was tall, he had broad shoulders and a narrow waist, and his jawline was so pronounced you could slice a block of cheese with it. His black hair and light blue eyes made him look otherworldly, and the best part was that he didn't even seem to realise any of this. He was kind and funny and a pretty good dancer. There was probably no one else like him in a one-hundred-mile radius and yet, he was not the one gnawing at Ava's insides.

'I see your point,' Ava said. 'Would you like me to give him your number?'

Kate shook her head. 'He's eleven years younger than I am.'

'So?'

'So… it's bad enough I chose to be a single mother in this part of the world. If I go and seduce the town's only eligible bachelor, just for pleasure, they might burn me at the stake.'

Ava laughed. 'Now *that* would be a sight.'

For a second Kate studied her, a knowing smile on her lips. 'It's good to see you happy, though,' she said.

Ava frowns. 'What do you mean?'

'Oh come on, Ave. You were miserable back home.'

'Sorry, what? I wasn't miserable! Why would you say that?'

Kate sat up straight, palms out as though it was obvious what she was talking about.

'You're working temp jobs and sitting at home Friday nights watching Midsomer Murders with that vanilla boyfriend of yours, and you're going to work for Uncle Richard. You hate Uncle Richard.'

Ava's jaw dropped. '*You* hate him.'

'Everybody hates him,' Kate uttered, all fired up, throwing her arms up in the air.

She was right. The man was insufferable, but that was beside the point.

'That job has great prospects. And what's wrong with James? And vanilla, for that matter?'

'You're twenty-three. You shouldn't be thinking of your pension and insurance. And James represents all those things. Mum and Dad have brainwashed you.'

'What's got into you? I am happy, Kate. Really.'

Kate studied her for a moment, her eyebrows pinched, as though that would make it easier to spot the lie. 'Promise me you'll do something crazy once in a while?' Her voice was pleading, a bit sad even. Ava moved to sit beside her and wrapped her arms around her sister. 'I'll kick an old lady if I see one today, yeah?'

Later that morning, they drove to the nearest town to do the shopping for the upcoming week. On the way home Ava felt her phone buzz in her jeans pocket. Trying not to alert Kate in case it was Conor, she didn't check it. The drive home, although only about forty-five minutes, suddenly seemed endless. She knew this level of anticipation wasn't normal, but no matter how hard she tried to forget about it, her mind kept drifting to their conversation the night before. There had been something about him – something about herself she saw reflected in him that had disoriented her in a way. And now she found herself wanting to talk to him again, to see if she could figure out what exactly it was.

Back at the house, Kate sent Ava to the fishmonger's to pick up her order while she put George to bed and started on lunch. As soon as Ava was alone, she got out her phone and before checking the screen, took a deep breath.

Want to watch a film tonight? xx

Not the message she'd been expecting, but after the initial disappointment wore off, excitement took its place.

You're on. What time? Your place? x

Orla replied immediately with the time and before Ava could put her phone away, another text came in, telling her to wear pyjama bottoms. Ava laughed out loud. It was nice to have someone around to do these things with.

There was a queue at the fishmonger's and when she entered, they all turned to look at her. This was one of those towns where everyone knew everyone, and a newcomer never went unnoticed. Two weeks earlier it might have intimidated her, but now she knew to just go in with a big smile and a *howya* and she would be fine. She even recognised one or two of them who smiled broadly as she entered. When it was her turn, the woman behind the counter grabbed a plastic bag containing her order and reached over to hand it to her. 'Hiya, pet. You're here for Kate's order, right?'

'I am. Thanks,' Ava said as she took the bag from the woman.

'Ava, was it?'

'Yeah, that's right.'

'Well, it's nice to meet you, Ava. I'm Siobhan and that's Marc,' she said, pointing at the man next to her. He gave Ava a friendly nod.

'Nice to meet you both.' Ava opened her handbag to find her wallet.

'Oh no, pet, it's all been paid for. Give Kate my best, will ya?'

'I will. Thanks. Have a nice day.'

'Have a good one, love.'

As Ava left the shop, a cold gust of wind hit her in the face, and yet she couldn't help but think this was the warmest she'd felt in a long time.

The way home led past the grocery shop, which had not escaped her attention. In fact, it may have even been part of her reason for offering to go into town in the first place. Could she go in and pretend to need something for Kate's fish stew? It was plausible, and she was pretty sure she could pull it off without him questioning her true motives. On the other hand, she'd only seen him the night before and he'd said he would text. Or had he? Was she supposed to text him? What exactly had they agreed upon?

Oh my God, why was she even thinking like this? She had a boyfriend, whom she loved.

Lost in thought, chiding herself for her foolish behaviour, she started when her handbag suddenly buzzed against her thigh with a text message.

Are you lost?

When she looked up, he was there, behind the shop window, his phone in his left hand, the 'Out for Lunch' sign in the other. Ava forced down the enormous grin on her face and typed out a response.

Right now? Or in general?

Watching him read the message, she felt a flutter in her stomach. The night before in the pub she'd noticed for the first time how, when he smiled, the skin on his cheeks pulled back, forming two lines around the corners of his mouth on each side, as if his smile was bracketed, and what was said in between brackets was only meant for her.

He briefly looked up, cocking his head to the side, and typed.

Both. But maybe we should focus on the former and save the latter for when we go for that drink?

Another flutter of her stomach at the mention of their plans. She suppressed it and shook her head. *Not lost*, she mouthed.

What? he mouthed back.

I'm not lost, she tried again, this time more slowly, overly enunciating each word.

He shook his head and squinted, trying to make sense of her words. She turned to her phone in despair.

A: I'm not lost. Not at the moment. And also, this is ridiculous. You are literally right there.
C: I know. Want to come in?

Ava held up the bag and pointed at it. Instead of miming or texting, she decided to shout this time. 'I can't! Fresh fish! Kate's waiting!'

Conor nodded but didn't shout back. Ava assumed he was not the shouting type. For a couple of seconds they just stood there, each on their side of the glass, their eyes locked. His gaze was so intense, it was as though he was looking right through her.

When suddenly her phone rang, Ava jumped up. How long had she been standing there like that? Why had she even been standing there like that?

'Is everything okay? Are you lost?' Kate asked when Ava answered.

Ava couldn't help but laugh. Apparently nobody had much confidence in her orientation skills. This town basically had one main road. To get lost here was physically impossible.

'No, I'm not lost.'

This time Conor must've been able to read her lips, because he laughed, bearing all his teeth, even the crooked one. She made a face at him conveying her disbelief, and he did it again. She felt it all the way in the pit of her stomach.

'Then where are you?' Kate asked.

'I'm on my way. Be there in ten minutes.'

She hung up and noticed a text that had come in while she was on the phone.

Should I pick you up on Wednesday when we go for that drink? Wouldn't want you to get lost on your way to the pub.

Ava felt the corners of her mouth rise. Cocky bastard. She rolled her eyes ostentatiously at him and typed.

Oh, would you be so kind, milord? These streets are terribly hard to navigate for a young damsel such as myself. I would be forever grateful for the help of a kind gentleman.

As she hit send, she gave him a defiant glare to clearly convey her sarcasm, which he must have seen, as he appeared to have been looking at her the whole time she was typing. Even though she couldn't hear him, she knew he gave a short laugh when he read it.

Pardon my manners, milady. I'll meet you there at 8.

He bowed and, in an attempt at hiding her flushed cheeks, she curtsied, damning that burning feeling in her stomach.

Wild Waves
Chapter 7

Ava was waiting at the bar, talking to Mike, the barman, when Conor pushed through the swinging doors. Seeing her there with her back turned to him, he couldn't help but marvel at the ease with which she was talking to this complete stranger. When she turned and noticed him, she smiled and kissed him on the cheek, her sweet coconut scent enveloping them both.

'Hi,' she said.

'Hiya. What are you having?'

'Beer, please.'

'Make that two,' Conor said, addressing Mike.

Ava reached for her wallet, but Conor stopped her, placing his hand on hers. He hadn't thought that through. The touch of her hand was so soft and warm, he was sad to let go of it.

'Fine, but I'll get the next one,' she said. 'Thanks for keeping me company, Mike.' She took the drinks from the bar and headed for a small table by the window.

'Anytime,' Mike said, and Conor was certain he meant it. Who wouldn't want to keep her company?

Ava pulled back a chair and sat down. 'Mike's lovely.'

'Yeah, he is. The pub used to be his dad's, but he took over when Tom fell ill. I think he likes it, though.'

'Yeah, apparently he tried several other jobs but none of them stuck.'

Conor smiled. 'How long have you been here?'

Ava checked her watch. 'I don't know, five minutes or something.'

'And you already know more about Mike than I do? I've been here twenty-five years and we were in school together.'

'What can I say? It's my special talent,' she said.

'What other special talents do you have?'

Her eyebrows shot up in surprise, and it was only then Conor realised the many ways his question could be interpreted.

'I mean like things you would put on a CV or something,' he added.

'Sure you do.'

Their eyes met, and for a strange moment it was just the two of them alone in the world again. A blush appeared on her cheeks and she picked up her beer, taking a large sip as she averted her gaze. For all her cheekiness, it seemed she might have been just as flustered as he was.

'I didn't see you at the beach this morning,' she said. 'Finally opened your eyes to the dangers of the ocean, did you?'

'Hmm. My mate spotted a killer whale on Tuesday and tried to go *Free Willy* on it, but it wouldn't jump, so I figured it was best to stay home for a bit, you know, till it finds its own way home.'

'Did he have a harmonica on him?'

'No, he'd left it at home.'

'See, well, that's just foolish, isn't it?'

'He won't make that mistake twice, I tell ya.' Seeing his own amusement mirrored in her expression gave him gooseflesh.

'I didn't think that would stop you from swimming though,' she said.

'Yeah? Why's that?'

'It's just, you seem like a bit of a maverick.'

Conor couldn't help but laugh. 'A maverick?' He sort of liked that she thought that about him, when actually he hadn't really done anything with his life for the past five years.

'Yeah, with your ocean swimming and manifestos and condemnation of corporate souls and all…'

'Interesting.'

'Am I wrong?'

'I don't know. But if I'm a maverick, what are you?'

'Just a normal person.'

'A normal person?'

'Yeah.'

'What kind of a normal person believes sharks live in Ballybridge and wants to be a sales assistant?' He hadn't known her long, but he was almost certain she didn't want to take that job. He'd seen it in the way her gestures changed when she mentioned it in the pub. She'd started picking her cuticles, and her shoulders had set solidly, no longer moving in unison with the rest of her body. And now, he could see it in her expression. The frown line between her eyes deepened as she smiled at him, unconvincingly.

'A: Sharks are real – ask science. B: That job has prospects. I'm planning ahead.' She gave him a defiant glare that set his insides on fire.

'Sure, look, whatever helps you sleep at night.'

'A good pillow and a comforter,' she said, and finished the last quarter of her pint in one go. 'Another one?' She pointed to his glass and pushed back her chair.

Conor nodded and suppressed a massive grin. He hadn't had this much fun in a long time.

When she returned with their drinks, she rolled up the sleeves of her silk blouse and leaned her arms on the table, like she was preparing for battle. 'So, tell me about your story,' she said.

'It's not ready yet.'

'You know what it's about, though?'

He nodded.

'Then tell me.'

'It's about a screenwriter—'

'Ah, writers writing about writers. How meta.'

'Do you want to hear it or not?' he asked, faux-annoyed.

'I'm sorry, go on.' Her eyes shone with amusement.

'It's about a screenwriter who just pitched a story but got rejected halfway through it, and with no money left, he decides to give up forever and leave LA. Flights are too expensive, so he finds an ad online from someone who's looking for a co-pilot to drive a car across the country—'

'Oh, is someone going to get murdered?'

Conor cocked his head. 'Nope.'

'It feels like there should be a murder.'

'There isn't.'

'Hmm… Shame. It would really add to the tension, I think.'

'Do you, now?'

Ava shrugged. She was taunting him, and for some reason he actually wanted her to keep going. What was she doing to him?

'So what happens next then, if there's no murder?'

'You'll have to read it.'

She threw her arms in the air. 'But I can't – it's not finished.'

'Then you'll have to wait.'

'I'm a very impatient person.'

'Really? I wouldn't have guessed.'

Ava let out a huff. 'You seem to have made a lot of assumptions about me.'

'I'm sure you've made just as many about me.'

'See, another one.'

Conor couldn't help but laugh. This girl was exhausting, and he loved it. 'Prove me wrong, then,' he said. 'If you had all the options in the world and money wasn't an issue, what would you do? Would you still be a sales assistant?'

She gave an exasperated sigh, but then her eyes met his and there was something there – a hint of a dream she'd once had, perhaps?

'This again?'

'Go on,' he said, 'humour me.'

She grabbed her pint and slowly sipped it. A bit of foam remained on her top lip when she put the glass down, catching Conor's attention. Tiny drops of condensation slid down the glass as she wiped her lips with her thumb. It's not that he hadn't thought of kissing her before, but now it was all he could do.

'Fine,' she said, pushing a strand of hair behind her ear. 'When I turned sixteen, Kate gave me a camera for my birthday.' She took another sip, tauntingly slow, as though she wanted him to interject. But Conor didn't speak.

'I loved it,' she continued. 'I carried it around everywhere I went and took pictures of everything and everyone in my path. The more pictures I took, the more I wanted to take.'

'And then what happened?'

She shrugged. 'I grew up, that's what happened.'

'That's not an answer.'

'It sure is, Peter Pan. Photography is not a proper job.'

'Tell that to Annie Leibovitz.'

Ava sighed and rolled her eyes. 'Has anyone ever told you you're insufferable?'

His cheeks strained with the biggest smile. 'Loveable? Yes. Insufferable? Not so much, no.'

Wild Waves
Chapter 8 - July 2009

'I'm sorry I haven't made it over yet,' James said on one of their weekly calls. Since the day she left, a little over four months earlier, Ava hadn't had a chance to meet up with James. If he wasn't busy with work, she was the one who'd made plans, and time had rushed by without her realising it.

'That's alright. We've both been really busy.'

'I know,' he said. 'I miss you though.'

'I miss you too.'

And she did miss him, but in a way, she didn't mind that he hadn't come to visit yet. Ava had created a tiny world of her own in Ballybridge, and mixing it with her real life, with reality, somehow didn't feel right.

'Not long until you come home. Has your dad said anything about that flat?'

Ava's dad, a banker, had a Swiss colleague who owned a flat in London he hardly ever stayed at. He'd offered to rent it out for a friendly price to Ava and James when she got back from Ireland.

'Yeah, it's all sorted. The man's having a few things renovated this summer, but after that, he'll give the keys to Dad and we can move in.'

'Perfect.'

Ava removed her phone from her ear to check the time. 'Sorry love, I have to go now,' she said. She ruffled through her earring collection for a pair of gold dangles, and put James on speaker while she put them in.

'No worries, I'm off too. Meeting a few colleagues at the pub to discuss this new client.'

If it hadn't been James telling her that, she would've thought it was an excuse to go to the pub and get pissed, but knowing him, she saw it for what it was. The truth. He was going to sit there and discuss work with two middle-aged men, each drinking one glass of wine. Ava couldn't help but smile at the thought.

'Alright, have fun!' she said.

'I will.'

Ava hung up, sprayed some perfume and headed downstairs.

'You look pretty,' Kate said, the look on her face suggesting it was more a question than a statement.

'Thanks.'

'Meeting the lads at the pub?'

'Uh-huh.' Ava fastened the clasp on her sandal without looking up at her sister. She was actually only meeting Conor. Orla was out of town playing a gig somewhere near Cork, and Matt had offered to cover a colleague's night shift at the hospital.

'I thought Orla was in Cork tonight?'

Eyebrows raised, she turned to her sister. 'Is there something you want to ask me?'

'You and Conor seem to have got quite close.'

It was true, Ava had been meeting up a lot with Conor in the past months. Whenever neither of them was working, they would always end up together, often intentionally, but sometimes they'd just run into each other, as though there was no way around it. If the weather permitted, they'd go to the beach and talk or listen to music, and Ava found herself gravitating towards him more and more each day. He was a fantastic storyteller and even though they often disagreed, his way of thinking intrigued her. And when she talked, he listened, really listened, unlike most people who always seemed to have an answer prepared even before she'd finished speaking. He was such a good listener, she nearly told him everything. Nearly.

'Sure. I'm also close with Orla and Matt. Was I not supposed to make friends here?'

'Oh no, I'm thrilled you've made friends.' The smirk on her face would have been annoying if it hadn't been so comical. 'Especially Conor. He's such a lovely lad.'

'They're all lovely.'

'Oh yeah, definitely.'

That smirk again. Now it was becoming annoying. 'Maybe you should ask him out, if he's so lovely.'

'Maybe I will. If that's okay with you, that is.'

'Don't see why it wouldn't.' Ava grabbed her bag from the coat hanger. 'Are you done now? 'Cause I have to go.'

'All done. Tell Conor I said hi.'

'I'll give him your number so you can tell him yourself. Bye.' Before Kate could say anything else, Ava was out the door.

But on her way to the pub, the conversation with Kate played on her mind. Especially the part where she'd suggested Conor was more than a friend. It unsettled Ava because she loved James. And she was returning to London soon. But denying she'd never felt desire around Conor was ridiculous. The workings of his mind, combined with his broad swimmer's shoulders, dark blue eyes and bracketed smile, had occupied her dreams more than once, and in those moments they were definitely not just friends.

In the pub, Ava had become somewhat of a regular, to the point that Mike had stopped asking what she wanted to drink and just served it as soon as she walked in.

'Hiya, Mike!'

'Ah, my favourite customer.'

'I highly doubt that. How's Sinead?' She grinned. Mike had never spoken to her about Sinead, a flight attendant who lived the next town over but apparently always found the time to come to the pub on Friday nights. Whenever she was there though, Ava noticed the change in Mike – his usual swagger suddenly replaced with a softer, more timid approach. His cheeks flushed and he glanced around to make sure no one had overheard their conversation. Ava laughed. She enjoyed seeing Mike this flustered. But she also really liked him, so she let it go. 'Is Conor here yet?'

Mike shook his head.

'Tell him I'm out back when he comes in?'

'Will do.'

Ava headed for the small beer garden. She took a seat on one of the picnic benches, leaned against the wall and rested her legs on the bench. Just as she was about to start reading the book she'd brought, Conor walked up to her, pint in hand. He grabbed the base of his burgundy T-shirt to wipe at the sweat on his forehead, revealing his stomach. Ava quickly averted her gaze.

'Hiya, Bruce.'

The hairs at the back of her neck stood. The first time he'd called her Bruce, she'd asked him to clarify but he'd refused, told her to figure it out. It had taken her a few days until one rainy morning, she was in front of the telly with a sleepy George on her lap, watching *Finding Nemo*, when it clicked. Now, every time he said it, it made her insides go weak.

There were little drops of perspiration on his upper lip when he leaned in to kiss her on the cheek. It was all she could do not to run her thumb over it.

'I nearly went in the water today,' she said, mostly to distract herself. 'That's how hot it is – it's fear-of-melting-exceeds-fear-of-sharks kind of hot.'

Conor gave her a smirk. 'Want to go now?'

'I said *nearly*. I'm not mad yet.'

He smiled. 'I'll get you there.'

'In the water, or mad?'

'Both, I hope…'

There was something challenging in his eyes, as though he was pushing to see how far this conversation could go without being specific. He was also making it really hard for her to remember he was just a friend.

'Challenge accepted,' she said, against her better judgement. Conor's eyebrows shot up in surprise and Ava quickly turned away. The tables around them filled with more pub-goers, complaining about the heatwave which had been torturing every Irishman in the country for over a week. Ava had spent most of the days on the beach with George under a pink parasol, but even that had been too hot at times. They would all perish if they lived in warmer climates.

'Would you ever live anywhere else?' Ava asked.

His eyes met hers briefly but then he looked away. That was new.

'Sure,' he said. 'You?'

For some reason she didn't believe him. His answer, although quick, was too vague. Conor was a man of details and explanations. 'Like where?' she continued.

'Anywhere.'

'Yeah? You'd move to North Korea?'

'Sure. You?'

He was being evasive. Conor was never evasive. What was this? There was an old candle on the table in between them, softening from the summer heat. Conor picked at the wax and rolled it between his thumb and index finger.

'You're avoiding my question,' she said.

'No, I'm not. I said I would. You're the one not answering.'

'What's stopping you from moving?' She was onto something – she could sense it.

'To North Korea?' he asked. 'There's a few hurdles in the way, to be fair.'

'Funny.'

He looked up again and met her gaze. His eyes looked sad, but she couldn't figure out why.

'You know, for a guy who's always telling me I shouldn't go into corporate and I should follow my dreams, you're awfully rooted in Ballybridge.'

He smiled, but it wasn't a happy smile. 'Well, maybe that's my dream,' he said after a while.

'Is it?'

The staring match continued. Ava knew there was something he wasn't telling her, but she wasn't sure how to get it out of him. Now that she thought about it, it had always been him asking the questions. They'd never really discussed his life much. Sure, he'd given his opinion on almost everything, but how much did she really know about him? He was twenty-five and lived with his dad on a sheep farm. He worked weekends in the grocery shop, and he swam in the ocean to clear his mind. There was the writing, reading and his love of music, but that was it. Did she even know him at all?

'Want another drink?' he finally said. Before she could answer, he was up and gone.

Why would he not talk to her? It couldn't always be the other way around. For once, she wanted to be the one listening and asking the questions. She followed him inside and halted him by placing a hand on his elbow. Conor turned around.

'Let's get out of here,' she said. She grabbed his arm and led him outside. This conversation was not going to work in the pub. There was only one place Ava knew he would talk. They kept on walking, past a group of teens with empty beer bottles strewn around them, until they were completely alone. When he finally sat down in the soft white sand, facing the ocean, the orange glow of the setting sun fell on his face. Ava perched beside him, her shoulder softly brushing up against his. She pulled her legs close and wrapped her arms around them. With her head resting on her knees, she turned sideways, admiring the reflection of the sinking sun in his eyes.

'Sorry if I was a bit pushy earlier,' she said. 'If living here is your dream, then I'm happy for you. I really am. But I don't know, I think there's so much going on in that head of yours, this place can hardly be big enough to contain it all.'

He turned to face her, the intense blue of his eyes clouded with sadness. 'You know when people use your own words against you?' he asked.

Ava nodded. 'Horribly annoying, isn't it?'

'The worst,' he smiled.

'Sorry,' she said again.

Conor shook his head. 'Nah, you're right. Ballybridge might as well be North Korea.'

'What?'

'I mean, neither's ideal, you know?' He turned away again and ran his hand through his hair. The wavy locks immediately fell back into place. He was silent for a good few minutes and she let him be. In all her life she hadn't been one for silences, but with Conor it never felt uncomfortable.

When he finally spoke, his voice was heavy with sorrow. 'My mam died,' he said.

Olivia's heart cracked. 'Oh, Conor, I'm so sorry.'

Beside her, he shrugged. 'It's okay. It's been a while now.' When he turned to look at her, something inside her shifted. The small dam she had built to keep him at a distance caved. She placed her hand on his arm – a futile gesture, perhaps, but he gave her a soft smile anyway. How could she not have known this? Why hadn't Kate told her? She'd assumed his parents had just separated, but never had it occurred to her his mother had died. 'What happened?'

Conor lifted his shoulders in a minimal shrug. 'She just didn't wake up one day. Brain aneurysm, the doctors said. Nothing we could've done.'

Ava moved closer, allowing him to lean into her. He pushed the tips of his fingers into his eye sockets and took a deep breath. 'I was at uni, some party, I don't know. But I wasn't here. I don't even remember the last thing I said to her…' A single tear escaped the corner of his eye, and rolled down his cheek and onto his T-shirt, leaving a dark circle just below the collar. 'I've been trying to remember, but everything's just a blur. I can't see any of it clearly.'

Ava frantically searched her brain for consoling words to take away his pain, but none of them seemed substantial. Perhaps she should just listen. If there was one thing she'd learned from Conor, it was that listening was enough, most of the time.

'Do you talk about it with your dad?'

'No. It's just… it's been so long. I don't really talk to anyone about it.'

The way he said it made it sound as though he was afraid to bother people with his grief. Ava's heart broke at the thought of it. 'There's no time limit on grief, Conor. You can talk to me anytime, and I'm sure Matt and Orla feel the same.' She rested her head against his shoulder. They sat silently for a long time, watching the sun sink deeper and deeper into the ocean.

'What was she like?' Ava asked after a while.

He sighed and smiled at the memory of her. 'The opposite of my dad.'

'How so?'

'She was just… outgoing and ridiculous. Da used to say she was too wild for this world, and I often agreed with him.'

Ava swallowed as his deep voice travelled all the way to her centre.

'She lived her life the way she wanted to, you know? No *what will the neighbours think* or any of that. She was just herself, never pretended to be anything else.' Conor's hot cheek warmed her forehead as he finally leaned into her.

'I wish I knew how to do that.' Ever since uni, Ava had been trying to figure out what she was supposed to be doing, if she was on the right track. But was she living the life she wanted to live?

The sun disappeared into the ocean, painting the sky different shades of purple and blue.

Everything fell into place for Ava: the reason he was living with his dad, why he'd dropped out of university, why a big dreamer like him was stuck in a small town like Ballybridge. He was scared.

'Do you ever think about going back to uni?'

He shrugged. 'I've thought about it.'

'And?'

'I don't know. I mean… it's a bit late now, and my dad…'

'What about him? Do you think he doesn't want you to go?'

'No, nothing like that… I just…'

'Are you afraid something will happen to him if you leave?'

Conor didn't answer, but reclined onto the sand, looking up at the darkening sky. He was quiet for a long time. Lying down next to him, Ava waited for him to continue.

'I know it's not rational,' he said. 'I mean, the odds of the same thing happening twice are so small, but still, every time I leave the house and come back, I can feel my body unclench the moment I see him. It's like I'm just waiting for him to die too, you know?'

Ava found his hand and linked her fingers with his. 'Can I ask an annoying question?'

'You usually don't ask for permission to do that.'

Ava smiled. 'True, but considering the circumstances, I'd thought I'd give you the option now.'

'Go on then.'

'If you're always just going to stay here, then what? Your dad could still die. You can't stop bad things from happening, but not living your life will stop *good* things.'

Next to her, he sighed. 'I know,' he said. 'I know.'

A few stars shone bright in the darkening sky. The longer she looked, the more of them she discovered. Conor, for all his bravado, was a lot like the dark sky. The longer she looked, the more layers she uncovered, and she found that underneath all that talk of dreaming and changing the world was a boy broken by grief for his mother and paralysed by the fear of losing his father. Ava felt the heat of his palm in hers. It was unsettling, but she couldn't let go. After some time, Conor turned his head to face her. 'But what about you? Are you really going to be a sales assistant?'

Ah, he was clearly feeling a little better.

'Yes. It's a good opportunity,' she said.

'You keep saying that. Will it make you happy, though?'

Why was everyone so concerned with her happiness? 'Is a job supposed to do that? Or is it just a way to earn money, so you're able to do fun things in your spare time?' 'Maybe…' he said. He fell silent then, but she could almost hear him thinking. Before she could say anything else, he propped himself up on his elbow, a stern look on his face. 'You know what? No, I don't believe that. I do think your job should make you happy. Imagine spending eighty per cent of your day doing something you don't enjoy. What kind of a life would that be? It's 2009, Bruce — we have options now. We don't have to stay in the same job for forty years and be miserable every single day anymore.'

The fire in his eyes was back and at that exact moment, Ava realised she'd fight him till the end of days to keep that fire burning.

'You do realise the financial climate at the moment is less than desirable for the unemployed, right?'

'I vaguely remember reading something about that, yeah.'

'So what do you suggest I do then, Mr Life-is-supposed-to-be-fun?' she asked.

'I thought you were a photographer?'

'I never said that.'

'Sure you did.'

Ava shook her head. 'I told you my sister gave me a camera for my sixteenth birthday. It's hardly the same thing.'

'Yeah, and then you told me it was the best gift you'd ever got, that you were obsessed and had taken tons of pictures. Sure, look, isn't that the very essence of a photographer?'

'No… it's the hobby of a teenager. You can't make a living off that. And anyways, nowadays the fancy cameras do all the work for you. Everyone's a photographer.'

'So? Does that mean you can't be one?'

'You're exhausting.'

'No, I'm being serious, Bruce. If it's something you love, you should go for it. Don't give up just because you believe you're not good enough or that the world doesn't work that way. Prove the world wrong and change it for the rest of us.'

'Is that what you're going to do?' She propped herself up on her elbow to face him, slightly misjudging the distance between them. They were very close all of a sudden, and it was instantly clear she wasn't the only one taken by surprise. Right in front of her, Conor held his breath, and she swallowed.

'You jump, I jump, Jack,' he said after a beat, his voice barely a whisper.

His gaze was intense, and Ava was being pulled towards him, like Icarus to the sun. She knew how that had ended, and yet she couldn't find the strength to pull away. The waves crashed onto the shore, white noise drowning out the world around them. His warm breath tickled her cheek, the tip of his nose so close to hers they were almost touching. Even in the dark, his eyes pulled her in like a dangerous undercurrent, inescapable. There was not a buoy in the world that could save her now.

The balmy air only added more weight to the tension between them. She should not be doing this. A tiny voice at the back of her mind screamed at her to move away, but every other instinct in her body told her to move closer. Her eyes drifted to his mouth – those soft lips that talked of dreams and jumping together. But would he? Would he jump if she did? Was it worth the risk?

He inched closer and Ava felt the heat radiating off him. What was she doing? She could feel her heartbeat in her throat. Why couldn't she stop herself? The tip of her nose brushed up against his when the sharp squeal of a seagull startled them. Ava jumped up, guilt instantly washing over her.

'I should go,' she said, brushing the sand off her legs like her life depended on it.

'Oh… okay.' The confusion and disappointment in his eyes was devastating. What had she done?

She owed him an explanation, but telling him about James would ruin everything they had – a thought she couldn't bear. Even though she only had a few weeks left here, not spending them with Conor was unimaginable. But not explaining her sudden need to keep her distance would also push him away. He would think it'd all been a lie – every moment they'd spent together. But it wasn't. It was the most real she'd ever been with anyone. So what was she supposed to do now?

They walked back in tense silence, barefoot on the sand. Just before they reached the road, she stopped and grabbed his hand, making him face her.

'I'm going home in a few weeks.' She had to say something, and at least this wasn't a complete lie. Even if it hadn't been for James, she would have said the same thing. Life just didn't work that way.

She looked him in the eye, pleading for him to understand.

Conor smiled a sad smile. 'I know,' he said, and planted a kiss on her forehead, bringing tears to her eyes.

9

Olivia puts down the book, heartache radiating throughout her entire body. The salty ocean air, his palm warm in hers, the burn of his lips against her skin. She remembers each sensation as though she's on that beach right now. That was the moment, after months of convincing herself her life could go back to normal when she returned to London, she realised it might not be all that simple. Eamonn had got under her skin.

What would've happened had she not been with Joe, her boyfriend at the time – had she not been so convinced a secure future was more important than a happy one? She'd been so stuck in her thinking, so afraid of taking a risk that wasn't on the general life-path itinerary she had in mind, that she'd been blinded by it.

Is this a repetition of what happened then? Going to Canada with Graham is a risk and it terrifies her. If she goes, there's a ninety per cent certainty she won't ever have kids. He's been clear from the start that that's not what he wants. Most of the time, Olivia doesn't even think about it. But she's getting older, and somehow, still having the option makes her question it from time to time. Whenever she's holding Alex or Miles, a tiny part of her wonders what it would be like to have a child of her own – to have someone call her Mummy. But having children also means limiting her life. She won't be able to live the one she has now, and how can she be certain it's worth the sacrifice?

But Eamonn is a risk as well. If she decides to talk to him, there's a danger that she'll fall for him all over again. Is she willing to go there and lose everything she has? She wasn't back then, and she's regretted that for years. Is this the same?

Olivia groans, considering the book in her hands and then the drink on her nightstand. Tea is not going to get her through the next chapters. She wanders to the kitchen and opens a bottle of red, her cheeks still flushed from the memory of that near-kiss. But what surprises her now is not how much she still wants to kiss him, but how much she misses the friendship they had. Her life is very different from the one she had back then, and filled with great friends, but the connection she had with Eamonn is something of an entirely different category. Yes, there was desire and infatuation, but there was also a profound love for the other person. Perhaps that is why it's been so hard to understand what happened. Where did all that love go?

With a very full glass of red in hand, Olivia settles back under the covers, desperate to find out.

Wild Waves
Chapter 9

Halfway through summer, Orla suggested they all go on a camping trip together in the last week of August. While Matt and Conor immediately agreed, it had taken an awful lot of convincing to get Ava on board. Questions had to be answered, like: where would she go to the toilet, would there be bugs, where would she shower and, most importantly, why on earth would anyone voluntarily sleep on the ground, protected only by a thin veil of nylon, when there were perfectly comfortable B&Bs available? Conor had answered each question to the best of his abilities without mocking her, but it wasn't until he'd shown up at Kate's a week before the trip – with a care package containing bug spray, a mosquito net and a map with all the places highlighted along the way where she could use the toilet – that she'd finally agreed to tag along.

Since their near-kiss on the beach, Ava had been somewhat distant around him. Not so much that other people would notice, but enough for him to get the message. Nothing was going to happen. She was moving back to London, and he was staying in Ballybridge.

It killed him that she saw the world the way she did, all rigid, like there was only one way of doing things right. A small part of him remained hopeful though. Perhaps he could still show her that things could be different. He had five days to convince her – five days to show her they could figure something out.

The Delaneys' kitchen at the back of the house wasn't much: a small round table with four chairs, a basic mahogany IKEA set-up with sink, electric stove, oven and dishwasher, and a few presses. Nothing to write home about, and yet it was Conor's favourite place in the house. Thanks to the sliding glass door that offered such a stunning view of the farm and the surrounding hills, it was as though you were part of the scenery around you. He poured himself a cup of tea and waited until he saw Matt's car pull up in the driveway. He parked behind the barn, opened the boot and got his backpack out. Conor switched the kettle on a second time and grabbed a mug from the counter.

'Mornin',' Matt said cheerfully, wiping his shoes on the mat. For as long as Conor had known him, he'd been a morning person, always the first to arrive anywhere and never in a foul mood, which was probably a big part of why the patients and staff of the Galway hospital loved him so much. That and his excellent nursing skills, of course.

'Tea?' Conor asked.

'Cheers!' Matt got a paper bag from his rucksack and took out two slightly squashed raspberry muffins, handing one over to Conor, crumbs tumbling to the floor.

'Ah, you're a star, mate,' Conor said before taking a bite.

Matt placed the other muffins on the table, grabbed a chair and leaned back, eyebrows raised. 'So…'

'So?' Conor repeated, pretending he'd no idea what Matt was getting at.

'So, how's things with Ava?'

'Grand.'

'Are you two—?'

'Friends? Yeah,' Conor cut him off. Ava had made that perfectly clear when she suggested they make a pact at the start of the summer. Up until that moment, he'd hoped there was something more between them, but even if there was, she had no intention of acknowledging it.

Matt wasn't convinced. 'Conor, stop fecking about, it's just you and me here. You two are always together and when you're not, she's all you talk about. Don't tell me you're just friends – tell me what you're going to do about it.'

Conor shrugged. 'Nothing. She's made it very clear, on several occasions now, that she's going back to London. And anyway, what's the other option? Her staying in Ballybridge? What the feck would she do here?'

'Are you fecking messing? Have you ever considered going with her?'

Conor shook his head as though it was the most ridiculous suggestion he'd ever heard. But the truth was, he'd imagined it. He'd imagined moving to London and returning to uni, taking on a job and spending his spare time with her. He'd imagined them going on walks all over the city, visiting museums, going to the theatre, reading books together. He'd imagined a lot of things they would do together, but he'd never really considered it. Imagining and considering were two very different thought processes.

'I can't,' he said, and before Matt could react, Orla's Volkswagen van pulled up beside Matt's car. 'Don't bring this up on the trip, Matt, please?'

Matt studied him for a second, his eyes solemn. 'I won't, but promise me you'll think about what I said, Conor. It's time to start living again. You deserve to be happy.' With a pat on the back, Matt got up and opened the door for the girls.

A familiar warmth washed over Conor at the sight of Ava's smile when she met his eyes. She was wearing a rust-coloured hoodie, dark green cargo shorts and a pair of sturdy walking boots. Her hair was tied up in a bun, and a pair of sunglasses pulled back her outgrown fringe on top of her head.

'What do you think?' she asked when she stepped into the kitchen, twirling around, showing off her outfit. 'I had Kate take me to one of those camping shops. Who knew there were so many different styles of hiking shorts?'

Conor couldn't help but smile. He'd never seen her look like this. She was a casual dresser, but nothing had ever been this adventurous.

She looked at him expectantly, waiting for his opinion.

'No one could wear it better,' he said and snapped a mental picture of her, hoping to remember this moment forever.

'Muffin?' Matt offered the paper bag to Ava.

'Matt O'Connell, we haven't even left yet and you're already calling me *muffin*. Where's this gonna end up?'

'He's never called *me* muffin,' Orla said. 'Should I be grateful or offended?'

'Offended, obviously. Isn't it every girl's dream to be called *muffin*?' Ava replied.

'I don't know, guess I'm more a *cupcake* kind of girl. You know, a little more delicate.'

Conor laughed.

'You two are going to be exhausting, aren't you?' Matt said.

They both grinned and grabbed a muffin.

'So, where are we going?' Ava mumbled, mouth full of cake.

Matt took a map from his backpack and laid it out on the table. 'We were thinking about heading south along the coast, past Galway, on to Dingle, then maybe down to Cork, depending on the weather.' His finger traced the coastline on the map and then turned inwards to the countryside, crossing over to the east coast. 'Then perhaps on to Wexford and up to the Wicklow mountains before coming back here,' he said, closing the imaginary circle on the map with his index finger.

'Did you remember to bring rain clothes?' Matt asked Ava.

'I live in London, not Hawaii. I know about the rain, babes,' she said in an exaggerated posh voice.

'Right. Off we pop then.' Matt's English accent was dreadful, making everyone laugh.

Orla jumped up from her seat and was the first out the door, heading for the van.

'Do you have things in the car, Matt?' Conor asked, but Matt wasn't paying attention. Conor followed his gaze, and was not surprised when it led to the van where Orla was making space for the boys' bags. The look in his eyes confirmed Conor's suspicions; this was going to be an interesting trip.

'So, here's how I see it,' Orla said. 'I take the first stretch to Dingle today. We stop for food in Tralee and then drive on to Ventry Beach. There, we find a place to park and sleep and tomorrow, we decide what we'll do next. Take it day by day, see where life takes us.' She looked around to see if everyone agreed.

'Sound,' Conor said, and the others nodded. The sky was grey, but the air felt soft and warm. They opened the windows and, with their hair dancing in the wind, headed south.

After discussing the playlist and possible activities for the days ahead, the initial excitement wore off and they fell silent. As Conor stared out the window, Matt's words played on his mind. Was going with Ava really an option? Theoretically, it would be possible. There were plenty of places where he could study and work in London. But practically? Leaving his father behind, not just for a different city but a different country entirely, still frightened him. The thought of losing his father was paralysing, but he was beginning to understand that staying home would not prevent that from happening.

Sitting in the backseat behind Ava, he caught her reflection in the side mirror. She had her eyes closed, her head leaning on the headrest, one arm dangling from the open window, fingers outspread, pushing against the wind. Once in a while, a hint of coconut reached him, drowning him in a mix of longing and sadness. To let her slip through his fingers seemed like something only a fool would do. Was he being a fool?

A guitar intro announced the Gallagher brothers through the speakers. Orla turned up the volume and, one by one, they all joined in. Ava opened her eyes and as she looked at Conor through the mirror, he wondered if she was gonna be the one that saved him.

Wild Waves
Chapter 10

Driving through Dingle town, they passed several tourists packing cameras, trying to catch a glimpse of Dingle's famous dolphin, Fungie. Ava had brought one too. Soon after her chat with Conor on the beach, she'd found her sister's camera and started taking pictures of George, then of Kate, and by the time she felt confident again, of Orla, Matt and even Conor. It had been a long time since she'd held a camera in her hands, from before uni, and she'd almost forgotten how much she loved it, especially capturing people. It was easier than landscapes and much more rewarding. A photograph taken at the right moment, in the perfect light, could capture many layers of a person – things they might not even be aware of themselves. People were rarely honest about how they truly felt, but in their expressions, their posture, their eyes, lay so many things begging to be read, especially when they thought no one was looking. That was what Ava loved most. She got a chance to see them, really see them, and then show the world what she'd found.

When they arrived in Ventry, they parked behind the dunes and took their sandwiches to the beach. Along the shoreline there was a group of people riding ponies. The tide had just gone out, giving the sand a glossy surface and turning the beach into one big mirror. As the sun broke through the dark clouds, the ponies' reflection on the wet sand begged to be photographed. Ava moved closer, catching the light in different ways, changing the feel of each frame. When she turned to rejoin her friends, Conor jogged towards her, wearing nothing but his swim shorts. Ava's breath caught in her throat at the sight of him. How was she ever going to survive this road trip?

'I didn't get my morning swim,' Conor explained as he sped up and jogged past her.

Ava picked up her camera again and zoomed in on her new subject. Since that first time she'd seen him in his swim shorts, his skin had bronzed slightly, giving more definition to the freckles on his shoulders. His hair was maybe a bit longer on top, but everything else about him was exactly the same. It was only in her eyes that he'd changed entirely.

Through the lens of her camera she watched him run, the muscles on his back and shoulders contracting with every arm movement. The moment he hit the water, he moved as if in slow motion, his legs pushing against the waves, drops of water splashing up around him, a perfect picture. Intense desire and unrelenting guilt battled inside her. It was impossible to deny her feelings for this man any longer. Every time his dark blue eyes focused on her, a tiny part of her came back to life. Just the fact that she was holding a camera said it all. But her life in London was good. James was good. And he deserved much better than this.

Lost in thought, she didn't hear Matt and Orla until they were standing next to her. Orla pulled her close as if she'd read her mind, resting her head on Ava's shoulder. Conor wasn't the only one she would be leaving behind. Orla and Matt had become an essential part of her life too, making it all the more painful.

When Conor reemerged from the ocean, his skin was red where the cold water had burned him. He jogged towards them, big drops of saltwater falling from his hair and skin onto the sand, like breadcrumbs leading back to the ocean in case he lost his way.

'Who wants a hug?' he asked, spreading his arms wide.

'Oh, fuck no,' Matt said, side-stepping him. This however only encouraged Conor, and Matt, realising it just in time, turned around and sped off. Unfortunately, he wasn't fast enough and Conor caught up with him, pouncing on him from behind. They fell down in the soft sand, Matt shouting at Conor to get off him.

'Did we bring a first aid kit?' Ava asked Orla from behind her lens.

'Yep.'

'Good. I've a feeling we'll be needing it pretty soon.'

They watched the boys roll around in the sand for a bit, Ava snapping several pictures.

'Do you lads need some privacy or are you almost done, like?' Orla asked after a few minutes.

Conor had Matt pinned down underneath him and grinned. His eyes met Ava's lens as she zoomed in on his face. Without looking at the result, she knew this would be one of her favourite pictures. The boys got up and Conor, who was now caked in wet sand, grabbed his towel to rub it all off. A strong urge to go over and help him, to let her hands wipe the tiny grains off his back, to press her lips to his shoulder and taste the salt the ocean had left behind, made her skin itch.

'Who's up for a wee hike?' Orla asked, pulling Ava from her thoughts.

'Me!' she shouted. Anything for some distraction.

Their hike took them from Ventry to Dunquin and back. Ava hadn't been on many hikes before, but this one was extraordinary. The deep green hills and the sky-blue ocean looked photoshopped. It wasn't an easy hike though. The path was marshy and hard to navigate at times, but no one complained and, for some inexplicable reason, Ava enjoyed it. Maybe she was outdoorsy after all, or maybe, and more likely, having something to focus on freed her mind of all other worries, giving her a welcome break.

On the way back, there was a steep slope running through a meadow, the trail muddy from the rain the day before. Carefully choosing her step, Ava almost made it to the top, but when she trusted one of the cobblestones for support, her foot slipped and she fell face-forwards with a loud thud. Everyone gasped and, for a second, there was nothing but silence. Conor, who'd been walking behind her, helped her up, his expression a mix of concern and repressed laughter.

'Are you okay?' he asked.

'Fuuuuck!' she screamed, making the cows in the meadow below turn their heads. There was mud everywhere. Every inch of her body was covered in it. She tried to wipe it from her face, only to realise her hands were covered too, making it worse instead of better.

'If you wanted a spa treatment, you should've just said. We've got places for that in Ireland too, you know,' Matt said. Conor and Orla froze, their eyes going from Matt to Ava and back, unsure if Ava was up for the joke.

Ava looked at him with a straight face, not giving away a thing until his grin melted and doubt settled in his eyes. It was deeply satisfying to see his cocky grin wiped from his face.

'If anyone here needs a spa treatment, it's clearly you, muffin,' she said, levelly.

Matt released the breath he was holding and they all burst out laughing. Conor had in the meantime removed his jumper and used it to wipe the mud from Ava's face. 'Are you really okay?' he asked, his voice soft and warm, like a soothing blanket.

She nodded. 'Just feel like an idiot.'

His fingertips softly grazed her forehead as he pushed a strand of muddy hair behind her ear. Standing so close to him, she could smell the ocean on his skin and, when she looked into his eyes, she didn't care anymore about the mud or anything else for that matter. She'd stand there for another hour like that if it meant having him that close. It wasn't until Matt cleared his throat that she remembered where she was.

'Let's head back, lads. I think we could all do with a pint right about now,' he said.

Conor wiped away the last bit of mud from her face with his thumb, accidentally grazing her bottom lip. A shudder went down her spine, all the way to her toes. She was truly fucked.

With some fresh water from a tap by the parking lot, Orla helped Ava rinse out her hair and clothes while Matt got the disposable barbecue going. They gathered around, exhausted from the hike and starving. The cans of beer they'd put in a cooler box filled with ice earlier that day were still cool, even though the ice was long gone. Ava rolled one of the cans over her forehead and cheeks. Her sunscreen and the mostly clouded skies had not prevented her from burning, and the cool aluminium against her skin provided a welcome relief.

They ate in near-silence, staring out at the ocean. Ava's heart swelled with love as she watched her friends eat. Six months earlier, she'd been so reluctant to come to Ireland, and if anyone had told her then that she'd end up on a stunning beach, surrounded by the most wonderful people she'd ever met, she wouldn't have believed any of it.

'I finally found a drummer for my band,' Orla said, breaking the silence. 'She's only seventeen and she's had zero training, but she's a fecking genius, like.'

'Oh, that's fab! Was it the girl you were meeting last week?'

'Yep. She came in all nervous and shy, fiddling with her drumsticks, but the moment she sat down and started playing, she transformed into an absolute beast. You should've seen her. It was like Hulk but with drums.' Orla glowed with admiration.

'Have you started rehearsing yet?' Conor asked.

'Yeah, we've got together a handful of times and it's going really well, like. I think this might just be a perfect set-up – touch wood.' She looked around for a piece of wood but when she couldn't find anything, she put her hand on Matt's head, making the others laugh.

Matt pushed it off but held on to it a few seconds longer than necessary. Ava couldn't help but smile. She hadn't really spoken to Orla about it, but she was pretty sure there was something there, and she wanted to be in the front row when it happened.

'How many are ya?' Conor asked.

'Four. Drummer, bass, keys and me on guitar.'

'I can't wait to hear you play.' The moment she said it, Ava realised she might not be around long enough to do so. A dull ache burrowed in her chest.

'Do you have a band name yet?' Matt asked.

'That's still up for debate. We've got two options, but I'm not sure either of them's the one.'

'Let's hear 'em.'

'So, there's The Lactose Intolerant Chocolate Lovers, or The Fish Finger Fanclub.'

Conor laughed. 'It's always going to be about food with you, isn't it?'

Ava thought about both names for a second. 'I suppose it depends on what you're going for, but the first one implies you have chronic diarrhoea, and I'm not sure you want people thinking about that when they see you. So maybe the fish finger one is a bit sexier? Although I do associate fish fingers with Captain Birdseye, and I'm not sure sexy applies to him. He's more the cuddly type, isn't he? Are there no other options?'

'Nothing better than these two, anyway.'

'Mmm.'

'Is the music better than the band name suggestions?' Matt asked.

Orla shot him a defiant look and, without a word, stalked off in the direction of the van, returning moments later with her guitar in hand. She plopped down in the sand, took the plectrum out from between her teeth and strummed the first chord of one of her own songs. Ava had heard her play many times before, but never under these circumstances. A lump formed in her throat as Orla's light and fragile voice blended with the wind and the waves. All the emotions she'd been trying so hard to keep at bay washed over her like a tsunami of sorrow. But she wasn't the only one struggling. The look in Matt's eyes spoke louder than words and as for Conor, she was afraid to look at him. It would only break her heart.

Nobody spoke when the song ended and Orla continued to strum the guitar softly as they sat in silence, watching the sun set, melancholy weighing down on them like a sumo wrestler on his opponent.

'Alright, let's sing some songs, shall we?' Ava said, unable to bear it any longer.

She held out her hand to Orla who gladly handed over the guitar.

'How about…' She trailed off, searching her mind for the chords to 'Zombie'.

The moment she started playing, Orla grabbed the cooler box and repurposed it as a bongo. Before long they were all singing along and the mood was lifted once again. They played human jukebox for a bit with the guitar, and when they ran out of songs to play, Ava got the iPod and a set of speakers from the van – Orla's playlist of nineties pop and Britpop easily transporting them to their teenage years.

The increasing amount of empty beer cans seemed to be in direct relation to the volume of their conversations and, after her fifth beer, Ava could no longer sit still. She jumped up, twirled round, arms in the air, her bare feet kicking up the sand as she danced. She felt wild and free and capable of taking on the world. Orla and Matt joined her for a bit while Conor looked on and managed the playlist. Half an hour later, Matt and Orla fell down in the sand, panting, no longer able to stand upright. All the while, Conor did not take his eyes off Ava. His gaze fuelled her, spurred her on, made her invincible. It might have been the sixth beer or the high from his undivided attention, but suddenly she stopped, looked at him, and with a wide grin on her face, turned and ran towards the ocean. She had no idea what she was doing but, somehow, she couldn't stop. She peeled off her dress and ran into the water, wearing nothing but her bra and pants.

'What the fuck are you doing, Bruce?' Conor shouted. The thump of his footsteps on the wet sand became louder as he caught up with her. But she was already waist-deep in the ocean and didn't look back.

'Oi, you wee fuckers, where are you going?' Matt called out.

'Eejits!' Orla joined in.

When Ava finally turned around, Conor stood behind her, knee-deep in the water.

'Fuck, fuck, fuuuuck!' she shrieked, the icy temperatures reaching her brain. 'What the fuck am I doing?'

She turned to swim towards the beach, but Conor stopped her, his arm pulling at her waist.

'Come on, Bruce, don't be such a girl,' he said, choosing those exact words to taunt her.

'You sexist twat!' She placed her hands on his shoulders and tried to push him down. Unfortunately, Conor was too strong, and before she knew it, she was the one going under.

When she resurfaced, she gasped for air and immediately launched a counterattack. She jumped on his back, threw her arms around his neck and wrapped her legs around his torso, using all her strength to pull him down. This time she succeeded, surprising herself even more than Conor.

'Look who's secretly a ninja assassin,' he said, slicking his hair back. 'Wonder if you'll be this feisty when a shark swims up to you.' He reached for her leg underwater and softly pinched her thigh. In all her excitement Ava had completely forgotten about the sea creatures. She froze. 'Fuuuuck,' she whispered, suddenly feeling the need to be quiet so as not to disturb the sharks. In her stillness, she almost forgot to breathe. Conor laughed, took hold of her arms and draped them around his neck. 'Don't worry,' he said softly, 'I'll keep you safe.'

He wrapped his own arms around her waist, pulling her in close. The ocean was calm, the gentle movement of the waves rocking them back and forth in the darkness. The alcohol seemed to have evaporated from Ava's system, heightening all her senses. She was acutely aware of where his skin touched hers, where her breasts pushed up against his chest, where his hips pressed into her stomach. His lips were only inches away, so close she could almost taste the warm breath escaping them. The night covered them in a cloak of darkness and with nothing but the sound of the wind and the waves, they were the only two people on earth. Ava's last bit of resistance melted away in the water and, when his nose brushed up against hers, his lips grazing her cheek, she finally surrendered to the pull and found his lips with hers. Instantly heat rushed through her veins, the cold of the ocean forgotten in mere seconds. His lips were soft, his touch careful, as though he was afraid she would reconsider. Ava pulled back, opened her eyes and looked right into his. Even in the dark, he could read her gaze. He brought his hand to her neck then, his thumb resting on her cheek, and kissed her again, this time with an urgency she recognised. It was the same urgency that had been roaring inside of her for weeks. When he pushed her lips open with the tip of his tongue, a shudder travelled from the top of her spine all the way to the base. He tasted of beer and salt and something sweet. She wanted to inhale all of him, swallow him whole. As she ran her fingers through his wet, wavy hair, everything around them disappeared. All her fears, the shock of the cold water, her life in London, all of it was gone. Ava's mind was blank. There was no more thinking, only feeling, and it was the greatest feeling in the world.

Wild Waves
Chapter 11

Conor couldn't sleep. Every time he closed his eyes, he saw her face, felt the touch of her soft skin on his fingertips, the weight of her arms around his neck. The urge to kiss her again was unbearable, and not knowing what all of it meant only made it worse.

Was there hope after all?

He woke early the next morning, put on his swim shorts and headed for the sea. He'd barely got any sleep and, although he was tired, the adrenaline from the night before still coursed through his veins. The shock of the cold water was a welcome relief from his thoughts, but the effects didn't last long. When he closed his eyes, her face appeared again, her golden-brown eyes reflecting the moonlight, the smell of coconut mixed with ocean water. In despair, Conor threw his head back and went under. He liked being underwater, where everything was quiet, and he moved in flow with the current, but this time the silence only amplified his thoughts and so, after a few minutes, he gave up and wandered back to the van.

With a towel wrapped around his shoulders, Conor turned on the gas heater and made himself a cup of instant coffee. Cradling the drink in his hands, he stared out at the ocean. There was a solution, he knew there was. But was he ready?

When he heard movement behind him, he turned. Ava made her way towards him, pulling her hair up in a bun. His heart skipped a beat, but when he saw the look on her face, it dropped into his stomach. She regretted what had happened – he could tell from the lack of conviction in her smile.

'Morning,' she said.

The ocean water had made her hair curly and wild. She'd never looked more beautiful.

'Coffee?'

She nodded. He turned on the heater again and grabbed a mug.

'Did you sleep okay?' she asked.

'I've had better nights.'

'Yeah, me too.'

Was he supposed to say something? Or were they going to ignore the whole thing altogether? He added some more water to the small pan and waited for it to boil. Beside him, Ava pulled her knees close and inhaled audibly. 'I have to tell you something,' she said after what felt like an eternity of silence.

Her tone, her demeanour, everything about her told him to fear what came next. 'I'm not going to like what you have to tell me, am I?'

She shook her head slowly and Conor's heart sank even deeper. He didn't want to hear that it was a mistake, that she was leaving. For a few more days he wanted to pretend everything would work out. 'Can you tell me when we get back home?'

She frowned. 'Really? Is that what you want?'

What he wanted was to kiss her again, but that clearly wasn't going to happen. 'Will it make much of a difference if you tell me now?'

Raking her teeth over her lower lip, she shrugged. 'I don't know, I suppose not.'

'Yeah, then that's what I want.'

After breakfast, they gathered their belongings and set out on the road again. Everyone was quiet. There was a tension in the air that made Conor fear for the rest of the trip. Even Matt and Orla seemed off. With everything going on between him and Ava, he hadn't really paid attention to them, but something must've happened. They were too quiet.

Conor offered to drive in the hope it would keep his mind occupied, but the silence didn't help. Thankfully, Orla had made the perfect playlist. It was not the first time the Spice Girls had saved the day, and it wouldn't be the last.

Initially, it was just the girls singing along softly, but by the time they arrived at their next destination, they were all chanting their favourite tunes and their spirits had lifted considerably. Conor pushed his worries to the back of his mind. After all, these were the last days he had with her – it would be foolish to waste a single minute.

The following days, they drove from town to town, switching drivers every so often. They went on hikes, played cards and made music. On the third day, they found a town with a communal swimming pool where they used the showers to wash off all the mud and salt they had gathered. With only two days left, they decided not to head to the east coast. Instead, they drove all the way down to Cork, before returning north again. On their last night, they set up camp in Doolin, a tiny town not too far from home, where they had dinner in a pub before returning to the ocean. It was a warm, dry night and so they set up camp on the beach, under the stars – the girls in the middle, flanked by the boys on either side. They all lay quiet. After a while, Matt broke the silence, pointing at the starry sky. 'There's only one constellation I'm sure of and that's Orion's belt.'

'Oh, don't start. I don't believe in that,' Orla said.

'What do you mean? You don't believe in that? It's not like Santa. It's a constellation,' Matt argued.

'I'm sorry but it's like when people show you an ultrasound and all you can see is black and grey spots. It used to make me feel really stupid that I couldn't see the baby, but now I've figured it out. It's all just a big scam – no one can see it, everyone's just pretending.'

They all laughed.

'It's not, though. Here, I'll show you,' Matt said.

'I wouldn't bother if I were you. I won't see it, like.'

'Honestly, woman, will you at least let me try?'

'Fine. Knock yourself out.'

Matt moved his head closer to hers and grabbed hold of her hand, pointing her index finger up at the stars. 'Can you see those three stars forming a row? One, two, three.'

'Yeah, I can see that. I'm not blind.'

'That's it. That's his belt.'

'What? That's it?'

'Yeah, that's it. And then, dangling from the belt is his sword. You can see it right there,' he continued, again directing her hand to the thin line of stars beneath the three prominent ones.

'Huh,' Orla said, turning her head to Matt. Conor couldn't see, but from their silence, he gathered they were enjoying the moment as much as he was.

'What do you think is out there?' Ava asked. 'We can't be the only ones, can we?'

'Are you talking about aliens?' Matt replied.

'No, I mean… I'm no Fox Mulder, but don't you think it's quite arrogant of us to believe that in the entire universe, earth is the only planet that has life on it? Maybe, lightyears away, there's another planet like earth, with people just like us…'

'I can't think about things like that,' Orla said. 'Really, it does my head in, like. Once I start thinking about all these abstract things, it's like I get sucked into the rabbit hole and there's no way out.'

'Don't you think we would've found evidence of that by now?' Matt said.

'Took us long enough to figure out earth wasn't flat though,' Ava replied. 'What do you think, Conor?' She turned her head to look at him.

'I'm not sure about other planets with people on them, but I do believe there's more to it than just this. I mean, what are we doing otherwise? We're born, we get a few years and then we die and in between that, we're just trying to survive for as long as possible. If you think about it… in the grand scheme of things, we're quite pointless, aren't we? But there must be a point to it, right? Why bother, otherwise?'

Nobody spoke at first. He could feel Ava's eyes on him. She removed her arm from her sleeping bag and reached for his hand. When she linked her fingers with his, he turned his head sideways to face her. It dawned on him once more that these were the last nights they would ever spend together. He felt a dull pain in his chest. Life would never be the same again. How could he return to his life in Ballybridge, knowing she was not coming back?

'Feck,' Orla said. 'Now I can't stop thinking about how meaningless everything is. Someone talk about something else or I'm going to spiral into some serious anxiety.'

'Yeah, cheers Conor,' Matt said. 'Do you do weddings as well?'

Conor laughed. 'Why, got a wedding coming up?'

Matt jumped up, pretending he hadn't heard Conor's reply. 'Anyone want a drink?'

'More than ever,' Orla said.

He returned from the van with a bottle of liquor and the leftover cans of beer.

'Where'd you get that?' Orla asked, pointing at the bottle.

'Brought it from home. I was saving it for a special occasion and now that Conor's got us questioning our entire existence, I thought, this is it. If we're going to be pointless, we might as well be drunk and pointless. Right?'

They all passed the bottle around. Conor took a large swig, hoping to dull the sound of the ticking clock inside his mind.

'Can we do this until the end of time?' Orla asked.

'Yes please,' Ava replied quietly, locking eyes with Conor.

The soft glow of the rising sun woke Conor from his sleep. Ava's head was resting against his chest, his arm draped around her, her hand on his stomach. He breathed in her familiar scent and kissed the crown of her head, moving very cautiously so as not to wake her. If he could've picked any moment for time to stand still, this would've been it. But instead of standing still, time seemed to be moving faster than usual. Was he really just going to give up? Was he willing to let her go, without even so much as trying? He was twenty-five. He couldn't stay with his dad forever, just in case something happened. No. It was time for him to take a chance again. If ever he'd had a good enough reason to risk it all, this was it.

The past week, he'd become more and more convinced of her feelings for him. But the thing with feelings was, as long as they were unspoken, there was no way of being sure. And then there was the elephant in the room Conor had refused to face. Ignoring it, however, had not kept it from taking up space in his mind. But perhaps none of it would matter anymore once he decided to come to London with her? Perhaps she would no longer feel the need to say anything, once she knew he was all in? The higher the sun rose, the stronger his resolve became. He would go back to uni. He would go back to uni in London. He had nothing to lose and an entire life to win. Most importantly, a life with Ava.

To his right, he heard someone stir. When he looked, Matt had just opened his eyes and found Orla curled up against him. Like Conor, he moved carefully and the look in Matt's eyes told Conor he was not the only one with the desire to stop time at that exact moment.

Before they drove home, Conor suggested going for one more swim. To his surprise and joy, they all joined in, even Ava. He watched her lift her dress over her head, revealing her black high-waisted knickers and black lace bra. That first night she'd done the exact same thing, but it'd been dark and Conor had been so surprised by her sudden sprint to the ocean, he hadn't paid much attention to anything else. This time it was a very different story. He couldn't keep his eyes off her. More than anything he wanted to feel her pressed up against him again, let his hands slide down the soft curves of her body. She stepped into the ocean, Matt and Orla by her side, and turned around. 'Oi, are you coming?'

'Yeah,' he said.

I'm coming. All the way to London.

'I can't believe this is it,' Ava said later, when they were all lying down on their towels, hoping to dry from the wind and the sun.

'Don't,' Orla said.

'When will you be back?' Matt asked.

'I don't know. I might visit for Christmas.'

The sadness in her voice broke Conor's heart. If only he could tell her he was coming with her.

But he wasn't ready. He needed more information: to research possible unis, check tuition fees, look at flats... And it wasn't just the practical stuff. He needed to tell his father first. He owed him that much. So for now, he remained silent, even though he could see her hurting.

'We should be off,' Matt said, brushing the sand off his boxers and stepping into his jeans. They dressed in silence and packed up the last of their belongings. As they walked to the van, Ava grabbed onto Conor's hand. He pulled her in, draped his arm over her shoulder and kissed her on the temple. With his thumb, he wiped away the tear rolling down her cheek.

'We'll be alright,' he whispered into her hair. 'I promise.'

10

The sound of keys in the door startles Olivia. She checks the clock and is surprised when she sees it's only quarter past ten. Before she knows it, Graham is standing in the doorframe, the light coming from the living room behind him, reducing him to a silhouette.

'You're home early,' she says.

He kicks off his shoes and joins her on the bed, wrapping his arm around her. 'I felt terrible for leaving you after the day you'd had. I told Turner I'd have lunch with him tomorrow instead.'

What did she do to deserve someone like him? Graham kisses her and pushes a strand of hair behind her ear. 'What are you reading?'

'Oh… uhm… just a silly little romance I picked up at *Pages & Leaves* this afternoon.' She hates herself immediately for the lie. And then a little more for slagging off Eamonn's book and the entire romance genre in general. And then a lot more for calling what she and Eamonn had a *silly little romance*. It clearly was a lot more than that.

Graham looks at the now closed book in her lap. 'I like that cover. Quite different for the genre, isn't it?'

Olivia shrugs. 'Small independent publisher.'

'I'm going to have a quick shower, and then maybe we can watch another episode of *Slow Horses*?'

'You don't mind being in bed this early?'

'Livvie, I'd be in bed with you all day every day.' He rolls on top of her, the book tumbling to the ground, and kisses her deeply. Olivia wants to sink into it, but when she closes her eyes, all she can see is Eamonn and that kiss in the ocean. It's unfair to Graham, but the more she tries, the more she sees Eamonn's dark blue eyes.

'Are you alright?' Graham pulls back, giving her a quizzical look.

'Uh-huh, yeah, just tired.'

From his expression, she gathers he doesn't quite believe her.

'I had some wine – it's making me a bit hazy.'

Graham's eyes travel to the empty glass beside her, aware that Olivia is not a big drinker, especially not when she's home by herself. 'You sure nothing else happened today?'

'I'll be alright tomorrow,' she says, and gives him what she hopes is a reassuring smile.

Graham pushes himself up from the bed and makes his way to the bathroom. As she watches him go, the guilt tears at her insides, making her want to down the entire bottle of wine in one go. She has to tell him. But there's one thing she needs to do first. She grabs her phone and types out a message.

I'm at the women's arts centre tomorrow from 10 to 3. If you're still here.

It takes mere seconds for his reply to come in.

I'll be there

When she hears the water in the shower running, Olivia finds her spot in the book. Two more chapters until the end of Part One. Two more chapters until she has to pretend everything is fine again.

Wild Waves
Chapter 12

On her last full day with Kate and George, Ava found herself conflicted. On the one hand, she was happy to be returning to her normal life, to James. Her stay at Kate's had been wonderful, but it was not real life and this wasn't sustainable. James was real, her upcoming job was real, and once she was back there, this would all just be a memory.

But the thought of leaving also made her terribly sad. The past six months had been so much better than she could've imagined. In London she was often alone, with both her parents not exactly the warm family types, but here the three of them had formed their own little pod and she'd loved being a part of that. With Kate and George, she'd felt a sense of belonging. And it wasn't just them. She'd pushed her boundaries, swimming in the ocean and going on a camping trip. She'd learned to sit in silence and actually enjoy it, and she'd been reminded of her love of photography. As a career it was not an option, but the idea of spending her spare time taking pictures gave her a little jolt of excitement each time she thought of it.

And as if that wasn't enough, she'd been welcomed with so much warmth by these people in this small Irish town, and she'd made the best of friends. Friends she hadn't known she was looking for, but were now a part of her. Her people.

And then there was Conor. The sharpest, sweetest, most beautiful man she'd ever met, and she'd fallen for him. She had tried not to, she really had, but it'd been impossible. He challenged her, understood her, encouraged her, and saw her for who she really was and could be. He was the one she wanted to talk to all the time, and the one person she wanted to be silent with. He'd woken things in her she'd forgotten were there. He'd made her feel alive again.

But perhaps that was why life had brought them together. To open her eyes and see there might be more to it than just securing a future. And she hoped she had helped Conor in a way, too. Perhaps one day she'd find his novel in a book shop, and knowing she was there when he'd started writing it would be enough.

As she lay in bed and stared up at the ceiling, a lump formed in Ava's throat. Not only was this her last day – it was also the day she had to tell Conor about James. It would break him. But there was no way around it. And perhaps it was for the best.

George was running around the kitchen when Ava came down.

'Ayaaa!' he squealed, running towards her and wrapping himself around her legs. Over the past six months, his vocabulary had grown, and Ava had seen him go from a crawling, babbling, drooling baby to a walking, talking, still drooling, toddler. She picked him up, kissed his chubby cheeks and held him tight, trying to squeeze out every last minute with him. Her eyes burned when she put him back down and walked through to the kitchen.

'Good morning, love,' Kate said.

Seeing the breakfast laid out, Ava could no longer hold back her tears. Smiling through them, she walked over to Kate and hugged her tight. 'I'm going to miss you so much.'

'Stop it or I'll cry all day,' Kate said through her tears.

'I'm sorry.'

'You should be.'

This made Ava laugh, but she didn't let go for another while, until George pounded their legs for attention. 'Come on, let's have some breakfast and not think about anything else for a bit, okay?'

Ava nodded, pulled back a chair and let herself be served. She took one of the scones and inhaled its scent. 'This is amazing.'

'I know, I've really outdone myself.' Kate poured them both a cup of coffee while Ava handed a scone to George, who didn't hesitate and immediately pushed it into his face. 'You're such a little piggy,' Ava chuckled, watching him get all the crumbs in his hair and on the floor.

'So, I was thinking, after breakfast we could go into town and do some shopping, and in the afternoon we could go to the beach. What do you reckon?'

'Yeah, sounds great, I'd love that.' Ava scooped the fruit salad into a small bowl and added some yoghurt.

'Are you seeing Conor tonight?' Kate asked, hesitantly.

'Uh-huh.'

When Ava had returned from the camping trip the day before, she'd finally confided in her sister and told her about her feelings for Conor and what happened in the ocean. When she admitted she'd never told Conor about James, Kate had been surprised yet understanding. In a way, Ava had hoped Kate would've chided her for her behaviour – she'd cheated on a lovely guy who'd been nothing but kind to her and she'd messed with Conor's feelings on top of that. But Kate had given her a hug and told her to sleep on it.

'Are you going to tell him?'

Ava nodded. 'Tonight.'

'Do you really have to?'

This surprised Ava. Of course she had to tell him – what else was she to do? She looked up at Kate with questioning eyes.

'I mean, have you considered all your options, Ave?'

Ava shook her head, confused by what her sister could possibly mean. 'I'm going back to London tomorrow. I have a boyfriend there, a job waiting for me.'

'Do you love Jason?'

Ava rolled her eyes at her sister. 'Really, Kate? You know it's James. We've been together four years. He was at George's baby shower.'

'Jason, James; potato, potahto.'

Ava laughed. She knew Kate was just trying to lighten the mood. But when she didn't answer, Kate repeated the question. 'Well, do you love him?'

'Yes.'

'You're shaking your head.'

Was she? 'No, I'm not.'

Kate opened her eyes wide, staring Ava down. '*Really* love him?' she pushed on.

'Yes! Why are you so adamant on proving that I'm not happy in London?'

Across from her, Kate's expression suddenly turned serious. 'Because, Ava, you're not! You've let Mum and Dad get into your head. You used to be adventurous and creative and a little wild, and now all I hear you talk about is good financial opportunities and proper jobs and *Midsomer* bloody *Murders*.'

'Again with the *Midsomer Murders*? What have you got against Barnaby?'

Ava's attempt at humour had no effect on Kate. 'I lied, you know,' she went on, leaning back in her chair.

'What?'

'I had plenty of au pairs lined up.'

It was like being slapped with a wet towel. 'What the fuck?' Blood rushed to her cheeks as she pushed away from the table, unable to think straight. She'd uprooted her entire life, her long-term relationship, because she thought her sister needed her. And now it turns out it was all a set-up?

'You brought me here for nothing?'

With her arms crossed and eyebrows raised, her sister's posture screamed defiance. 'I don't regret it. You came back to life here.'

Anger bubbled up from her stomach to her throat and Ava exploded. 'I WASN'T DEAD!'

George looked up at her, his big eyes confused as to why she was shouting, but Kate didn't even flinch.

'You might as well have been. And sit down, you're upsetting George.'

Raging with anger, Ava was about to tell her sister to fuck off, but when she saw the fear on her beloved nephew's face, it was the only motivation she needed to force herself to calm down. They were silent for a while and, even though Ava felt completely betrayed by her sister, the anger slowly traded places with disbelief.

'Why didn't you just talk to me?' she asked.

'Because I knew you wouldn't listen.'

'That wasn't your choice to make, Kate.' Ava got up and walked away from her sister.

'Look, I'm sorry. I shouldn't have lied. But please think about it before you talk to Conor. There could be another way.'

Ava stopped, turned and looked her sister in the eye. Yes, she wouldn't have come to Ireland if Kate hadn't lied. But perhaps it would have spared her from this moment. If she'd never met Conor, she wouldn't have fallen for him. And she wouldn't have been about to crush his heart.

'There is no other way,' she said, and walked out the door.

Wild Waves
Chapter 13

His dad took the news well. A little too well, if he was being honest. The word *finally* fell a few times too many in Conor's opinion, but he was relieved nonetheless. As he had come to see it had never been his dad standing in the way of his life. He was still anxious about leaving him behind, but for the first time in a long time, he'd found a good enough reason to push through the fear.

At Paddy's, the thought of revealing his plans to Ava later that night and the prospect of his bright new future put him in such a great mood that he voluntarily engaged in small talk on several occasions, smiling brightly at every customer who entered the shop. Before he knew it, the day was over. He flipped the sign on the door from 'Open' to 'Closed' and locked up behind him.

At the sight of Ava walking towards him, her plait bouncing on her shoulder with every step, a wave of excitement washed over him and his face broke into a bright smile. She was wearing a mustard-coloured cardigan with a black blouse tucked into a pair of faded jeans and her yellow Doc Martens boots. She looked as beautiful as ever, although perhaps slightly less bright-eyed. When she kissed him on the cheek, he inhaled deeply.

'How was your day?' she asked.

'Class, yeah,' he said. 'I've something to tell you.'

She nodded. 'Me too.'

Conor shook off the sense of dread her tone instilled in him. She still thought they were parting ways the next day. She'd feel better once she knew he was coming with her. Right? It was hard to imagine how she would react, and an undeniable dose of anxiety gripped his heart. What if he'd misread the signs? No. Impossible. She'd kissed him, not the other way around. He was doing the right thing. 'Not here, though – let's find a place to sit,' he said.

They headed for their spot in the dunes, shielded by shrubs, sheltered from the wind and the few people who remained on the beach. The day had been warm and sunny, but at the end of August, temperatures dropped rapidly once the sun began to set.

The moment they sat down he turned to her, but before he could say anything, she squeezed her eyes tight. 'I have a boyfriend,' she blurted.

His mind went blank and the air left his lungs. The entire world came crashing down on him, the anticipation and joy he'd felt earlier that day buried under the rubble. For a moment he hoped she was messing. Even though it would've been the cruellest joke ever, he would rather that than it be reality. Beads of sweat gathered on his forehead when he forced himself to look her in the eye and found nothing but the truth behind her tears.

'I don't understand,' he said, forcing the words through his throat.

'That's what I've been trying to tell you, Conor.' The tears spilled from her eyes and Conor bent his head so he wouldn't have to look at her. How had he ended up here? They'd spent the past six months together and not once had she mentioned him. How is that even remotely possible? How could she not have told him? Who leaves their boyfriend for six months and never even mentions him? Conor thought he might be sick.

Ava shuffled towards him on her knees, bringing her hands to his face. 'I'm so sorry. I should've told you sooner.'

Disoriented, he pushed her hands away, got to his feet and ran. The only thing he could think to do now was get into the ocean. He needed to get away from her, away from everything, and the sea was his only solace. The cold water burned his skin but he kept on swimming, desperately trying to drown out the world. This could not be happening. If only he kept on swimming, maybe it would all go away. Stroke after stroke, the ache in his muscles intensified, but he kept on going until the pain in his limbs became worse than the one in his heart. He was unsure how much time had passed, but when he finally got out of the water, she was still sitting where he'd left her, her tear-soaked hair stuck to the side of her face, her eyes red and puffy. He picked up his shirt and pulled it over his head, the grains of sand scratching his burning skin. He welcomed the sting.

But even though he couldn't bear to be around her, he somehow couldn't walk away yet either, and so he crouched down beside her, his eyes fixed on the horizon. Water dripped from his hair along his temples, darkening his T-shirt's collar. Neither of them spoke for a long time, not until darkness fell over the beach and the remnants of the day faded away, leaving only heartache in its wake.

'I'm sorry,' she said after a while.

The words didn't mean anything to him.

'I know I should've told you.'

Why hadn't she? If she had no feelings for him, she could've told him, it wouldn't have made a difference. Did that mean he hadn't imagined it all?

'But to be fair... I did try and tell you before, you just... didn't want to hear it.' Her voice cracked. She was trying not to cry but her eyes glistened.

'You must be messing,' he said. 'You tried to tell me last week, for fuck's sake. What about all those months before that? You never even mentioned him.'

Ava flinched at the anger in his voice. 'I know. I should have. I don't know why I didn't.'

Conor scoffed. 'Don't you?'

The moment he looked her in the eye, she turned away. 'Even if it wasn't for him, I would still be going home. This, whatever this is, was always going to end tomorrow, Conor. Or what, were you going to come with me to London? Or were you expecting me to stay here? Because that dreamworld you live in, is not how people live their lives, you know!'

Another wave of nausea came over him, so he stood up and stalked off. He wanted to scream. He wanted to cry. He wanted to ask her if she loved him, but he didn't. Either answer would be too painful. When he heard her footsteps coming up behind him, he stopped.

'I was actually going to tell you I was coming with you,' he said, not turning around.

Ava didn't speak at first, but from the sniffing of her nose, he knew she was right behind him.

'What do you mean?' she said then, her voice fragile and shaky.

'I'm going back to uni, in London.' He gave a short, humourless laugh. 'Well, I was anyway.' Without looking at her, he continued his way home. Almost six months earlier they'd walked that route together for the first time. Her arrival in town had been the bolt of lightning he'd needed to shake him out of his lethargic existence. She'd made him feel alive again, and now he wished he'd stayed dead. Numbness was always preferable to this, he thought.

In his bedroom, Conor put on the Arctic Monkeys album they'd listened to on repeat that summer. He skipped to 'Do Me a Favour', Ava's favourite song, and wondered if she always knew it was going to end this way. As Alex Turner told him to hold on to his heart, Conor grabbed his phone and typed the lyrics of the second verse into a text message.

He hit send, turned off the light and switched off his phone.

11

When Olivia wakes, Graham is still beside her, his arms thrown wide over his head. She watches him sleep for a bit, his black, short-cropped curls shiny with the coconut oil he'd massaged in last night, making them look even darker. His beard is greying and the lines on his forehead are visible even as he sleeps. When Olivia first met him, he'd had tiny crow's feet around his eyes, but only when he smiled. Now they're always there, and she loves them.

Lying there, watching his stomach rising and falling to the rhythm of his deep breaths, she can't help but compare him to Eamonn. Apart from the obvious difference in skin colour and predominant features, Graham's mum being Nigerian, they seem to have the same build. Not trim, but not chubby either. Somewhere in between. The internet would probably call it a 'dad bod'. In 2009, Eamonn had had broad shoulders from swimming, but was otherwise quite slim. When she saw him yesterday, she'd noticed he'd put on some weight, like he'd grown into himself somehow. She'd also noticed the swoop of her stomach when they were standing so close in Primrose Hill. The memory unsettles her. She swings her legs over the side of the bed, but then Graham stirs beside her and pulls her back in, his arm around her waist. 'Morning,' he says, his voice raspy but soft.

Olivia gives in and lets him draw her close. 'Morning.'

His bare chest is warm against her cheek.

'Did you sleep well?'

'Uh-huh.' She didn't. Falling asleep was fine, but a few hours later she woke again and stayed that way until five in the morning, the cogs in her brain working overtime.

'I've made reservations for dinner tonight,' he says. His hand is in her hair, his thumb drawing circles at the base of her neck. Olivia sighs when he hits the spot where all her tension is gathered. 'Where are we going?'

'You'll see.'

Eating out is not unusual for Graham and Olivia, but him not telling her where they're going is, and Olivia isn't sure she can handle any more surprises. 'Is it Honest Burgers?'

A shake of his head. 'You'll see.'

'Please tell me.' With her index finger she pokes him in the ribs, making him squirm.

'Ouch! It's a surprise, okay?'

Olivia grunts in protest but folds herself around him again.

'You feeling better today?'

'Uh-huh.'

'Good.' He nuzzles her neck and his hand travels from her shoulder to her hip and back up again, under her tank top, until his thumb grazes the underside of her breast. Goosebumps line her skin when she feels him harden against her thigh but before desire can fully take over, guilt floods Olivia's senses, erasing the goosebumps and filling her with dread instead. In about two hours she's meeting Eamonn, and Graham knows nothing about it. He doesn't even know there's an Eamonn to meet. This is wrong.

'Graham, we don't have time,' she says.

'It won't take long, trust me.'

Softly, she places her hands on his chest, creating distance between them. 'I'm serious. Amira is expecting me to open up.'

'Ten minutes, tops.' Graham takes her face in both hands and kisses her, his tongue firm and soft, but Olivia pulls back and gives him a gentle smile. 'Maybe later, yeah?'

As his eyes scan her face, a thin frown line on his forehead appears. A warning he might be on to her. Before he can say anything, she slips out of bed and heads for the bathroom, closing the door behind her.

An hour later, Olivia lets herself into the arts centre and dumps her belongings behind the bar. She has another half hour before it opens to the artists, and an hour before they let the public in. On her way over, she stopped at Pret for a 'very berry' croissant and an oat flat white, even though there's plenty of coffee and pastries in the café. It's become part of her morning routine over the years. Before doing anything else, she settles in one of the red velvet chairs in the exhibition room with her cup in one hand and the pastry in the other. This place has been her home for over a decade: it's where her pictures first found an audience, where she finally met like-minded souls, and where she not only found a community but helped build one too. It's the place in London she's going to miss most of all.

A new painting in the middle of the back wall catches her attention: a swirl of different hues of blue, wild and stormy. It might not have been the artist's intention, but to Olivia it looks like wild waves. She laughs a bitter laugh at the cruelty of the universe. 'Fuck me.'

As if the day wasn't hard enough. The knowledge that Eamonn will come over and they will finally have their long-overdue conversation makes her fidgety. Not just for the conversation, but for having him around again. Just the sight of him nearly knocked her over with love yesterday, and even though she's prepared now, she's not sure it will be any better.

Too anxious to enjoy her morning ritual, she heads to the bar to get the place ready. When the door swings open at exactly 9.30 a.m., Olivia jumps.

'What have you got to hide?' Lou, the resident sculptor, says, grinning at Olivia's reaction.

'Ha! If I told you, I'd have to kill you.'

'Never mind, then. Is this your final week?'

Olivia juts her bottom lip out in a pout. 'Yeah.'

'We're gonna miss you.'

'Me too – I'll miss you that is, not me.'

Lou grins again, not being much of a loud laugher, and heads for the exhibition room. 'I'll be back for coffee in a bit.'

Olivia salutes them and returns to organising the showroom fridge where they stock the pastries. It's quiet and she puts on her favourite playlist. Chappell Roan aptly kicks off with 'My Kink is Karma' and as Olivia wipes down the coffee tables, Paolo Nutini takes over.

At ten, she opens the doors and takes the chalkboard sign out to the footpath to lure people in. A few regulars enter with their laptops and install themselves at the coffee tables. She knows most of their orders by heart and anticipates by steaming the oat milk for Ginnie, a woman around the same age as her, with two young kids and a thriving YouTube channel on vegan cooking for children. She expects to see Ginnie at the bar when she turns around but instead of a beautiful woman, there's a painfully beautiful man smiling at her.

'Hiya,' he says.

On her way over to the centre, she made a list of all the things she wanted to say to him, but the simple sight of his dark blue eyes has every item instantly evaporating from her mind. She's not even sure how to say hello anymore.

'Hi.' It comes out as barely a whisper. The little jug of milk wobbles in her unsteady hand.

He looks tired, his eyes somehow darker than the day before, a nine o' clock shadow dusting his jaw. And yet, he's still lovely, in every way possible. Neither of them speaks and then Ginnie comes up from behind Eamonn. He takes a step aside and gives her a smile.

'Is that for me?' she asks.

Olivia nods, grabs the mug with coffee and tries her best to pour the milk in the shape of a heart. It's never been one of her strong suits and now, with her fingers trembling as they are, it's an absolute atrocity.

'Sorry about that,' she says, jutting her chin in the direction of the milk-blob.

'You're alright. I'm not here for the coffee art,' Ginnie says.

'Do you want one?' Olivia asks Eamonn.

'Yeah, cheers.' He pulls back one of the high stools and settles at the bar. She can feel his eyes following her every movement and it's not helping with her hand-eye coordination. Is she supposed to make a heart in his coffee too? Or will that make things awkward? Maybe not doing one will make it even more awkward? Is there a protocol for situations like these? Like, if your long-lost love shows up, this is the coffee art you serve them. Maybe a leaf is more appropriate. Olivia gives it a shot, but shakes her head as she watches her own failure take form. Then, nearly spilling his coffee, she slides it over to him, the supposed leaf blending with the dark roast.

'Missed your calling there,' Eamonn says, staring into his cup.

Olivia lets out a surprised laugh. 'I'm sorry, you think you can do better?'

'A fingerless child can do better.'

Her jaw drops at the audacity. After yesterday, after the past decade, really, he's making fun of her coffee art skills? She's laughing though, and she hadn't seen that coming either. Before she can retort, another person comes up to the bar to order a cappuccino. 'Go on then, have a go,' she says, pushing the jug of steamed milk towards him. His eyebrows shoot up in incredulity but he takes the handle and the cup, and slowly creates a perfectly shaped heart.

'See,' he says. 'Easy.'

'When did you learn to do that?' The words haven't fully left her mouth before she realises what she's said. Eamonn meets her eyes and lifts his eyebrows ever so slightly. Right. Probably somewhere in the past fourteen years. Is this how the conversation is going to continue?

Olivia finishes up with the customer while she searches her mind for safe topics. 'How's your dad?' she finally asks when they're alone again.

His eyes light up at the question. 'He's grand. He and Zarah got married a few years back.'

'Really? Oh, that's lovely. He deserves to be happy.'

Eamonn nods. 'Yeah, it's good seeing him like that. They're going away in August – a road trip in Italy.'

'What about the farm?'

'They retired last year, actually.'

'Wow, that must've been massive for him. Does that mean you get to see him more now?'

Eamonn finishes his coffee and slides the cup towards Olivia. 'Yeah, I do. It also helps that I live around the corner from them.'

Taking the cup, Olivia smiles.

'You're not surprised?' he asks.

She's not. Eamonn belongs in that town, the way he belongs in the sea. 'You missed the ocean.'

'I missed the ocean.'

Their eyes lock and understanding passes between them. It doesn't matter how many years have passed. They know each other.

'So, you own a house?'

'Yeah. Jono's mam went into care – you know Jono, your man from the shop?'

Olivia nods and leans on the counter.

'Well, he rang me and said I could buy her house if I wanted to. It wasn't in the best of conditions, but I think I've managed not to make it worse.'

Immediately a picture of a cosy, old house comes to mind and a certain longing awakens in Olivia's chest, making the hairs at the back of her neck stand. 'What's it like?'

'It's small. Sitting room, kitchen, two bedrooms, a bathroom. Nothing out of the ordinary.'

Olivia wonders how he's decorated each room. Are there curtains? Is there a place just for him to write? What colours are the walls?

'Are you close to the ocean?'

'I have a small garden with a gate that opens up onto the beach.'

'Oh Eamonn, that sounds perfect.'

'It still needs a lot of work.'

'I'm sure it's already wonderful.'

He smiles, but there's a hint of sadness in his eyes. He's about to say something else, when Lou comes to the bar to order. Olivia serves them, but it's like they've triggered an avalanche of orders and a queue forms.

'Do you need a hand?' Eamonn asks.

'Do you mind?'

He gets up from his stool and joins her behind the bar. It's a narrow space and being so close to him poses its problems. Her hands tremble even more and when he notices, he takes the jug from her hand. 'I'll do the coffee,' he says. 'You can do everything else.'

If it weren't for her racing heart, she'd tell him off again for mocking her skills, but she doesn't. Instead, she sticks to the other side of the bar and starts taking orders. Fifteen minutes go by as they work in unison, side by side. Like it's always been that way. Like it *could* always be that way. She can see herself in his house by the sea, reading a novel by the window while he's making dinner, painting a room together, deciding whether or not to plant wildflowers in the garden. It's so easy to imagine, she has to forcefully stop herself from doing so by focusing on her tasks at hand.

'Sorry about that,' Olivia says afterwards.
'I don't mind. I like helping you.'
The words reach her heart as he pushes past her to return to his side of the bar. It takes all of her strength not to grab hold of his arm and pull him close. The longer he's there, the more it seems like they've never parted ways. It's so easy to be comfortable around him, even when it's not. Olivia dreads the moment he'll say goodbye. He'll return to Ballybridge and she'll be on her way to Vancouver. The full circle moment hits her like an overhead wave in an otherwise peaceful ocean.

'If you've got time, maybe we can grab lunch later?' Her voice rises a little too much at the end of her question, desperation oozing from it. She'll do anything to hang on to him a little longer.

But Eamonn answers without wasting a beat. 'I have time.' And relief washes over her.

'Have you got any pictures up there?' He points to the exhibition room, where a long time ago, they'd stood side by side, looking at a picture she'd taken of him.

'I do.'
'Can I see?' His hopeful gaze makes her smile. Isn't she supposed to be upset with him? This is not going as planned.
'Sure. Go on ahead, I'll be there in a minute,'
Olivia waves Lou over to take her place for a bit as Eamonn makes his way to the exhibition room. But before she joins him, she makes a quick stop in the loos. Staring at her reflection in the mirror, she shakes her head. What is she doing?

She's supposed to be confronting him about broadcasting their relationship for all to read. She's supposed to be asking him why he broke her heart – if he ever really had the intention of meeting her for their pact. She's definitely not supposed to be in love with him anymore.

For fuck's sake.

12

Standing in the exhibition room, Eamonn is glad to get a minute to himself. He needs to recalibrate, or he will end up with even more regrets. Ben is right: there are things he needs to ask her and things he wants to say. And time is running out.

It's hard to believe they'll be oceans apart in just a few days. The way they moved around each other behind the bar, completely in flow, no words needed, makes him wonder if that's what life would be like if they shared it. It makes his heart ache, knowing he'll never find out.

'So? Which ones are mine?' Her voice comes from behind him.

Eamonn turns to look at her and smiles when her golden eyes meet his. Then he turns back to the room. One wall is reserved for paintings and the other two are lined with photographs. There must be at least fifty, but it doesn't take him longer than a few seconds to find Olivia's work. Three black-and-white portraits of female artists hang side by side. They're working on their art, intense focus in their gazes – all so different, and yet there's something that binds them. Without speaking, he takes a few steps in their direction. Below each picture, there's a plaque with information about the artwork along with her name. Each one is a different type of artist – a dancer, a painter and a sculptor – but they all have the same look in their eyes: longing.

'That was quick,' she says as she joins him.

Eamonn shrugs. 'They're very *you*.'

'Yeah?'

He nods. 'They're class.'

Beside him, Olivia is quiet as she studies her own photos. Eamonn glances sideways, taking everything in. Her short bob is tucked behind her ear, revealing a few gold, helix piercings that match the thin ring in her left nostril. The freckles are still there – more of them, even – and thin lines grace her temples. She's only got more beautiful as the years have passed. Lost years, he thinks – years he should've been with her, even just as a friend. It makes no sense at all, like there was a glitch in the universe and everything is the wrong way round. How did they fuck up so astronomically?

Her pinky brushes up against his and for a second or two, she leaves it there. It's maddening how a light touch can cause a heart to break.

'They're some of the people I've mentored over the years,' she says, pulling her hand away, at once leaving him feeling unbalanced.

He clears his throat to regain composure. 'Do you enjoy that – mentoring?'

'I love it. It's something I never thought I'd do, and now I'll be...' Olivia trails off, but he knows where she was going with that sentence. She was about to tell him about her mentoring project in Canada, but for some reason thought better of it at the last moment. He's glad she didn't. He wants to pretend for a little while longer that they're not parting ways again in a couple of hours, and that whatever happened in the past is irrelevant. Even if that makes him delusional.

'Well, you were always good with people.'

'You think so?'

'You were good with me.'

Olivia meets his gaze, her eyes reflecting the sadness in his heart. 'Eamonn...'

Her voice is heavy and he shakes his head, cutting her off. 'Just a couple more minutes.'

She doesn't ask him what he means, doesn't give him a quizzical look. Instead, she nods and rests her head against his shoulder.

'I have a dog,' he says when they're back at the bar, surrounded by strangers who have no idea how important this moment is.

'Really?' Her eyes are wide with surprise.

'A black lab.'

She laughs.

'What?'

'That's basically you, personified.'

'Are you saying I'm meek?'

She laughs again, louder this time, from her belly. It's a sound he's missed with his entire body.

'I'm saying you're kind and playful.' Her cheeks flush and she busies herself wiping the bar. The words take him by surprise. Yesterday she had not seemed to think he was kind and playful at all. They fall silent as Olivia serves another handful of customers. Even though it feels like they're back to how it used to be, Eamonn can't help but notice she hasn't shared much personal information about herself. From her work at the centre, however, it's clear that she's doing really well. Her art is stunning, and it looks like she's found her true calling, combining mentoring with photography. She's come a long way from thinking she wanted to be a sales assistant. What if she made the right decision all those years ago by ignoring him and focussing on her future? Would she have made it this far if they'd been together?

Around one p.m., Olivia calls Lou over and then turns to Eamonn. 'Shall we get some food?'

'Yeah, alright.' After lunch he really has to go, or he'll miss his flight. He has a decision to make. Is he really going to tell her he loves her?

A tightness in his chest. A lump in his throat. An impossible decision.

'Okay if we grab something from Tesco's and eat it by the canal?' Olivia adjusts her handbag over her shoulder and gives him a questioning look.

'Sound, yeah.'

As they walk side by side on the footpath to the nearest Tesco, they are both quiet, like each is waiting for the other to break the illusion, but hoping they won't. It's another warm and sunny day and everyone in the shop is looking for barbecue meats, salads and ice cream. Eamonn and Olivia settle for a meal deal and then silently, Olivia leads the way to a bench by the canal where they sit down and unwrap their sandwiches. The bench is wide enough to fit at least four, but their shoulders touch anyway. She no longer smells of coconut and yet sometimes, he thinks he catches a whiff of it. It's happened more than once over the years and every time, it's been a shock to his system. Especially once he realised she wasn't there.

When he finishes his sandwich, he folds the paper and plastic wrapper and stuffs it in his jeans pocket. He can almost hear time ticking by as people walk past them and yet he remains silent, all the words of the English language stuck in his throat.

But then, Olivia turns on the bench, clenching her empty wrapper in her fist. 'I'm moving to Canada,' she says, and then a bit more quietly, 'with my boyfriend, Graham.'

There it is.

Eamonn nods as he processes the facts for a second time in less than twenty-four hours. Hearing her say it somehow makes it final, like there's no coming back from it now.

'Ben told me yesterday.' He weighs his words. 'I'm, uhm…' But they're too heavy and he falls silent again. Everything he's been doing in the past couple of years has been leading up to this moment, but as more people stroll by, their sunglasses shielding them from the bright midday sun, Eamonn finally realises he has no right to tell her how he feels. She made her choice years ago, and it's about time he accepts her decision. It's time to move on, to let her go.

'Ben said you'll be mentoring teens over there?'

Her eyes light up and her shoulders relax. It nearly kills him.

'Yeah, I think we'll be doing a good thing. I love photography so much, but I only realised that because I grew up as privileged as I did. My sister gave me a camera for my sixteenth birthday… I mean, that's just mental. How many kids get those opportunities?' The passion radiates from her body as she goes on. 'Like Graham: he grew up in Vancouver with a Black single mum. It was tough for him in ways I can't imagine. But he had a teacher in secondary school who made sure he kept on writing – gave him extra assignments outside of school. She guided him towards scholarships and helped him with his applications and now he's a highly commended journalist. Without that woman, that might never have happened.'

Listening to her talk about Graham makes his actual heart ache, but still he smiles.

'So how will it work?'

'Well, we've rented this old industrial building in town. It's quite dilapidated, but the structure is gorgeous. We'll be fixing it up this summer and then, come autumn, we want to start going round to schools and community centres, maybe get a few competitions going on social media to find talented kids.'

'Sounds class.'

For a few moments they are silent. There's a pebble on the ground and she rolls it around, using the tip of her shoe, turning her face away from him. 'It's scary, though.'

'Yeah?'

Olivia nods. 'We've put all our money into this, and I don't know, I sort of feel I'm at this important crossroads and if I take the wrong turn, I won't be able to find my way back.'

'Yeah, I get that,' he says.

Maybe he took the wrong turn in 2010. Maybe that's why he lost her, and maybe there's no finding his way back from that? But what if that was always supposed to happen? It's impossible to know for sure.

'I think you're going to be grand,' he says.

She turns to face him again and their eyes lock. For a few seconds, neither of them moves. Eamonn is acutely aware this might be the last time he'll see her, if not forever, then for a very long time at least.

'I should get back to the centre.' She shifts uncomfortably. The empty wrapper in her hand crinkles when she turns it between her fingers.

Eamonn gives a small nod. 'Sure, yeah. I should go too.' Neither of them moves. Her lips part slightly, like she's about to say something, but then she doesn't. The wind blows her hair across her face and without thinking, Eamonn reaches for her forehead and pushes the strand behind her ear.

'Eamonn…' she starts, but she doesn't pull away. Instead, she covers his hand with hers and links their fingers.

'We're really bad at timing,' she says, pressing her cheek to their linked hands.

Eamonn moves closer, his forehead touching hers, letting the warmth spread through his body.

'Yeah, I wouldn't hire us for a time-sensitive assignment.'

Her eyes are closed, and she smiles a sad smile. 'Maybe in the next life.'

'Yeah, definitely.'

Olivia opens her eyes again and for a few silent moments they sit like that until, with a deep sigh, she finally pulls away. It's like he's suddenly naked on a freezing day.

Taking the plastic wrapper from her hand, he pushes himself up from the bench. 'Good luck in Canada. Maybe you could let me know how you're getting on?'

Relief softens her features and she nods. 'Yeah, I'd like that.'

He half turns to leave but then feels her hand on his elbow, halting him. She throws her arms around his neck and pulls him close. 'Thank you,' she whispers.

For a final moment, he buries his face in her hair. 'Bye, Bruce.'

Olivia kisses him on the cheek, and without another word turns around and walks away, leaving one of her tears lingering on his lips. As he watches her go, Eamonn slumps back onto the bench. Only twenty-four hours ago he'd secretly hoped the universe had offered him another chance at making it work, but now he realises it was only a chance for closure.

13

Olivia's heart feels raw, like if she looks down now, she'll find it bleeding through her skin. This is not the first time she's said goodbye to Eamonn, but it feels like the last. Her body aches in the places they touched, like some kind of phantom pain where her brain hasn't caught up yet with the severing of what once sustained her.

She didn't ask him about the pact, or the book, or anything that happened in the past. Not because he'd given her the answers, but because it didn't matter anymore. It's clear that he had his life in Ireland, and she just didn't fit into that. After all, she had hers in London too. They were at different junctions at the time, leading in opposite directions. There's no point in continuing to read his book now. It'll only bring back more memories and it won't change a thing. Tomorrow, she'll take it to one of the charity shops in Kentish Town, where some lucky reader can purchase it for a few quid. She got her goodbye today, and now it's time to look towards the future.

When she returns home after work, Graham is not there, but there's a note on the kitchen counter.

Meet me on Parliament Hill at 7 <3

Olivia checks the clock. She stayed late at the centre, chatting to Lou, and now she only has a little over an hour to get ready and make her way to Hampstead Heath. Tonight she wants to tell Graham everything that happened in the past thirty-six hours. It's daunting, and she's not sure which words to use, or how to explain her reasoning, but if the past has taught her anything, it's that she needs to be entirely honest with Graham. If they're going to make Canada work, they'll need to be able to trust each other completely. It might be a difficult conversation, but part of the reason why she and Eamonn never worked out was because of their inability to have difficult conversations. They're so similar in that regard, both always sticking their heads in the sand, but it clearly has never worked to their advantage. It needs to be different with Graham.

Olivia's Uber driver doesn't say a word on the way over and usually that would unsettle her, but not today. Today she's grateful for the silence as she practises her lines in her mind, as though preparing for a Shakespearian tragedy.

The car stops at the entrance in Dartmouth Park and Olivia makes her way up the hill, clutching the skirt of her maxi dress in her fist so she won't trip. The summer breeze is soft on her skin, the scent of warm grass rising up from the ground. There are a lot of people in the park, but her eyes are fixed on the top of the hill. As she draws closer, she sees him, a single orange gerbera daisy in his hand – her favourite flower. He's wearing a faded yellow T-shirt and navy-blue slacks, his white runners smudged as always. Since she saw him this morning, he's had a haircut and something happened to his beard, although it's hard to tell what. It's not shorter – he usually keeps it close-cropped – but it's fancier somehow.

'Hello, my love,' he says, his eyes shining with delight.

'Hi.' Olivia smiles when he hands over the flower and leads her away by the hand.

'Right this way, madam.'

'Where are we going?'

As they pass the highest point of the hill, cheering erupts and then she sees them on the downward slope.

'Surprise!'

All of their closest friends are there: Ben and Erin, Amira and her partner, Andrew, Turner and Mark, and Sam and Suze. Olivia is stunned into silence.

'Surprise,' Graham whispers in her ear, folding his arms around her waist from behind. She turns around to face him. 'You're unbelievable.'

His hazel eyes shine bright. 'If we're leaving London, we're not doing it quietly, Livvie. We deserve to go out with a bang. Together.'

Behind her a bottle is uncorked as though on cue, and delightful cheers erupt from the people she will miss with all her heart. The emotional rollercoaster she's been on since yesterday reaches the deep downward plummet, scaring the life out of her. How can she feel so many things all at once?

She presses her lips to Graham's. 'I love you,' she says.

His hands travel from her waist to her warm cheeks and he looks her dead in the eye, shaking his head ever so slightly. 'You have no idea,' he says.

She doesn't need anyone telling her Graham's love for her is the real thing. He's doing a perfectly good job of that himself. But it feels undeserved, still. She desperately wants to tell him about Eamonn, but doing so with all their friends around is not an option. She'll have to wait and, in the meantime, somehow suppress the ever-increasing guilt.

'Oi! Stop being so horny and get over here,' Turner, one of Graham's best friends from uni, shouts.

Olivia laughs, pulls herself away from Graham and makes her way over to the group. They're all seated on the grass in a semi-circle, facing the park below instead of the London skyline behind them. Olivia and Graham close the circle and Amira hands them a glass of prosecco. When everyone is served, they raise their glasses.

'To Olivia and Graham, for fucking off and leaving us all behind,' Turner says. He's an acquired taste. He can be blunt and arrogant at times – especially, Olivia has learned, when he's feeling emotional.

'Lovely sentiments there,' Graham says, shaking his head. 'Remind me to invite you over as soon as possible.'

'I think what Turner is trying to say,' Mark, the third of the journalism musketeers, chimes in, 'is that you'll be missed terribly.'

Turner shrugs as though those were his exact words, making everyone laugh.

'Thanks, Mark. I think it's clear Olivia and I will miss you all too. We couldn't have wished for a better team.'

The lump in Olivia's throat grows bigger with every word that's spoken. This is definitely going to end in tears. Beside her, Erin leans in, her eyes a little more watery than usual. 'I'm sorry,' she whispers, 'I shouldn't have been so harsh on the phone.' The sorrowful look in her eyes makes Olivia wrap her arm around her best friend. 'Let's talk later, okay?' She really wants to tell Erin what happened with Eamonn today, but even after this apology, she's still not a hundred per cent sure that's a good idea. Something seems off about Erin, and Olivia is fairly certain it has something to do with Eamonn.

'So, are you all set to go?' Suze asks.

'Mostly, yeah. There are a few things we can't pack yet, but the rest's sorted.'

'And by the time Livvie gets there, we'll have running water and everything.'

'What do you mean?' Mark asks.

Graham explains the issue with the plumber and somehow makes it sound like a riveting story. Even Olivia can't help but be entertained, even though she was less than thrilled the first time she heard it.

'Oh shit,' Sam says. 'Is that why you ran out of the shop yesterday?'

It takes a second for Olivia to find a response but before she can say anything, Suze chimes in, 'Right! We forgot to tell you. Eamonn, you know, the author, seemed to know you. We gave him your number. I hope that's okay?'

Olivia's stomach drops. *No, no, no.* Afraid to look at Graham, she keeps her eyes fixed on Sam. 'Uhm, yeah, no, that was, uhm, my sister calling for my dad's birthday.'

Next to her, Graham turns. 'Is that the book you were reading?'

'Uhm, uh-huh, yeah.'

'And you know the author? That's so cool. How come you didn't tell me?'

When she finally turns to face him, the enthusiasm in his gaze fades and her palms become sweaty.

'Should we grab something to eat?' Erin comes to the rescue. 'Maybe we can go get a few snacks and bring them back here?'

'Good idea.' Amira pushes herself up and offers Andrew a hand. 'You two stay here to guard our spot and we'll be back in a bit.' Even though Olivia hasn't told Amira about the recent events, she's met Eamonn once and knows a thing or two about their history.

'Do you really need six people at Tesco's?' Turner asks.

A withering glare from Amira follows and without a word, he gets up and joins them.

Olivia and Graham wait silently until their friends are out of earshot, her stomach twisting itself in knots. She should've told him. Now he's heard it from someone else, it seems a lot more damning than she'd hoped.

'I need to tell you something.'

'It wasn't just your mother that upset you yesterday, huh?'

She shakes her head. 'It wasn't. I ran into someone from my past. Well, I didn't. He was there. I had no idea. I just wanted to buy a book. I—'

'You're not making much sense.'

'I saw Eamonn. Ben and Erin's friend.'

'Alex's godfather?'

'Yeah, him.'

'You know him?'

'I do.'

Confusion clouds Graham's eyes. 'But we've never met him.'

'He lives in Ireland,' she says, as though that is enough to explain the whole thing. But it doesn't and Graham goes on.

'Still, he's Ben and Erin's best friend. And so are you. You share a godchild. They never even mention him. How is that possible?'

'It's a long story.'

'You're a fast talker. Why don't you give it a try?'

There's a bite to his tone and although she knows she had it coming, Olivia is still taken aback. She faces away from him as she continues. 'You know how I met Erin and Ben when I went to live with Anna in Ireland for a bit, yeah?'

Graham nods.

'Well, that's how we all became friends. The three of them grew up together and it's a very small town so when I got there, we hung out a lot.'

'And?'

'And... we uhm...' She falls silent, pulls at a blade of grass and runs it through her fingers.

'You fell in love,' Graham concludes for her.

At this, she meets his knowing gaze and nods slowly. 'Yes. We fell in love.'

They're both silent for a while. Olivia looks away again, but feels Graham's eyes still on her. It's like he's contemplating his next move, or maybe waiting for her to make one.

'So what happened?' he asks after a while.

There are a few seconds where she considers telling him everything, from start to heartbreaking finish. But the others will return soon, and this is not a conversation she wants to be having in the middle of a park anyway.

'It didn't work out.'

Graham scoffs. 'That's it? It didn't work out?'

'Look, a lot happened, but I'd rather tell you some other time. The others will be here any minute.'

Graham looks over his shoulder and then turns back to her. 'Why have you never mentioned this?'

'Because, before yesterday, I hadn't seen him in fourteen years. It was irrelevant.'

'Clearly it's not irrelevant.' He waves a hand at her. 'You have best friends in common, a godchild. If this was all irrelevant, we'd have seen the guy at least once since Alex's birth.'

Olivia knows he's right, but she really believed it was irrelevant all those years. She thought it was in the past and that she'd closed that chapter. Until yesterday. 'It's complicated.'

Graham lets out a short, humourless laugh. 'Clearly.'

Does she really owe him all the details of her relationship with Eamonn? She doesn't know the intricacies of his previous relationships, and she's fine with that. They're over. That's the only thing that matters.

'Look, Graham, I understand you're upset because I didn't tell you, but I don't see why you need to know my complete dating history. Yes, I was in love with Eamonn fourteen years ago. Yes, it was complicated and painful but we both knew it couldn't work. Seeing him yesterday threw me, I won't lie about that, but he's gone back to Ireland now and we're moving to Canada. So the way I see it, it's not relevant.'

His expression is blank. 'Did he text you?'

'What?'

'Suze said she gave him your number. Did he text you?'

Of all the reactions she'd anticipated, anger was not one of them. In all their time together, Graham had rarely been angry, and maybe only once or twice about something she'd said or did. If she tells him about meeting up with Eamonn today, he's only bound to get more upset. But lying now would only make it worse and, even though his anger feels somewhat disproportionate, she owes him the truth if she doesn't want to lose him.

'Yes, he texted me.'

'And?'

'And we met up today.'

Graham's eyes grow wide.

'We just had a chat. That's all.'

'Did you know you were meeting him this morning?'

'Graham...'

'Did you?'

She nods.

'Oh my God, Olivia, seriously?' His voice is high-pitched, and even he flinches at the sound of it.

'I'm sorry, okay? I didn't tell you because it's... it's...'

'Complicated?'

She closes her eyes briefly and lets out a sigh of defeat. 'I'm sorry. But nothing happened. We talked. We had lunch. He left.'

Graham gets to his feet and fear grips her heart.

'I've put everything I have into us, into Vancouver, because I thought we were solid. I thought I knew you.'

Olivia gets up too, wraps her hand around his arm to keep him in place. 'You do know me.'

'You lied, Olivia.'

'I'm sorry. But meeting up with Eamonn has nothing to do with us.'

He laughs now, a mocking kind of laugh. 'If you really think that, then you're not only lying to me, but also to yourself.' He pulls his arm from her grip. 'I need some time to think. I'll see you at home.'

'Graham...'

But he's already walking down the hill, in the opposite direction from where their friends have reappeared, just in time to watch her burst into tears.

14

Graham is by the door, two large suitcases at his feet while Olivia leans against the fridge, silently watching him. It's still dark outside, but his only option to fly out was early Friday morning and so the alarm went off at four a.m. Ever since the surprise party he's been quiet – not angry exactly, but closed off, contemplative. Graham is not a quiet guy. If anything, he's usually even chattier than Olivia. They've never run out of things to say, until now. Olivia has tried to talk to him several times – the idea of him leaving without having discussed the whole Eamonn thing terrifies her. But Graham has avoided the subject entirely.

'I'm gonna miss you,' Olivia says, taking a step closer in his direction. He looks at her briefly and then his phone buzzes in his palm. 'That's my ride,' he says. With one hand he picks up his suitcase and with the other, opens the door. 'I'll call you when I land.'

Olivia stands defeated, unable to find the right words to make him turn and talk to her, tears pricking her eyes. 'Okay,' she says. 'Have a safe flight.' What a stupid expression, she thinks. It's not as though he has any control over the safety of his flight. But what else is there to say when he won't hear any of it?

He's about to close the door when he stops. 'Liv…'
Hopeful, Olivia's heart jumps. 'Yeah?'
'Before I go, I need to say something.'

She holds her breath and waits for him to continue.

'I read the book.'

Of all the things she thought he might say, this is not one of them. She shakes her head in confusion. 'What?'

'I needed to know.'

'Know what? How much I loved him? If I love you more? Have you never been in love with anyone before me?' Her voice is whiny and desperate, and she hates the sound of it.

'Have you finished reading it?' he asks, not answering any of her questions.

'No, and I won't! Because I don't need to. It's in the past – it doesn't matter.' She steps forwards, reaching for his hand, but he pulls back.

'I want you to read it.'

Baffled, she stares at him. 'What are you on about?'

'I want you to read it all.'

This makes no sense to her whatsoever. She throws her head back in exasperation. 'Fuck, Graham, why?' His reasoning is incomprehensible. And it's infuriating.

'Were you there? On the day of the pact?'

Tears fill her eyes as she reaches for his hand again. 'Graham, it doesn't matter. That was years ago.' The words come out slowly, as though having to say them over and over is making them heavier.

Graham smiles a sad smile. 'It does. You say you both decided it couldn't work. But that's not what happened, is it?'

'It is!'

'It's not.' He pulls his hand from her grip and picks up his suitcase. 'Just read the book. I'll call you when I land,' he says again, closing the door behind him without looking back.

Dizzy with confusion, Olivia slumps against the door, the entire conversation rolling around her mind, over and over, relentlessly. Why did he wait until the last moment to drop this on her? She's been trying to get him to talk for two days. And now he's gone, soon to be across the ocean. She drags herself to the bedroom and hides under the covers. The sheets on his side of the bed are still warm, and his soapy scent lingers. With his words running never-ending circles around her brain, it's impossible to go back to sleep, so instead she just lies there, breathing in what's left of him.

It could be moments later or hours when her phone buzzes on the nightstand – Olivia has no idea. This whole morning seems to be playing out on a different timeline entirely. Without turning around, she reaches back and feels around the nightstand until her hand touches the smooth, glass screen of her phone. The cold white light hurts her eyes. She blinks. Once. Twice. Before she can read the message.

Liv, I want you with me in Canada. I really do. But I want you to be certain you want to be with me. And you can't do that without knowing the whole story. And I don't think you do. Please, read the book, talk to him, do what you need to do and if after all that, you still want to be with me, we'll talk. x

Nausea swells in her throat. *We'll talk?* What the fuck?

Wide-awake now and filled with dread, she buries her head in her pillow and screams. His words don't make any sense at all. Olivia knows what happened – she was the one who was there, after all. She showed up, Eamonn didn't. What more can there be to the story?

Unable to stay under the covers any longer, she marches to the kitchen and puts on a pot of coffee. As she waits for it to brew, the first question she had when she found out about the book comes back to mind. *Why would he write that, when I was the one left broken-hearted?*

Could Graham be right? Does she not know the whole truth about their story?

On the footpath below, people are making their way to the tube. They're in shirts and dresses, not a coat or umbrella to be seen, the air still warm from the day before. The perfect weather for her father's birthday party. Another fun event in an already fun-filled week.

With a cup of coffee cradled in her hand, Olivia returns to her bed and opens the drawer on her nightstand. The book is still there, exactly where she thought it had always been, but now knows it wasn't. Graham must've put it back when he finished reading. She stares at it for a long time, feeling a bit like Alice about to follow the white rabbit. There's no way of knowing where this will lead, but it seems she has very little choice in the matter. Dread fills her again as she picks it up and turns to Part Two. And with a deep breath, down the rabbit-hole she goes.

Wild Waves
Chapter 14 - January 2010

Conor was in the kitchen reading Frankenstein for a uni assignment when Jack entered, carrying three tote bags in each hand. They were stuffed with crisps, nuts, olives and so much alcohol, it seemed illegal. Conor looked up from his book and raised his eyebrows. 'How many people are we expecting, exactly?'

'Oh, don't worry about this – I'm shite at organising these things. I always get too much food.' Jack rubbed his hands where the bags had left indentations.

From the boyish grin on his face, Conor gathered he was overjoyed to be throwing his New Year's party. He'd been begging Conor for weeks, trying to convince him it would be a great way to meet more people. Ever since he'd moved to Dublin, Conor had had his hands full with studying and his job at Tesco, leaving little room to make new friends. Not that he necessarily wanted to. He still met up with Matt and Orla quite regularly and, after the heartache he'd suffered with Ava, he'd decided to keep to himself for a while. But Jack had been incessant and if consenting to this party would get him off Conor's back for a bit, it was worth the sacrifice. One night, that's all it was – one night of socialising, or at least pretending to.

'Where's our food?' Conor asked, watching Jack stack as many beer bottles as possible in the apparently empty fridge.

'Well, there wasn't much left to begin with and the few things that were in there are now hanging outside.' Jack pointed to the window at the other end of the kitchen.

'What do you mean, hanging outside?'

'It's cold outside. I put the food in a plastic bag and tied it to the window handle. Free fridge.' He shrugged as though it was the most natural thing in the world.

Conor looked out the window and there it was, the white plastic bag, swinging gently from side to side in the wind. He had to admit, it was quite clever. He grabbed one of the beers and, using a lighter he found on the counter, popped the crown cap off.

'Do you need a hand with anything?' Conor asked.

'No, we're good here, I think. All there's left to do is get ready. Do you mind if I shower first?'

'Yeah sure, I wasn't planning on showering anyway.'

Jack gave him an incredulous look. 'Oh, so that's what you're wearing?'

Conor looked down at his jeans and plain grey T-shirt. 'What's wrong with what I'm wearing?'

'It's a New Year's party. At least put on a clean shirt, Conor.'

'My T-shirt is clean.'

'It's also a T-shirt,' he said, emphasising the *T*. 'Wait here.' Jack left the room and reemerged a few seconds later, holding out a freshly pressed, navy-blue shirt.

Conor shook his head. 'No. It's this or I'm out,' he said.

'Fine, but don't come crying to me when no one wants to shift you.'

Conor smiled. 'I can't make any promises.'

Later that night, Conor was talking to one of Jack's friends he'd once met in the pub when Jack came up to them, followed by two women. This was what Conor had feared would happen.

'Conor, I'd like you to meet Julia and Sadie.'

'Hiya, how's it going,' he said. They smiled closed-lipped smiles.

'Julia and I went to school together,' Jack continued.

Conor nodded. He'd repeatedly told Jack not to try and set him up with anyone at the party and Jack had promised he wouldn't, but this looked an awful lot like a set-up.

'Jack told us you might be interested in working in a book shop,' Sadie said.

In surprise, he turned to Jack, who gave him a wide grin.

'Thought I was playing matchmaker, didn't ya?'

Conor's cheeks flushed. 'I, uhm…'

'Yeah, you did. Think you're such a catch, don't ya?'

'Ah, fuck off.' He gave Jack a playful shove.

'You know your Irish greats?' Sadie asked.

'I suppose I should. I'm doing literature, so…'

She gave a small shrug. 'Not that most customers come in asking for them. Usually they're just after the new Jamie Oliver or something.'

'Tall, lanky politician, right?' Conor said.

Sadie laughed. 'Close enough. Have you heard of The Sea of Books?'

'Yeah, of course. I love that place.'

'It's my mam's and we're actually looking for someone to help out on the weekends, occasionally weekdays too. Jack told me you'd be the perfect guy for the job, so… do you want it?'

'Just like that?'

'Just like that. My mam will obviously want to talk to you, but I'm pretty sure she'll be okay with it.'

From the corner of his eye he could see Jack beaming with pride, and when he noticed Julia and Sadie were holding hands, he acknowledged he might've been a bit too hasty to judge.

Conor couldn't believe his luck, but that was the thing about living with Jack – he was one of those guys who knew people.

With his plan changing from living in London to moving to Dublin at the last minute, there'd been no time to look for a proper flat. Fortunately, Matt knew someone who needed a flatmate and that's how he'd ended up living with Jack O'Keeffe. His parents owned a high-end car dealership and from a young age he'd been invited to almost every event in town. People liked him: he was charming, funny, but most of all, kind. You could ask him anything, and even if you *didn't* ask, he'd show up for you.

'So, what do you say, mate?' Jack gave him a pat on the shoulder.

'Count me in.'

Wild Waves
Chapter 15 - March 2010

'Did you remember to pack my red tie?' James asked from the kitchen.

'Yep. Although I think you should wear the charcoal one, it matches the suit better.'

'Well, my sister asked me to wear the red one, so there you go.'

Ava rolled her eyes as she folded her own clothes and arranged them in her suitcase. James was in a bit of a mood that morning. When his sister had given birth to her second child in December, he'd been named godfather, and the christening was the following day in Southend-on-Sea. In all the years they had been together, they'd never left London together, and it wasn't until the invitation that Ava discovered James hated leaving the city. When she'd asked him why, he had told her about all the compulsory family vacations he'd had in the countryside, forced to interact with nature, and it was clear he had no intention of ever reliving those memories again. Perhaps that was why he hadn't come to see her in Ireland?

Adding to that, he had just switched companies and was starting his career in insurance fraud investigations, and he'd repeatedly reminded Ava he didn't have time to go faffing about in the middle of nowhere. (His words, not hers.)

Ava, on the other hand, hoped their mini break would be good for them. When she'd returned from Ireland, she'd worked really hard to find her rhythm with James again. And to her own surprise, it had gone quite well those first few weeks. At first they'd been busy with the move and the start of their respective new jobs, but once the newness of it all had faded, they began slowly drifting apart. Ava's new job turned out to be rather stressful, and the strain on their relationship was beginning to show. They desperately needed some time away together.

Ava sometimes wondered if James suspected something had happened in Ireland, but he never actually confronted her and so she decided not to bring it up either. Conor was in the past and hundreds of miles away. She would most likely never see him again, so why break James' heart too? She'd broken enough hearts as it was.

This weekend was going to be the perfect opportunity to reignite the slowly extinguishing flame of their relationship. She was going to make sure of that, starting in the bedroom. It had been a few months since they'd last had sex and, even though she was mostly too tired herself to bother, she realised something needed to happen before they turned into nothing but roommates.

Determined to put an end to this drought, she walked over to the dresser in the bedroom to take out her best bra and pants. Ava was not the type to buy lingerie sets – paying twenty-five pounds for a pair of knickers was completely ridiculous in her opinion. Instead, she always bought black bras and black knickers, convinced no one would notice. The prospect of having sex again lifted her spirits a little and she decided not to address James' foul mood, hoping it would sort itself out by the time they got to their B&B.

When they arrived, the room wasn't ready yet and so they left their luggage at reception and went looking for a place to have lunch. They landed on a small seafood restaurant. Despite its size, it was light and bright with big windows overlooking the sea. For the first time in a long time, Ava let her mind drift to a different beach. In a way it all seemed as though it had happened years ago, but then again, she remembered it so vividly, it might as well have happened the other day. When the waiter came over to take their orders, she was pulled from her memories and quickly picked up the menu to make a choice. She could feel James' eyes on her but she pretended not to notice. They ordered – monkfish for her, mussels for him – and when the waiter left, they fell silent again until he returned with their drinks.

Ava raised her glass in a toast. 'Here's to us finally spending some time together.'

'Yeah, it's been a while, hasn't it?'

'It's like I see you less than before we were living together.'

'I know. But we've both been so busy.'

'I guess…' she sighed.

'Look at it this way,' James said. 'If we put in the hard work now, we'll be able to buy a place soon and then eventually things will calm down.'

'You think so?'

Conor's words echoed in her mind. People always want more. A bigger house, more cars, fancier cars, a massive garden, kids… but all of those things cost money. And in order to get that money, they need a higher paying job with lots of benefits. They don't care if they love their jobs, they just desperately need the pay. And so they become unhappy, but there's no way out. They're stuck.

'Yeah, it'll be nice, you'll see,' James said. He turned to look out the window, the empty beach stretching out in front of them, and shook his head. 'I can't believe Madeline and Thomas actually moved here.'

Ava shrugged. 'Why not? It's lovely.'

'It's dead though, isn't it?' James said.

'I like it. It's peaceful.'

With their plates in front of them, the conversation died down again.

'Food's great,' Ava said, hoping to keep a conversation going. James only hummed in agreement and so she gave up. They ate in silence until their plates were empty and James finished his glass of wine, signalling to the waiter for the bill.

'Let's go for a walk on the beach,' Ava suggested.

'I'm knackered, Ave. I think I might just head back to the B&B for a nap.' He checked his watch. 'Our room should be ready by now.'

'Okay, you go ahead,' she said, trying to hide the disappointment in her voice. 'I'm going to get some fresh air first.' So much for spending time together.

He kissed her on the forehead. 'I promise I'll be better company after my nap. We'll do something fun then, okay, muppet?'

Ava grabbed his hand and squeezed. Maybe they didn't have the most invigorating conversations anymore, but he still loved her, of that she was certain.

The icy wind hurled grains of sand at her as she walked along the shoreline, the squeak of seagulls and rushing waves taking her back to Ballybridge. When she closed her eyes she could see him, smell the warm salty scent of his skin, feel his fingers laced with hers. All the things she'd been trying to forget. Because the truth was, she sometimes questioned her decision. Would things have been different, had he come with her to London?

She got her phone from her coat pocket and opened the last text he'd sent her, not that she needed reminding. In some painfully ironic way, the words of her favourite song had been the most fitting for her heartbreak.

Since then, she hadn't heard from him, and standing there on that beach, she couldn't help but wonder how he was doing. Her thumb hovered over the tiny keyboard. Maybe she could text him? Just as a friend?

No. Of course she couldn't. What was she even thinking? Twat. She let out a growl of frustration, pocketed her phone and returned to the B&B, the ice-cold wind whipping her in the face, as though punishing her for even having considered it.

James had the television on and was sitting with his back propped up against the headboard, flipping through the channels. He looked a lot more cheerful than he did an hour earlier, and gave her a wide smile as she took off her coat and shoes.

'Someone looks well-rested,' Ava said.

He tapped the bed, inviting her to sit by his side. When she did, he wrapped his arm around her shoulders and pulled her close, kissing her on the temple.

'I'm sorry, muppet,' he said. 'I know I've been a bit of a tosser lately.'

'You've had a lot on your mind.' She rested her head on his shoulder.

'True, but still.'

Ava didn't reply, but turned her head and kissed him.

'Let's just stay here for a while. We can watch a film before we have to go to Madeline's,' he said.

The selection of DVDs was rather limited, and so they quickly agreed on *The Lion King*, James' favourite Disney film. They curled up on the bed together, and when Mufasa died, James pulled her in close. They laughed when they both needed a tissue, and James got up to get them. It'd been a long time since she'd seen him so relaxed. His black hair, usually combed back and set with products and spray, was now wild and messy from his nap; his T-shirt was wrinkled, but it was his demeanour more than anything that told her he was feeling better. The tense muscles in his jaw had softened, and the wrinkles around his eyes deepened when he smiled at her. With his long, dark eyelashes, high cheekbones and full lips, she'd been attracted to him from the moment she met him, but time had desensitised her to his features. His gorgeous face had become too familiar over the years, and it wasn't until now she remembered how much she'd once fancied him. When he returned to the bed she wrapped herself around him again, and by the time the movie ended, neither felt like untangling themselves to get ready.

'Do we really have to go?' James asked.

'I'm afraid so.'

'I mean, what would happen if we didn't? She's hardly going to come and find us, is she?'

'James, we have to go.'

'Oh come on, Ave, let's just stay here.' His hand slid down her side and under her top. Even though she desperately wanted him to continue, she pushed his hand away.

'We'll come back straight after dessert and then we can do whatever we want,' she said, leaning forwards and kissing him so deeply a moan escaped him.

'Fine,' he said. 'Let's get this over with, then.' He gave her bum a squeeze and disappeared into the bathroom to get ready. Ava smiled. Perhaps there was hope for them after all.

Madeline had gone all out with dinner. She'd cooked Beef Wellington with roast veg from a Nigella Lawson recipe, and for dessert she'd served them a homemade raspberry white chocolate cheesecake. Ava tried not to eat too much, with the prospect of sex in mind, but it was a challenge. Madeline was an excellent cook, and she loved nothing more than having people over for dinner. They drank red wine and discussed the christening the following day. The two godfathers, James and Tim, Thomas's younger brother, were asked to read something in church, and Ava, who'd brought her camera along, offered to take pictures. They'd hired a professional photographer for the official photos but Madeline wanted candid pictures as well and had welcomed the offer with open arms. Being expected outside the church at nine a.m. the next day, everyone went home after dessert, much to Ava's relief.

They walked back to the B&B, the cold air sobering them up slightly. James draped his arm over her shoulder and linked his fingers with hers. Even though Ava loved every moment of it, a tiny voice at the back of her mind couldn't help but wonder if all this sudden affection would continue beyond the evening. But why was she being so negative? He was clearly trying, so perhaps she should too. She silenced the voice and leaned into him.

Back in the room, Ava popped into the bathroom to change and when she came back out wearing only her bra and pants, James was lying on the bed, grinning.

'Come here,' he said. He put his hands on her waist, pulled her against him and kissed her. His mouth tasted of red wine and the cigarette he'd smoked on the way back. He was sitting on the edge of the bed and locked Ava between his thighs. With one hand he took off his T-shirt, pulling it over his head. Ava had always found that an extremely sexy move and this time was no different. The wine had made her frisky and when she felt him pressing up against her, she let out a soft moan and climbed on top of him. James kissed her breasts while his hands reached for her bra clasp.

'Scoot back a little, I'm going to fall off,' she said, lifting her hips so he could move. James shimmied backwards, his gaze focussed on her, his eyes hazy with desire. As she unbuttoned his jeans, James let himself fall back onto the bed.

There was a loud thud.

'FUUUCK!' he shouted.

Ava clasped her hand to her mouth and gasped, trying not to laugh. In all his enthusiasm, James had banged his head against the bed frame pretty hard. He reached for the sore spot and pulled his hand back immediately, a tiny drop of blood on his index finger from hitting the edge of the wooden frame.

'Oh my God, are you okay?' Ava asked, sounding more amused than alarmed.

'It's not funny,' he said. There was no anger in his voice, but she felt bad nonetheless.

Ava got a wet towel from the bathroom to press against the wound. The minimal bleeding stopped soon after, suggesting he wasn't in need of stitches. In a way she was relieved, but the odds of having sex had vanished the moment he banged his head and Ava had to work hard to hide her disappointment.

'I'm so sorry,' she said.

His expression was pinched, his hand pressed to the back of his head. 'It's not your fault.' He leaned in to rest his head against her chest. His cheek was warm against her bare skin. They sat like that in silence for a bit, Ava cradling him in her arms. 'Do you want to go to sleep?' she asked after a while.

He nodded and they got up to brush their teeth. Back in bed, James wrapped his arm around Ava's waist and pulled her close.

'I'm sorry,' he whispered. 'Maybe tomorrow, yeah?'

'I'm thinking about taking a photography course,' Ava said on the drive back to London.

'Photography?'

James' head was still hurting, and the painkillers she'd gone and bought for him appeared not to be effective. The whole day he'd been grumpy and unpleasant, and even the prospect of going home hadn't lifted his spirits.

'Yeah. I've always wanted to do it and today just reminded me of how much I love it, you know?'

He gave a small shrug and stared out the window, even though there was nothing to see in the dark.

'What do you think? Do I have what it takes?'

'Everyone's a photographer nowadays. The cameras basically do all the work for you, don't they?' he said.

Ava knew he wasn't feeling well, but his reaction hurt her anyway. The thought of getting back into photography had been so exciting, she'd even googled a few courses on James' laptop while he was taking their things to the car. The more she'd looked into it, the more energised she'd become. The daily grind and the stress of her job were getting to her and she desperately needed to have fun again. Taking pictures at the christening had reminded her of the ones she'd taken in Ireland, and once again, Conor's words echoed in her mind.

This time, she didn't keep them to herself. 'So what if everyone's a photographer? Doesn't mean I can't be one, does it?'

James closed his eyes. 'Sure, yeah.'

As soon as they got home, Ava retreated to the bedroom. Her laptop was on the bed and with her back propped up against the wall, she flipped it open and positioned it on her knees. She hesitated for a second but then, for the first time in six months, she opened the photos folder titled 'BB 2009'. Her screen filled with the images of what felt like a completely different life. First the ones of Kate and George came up, and Ava couldn't help but smile at the sweetness of it all. The love she'd felt in that house shone through these pictures all the way into her bedroom. She felt a certain amount of pride too – these images weren't bad. When the first photo of Orla appeared, Ava took a deep breath. This one was taken on the beach, wine bottle in her hand, laughing so hard her eyes were closed. They'd been having a lazy day somewhere in late June, and Conor had joined them later that night. They'd talked about the *Twilight* phenomenon, and what they would do if vampires were to invade their little town. Ava remembered laughing so hard she'd peed herself a little. That night she'd taken her first picture of Conor, and she knew it was coming up next. The moment she saw his freckles and the lines around the corners of his mouth, his hair messy from the wind and those deep blue eyes staring back at her, something inside her shifted.

Her next steps came almost involuntarily. First, she opened her browser. In the search bar she typed *photography course London*, and when the results came up she clicked on the one she'd seen earlier that day. Five minutes later, she'd enrolled in the first class on offer. Then, she moved on to Outlook and opened a new email.

> *Hey Conor,*
> *It's me, Ava – which you obviously already know from my email address. Silly.*
> *Guess I'm a little nervous. I've been thinking about you a lot these past few days, but I wasn't sure you'd want to hear from me. Guess I'll find out soon now.*
> *I was at the seaside this past weekend and it reminded me of you. I miss you, Conor. I really do and I'm sorry for how things ended.*
> *You're probably wondering if there's a point to this email. There isn't really, I just wanted to talk to you.*
> *I hope you're happy.*
> *Love,*
> *Bruce*
> *PS: I'm starting a photography course next week. Thank you. X*

Wild Waves
Chapter 16

Conor was in the shop window, reorganising the display, when a woman stopped on the footpath in front of him to tie her shoe. At first, Conor wasn't sure he was seeing things right but when he did a double take, he was certain it was her. The moment she got up and saw him, she seemed equally surprised.

Conor froze, unsure what to do next. She waved and, in response, he wiggled his fingers like a *Looney Tunes* character. *What the fuck?* Regretting his awkward move, he pushed his hands in his pockets. She shook her head, laughed and walked towards the door. Conor climbed out of the display, his legs suddenly a few pounds heavier.

'Conor Delaney, I'll be damned,' she said.

He pressed his lips together in an uncomfortable smile.

'What are you doing here?' she continued.

'I, uhm, I work here.'

'I should hope so. Most business owners don't approve of customers rearranging their displays.'

He gave a short laugh and felt his cheeks flush.

'Well, you haven't changed much.'

'Yeah, you too,' he answered. Apparently he had lost all powers of speech. Was this really the best he could do? Before he could make even more of a fool of himself, someone tapped him on the shoulder.

'Excuse me, could you tell me where to find the new Jamie Oliver?'

'Sure, I'll get that for you in a second,' he told the man, who was clutching his umbrella as though afraid Conor would take it from him. 'I, uhm, I should get back to work,' he said, turning to her.

'Do you want to get a drink some time, catch up?' she asked.

At least one of them was behaving like a normal human being.

'Yeah, sure, I'd like that.'

'Tonight?'

'Grand, yeah. I'm here till closing time.'

'Alright, we can go to the pub across the road. See you there at seven?'

'Seven, yeah, sound.'

'See you then, Conor.' She gave his arm a soft squeeze before she turned around and walked away. The man looking for the cookbook was still standing next to him and gave a little cough to get his attention. When Conor turned to him, he could swear he saw pity in his eyes.

'Right,' he said, walking over to the enormous stack of Jamie Oliver books next to the life-size cardboard cutout of him in the middle of the shop. He handed the man a copy and followed him to the till.

'Who was that?' Sadie asked when the customer had gone.

'I don't know, just some guy looking for Jamie Oliver.'

'Clearly that's who I'm asking about.' She rolled her eyes at him.

'Oh, you mean Niamh?'

'Yeah, the gorgeous woman you were just talking to. If you can call that talking, anyway.'

'Oi!'

Sadie laughed. 'Who is she?'

'My ex. We were together at uni, years ago. Hadn't seen her since.'

'What happened?'

Conor shrugged. 'Life, I suppose.'

The truth was, when his mother had died, he'd moved back home to Ballybridge and pushed everyone out of his life that reminded him of the fun he was having the moment her heart had stopped beating. Including his girlfriend.

Conor grabbed some books from the counter and walked away from Sadie, not willing to go into the details of it all.

'If you need some help before your date tonight, let me know, okay? We have a few books on people skills in the psychology section that I think could be very useful!' she shouted after him, chuckling at her own joke.

Before he left, Conor popped into the loo to check his reflection in the mirror. His eyes had dark circles under them and the first signs of stubble had appeared around his mouth because he hadn't bothered shaving that morning. He stood facing the mirror for a while, not really looking at himself but lost in thought. Seeing Niamh had unsettled him. The first months after their break-up, he'd been consumed by guilt for pushing her away. She'd done nothing but support him, but he'd felt suffocated by grief at the time and had been unable to talk about it. After a while, his pain had softened and he'd realised what he'd done, but by then it had been too late.

He splashed some water in his face and, with his hands still wet, shaped his wavy hair until he looked presentable enough. When he emerged from the toilet, he threw a questioning glance at Sadie.

'You look exactly the same as you did five minutes ago,' she said.

'Cheers, mate,' he replied, anxiously ruffling his hair again.

'Oh Conor, I'm only messing. You're so pretty.'

'Eejit.' He bumped her with his hip just hard enough to unbalance her on his way out.

The icy wind was a shock to his senses. He'd been inside the warm shop all day and had no idea it would be that cold when he closed the door behind him. It was dark and the air felt pregnant with snow. When he approached the pub, she was standing there, her hands deep in her pockets, an enormous scarf covering half her face. A peculiar mix of excitement and sadness settled in his chest.

'Hi,' she said.

'Hiya.'

'Let's go in before we freeze.'

There were a couple of tables left in the back of the pub and while Niamh found them a spot, Conor ordered two Irish coffees. Leaning against the bar, he watched Niamh unwrap herself, first removing her shoulder bag, then her scarf, hat and coat. Sadie was right. She was gorgeous.

'Cheers,' she said when he put down the coffee in front of her.

'Here, I'm sorry about earlier.' Conor pulled back a chair and took off his coat.

'Sorry about what?' she asked.

'My lack of conversational skills, I suppose. It's just that I didn't expect to see you there and well, I guess you could say I was surprised.'

'I noticed that. I was a bit surprised myself, really. I walk by there so often and I've never seen you around. Have you been working there long?'

'No, I started a couple of weeks ago, but I only work weekends. I'm back at uni, actually,' he said.

Niamh had always wanted him to go back to uni, and they'd had so many fights about it, Conor instantly regretted bringing it up. But he should've known better.

'That's fab, Conor. Fair play to ya.'

How was she this nice to him, after everything he put her through?

'What about you?' he asked. 'What have you been up to?'

'I've been working as an editorial assistant.'

He grinned. 'You always said you would.'

'Yeah, the plan hasn't changed much, really.'

Niamh and her plans. Just like Conor, she'd studied literature, but unlike him, she'd wanted to start her own publishing company. They'd fantasised about it a lot. Conor would write his novels and she'd edit and publish them. They'd live in Dublin, somewhere on the coast, but close enough to have the best of both worlds. Would it all have happened, had he not broken her heart?

'How's, uhm… What's his name?' From the look on her face, he could tell she saw right through him.

'You don't have to pretend you don't remember his name, Conor.'

He smiled. 'Fine, how's Sean then?'

When Conor had refused to return to Dublin, Niamh had met Sean and eventually left Conor for him. He'd hated it, but he knew there was no one to blame but himself.

'Sean's grand.'

'Oh?'

They held each other's gaze for a bit, trying to size each other up.

'But we're not together anymore. We split up a couple of months ago.'

A smile tugged at his lips but he forced it down. 'I'm sorry.'

'Are ya?'

He shrugged. 'I am sorry about everything else, though,' he said softly, suddenly feeling the need to apologise for everything he'd done to her.

Their eyes met and for a few seconds, neither of them spoke.

'I know,' she said eventually.

'I was in a bad place when Mam died. All the things that mattered to me most, all the people who mattered to me most… I just, I suppose I pushed them away, and I don't know why I did that.'

With his thumbnail, he scratched a bit of candle wax off the table.

'Everyone copes with grief in their own way,' she said.

'I suppose. I regret doing that, though. I know I hurt you, and you have to know you were the last person I wanted to hurt.'

'I know,' she said again. She reached across the table and gave his arm a squeeze, sparking something in him he hadn't anticipated. Goosebumps covered his arms and heat rose to his cheeks, making him grateful for the dim lighting in the back of the pub.

They ordered another round of drinks, and Niamh talked about her job and the people she worked with. From everything she told him, he gathered she was single and living with two housemates, not too far from him. He told her about his classes and his inability to comprehend the twenty-year-olds at times. But also how he loved being back at uni, and how one of his short stories had recently been longlisted in a competition. The conversation flowed so naturally it was easy to forget they hadn't seen each other in five years.

'Are you hungry?' Niamh asked somewhere into their third drink.

'Starving,' he replied.

'Want to order here or…'

A thought popped into his head. 'No, not here. I have an idea,' he said.

She gave him a puzzled look, but he kept his plan to himself. 'You'll see.'

They'd been walking for about twenty-five minutes when Conor suddenly stopped. Niamh gave him another questioning look. 'What is it?' she asked.

'Look!'

They were standing across the road from a café named Crumbles, with lettering on the window that said 'All Day Breakfast'. Niamh turned to Conor with a massive grin on her face. 'I completely forgot about this place!'

When they were together, they would come here on Friday nights after class. Niamh loved breakfast. She'd eat it all day every day if she could. It was one of her quirks Conor had never ceased to find endearing.

'Good idea?' he asked.

'The best.'

Conor ordered a vegetarian fry up, sticking as close to a regular dinner as he could, but Niamh went all in with pancakes, a muffin and a large caramel macchiato.

'So, what are you reading at the moment? Anything we've published?'

He shook his head. 'Uni stuff, mostly. But I've seen a few good things come into the shop. If I ever have time to read for fun again, I'm sure I'll have a stack waiting. How about you?'

'I'm editing a manuscript by a new author. It's the first one on my list and it's genius.'

'Oh wow, congrats. What's it about?'

'It's about a group of friends living in London. You follow each character's story line and see how it affects the group dynamic. Very millennial, but I really think it's gonna do well.'

'Sounds like an interesting premise.'

She considered him for a second and then ran the tip of her tongue across her upper lip, the way she always did when she had an idea.

'Do you want to read it?'

'Is that allowed?'

'I think so. You're not gonna plagiarise it, are you?'

'Not unless it's really good.'

She laughed. 'I actually have an extra copy at my place. I could give it to you on our way back?'

From the bus stop, it was only a short walk to her apartment. A sense of anticipation had settled in Conor's stomach when they'd left the pub. Niamh had always been a straightforward person and if he could trust his intuition, he knew where this night was headed. But his intuition had been off lately, so he remained hesitant.

Long before they reached the door, Niamh got out her keys. She didn't even have to rummage through her bag to find them. Conor smiled to himself. She hadn't changed a bit. She was and would always be prepared for what came next. As she walked in, Conor waited on the doorstep.

'What are you, a vampire?' She laughed. 'Come in.'

There was a bicycle in the hallway, a helmet dangling from its handlebars. They walked past it, through to the living room. Niamh flicked the switch on a floor lamp in the corner, dimly lighting the room in a warm yellow glow before taking off her coat.

'My housemates are out of town,' she said. 'Do you want a drink?'

'Uhm yeah, sure, anything's fine.'

With his hands thrust deep into his pockets, he just stood there, looking around.

'The sofa's not drenched in holy water, Conor,' she said, disappearing into what he assumed was the kitchen. He heard the clink of glasses and then the soft pop of a cork, as he settled on the sofa.

When she came back out carrying two glasses of red wine, Conor was studying the blurb of a book he'd found on the coffee table and she quickly put the glasses down. 'Right, the manuscript,' she said. 'Won't be a sec.'

Her footsteps sounded up the stairs. The manuscript was probably in her bedroom. The thought of her bedroom sent his blood rushing downwards. The last time he'd had sex had been with her, and even though the details were vague, the muscle memory was apparently still there.

'Found it,' she said, entering the living room again and handing him a stack of A4s.

'Thanks.' He flipped through the pages, reading a couple of sentences here and there.

Niamh plopped down next to him. 'You don't have to read it now, though.'

He looked at her and smiled. Her black hair was still cut in a short, blunt bob but she'd grown out her fringe, making her dark brown eyes stand out even more.

'What?' she asked.

'Nothing.'

'No, tell me.'

'I was just thinking how funny it is that we're here like nothing has changed, and yet everything is different.'

Niamh nodded. 'Funny yeah,' she said, taking a sip from her wine and moving a bit closer towards him. The warmth radiated from her body, making him acutely aware of their proximity. The silence in the flat crackled with intensity. He cleared his throat again before he spoke. 'Are you seeing anyone now?'

She shook her head. 'You?'

'No.'

At this, Conor moved closer too, the wine in his hand nearly spilling from the movement. Niamh put her glass on the coffee table and then took his from his hand to do the same. They were only inches apart. He could smell her perfume and the sweetness of the red wine on her breath.

'Do you have all the information you need now?' she asked.

He gave her a questioning look.

'Just kiss me already, Conor.'

He laughed. 'You are incorrigible, do you know that?'

The corner of her mouth lifted. 'I just know what I want, that's all.'

Conor brought his hands to her cheeks and pressed his lips to hers. It was a deep kiss, a kiss full of memories and yet entirely novel. He pulled her closer, wanting more, and in response she ran her fingers through his hair and opened her mouth, her tongue finding his as she reclined onto the sofa.

Conor's blood rushed through his body, waking up all the tiny nerve cells that had lain dormant for a long time. She moaned softly as he kissed her neck and collarbone, the sound vibrating in his ear.

'Are you sure you want to do this?' he asked, before sliding his hand under her shirt.

She was breathing heavily and nodded. 'Are you?'

'That's pretty obvious, isn't it?'

She glanced down briefly to where he was pressing into her and smiled. 'So not car keys then, huh?'

Conor laughed.

'Let's go upstairs,' she said.

She unbuttoned his jeans, his stomach muscles contracting at the cool touch of her hand against his skin as he fiddled with the buttons on her blouse. The feel of her body against his ignited him instantly.

'I haven't done this in a while,' he said, feeling the need to explain.

'That's okay,' she whispered. 'It's like riding a bike.'

'I'm not sure I ever got this excited riding a bike,' he replied.

'I should hope not.' She slid her hand down his boxers, making him gasp.

'Really, though,' he said. 'I think we need to slow down a little, otherwise this might be over very soon.'

'Okay.' She pulled back her hand and ran it up his chest, her fingers still cool from their walk home.

It was the lightest touch, but still his body reacted ferociously. To stop himself from losing control, he turned his focus completely on her, kissing his way down her neck, to her shoulder and then to the exact spot on the inside of her arm he remembered she loved to be touched.

Niamh moaned. 'You remembered.'

'I remember everything,' he said in between kisses.

A sharp laugh escaped her. 'Are you quoting *Dawson's Creek* on me?'

Conor grinned, pleased she'd figured it out. 'That was your favourite scene, right?'

'Yeah, but you're in dangerous territory here. Reminding me of Pacey Witter in a moment like this… Are you sure you can live up to his legacy?'

'Not at all. But then at least you'll have him to think of.'

She laughed again and pulled his lips to hers. 'I think I'm alright with just you, thanks.'

Conor bit her lower lip softly in a satisfied response and then rolled on top of her.

'Are you ready?' Niamh asked.

He nodded, even though he wasn't sure. 'Do you have a condom?' he asked, softly kissing her clavicle.

'What? You don't bring condoms into work with you?'

'Used the last one yesterday,' he said, making her laugh so hard the vibration of her throat sent a shiver down his spine. She got one from her bedside table but as soon as he was inside her, he could feel the pressure building instantly. Before he knew it, a groan escaped him and it was over. He closed his eyes and buried his face in the crook of her armpit, before rolling off while uttering his apologies. 'I'm so sorry. Fuck.'

'That's okay, I don't mind.'

'No, it's not okay.' He covered his face in his hands and repeated his apology again.

'Really Conor, don't worry about it, I'll take it as a compliment,' she said, stroking his chest.

'I just… it's been a while.'

'What's a while?'

After a few seconds of silence, Conor turned sideways to face her. 'You,' he said.

Niamh's eyebrows shot up. 'Oh, okay, that is a while.' She brought her hand to his cheek and he kissed the soft flesh under her thumb.

'Has there been no one since?'

He shook his head. 'Not like this.'

He got up to dispose of the condom but refused to leave it at that. Niamh deserved better. He kneeled before the bed and pulled her towards him by her ankles. Her shallow breath intensified as his lips moved up her inner thigh. The moment he took her in his mouth, she grabbed his hair and let out a guttural *fuck* until her entire body shuddered under his lips.

Afterwards, when they lay staring at the ceiling, she said, 'Now that wasn't too bad, was it?'

He smiled and turned to kiss her forehead. 'I'll do better next time,' he promised.

'Next time?'

'Well yeah, if this didn't get you hooked, I'm not sure what could.'

Niamh kissed him, her smile against his mouth reassuring him he'd get a second chance.

The next morning, Conor woke up early so he could go home and change clothes before work. He'd not intended to sleep over but when she'd asked him to stay, he'd been unable to resist. Not only was he reluctant to leave the warm covers – the touch of her bare skin against his had been so addictive, he couldn't bear the thought of untangling himself.

He tried not to wake Niamh but as he put on his jeans, he heard her stir between the sheets. She opened her eyes and smiled.

'I didn't want to wake you,' he whispered.

'Walk of shame, is it?'

'No. I have to get to work.'

She turned around to check the clock on her bedside table. 'I thought you said you didn't start work until ten, it's only half seven.'

'That's right, Sherlock, but I want to go home first and shower.'

'You can shower here.'

'I can, but I need fresh clothes and I really need to shave.' He rubbed his hand over his stubble.

'Come here.'

Conor sat down on the side of the bed and she reached out to stroke his face.

'I like it,' she said, before kissing him and trying to pull him back into bed. It took all his strength to resist. 'I should really go,' he repeated, nuzzling her neck.

'Fine. Go be responsible.'

'What are you doing tonight, though?' he asked.

'Can I say *you*, or is that cheesy?' She grinned.

'I'll allow it.'

Back home, he was glad to see Jack wasn't up yet. He was existing in his delicious bubble from the night before and afraid it would burst if he let other people in. The intense desire was still raging through his veins, and he wanted to savour every detail: her legs entangled with his, her ragged breath against his ears, the citrusy scent of her skin, the taste of her wine-soaked tongue…

He poured himself a cup of tea and opened his laptop to write it all down, hoping to commit it to memory. But the moment his laptop connected to the internet, a pop-up appeared.

1 new email, sender: Ava Kingston

The burst of his bubble was almost audible.

Blood drained from his face, taking his breath along with it. Then, all the thoughts came flooding in, followed closely by an intense wave of nausea. Why would she do this? After seven months of silence, why did she choose this exact moment to email him? Why couldn't she just leave him be?

The cursor hovered over the message, but he didn't click it. He didn't do anything. He felt frozen in time. He wasn't sure how long he'd been staring at his screen when his phone buzzed on the table next to him, jolting him from his hypnosis.

N: You didn't even take the manuscript. Part of your big scheme to get into my pants?

The thought of Niamh's husky voice brought him back to the present, and he couldn't help but laugh at her text.

C: Been planning it for months. The manuscript's a fake. All part of it.

N: A regular Danny Ocean. I like it. Got any other tricks up your sleeve?

C: I'll show you tonight...

He smiled, closed his laptop, grabbed his phone and left for work.

Not today, Ava.

Wild Waves
Chapter 17

The first week of April, Orla called Ava to tell her she'd been offered a job at a radio station in London, which meant she would have to move as soon as possible. Ava was ecstatic and offered her their spare room while she looked for a flat. She secretly hoped it would take her a long time to find something, because even though they called each other at least once a week, she missed having her best friend around.

But it wasn't just that. Her relationship with James had gone from bad to worse since the christening. They hardly saw each other anymore and when they did, they were both too tired to talk. There was no animosity between them, but Ava wasn't sure there was much love left either.

The morning of Orla's arrival, Ava was having her coffee when James entered the kitchen.

'Orla arrives today. We're going for a drink tonight,' she said between sips.

'That's okay. I won't be home before nine, anyway.'

James was looking his finest, wearing a navy-blue suit and tie with a cream-coloured shirt, his hair combed back and fixed with gel, his face soft and smooth. Ava put down her magazine and eyed him up and down. 'Important meeting today?'

'The Americans are flying in.' He flicked the switch on the kettle and a soft humming sound filled the room. Ava chuckled.

'What's so funny about that?'

'It's very Daniel Cleaver, that's all.'

James didn't get the *Bridget Jones* reference, and Ava was too tired to explain.

'See you later,' he said, giving her a peck on the cheek like a brother saying goodbye to his sister.

Work was a nightmare. As she was finishing up a sales report that was due at the end of the day, something went wrong with the pivot tables and she had to start all over again. Excel had never been her friend, but it was rapidly becoming her arch nemesis, much like her Uncle Richard who seemed to be even more of a dick at work than in family circles. His love of arbitrary assignments and power-posing didn't go unnoticed in the office. In fact, there was a game called 'boss bingo' going on in his sales team. 'Leans back in chair', 'stands over you while glaring', and 'manspreads in meeting' were some of the categories Ava had managed to tick off within an hour. But he'd promised her a promotion, with a significant pay rise by the end of the year, and so she ploughed on, hoping it would be worth it. A throbbing headache demanded all her attention at the end of the day and so as soon as she got home, Ava popped some painkillers and settled on the sofa for a nap, hoping to feel better by the time Orla arrived.

When the doorbell rang an hour later, Ava was pleased to find her headache had mostly gone. She rushed to the door and when she opened it, the brightest face smiled back at her. It was more effective than any medicine she'd ever taken.

'Avaaaaa!' Orla shouted as they fell into each other's arms.

'Oh, I'm so happy you're here!'

'So much, you're willing to choke me to death?'

Ava hadn't realised how hard she'd been squeezing her friend, and quickly loosened her grip. 'Sorry, I'm just so glad. Come in!'

On Orla's back there was an enormous rucksack, and a black guitar case dangled from her hand, covered in stickers of indie bands Ava had never heard of. Ava took the guitar from her and led the way into the kitchen.

'Would you like to put your things in your room first, *fräulein*?'

'My room? I get a room all to myself?'

'Of course, silly. You didn't think I would make you sleep on the sofa, did you?'

'I guess I just never imagined you having a two-bed flat in London. I mean, the rent must be too dear, like?'

'Honestly, we got lucky. We're renting from a friend of my dad's who's living in Switzerland at the moment. He doesn't ask much – just that we keep the place in order, water the plants, you know.'

'Note to self: change families and make rich friends.'

The room was small but cosy with a single bed, wardrobe, desk and chair. On the wall above the bed's headboard, Ava had put up a picture of the two of them on the beach in Ballybridge.

'Oh Ave, I love it!' She ran towards the windows and made a bonnet out of the curtains. 'All my favourite things!' And oh my God, look at the picture, it's perfect – it's picture perfect!' Orla threw her hands around Ava's neck again.

'It's not much, but the mattress is comfortable.'

'No, seriously, it's fab. Thanks for letting me stay, Ava. It means so much.'

'No, thank you, really,' Ava said, certain Orla was doing her a favour instead of the other way around.

Orla gave her a questioning look. 'Is everything okay?'

'Yeah, it's fine. I'll explain later. Have you eaten?'

'No, just some crisps at the airport.'

'Great, there's a Lebanese place not too far from here that serves the best falafel in London, and afterwards we can go for a drink if you're not too tired.'

'Lebanese food and drinks? The day I get too tired for that, just put me down, like.'

'I still can't believe I get to keep you with me in London,' Ava said, digging into her falafel.

'I know. I got so lucky. It's mental.'

'When do you start working?'

'In two weeks. I'm hoping that'll give me enough time to find a place to live.'

'You're welcome to stay as long as you want. I really, really, don't mind.'

'What's going on there? James?' Orla put down her fork and used the napkin to wipe some garlic sauce off her chin.

'Yeah, it's getting worse.' After Ireland, she'd filled Orla in on what had happened between her and Conor. Other than Kate, no one had known about James, and when she'd told Orla, she'd been surprised to say the least. But like Kate, she hadn't judged Ava, not once, even though she deserved it.

'Are you fighting?'

'No. You'd have to talk to each other for it to be classified as a fight.'

'Oh, I see…'

'It's like we're roommates now, really.'

'Do you think he feels the same?'

'I don't know. He's been so busy with work, he's hardly ever home anymore, and when he is, we don't have anything to say to each other. Surely it must be easier than this?'

'How's the sex?'

'What is this sex thing you speak of?'

Orla let out a hearty laugh. 'Seriously, though, when's the last time you had sex, like?'

'We tried—'

'You *tried*?'

'Let me finish.'

'Is that what *you* said?'

'Seriously, Orla…' Ava rolled her eyes and they both laughed.

'Sorry… Too easy.'

'We tried to have sex a couple of weeks ago, when we were at that B&B for his goddaughter's christening.'

Orla nods knowingly. On the phone, Ava had told her all about their trip, but James had been around and so she'd left out the sex fail part.

'It was all going quite well actually, but then he banged his head against the headboard and that was the end of it. We just went to bed and haven't talked about it since.'

'Ouch. And before that?'

'Somewhere around Christmas?'

'Oh Ava, I'm anything but an expert at this, but it should definitely be easier than that.'

'Yeah, I figured.'

Orla finished her water and gave her a compassionate smile. 'Pub?' she asked.

'Pub.'

The first signs of spring were in the air as they strolled, arm in arm, past brightly lit shop windows, stopping once in a while to either mock or admire the displays.

'What did Matt say when you told him you were moving to London?' Ava asked.

Orla hadn't said a word about Matt all night, and that wasn't like her. Usually, she couldn't go two sentences without mentioning him. Not only was Ava wondering what was up, she also hoped that asking about Matt would eventually lead to talking about Conor without actually having to bring him up.

Orla shrugged. 'It's complicated,' she said.

'What do you mean?'

'I don't know, it's just been weird between us.'

'Why?' Ava asked, although she had a pretty good idea.

'Can we talk about something else?'

'No.' Ava stopped, her arm tugging at Orla's, grinding her to a halt as well. A woman came up from behind them, swearing under her breath as their sudden halt had clearly surprised her. Ava apologised and pulled Orla to the side.

'What happened?' she asked, still holding on to Orla's arm, keeping her in place.

'He sort of told me he was in love with me,' she mumbled.

'Oh my God, he said that? That's fantastic!'

The look on Orla's face suggested otherwise.

'Isn't it?'

'No it's not, it fucked everything up.'

'What do you mean? You love him too, don't you?'

Shock and disgust contorted Orla's features at the insinuation.

'Bollocks!' Ava retorted.

Orla pulled her arm from Ava's grip and stalked off. 'I don't do relationships, Ave, I just can't,' she said, throwing her arms in the air.

'I don't understand.'

'No one understands, not even me.'

'But—' Ava started.

'Is this the place?' Orla cut her off.

They'd stopped in front of a pub and Orla, who was now quite agitated, gave Ava an impatient, questioning look. Ava nodded and, before she could say anything else, Orla pushed through the door of the pub and disappeared inside.

'Okay…' Ava followed her to the bar, where Orla was already ordering them a round of tequila shots. Ava hated the taste of tequila but she licked the salt off the rim, downed the drink in one big gulp and then sucked on her lime wedge anyway.

'God, if it takes this many things to wash away the taste of it, should it even exist?' She winced, still feeling the burn down her throat.

They made their way over to a small table, each carrying a pint of Stella.

'Go on, try and explain it to me,' Ava said, giving Orla an encouraging nod as they sat down.

'I don't know how. I can't even explain it to myself.'

'But what do you mean when you say you don't do relationships? Is it that you don't want to be in a relationship?'

'No, it's not like that. I just… I've never been in one and I don't know how.'

'Okay, that's not so bad. I'm sure plenty of people our age have never been in a relationship, and no one knows how to do it, really. We're all just sort of winging it.'

'I've also never had a one-night stand… or anything…' Orla added, turning her head away from Ava.

Oh. This she had not expected. Orla was such an outgoing, joyful, enigmatic person, the thought of her never having been intimate with anyone didn't really compute for Ava.

'Babes, look at me.' She reached for Orla's hand, making her look up, her eyes watery with tears. 'It doesn't matter, okay? You're still an amazing person. There's nothing wrong with never having been with anyone. None of that matters, really.'

Orla shrugged. 'The problem is that when the opportunity presents itself, I lose it. There have been times when I could've… you know. Like, I once shifted a guy in the pub, but as soon as his tongue left my mouth, I legged it.'

'What do you mean, you ran?'

'I literally ran. I was there with a friend. She was chatting to this fella and I ran over and tried to get her to leave. She looked at me like I was mental. We'd only been there an hour, like, and she was really enjoying herself. So I just grabbed my coat, called a taxi and left. Apparently the guy asked for my number, not knowing where I'd gone, and he texted me the next day but I never texted back and blocked his number. That's what I do – I go mental and I can't function properly anymore until I know the threat's gone.'

Orla's eyes were filled with despair and Ava's heart broke for her friend.

'Maybe you just knew this guy wasn't right for you?'

'I don't know. The fear is just so overpowering that I can't tell which end is up. I have no idea why it happens. It's not that I don't want to be with someone. I really do. I just have no idea how to fix this.'

'Have you talked to Matt about this?' Orla laughed. 'Matt's a great guy, I'm sure he'd understand.'

'I can't, Ava.'

'So what did you say to him, then?'

'Nothing. I just ran again. This time I got on a plane instead of into a taxi.'

'Yikes…'

'Yeah… I know.'

Ava felt for her friend, but her heart also went out to Matt. Imagine someone leaving the country after you tell them you love them. A flash of Conor telling her about uni in London passed before her eyes. Did she do the same to him?

'Enough about my drama – back to yours. Have you heard from Conor?' Orla asked.

Ava pointed at the empty glasses. 'We're going to need more of these first.'

'On it!' Orla left and returned minutes later, carrying a tray with four tequila shots and two pints. 'So, Conor? Go!' she said, slamming back one of the shots. Ava followed her example, wincing once again at the taste of the disgusting drink.

'Haven't heard from him since the day I left. Nothing. But I know that's on me. I really fucked up,' she said, washing down the tequila with a sip of beer. 'Guess you're not the only one who gets scared and then acts foolishly. Never in a million years did I think I'd fall for someone else, but then Conor…'

She trailed off, staring at her glass, tracing the drops of condensation with her finger. 'I just miss him so much.'

'I bet he misses you too,' Orla said.

'Hmm. I sent him an email a couple of weeks ago, but he hasn't replied.'

'Just give him some time. You know Conor – he processes things more slowly than you. He's probably writing an entire book about it first.'

Ava smiled. 'Have you spoken to him recently?'

'Yeah, well, not about that, but he's back in uni. He moved to Dublin shortly after you left.'

Ava sighed with relief. During their phone calls she'd always managed to keep Orla from talking about Conor. She'd figured it was better not to think of him at all. But she'd always wondered what happened after she left, and knowing he hadn't given up on his plans because of her comforted her slightly.

'Good. Guess I didn't fuck *everything* up then.'

They ordered another round and, even though Ava desperately wanted to help her friend, she wasn't sure she could. The fear Orla described was something she'd never felt, and who was she to help anyone with relationship problems anyway? Her own relationship was fizzling, and the man she loved lived in another country and didn't want to talk to her. One thing was clear, though: she needed to end things with James. She'd been thinking about it ever since that night in the B&B, but a tiny kernel of hope that all could still be alright had kept her from doing so up until now. But maybe it was time to start being honest. With herself, in the first place.

Having Orla with her gave her courage, though. For the first time in years, she had a true friend to support her when her life went off the rails. Knowing Orla would be with her, cheering her on along the way and comforting her when she didn't quite make the finish line the way she'd expected, was one of the best feelings in the world.

Wild Waves
Chapter 18

Niamh put four slices of bread in the toaster and yawned. 'Want to get lunch together, today?'

'Can't. I only have half an hour between classes on Mondays,' Conor said, filling two mugs with coffee.

'Right, I forgot.'

They'd fallen back into their old patterns so easily, Conor barely remembered his life in Dublin without her. If he wasn't in class, he was at her place or they were out and about in Dublin, going for walks in Monkstown, taking the bus up to Baldoyle where Conor would go for a swim, or having breakfast at Crumbles. It felt so organic, Conor wasn't always sure it was a good thing. Was it supposed to be this easy?

'Will you come over tonight, then?' she asked.

'I thought you were going out with your friends?'

'Yeah, but it's just dinner. I'll probably be back around ten.'

'Sure, just text me when you're on your way back.'

'Wait,' she said, and promptly left the kitchen.

Conor buttered his toast and reached for his book on the windowsill. When she returned, she placed a key in front of him on the table. 'Here. Now you don't have to wait for me to text you.'

Conor laughed and shook his head.

'What?' she said.

'Classic Niamh Byrne. Handing me a key to her flat as if she were handing me a cup of coffee. Just like that.'

She laughed too now. 'I thought you liked coffee?' she said.

He pulled her onto his lap and kissed her. 'Oh, very much so.'

Niamh giggled as his hands travelled up her thighs and under her pyjama top. 'I'm going to be late for work,' she mumbled against his mouth.

Conor pretended he hadn't heard and stroked the curves of her belly, his thumb dipping just below her belly button. A little gasp escaped her and then she slowly pulled away, her fingers raking his hair. 'We'll continue this tonight,' she promised.

Conor gave a low growl of protest but let go of her anyway.

As she hopped off his lap, he took the key from the table. 'You're sure about this, right?'

She was still standing between his legs and bent down to kiss him. 'Just don't break my heart again, okay?'

After his last class, Conor wanted to find a gift for Niamh as a way to thank her for the key. There was a The Shins album he'd borrowed once but never returned and when he'd checked her CD collection that morning, he'd found she hadn't replaced it yet. The record store was on his way home and as he walked along the canal, Conor thought of Niamh, how being with her was so easy, effortless and clear. There was no question about it: she was all in.

With Ava, he'd never known. He thought his feelings for her had been obvious, but maybe they hadn't been? And what about hers? Neither of them had ever told the other how they felt. This lack of communication would not be an issue with Niamh, of that he was certain.

But Ava's email had taken up space in the back of his mind – never prominent, but always present. There was a reason he hadn't simply deleted it. A part of him longed to see her, talk to her, even though he wasn't sure his heart could take it. For weeks now, he'd left it sitting in his inbox, waiting for the right moment. But the longer he waited, the more he came to see there was no such thing as the right moment. Perhaps he should just get it over with.

The album was easier to find than he'd expected and so he continued to flip through the CD cases, hoping to get something for himself as well. Even though most of his friends had stopped buying CDs, Conor was not prepared to let go just yet. He liked having something to hold. The actual act of opening the case, inserting the disc and then choosing the song, somehow had a calming effect on him. He loved sitting on his bed with his headphones on, listening to each song, letting the lyrics sink in as he flipped through the booklet.

When he got back to his flat, Jack was in the kitchen cooking dinner.

'Would you look at that... He's alive!' Jack mocked as Conor entered the room.

'Hiya.'

'I thought you'd moved in with her.'

'No, still here.' Conor considered telling Jack about the key, but changed his mind. He was in a good place, and any questions Jack might ask that he hadn't considered himself might jeopardise that.

The kitchen counter was covered in chopped veggies, herbs and at least two different oils.

'What are you cooking?' Conor asked.

'Curry. Want to join in?'

'Yeah, thanks mate.'

'Should be ready in about an hour.'

'Need help?'

'No, I'm alright.'

'Cheers. I'm heading over to Niamh's again tonight – just gonna grab a few things from my room and check on some emails. I'll be back in a bit.'

Jack shook his head and burst out in song. '*On my own, pretending he's beside me…*'

After fumbling with the plastic around his new Paolo Nutini album, he finally got the disc out and inserted it into his laptop. With his headphones on, he closed his eyes for a bit and skipped through the songs for a feel of the album. It was a mix of really fun, upbeat songs and slower tunes filled with raw emotion, the grainy sound of Nutini's voice going straight to Conor's heart. After a first round, he skipped through to 'No Other Way' as he opened his emails and finally clicked on Ava's message.

Like Paolo's voice, Ava's words found their way straight to his heart.

> *Hey Conor,*
> *It's me, Ava – which you obviously already know from my email address. Silly.*
> *Guess I'm a little nervous. I've been thinking about you a lot these past few days, but I wasn't sure you'd want to hear from me. Guess I'll find out soon now.*
> *I was at the seaside this past weekend and it reminded me of you. I miss you, Conor. I really do and I'm sorry for how things ended.*
> *You're probably wondering if there's a point to this email. There isn't really, I just wanted to talk to you.*
> *I hope you're happy.*
> *Love,*
> *Bruce*
> *PS: I'm starting a photography course next week. Thank you. X*

He read the message maybe five or six times, his fingers itching with the urge to write back. But was that such a wise idea? Reading how she was taking a photography course made his chest tighten. He was so happy for her.

Could he really leave it at this? Or did he want to be a part of her life, even just as her friend? The answer was clear even before he'd asked himself the question.

> *Hiya,*
> *I'll be honest, for a moment there I wasn't sure I was going to read your email. I'm not upset or anything, but it took me a while to leave everything that happened between us behind me. I'm not blaming you. You tried to tell me, and I wouldn't listen. I should've listened. But the thing is, I'm not sure it would've mattered. I probably would've still let myself believe whatever it was I wanted to believe.*
> *But whatever happened, good things came of it too. I'm living in Dublin, I'm back at uni and I'm working in a bookshop. I like it here. (Although I do miss the ocean.) I've made some friends and things are good. And you're going to be a photographer. At least we did that for each other, right?*
> *Let me know how you are?*
> *x*

Without thinking it through any more, he hit send and closed his laptop, already eager for her reply.

Wild Waves
Chapter 19

On Saturday afternoon, James was sitting at the kitchen counter, drinking tea and reading the paper, when Ava entered the room. She'd been waiting for Orla to leave the flat to talk to him but now they were alone, her chest tightened at the thought of it. As she watched him turn the page of the economy section of the paper, she knew it was the right thing to do, but the certainty didn't make the actual act any easier. This was a nearly five-year relationship she was ending – a significant portion of her life at twenty-four.

To give herself a few more seconds before she confronted him, she turned on the kettle, the sound of the boiling water like a count-down clock, the ever-increasing bubbles telling her the moment had come. With her mug in her hands, she took a seat opposite him and cleared her throat. 'James?'

He lowered his paper and, from the look in his eyes and the slumping of his shoulders, she could tell he knew what was coming. How long had he known? Her stomach tightened.

'I, uhm, I don't really know how to say this, but I don't think this is going well – you know, uhm, you and me?'

He smiled a sad smile, confirming her suspicions. Of course he knew what was coming. This couldn't be a pleasant situation for him either. He took a deep breath. 'What happened to us?'

Tears burned behind Ava's eyelids. 'I don't know.' And she didn't. There was no specific moment in the past few years she could point to and say: that's when everything changed. It had happened gradually. Meeting at Business School had been the thing that bound them together, the thing they'd had in common. But when that fell away, there was not much left.

James got up and put his cup in the sink. The sound of the tap as he rinsed it filled the otherwise silent apartment.

'Was it Ireland?' he asked, his back still turned to her.

For a long time Ava had thought it was Ireland, but now she understood they'd been wrong for each other all along.

'No,' she said, when he turned around to face her. 'You know it wasn't. We weren't working before that, otherwise I wouldn't have gone, or you might have visited.'

James nodded. 'We're very different, aren't we?' He reached out his hand and when she took it, he pulled her in, his arms wrapping around her shoulders.

'What do you think we should do?' Ava asked.

'I got an offer to work in the New York office.'

Surprised, Ava looked up. 'Really? When?'

'Last week.'

'Oh.'

Resting her head against his chest, the tears fell from her eyes, staining his shirt. Even though this was over, she would still miss him with all her heart. 'I think you should take it,' she said. 'It's what you've been working for, and if anyone deserves it, it's you.'

James sighed and kissed her on the temple. 'I still love you, though,' he whispered into her hair. A tear fell from his eye onto her forehead.

'I love you too.'

She would always love him in a way. He'd always been a good friend to her – someone she could count on. Perhaps their romance had died, but he would always be an important part of her story.

They stood, holding each other in silence for a few minutes, both knowing it was time to let go, but not quite ready yet.

'I'll go and stay with my parents for now,' James said. 'If I take the job—'

'*When* you take the job.'

'*When* I take the job, they need me in New York at the end of next month anyway.'

'Are you sure about moving out now? I mean, there's no rush.'

'I don't want to make it harder. I'll take a few things now and come back for the rest later.'

Ava lifted her chin to look him in the eye and nodded. With a deep breath, he let go. It took him about half an hour to gather his things and Ava just stood there, the sudden reality of their goodbye immobilising her.

With his bag by his feet, his eyes dark and solemn as he gazed into hers, he brought his hands to her wet cheeks and kissed her one last time. 'I'll miss you, muppet.'

Ava closed her eyes and when she opened them again, he was gone.

An hour later, when Orla came home, Ava was sitting on the kitchen floor where he'd left her, her cheeks papery with dried tears. Orla crouched down beside her and wrapped her arm around Ava's shoulders.

'How did it go?' she asked.

'Not too bad…. I suppose.'

'Are you okay?'

'Yeah, I think I am… I will be, anyway. I know it wasn't working, but it still hurts, you know?'

Orla nodded and pulled her closer.

'Not being right for each other doesn't mean you stop loving them. It's okay to be sad.'

Ava rested her head on Orla's shoulder. 'I'm so happy you're here. Tell me about your day, please.'

As they remained on the kitchen floor, Orla told Ava about a new record store she'd discovered and the tattoo she was thinking of getting. The pain in Ava's heart slowly subsided and then her new situation dawned on her. 'I think I need a new flatmate,' she said.

Orla's eyes gleamed with the same realisation.

'Want to help me find someone?'

'*Badum tsss*,' Orla said, and they both laughed. They stayed on the kitchen floor until they were starving and then realised there was not much food left in the flat. They ordered sushi and spent the rest of the afternoon watching *The Holiday*. When the film was finished, Ava did some quick research on the main characters' ages, and they agreed there was still hope for them. If it wasn't too late for Kate and Cameron, it wasn't too late for them either.

Before she went to bed later that night, Ava checked her emails. She was no longer consciously expecting to see a reply from Conor, but once a week she checked anyway, unable to completely let go.

When she saw his name pop up on the screen, her heart leapt in her chest and she held her breath a couple seconds too long, equally afraid of what it would say as she was excited to read it. Maybe he just replied to tell her to fuck off, or maybe it was something entirely different. Was there still hope? Like a child, she crossed her fingers for a split second before she clicked on the email. After reading it the first time, her nerves settled and the tension in her body melted away. He didn't hate her. He wasn't even angry with her. They could be friends, she thought. She wanted to send her reply immediately, but decided to wait until the next day.

It took a long time before she finally fell asleep, images of James and Conor taking turns in keeping her awake. She composed at least twenty replies in her mind until she'd found the perfect one, knowing full well she wouldn't remember any of it the next morning.

15

Around eight a.m., a loud sound startles Olivia, making her look up from her book for the first time since she caved to Graham's demands. It takes her a moment to understand her phone is buzzing on the nightstand, and then another moment to understand it's her mum calling.

'Mum? What's wrong?'

'What do you mean, what's wrong?' Her voice is snippy from the first word.

'It's eight. You never ring me this early.'

'Sure I do. Anyway, it's your father's party tonight, remember?'

Olivia rolls her eyes. 'Is that tonight? Huh, I thought it was next week.'

'Don't be funny, Olivia. I need you to pick up some things for me this morning.'

A suppressed sigh nearly escapes her lips. 'I don't really have the time, Mum.'

'Is that right? What are you doing, then?'

'I'm, uhm...' How could she explain this? She can hardly tell her mother she's busy all morning reading a book about herself in the hopes of fixing two of the most important relationships in her life. 'I'm doing research for Canada.'

It's not a complete lie.

On the other end of the line, her mother scoffs. 'Well, you can do your research on the tube. It's your father's seventieth birthday, and then you're leaving us for God knows how long. Maybe you can do him this one last favour, if it's not too much to ask. We've only taken care of you for the better part of our lives.'

And there's the sigh. 'Fine. What do you need?'

While her mum gives the instructions to pick up the cake and her father's present, Olivia makes her way to the bathroom. Glimpsing in the mirror, her eyes are swollen and red from the early morning alarm and the tears she spilled reading *Wild Waves*. She'd never realised how ill-timed her email to Eamonn had been. It was an entirely selfish thing to do, but she'd needed him so badly to be her friend again, she had thrown all common sense to the wind. Is that how he'd felt when he wrote the book?

Apart from that, and a few scenes from her perspective that never really happened exactly the way he described them, the book is progressing in a way she expected. No shocking new information has come to light yet, and it still seems unlikely it will.

While her mum explains both locations in extreme detail, as though Olivia hasn't been living in London her whole life, a deep desire to continue reading claws at her, but bawling her eyes out on the tube is not an option, and bailing on her mother apparently even less so.

She ends the call, promising she won't take all day to get going, and reluctantly gets dressed. Might as well get it over with.

The place where she needs to pick up her father's gift – an old watch her mother's had repaired – is right around the corner from Ben and Erin's place. It's been a while since she's had a chance to talk to Erin, and so Olivia shoots her a text.

You home?

After Graham left her on Parliament Hill, Olivia had briefly explained the situation to Erin, but she hasn't seen her since.

With Graham leaving her no option but to go digging in the past, she desperately needs her best friend to offer some clarity on the matter. After all, Erin is probably the one person who knows exactly what happened.

Ever since Alex was born, Erin has been terrible at replying to messages, and when Miles arrived, it was like she didn't even own a phone most of the time. Olivia holds out no hope today will be different, and so she pops into the nearest café while she waits for an answer. She's about to place her order when a reply comes in, much faster than she'd anticipated.

Yep if you're coming over be a star and bring me a coffee will ya

Olivia smiles at the phone in her hand and orders two cappuccinos instead of one. Even though things have been a bit off between them, the thought of seeing Erin comforts her. She'll miss her most of all.

When Erin lets her in, she's wearing Ben's old hoodie and a pair of worn-down joggers, her wild blonde curls escaping the top bun, a tiny baby draped over her shoulder.

'My hero,' she says, taking the coffee from Olivia and showing her to the sofa.

'Where's my Alex?'

'Ben's taken her for a walk. I had a gig last night and didn't get much sleep.'

'Oh, so you don't look like shit because of the baby?'

Erin shakes her head and settles in the rocking chair by the window. 'No, that's why Ben looks like shit.'

Olivia laughs. 'Good to know.' She clears away some dirty clothes and a few toys and finds herself a spot on the sofa.

'Why do *you* look like shit, though?' Erin counters.

'Well, for one, Graham's Uber picked him up at 4.20 this morning.'

'Ouch. That's painfully early. How's things with you two, anyway? Did you talk after the party?'

Olivia leans her head on the backrest and looks up at the ceiling, sudden tears burning her eyes. 'It's a mess, Erin. I don't know what to do. Graham didn't talk to me for two days – well, not about anything important, anyway – and then this morning, right before he leaves, he tells me he's read Eamonn's book.'

Erin briefly closes her eyes and sighs, like Olivia is one of her children who just really disappointed her. 'Did you tell him you'd put it behind you?'

'You know I did. At the party.'

'And still he went ahead and read it?'

Her tone is accusatory, like all of this is Olivia's fault. 'I don't control his actions, Erin.'

On Erin's shoulder, Miles coos, lifting his head from one side to the other. If Olivia wasn't so offended by Erin's reaction, she'd be swooning over the baby noises.

'So what are you going to do?'

'He said I have to read it before I make a decision about Canada.'

'What?'

'He claims there are things I don't know, and I need to read it all.'

Erin groans.

'I've finished the first half this morning.'

Shaking her head, Erin gets up. 'I think you're making a massive mistake.'

'Yeah, you've kinda made that clear. Maybe you should tell me what's in the book if you don't want me reading it. Clearly, a lot of his inspiration came from you.'

Erin lifts the baby from her shoulder and hands him to Olivia. 'Please hold him for a sec.'

She disappears from the room, leaving Olivia cradling the four-month-old.

'Where did Mummy go, Miles?'

Miles' big grey eyes stare up at her, completely unaware of what's going on around him. For a second, Olivia wonders what it would be like to hold a baby of her own in her arms. What would they look like? And most importantly, what would her life look like? Could she still be a photographer who travels around? Maybe. Erin is managing her career as a musician with two kids, so in theory it's possible.

Graham is adamant he doesn't want to be a father, but what about Eamonn? Would she have had them already if he'd been there on the day of the pact? Is it possible her desire for kids depends on the person she's with?

Her thoughts spiral as the minutes pass. She's so caught up in her insecurities, it takes her a while to realise half an hour has gone by and there's still no sign of Erin. Olivia puts the baby down in his cot and sets out in search of her friend. She finds the bedroom door ajar, Erin spread out on the mattress like a starfish, clutching a nappy in one hand and a bib in the other. Her eyes are closed, her chest rising and falling with her slow breaths. In Olivia's back pocket, her phone buzzes. She closes the door behind her and heads back downstairs as she answers the call.

'What's keeping you so long?'

'Hi, Mum,' she says quietly, hoping her mother will tone it down too, just for her sake.

'Where are you?'

'Erin's.'

'What are you doing at Erin's?'

Good question. 'I'll be there in a bit.'

'I need some help at the house, Olivia. Please come now.'

At that moment, the front door opens and Ben walks in, balancing Alex on his hip.

'Livvie!' Alex squeals and immediately wriggles her way out of her father's arms to cling to Olivia's leg. Olivia bends down to pick her up. 'I'll be there in a bit, Mum. Bye now.'

Another protest is uttered at the other end of the line, but Olivia hangs up. 'Hello, cutie,' she says, kissing her goddaughter on the cheek.

Ben wraps them both into a hug. 'I didn't know you were coming around.'

'I wasn't. My mum sent me to pick something up not too far from here, so I decided to pop in.'

'Livvie, look!' Alex shoves a cuddly toy in Olivia's face. 'Shawk!'

'A shark! Wow! That's very cool, Alex. Did you get that from Daddy?'

She shakes her head so adamantly she loses her balance a little, and Olivia has to tighten her grip on Alex so she doesn't tumble to the floor.

'No? Who gave it to you, then?'

'Eanonn!'

Olivia's stomach flips. Of course she got the shark from Eamonn. The thought of him holding their goddaughter and being all sweet and loving with her makes her dizzy.

Ben shrugs apologetically, as though everything that's happened in the past few days is his fault.

'Well, that's very sweet of Eamonn, isn't it?'

Alex nods. 'I wuv Eanonn.'

The toddler's words ring so true in Olivia's ears, it's hard not to agree with her out loud.

'Where's Erin?' Ben asks.

'Asleep.'

'Did she hand you the baby and make you believe it was only for a moment?'

'Exactly that.'

'Yeah, she does that sometimes. Sorry about that.'

'It's fine. Is she okay, though?' Olivia puts Alex down and grabs her handbag.

Ben frowns. 'Yeah, just tired I guess.'

'Why didn't she tell me about the book, Ben?'

Ben turns on the telly and within seconds, Alex is standing in front of it.

'Sofa,' he says. Without taking her eyes off the screen, Alex backs up until she hits the cushions and then crawls onto the sofa.

'Have you asked her?' Ben replies.

'She's being evasive and she's acting as though all of this is my fault.'

'She just wants you to be happy, Liv.'

'I don't know what that means.'

'I know. I'll talk to her, okay?'

Olivia wraps her arms around Ben. 'Thanks. I have to go now. My mum is set on making my life miserable until the very last minute.'

'Thanks for watching Miles.'

'My pleasure. Bye, cuties!'

'Bye, Livvie.'

When Olivia arrives at her parents' house forty-five minutes later, her mum is in the garden instructing two people Olivia's never met before as they're putting up a white pop-up gazebo. Olivia greets them and they give her a polite smile in return.

'Good. You're here. I need your help with dinner.'

Olivia is not a cook. In fact, Olivia hates cooking. And her mum is perfectly aware of that.

'Why didn't you just hire a caterer?'

A mean look is thrown in her direction. 'Your father loves my lamb roast, and that's what he's getting for his birthday.'

'*Your* lamb roast,' Olivia mumbles while they head inside.

'Where did you put the cake?'

'Fridge.'

'And the watch?'

Olivia takes it from her bag and hands it over. Waiting for a thank you is something she's stopped doing a long time ago.

'Alright. I've made a list of what needs chopping and how.' A neatly written note is on the kitchen island next to the enormous wood chopping board. Why a wealthy woman would choose to cook a lamb roast for twenty-five people, instead of getting a caterer to do it, is beyond Olivia. But that's her mother. Pride and appearances matter more than comfort. Picking up the enormous list and skimming it, Olivia sighs.

'Oh, I'm sorry, is your father's birthday getting in the way of your fun-filled life?'

The urge to massage her temples and recite a zen mantra is strong, but she suppresses it as best as possible. Instead, she sticks her hands under the tap and washes them with soap, scrubbing so hard it hurts a little, before getting the ridiculous amount of carrots from the fridge, hoping it'll be the last time she ever has to do this.

16

Elvis is still sound asleep in his dog bed when Eamonn wakes on Saturday. Just like the day before, and the one before that. Sleep hasn't come easy since Eamonn's return from London. While he waits for his coffee, he makes his way outside, through the garden, onto the beach and into the ocean. He's been swimming a lot these past few days. Later today he has a meeting with his publisher, and there are deadlines to meet, and if he'd had to deal with all of that, and Olivia, without an ocean to carry him through, he'd be ruined.

When he gets out of the water, his arms heavy with exhaustion, an Australian Shepherd runs towards him, his owner calling out from a distance: 'Louis!'

Eamonn crouches down to pet the dog and when he looks up again, he's happy to find his colleague, Juliette, there. '*Bonjour*,' he says to the French teacher.

She laughs. 'Hi Eamonn, sorry about that. I didn't think there would be anyone on the beach this early, so I let him run free.' The wind has tousled her long, dark blonde hair and she pushes a strand of it behind her ear.

'I don't mind. He's lovely,' Eamonn says, taking in Louis' multi-coloured fur coat. 'I didn't know you had a dog.'

'He's my friend's. I'm dog-sitting for the weekend.'

Eamonn scratches Louis under his chin once more and rises, suddenly very aware of being half naked. Why does he never bring a towel anymore?

'You were swimming,' she says. Her eyes drift to his chest but then quickly look away. Are her cheeks flushed?

'Yeah, I couldn't sleep anymore.'

'Hmm, same.'

'How come?'

She shrugs. 'We finalised the divorce yesterday.'

'Oh. I thought you were already divorced.' Eamonn remembers her telling him something about that, but it was a long time ago and he figured it would be over by now.

'We've been separated for two years, but the technicalities and paperwork took some time.'

'I see.' He wants to ask her how she feels but is afraid she might not want to discuss it with him. When he opens his mouth and closes it again, she smiles.

'I'm alright,' she says. 'Just tired and relieved it's finally over.'

Eamonn smiles back. He likes Juliette. She'd been working at the school long before he got there and got tasked with showing him around on his first day. They've been friends ever since. She's very calm and gentle, and being around her is easy. Even the teenagers in school like having her there. For some reason they do as they're told around her, no need for shouting or threatening to take away their phones. She commands their respect without having to command anything. And apart from all that, it hasn't escaped Eamonn's attention that she's pretty, too. Once in a while, he catches himself thinking of her, not as a colleague or a friend, but something he hasn't been able to name yet.

She wraps the leash around her wrist, getting ready to walk on.

'Would you like a cup of coffee?' Eamonn points towards his house, not ready to say goodbye to her just yet. 'I've got a fresh pot brewing.'

Juliette touches his arm briefly. 'I'd like that.'

Her touch makes him smile. 'Grand. I'll be right back.'

As she sits down in the sand, she unleashes the dog again and Eamonn quickly makes his way to the house. At the back door, Elvis is awake and waiting for him, wagging his tail.

'We've got company, mate,' Eamonn says, while he finds a towel to dry himself off. The dog runs into the garden and waits by the gate, looking impatiently towards Eamonn. 'Just a sec,' he says. He runs up the stairs for a change of clothes and a quick look in the mirror. The cold water must've soothed the bags under his eyes, because he doesn't look half as bad as he did when he woke up this morning. Pleased, he jogs back down, fills two mugs with coffee and kicks the gate open. Elvis looks up at him, trained to wait for a signal, and when Eamonn nods, he sprints off. Both dogs immediately go wild, running circles around each other, trying to sniff whatever it is they're looking for.

Juliette takes the cup from his hand. 'Thank you.'

'Do you need milk or anything?'

'No, black's fine.'

Eamonn finds a spot on the soft sand beside her, the morning sun warming their backs. They're silent for a while, watching the dogs jump and run in and out of the water.

'So, do you have plans for the summer?' Eamonn asks, twisting his cup into the sand so it won't tip over.

'I'm going to my parents' cottage in the South of France for a couple of weeks.'

'That's nice. Will they be there?'

Juliette shakes her head. 'They only go in winter. Too hot for my dad, otherwise.'

'Fair enough.'

'What about you?' She pulls her legs close and buries her toes in the sand.

'Nothing much. Writing, editing... fixing up the house.'

She gives him a little nod and studies him for a moment. 'If, uhm...' she starts, but when he meets her eye, she stops and shakes her head, her cheeks slightly flushed. 'Never mind.'

Eamonn nudges her with his elbow. 'What?'

She twists her lips in consideration and then gives a tiny shrug, as though she has nothing to lose. 'If you'd like to get away for a bit, you could come and stay. There's a guest room, and it's by the ocean, and you could write, or…'

The invitation is as much a surprise as it isn't. He's thought of asking Juliette to spend more time with him too. But the timing couldn't have been worse. He's been down this road before, and committing to someone when he hasn't fully processed what happened with Olivia is not a path he wants to take anymore.

'I, uhm, I'm not sure that's a good idea.' His smile is apologetic and in response, Juliette looks away.

'That's okay. I understand.'

Immediately he's sorry for what he said, but there's no taking it back now.

'I want to,' he says. 'But I—'

'It's fine,' she cuts him off. 'You don't have to explain.'

They fall silent again. Juliette sips her coffee and the dogs keep on running. The sun climbs higher and more people walk past them. Everything keeps moving forwards. Everyone. Except Eamonn.

When he arrives at the pub later that afternoon, Mike is behind the bar, but other than him, the place is mostly empty. It's too early for the Friday crowd. After a quick catch-up, Eamonn finds a picnic bench and settles in the beer garden, his black lab's chin resting on his right foot.

Ruby, his editor-slash-publisher, texted him after his book signing in London, wanting to check in on his event and on the progress he's been making with his edits. She said she would be in the neighbourhood and asked to meet up in the pub instead of over Zoom, much to Eamonn's relief. He absolutely hates Zoom calls.

When she arrives about five minutes later, Elvis jumps up, his tail wagging like crazy. Her big brown eyes shine bright at him and then turn their radiance towards Eamonn. 'Hello, super star.'

Eamonn stands to give her a hug and a kiss on the cheek. 'Hiya, Rubes.' Behind her, Mike appears with two coffees. She must have ordered them when she walked in.

'So, how was London?' Ruby asks, after taking a sip.

'It was, uhm, interesting.'

A frown appears between her brows. 'How so?'

'Turns out *Pages & Leaves* is owned by Olivia's friends.'

Ruby lets out a short, surprised laugh. 'No feckin' way! Was she there?'

He nods slowly, still amazed himself at the serendipity of it all. 'She was there.'

Ruby reaches for his arm and gives it a soft squeeze. 'Oh, Eamonn. Of all the bookshops in all the towns in all the world, you had to walk into hers.'

'Yeah, she was less pleased than Bogart, though.'

'What happened?'

Eamonn walks her through the events of the past few days, from the moment he spotted Olivia in the audience until their bittersweet goodbye on the bench in Camden. It's nice to be able to share this with Ruby, after all they've been through. She's always been a great friend to him, no matter what their relationship status. And as was to be expected, she's also an excellent publisher. When he's finished telling her about how he and Olivia left things, Ruby takes a deep breath. 'Do you think it's possible she never got your message?'

Eamonn leans back in surprise. 'What? No.'

'Are you sure?'

'What makes you leap to that conclusion?'

Ruby gives him an *isn't it obvious?* look. 'She said: "I already know how it ends." Would she say that if she'd got the message? Like, is it possible she was there on the day of the pact?'

The outrageousness of her suggestion throws him and a high-pitched, ridiculous laugh escapes him. 'You're mad,' he says. 'She would've said something then, wouldn't she?'

'Like you did, when you didn't hear from her again?'

God, it's annoying when she points out his flaws to him. They roll their eyes at each other simultaneously.

'You two are the worst communicators since Harry and Sally.' She takes another sip from her coffee while Eamonn mulls over her words. Is it possible she never got his apology? And if so, what does that mean? Would she have accepted it, if she'd got it?

'It doesn't matter, anyway – she's got a good life going for her.'

Ruby puts down her cup of coffee and points a finger at him. 'You know what your problem is?'

Eamonn sighs in defeat. 'Please, enlighten me.'

'You're afraid to really love someone, because it hurts too much – because you're already thinking of losing them again.'

'Lovely. You and Ben should start a double act.'

Ruby shakes her head. 'Stop making jokes about it, Eamonn. Your inability to tell her how you feel has cost you dearly over the years, and once again, you haven't done it. I'm not sure what will become of you, to be honest.'

Blood rushes to his cheeks, frustration getting the better of him. 'She's moving to Canada, with her boyfriend, on Wednesday. It's too late.'

'It's never too late to tell her how you feel, regardless of what happens after. At some point in your life, you're going to have to let people in again – *really* in – if you don't want to end up all alone.'

Is that what he's been doing – keeping people at a distance? His mind drifts to Juliette for a split second, to her invitation. And then to the woman sitting in front of him. His once nearly-perfect girlfriend.

'Did I not let you in?'

Ruby puts down her cup and gives him a sad smile. 'I think you really tried to love me, but it just wasn't there.'

'I—'

'It's okay. We're better like this. But don't you want someone with you over here in this ridiculously small town – someone who's not Elvis?'

At the sound of his name, the dog's ears perk up and Eamonn scratches his head. 'I like Elvis.'

'I do too, but I don't wanna have his babies. Do you?'

'Do I wanna have my dog's babies?'

'You know what I mean.'

Eamonn looks at her for a while without answering. Most parts of his life are going really well, but some days, loneliness catches up with him. The deafening silence of his empty house can be so overwhelming at times, he can't bear to be inside. Just this morning, he had been so grateful to have Juliette with him.

'Yeah, I know what you mean.'

Ruby finishes her drink and pushes the cup to the middle of the table. 'So? What are you gonna do about it?'

17

As soon as Olivia finishes all her tasks, she rushes home for a change of outfit, and when she gets back to West London, Anna and Charlie come walking down the road.

'Charlie!' She throws her arms around him, noticing how he's outgrown her since the last time she saw him. 'Not to sound like an old woman or anything, but you've grown so much!'

'Just saying *not to sound like* doesn't make it go away, you know?' Anna counters.

Charlie beams, his black curls covering the acne on his forehead. 'Hi, auntie Liv!'

They might not see each other often, but the deep bond they created when Charlie was a baby is still there. Olivia calls him at least once a week and tries to visit every other month. It's sad to think that will all change soon.

'Did you only just get here?' Anna asks.

'I wish! I've been running around London all morning for Mum, and then she made me cook half the dinner.'

'You cooked? There goes the only good thing about this party.' Anna's expression is one of intense disappointment.

'Fuck off. I chopped the veg and made shrimp cocktails.'

'Charlie, you've heard your auntie. Stay away from the shrimp cocktails.'

'I'm vegan,' he says, rolling his eyes at his mother.

'Well then, definitely stay away from them.' Anna says.

Olivia shoves her sister towards the door. 'Go on in. It's your turn now.'

Anna grabs the key from Olivia and lets them into the house. 'Did you ring the bell?' Olivia asks.

Anna shakes her head. 'You don't always have to obey Mum, you know?'

'Does that mean I don't have to do what you tell me?' Charlie asks.

'In your dreams, Charlieboy.'

There are twenty-five guests in the garden, Olivia, Anna and Charlie included. There are twenty-two guests Olivia doesn't care for. They're all friends or co-workers of her parents and the majority of them are privileged white men and their wives. Seeing them all together, it's like a Poirot novel come to life. Any moment now, affairs, debts and drug addictions will come to light and one of them will be viciously murdered. Olivia hopes it's Simon Stringfellow. What a twat.

However, the silver lining of this set-up is that the three of them are completely ignored. As soon as the appetisers are served, Charlie disappears to the guest bedroom, where a giant television with all the streaming services is set up, just for him. In the meantime, Olivia and Anna take it one step further and leave the house for a stroll through the quiet West-London streets.

'How's Mr IT?' Olivia asks.

Anna smiles, her cheeks turning the colour of her hair. 'He's grand.'

'Don't lie to me. He's more than grand. You have that look.'

'What look?'

'The I-have-sex-so-often-it-should-be-illegal look.'

Anna thumps her on the shoulder. 'I do not!'

'Yeah, you do. You like him, don't you?'

'I'm fifty-one, Livvie.'

'So?'

'So…'

Olivia grins. 'Go on.'

'Fine. I like him. A lot.'

'See! And the sex?'

Now Anna is grinning too. 'It's good. He's good.'

'Oh, my big sister is sexually satisfied. It's everything I've ever dreamed of.'

Another punch on the arm. 'Gross.'

They both laugh and continue to walk through impeccably maintained streets with identical white houses. The evening air smells of warm concrete and gardenias, sweet and summery.

'Have you heard from Graham?'

Shaking her head, Olivia checks her phone for the time. 'He's probably on his way to the warehouse.'

'I miss him,' Anna says. 'He would've livened up that party like no other.'

Olivia hooks her arm through Anna's. 'I have to tell you something.'

Anna stops, her eyebrows bunched together in confusion. 'What is it?'

'Let's go in here,' Olivia says. In the middle of the block of houses, a private park for residents sits quietly. Olivia takes the key from her mother's keyring and opens the iron gate. Everything in the garden is lush, green and beautifully kept.

'Remember when I called you from Mum's, when I was heading for the bookshop?' Olivia asks, walking ahead of Anna through a narrow pathway.

'Yeah?'

'Eamonn was there.'

Anna's jaw drops; her eyes widen. 'What the fuck?'

'It gets worse. We should sit down.'

They make their way to the middle of the park and find a bench to sit on. Olivia turns to her sister. 'He wrote a book about us.'

'You and me?'

'Yes, Anna, he wrote a book about you and me.'

'Oh, sorry, you and him. Go on.'

'He was doing a reading.'

'Wait, what? He published the book?'

'Yeah, Anna, why else do you think I'd run into him in the bookshop?'

'Because he likes to read?'

'He lives in Ireland.'

'Well, that would've been less of a stretch than you running into him because he wrote a book about you and was reading from it the moment you happened to walk in.'

Fair enough.

'Anyway, the book's about the pact and everything that happened before and after we made it.'

Anna frowns, and shakes her head. 'But... he never showed. Why would he write about it? That's like explaining a crime when you haven't been caught.'

'Exactly! That was my first reaction too. Well, after the awful shock of seeing him.'

'Did you talk?'

'Not at first, but then...' Olivia walks Anna through the past couple of days, and the rollercoaster of emotions she's been on. Once in a while Anna nods or asks a question, and when finally Olivia has told her everything, even about Graham pushing her to read the book, she falls silent for a while.

'What are you thinking?' Olivia asks.

'I'm thinking Graham might be right.'

It's the answer she needed to hear, but wasn't ready for. She closes her eyes and sighs. 'Really?'

'I love Graham. You know I do, right?'

Olivia nods.

'But I was there when you fell in love with Eamonn, Livvie, and it was the first time I had seen you so completely changed by a person in a good way. The way that boy loved you, and you him…'

'What are you saying?'

'I think, if Graham is right, and your story with Eamonn doesn't end the way you think it does, you owe it to yourself to find out what happened. Him not showing up really wrecked you, and I'm not sure you ever really got over that.'

'I thought I did.'

'If you did, none of this would be as complicated as it is.'

Olivia throws her head back in despair. 'But why didn't Eamonn just tell me?'

'Oh hun, you know Eamonn. Has he ever been good at saying what he really feels?'

'He's forty now, though.'

'Yeah, well, you're thirty-eight and you didn't tell him how you waited for him on the beach for hours until I found you shivering and forced you to come home.'

The ache in her chest, the cold in her bones, the disillusionment of that rainy Sunday, all come rushing back as though it happened only yesterday. Tears burn behind Olivia's eyes. 'I hate this.'

'I'm sorry love. I know it's hard.'

For a few minutes they sit in silence, Olivia's head resting on her sister's shoulder. She knows Anna is right, about all of it, but it doesn't make it any easier. She's afraid that if the book reveals a different truth, she'll question everything even more. It's clarity she needs, not more questions.

A bird sings in a tree right above them, his song cheerful and light, not a care in the world. In her next life, she might want to be a bird.

'Is it possible to love two people equal amounts?'

'Hmm, I think so, but I don't think it's a matter of who you love more, Livvie. I think the real question is, how much do you love yourself, and what sacrifices are you willing to make to be happy?'

'Fuck.'

Anna wraps her arm around Olivia's shoulder and pulls her close.

'Are you happy?' Olivia asks after some time.

'With my life choices, you mean?'

'Yeah.'

'I am. Having Charlie on my own was the right decision for me.'

'Do you think *I* should be a mum?'

'Do *you*?'

'I don't know.'

'I think you do. It's just another hard thing to decide.'

A groan escapes her. 'Seriously, does life ever get any easier?'

Anna laughs and cradles her sister's face. 'No.'

Wild Waves
Chapter 20 - October 2010

Conor found a window seat in the back of the bus where he could sit quietly. Not having been home in a while, the prospect of seeing his father brought a sense of calm over him, as though by seeing him, he could finally be certain his dad was okay, and that his decision to leave home had not been a grave mistake.

The long bus ride home gave Conor plenty of time to jot some things down in his notebook. He was working on a new short story, set in the 1920s, and it was a relief to have a completely different world to focus on as his real life was becoming more and more complicated.

He'd been emailing Ava for a couple of weeks now, and found himself longing for her reply each time he hit send. No matter how much he knew it was wrong, it also felt entirely right, and it had felt that way from the moment she'd called him a madman for swimming in the ocean.

But both of them were steering clear of the subject of relationships. He hadn't mentioned Niamh and she hadn't spoken about James, like two ostriches in a head-in-the-sand competition.

And then there was Niamh herself. He hadn't told her yet, either, even though he was certain she wouldn't mind him being friends with Ava. So why was he keeping it from her?

There were only three people left on the bus by the time they arrived at the final stop. Immediately Conor spotted his dad's Renault and, to shield himself from the downpour, lifted his duffel bag over his head before making a run for it. His dad leaned over the passenger's seat and pulled the handle to open the door for him.

Conor threw his bag in the back and plopped down beside his dad. The warm soothing sound of Tom Waits' 'Time' sounded through the radio, making him smile at the predictability of his father. Always Tom Waits when it was pouring.

'Alright?' Jim asked, giving him a once-over.

'Grand, yeah. Yourself?'

'Not too bad.'

His dad was a man of few words, but when he leaned over to envelop him into a hug, Conor understood he wasn't the only one relieved to be reunited again.

Every time he came back to Ballybridge, Conor made a point of going swimming first. It was the one thing he missed most now he was living in Dublin. Sometimes he went up to the coast there, but between Niamh, studying and his job, he barely found the time.

And it wasn't just the ocean swimming. He'd been missing his hometown more and more lately, to his own surprise. Living in Dublin had its perks, but he was beginning to understand he was not a man built for city life.

He got out his old bike from the shed and, with nothing more than a T-shirt and his swim shorts, he sped through the rain to the beach. By the time he got there he was drenched, but it didn't matter. Conor loved swimming in the rain. He couldn't explain why, but there was something about being immersed in water while it was simultaneously falling from the sky that made him feel like he was part of something bigger.

After swimming for quite some time, he floated on the surface a little while longer before getting out, letting weeks of subconscious tension dissolve into the ocean. It was so effective, Conor understood in that moment he was made to live by the ocean.

Soaking wet, he cycled back home, changed into a dry pair of jeans and a woolly jumper, and headed to the shop for some fresh veg to get started on dinner. As he pushed through the door, the tiny bell chimed above his head, and in a matter of seconds, Conor was transported back to his old life. The place still smelled the same – a mix of cardboard and spices – and at first sight, everything seemed to be where it always had been. Conor smiled, pleased to be back, but even more pleased not to be behind the till anymore.

'Conor Delaney!' a cheerful voice shouted from the back of the shop.

'Hiya Paddy,' he replied, 'What's the craic?'

Patrick put down the cardboard box he was carrying and gave Conor a hug. 'Not too bad, mate,' he said mid-embrace, 'How's auld Dublin treatin' ya?'

'It's alright, yeah. Things are going well.'

'We miss ya around here. Loads of people coming in asking about ya.'

Conor smiles. 'Well, you can tell them I miss the place too.'

While Conor gathered his veg, Paddy filled him in on everything that had happened since he'd left and then sent him off with a complimentary bottle of wine. Outside the shop, Conor carefully placed the bottle in his rucksack.

'Having a party, then?' a familiar woman's voice sounded from behind him.

Startled, Conor turned to find Kate grinning broadly. He hadn't seen her in over a year and the sight of her instantly transported him back to those last days of summer in 2009. Even though she was a lot older than Ava, they still had the same smile. It hit him right in the gut.

'Oh, hiya Kate. How's it going?' he said. 'Got this from Paddy, actually.' He pointed at the bottle of wine and smiled.

'Visiting your dad?'

Conor nodded. 'Just for the weekend, yeah.'

'Ah, he'll be chuffed. I'm sure he misses you loads.'

'How's Charlie?' Conor asked.

'Oh, he's grand. Cheeky, but I feel guilty for working, so I let him get away with it.'

'Parenting 101.'

She smiled, and there was a moment of silence between them.

'He misses his auntie, though,' she said then. 'We both do.'

Conor swallowed. He hadn't expected her to bring up Ava and, as he wasn't sure how much she knew, he chose his next words carefully. 'I can imagine.'

Kate caught the truth of his words in his gaze, and gave his shoulder a light squeeze. 'It's good seeing you, Conor. I'm glad you're doing well.'

'Thanks. It's good seeing you too.'

On the way back, he wondered if she knew they were in touch again. A part of him wanted to turn around and ask her, just to have someone to talk to about Ava, but he didn't. Best let sleeping dogs lie.

His dad stepped through the sliding glass door of the kitchen, ostensibly taking a whiff. 'Smells good in here.'

'Should be ready in about five minutes, I reckon.'

'Alright, I'll go and get washed up.' He raised his palms to show the dirt on them, some of it ingrained into his skin from years of work on the farm. Conor heard him whistling in the shower and it had been such a long time since he'd heard that sound, it jarred him. His father had always been a cheerful man, always whistling, always positive. He was someone who actually enjoyed the small things in life. A lot of people claimed they did, but most of it was just talk. Not him. He found genuine joy in tiny things, like drinking his tea while he watched the sun rise over the hills. But when Conor's mam had died, his dad's *joie de vivre* had died along with her. He'd stopped whistling and talking about the different shades of orange he'd seen in the sunset, about how the salty ocean air made him crave a cold pint, or how the howling wind reminded him of a song he used to listen to growing up. His posture had changed and even the bounce in his step had vanished. He'd tried to stay positive and went on living his life, but Conor knew it had all been a façade for his sake.

During dinner, Conor filled his dad in on the latest news from Dublin. They talked on the phone once a week, but it was nice to see his father's face light up with each anecdote. He even exaggerated a few of his stories just to hear him laugh.

But then his dad told him about a storm they'd had a few days earlier, and Conor's chest tightened with guilt.

'I'm sorry I wasn't here to help.'

'It's not your job, son. Your place is at uni. How else are you gonna make enough money to take care of me in a few years, huh?' He laughed, but Conor didn't join in. To think his dad had had to deal with everything alone made him deeply sad. He should've been there.

The look on his face made his father push on. 'Really, I'm alright. I shouldn't have let you stay here for so long in the first place. It wasn't right.'

'It was my decision to stay, Da – you couldn't have persuaded me otherwise.'

'Well, I should've tried.' He put down his cutlery and refilled their two glasses with tap water. 'Now, stop worrying about it, alright? It all turned out fine.'

'I suppose.'

They were silent for a bit. Conor grabbed some bread to soak up the sauce, and cleaned his plate.

'There's something I've been meaning to tell you, actually,' his dad said tentatively.

'Oh?' Conor leaned back in his chair, eyebrows raised. It wasn't everyday his dad announced something so solemnly, and he had no idea what it could be. Was he retiring? Maybe. It would explain why he didn't seem too bothered about the storm.

His father cleared his throat and shifted in his chair before continuing. 'I, uhm, I've met someone.'

Conor could almost feel his brain short-circuiting. *What the fuck?* This was the last thing he'd expected his dad to say. Opposite him, a pair of expectant eyes was waiting for a reaction, but words failed him. Instead, he nodded very slowly as he tried to process the information, to capture the full meaning of what his dad had just said. He'd met someone. A woman, presumably. A woman who was not his mother.

Had he expected his father to stay alone forever? No, not really. His dad was only fifty-six, so theoretically it made sense. But until this moment it hadn't actually occurred to him this was a possibility. He just hadn't given it any thought at all.

Knowing he could no longer keep from responding, he gave his dad a small smile. 'Good for you.' He hoped it sounded genuine, but judging from the disappointment on his dad's face, it probably didn't.

'I hadn't planned on meeting anyone. It just sort of happened.' His father gave a shrug and then fell silent again.

A wave of deep sorrow came over Conor. He knew it made no sense, but it felt like now his mother was really gone. Gone for good. Erased from their lives and replaced by someone else. On the wall next to the press, the picture of the three of them together called his attention, and it took all of his strength not to glance over for a glimpse of his mother.

'Are you upset?' his dad asked, visibly afraid of what the answer would be.

Conor shook his head. 'No, no, I'm not. It's good. I'm happy for you, Da.'

That was a lie, but he knew it should have been the truth. He should be happy for his dad. The man deserved nothing less.

On the table by his elbow, Conor's phone buzzed, and he checked the screen. A text from Matt.

'I promised to meet Matt at the pub,' he explained.

'Go on. I'll clean up here.'

'Cheers.' As he got up, he patted his dad on the back. The sad smile he got in return broke his heart. What a terrible son he was.

'Tell me more about her later, okay?' he added, hoping to redeem himself somewhat.

At this, his father's face cleared up again. 'I will. Now go on. Tell Matt I said hi.'

Matt was leaning against the bar, one foot on the rail, deep in conversation with Mike. When they noticed Conor, Mike grabbed two pint glasses and filled them with a pale ale from the tap.

'How's things?' Matt asked as he straightened up to give Conor a hug.

'Good question.'

He greeted Mike with a curt wave and turned quickly in the hope of avoiding small talk. This was definitely not the time for it. It was a quiet night, so they had their choice of booths, and Matt walked straight to the one by the window. As he sat down, Conor noticed his face looked drawn, like he hadn't been sleeping well, the creases around his eyes deeper than usual.

'Still no word from Orla?' Conor guessed.

He shrugged. 'Not since her last text, no.'

'When was that?'

'About six months ago.'

Conor drew a sharp breath between his teeth. 'Oh, mate…'

'She said she needed some time, and that was fine, you know? I thought she'd call me in the next week or so, but six months? That's not *some time*, it's half a fucking year.'

Conor had no idea how to console his friend. When Matt had told him what had happened between him and Orla, Conor had been surprised, to say the least. He'd been pretty convinced Matt and Orla were a sure thing – he'd always thought it would just be a matter of time. But then, that's what he'd thought about him and Ava too, and look how that had turned out. Clearly this wasn't his area of expertise.

'Sometimes I wish I could take it all back just so we could be friends again. I miss talking to her, just having her around. I'm afraid I might have lost my best friend, Conor.'

'Cheers.' Conor raised his glass in mock offence.

'My best girl-friend,' Matt corrected, rolling his eyes.

'Do you want me to talk to her?'

'No, it's fine. I'll give her a couple more days and then I'll try calling her myself.'

After taking a big swig of his pint, Matt gave Conor a quizzical look.

'What's up with you? You look off.'

'Da just told me he's been seeing someone.'

Matt's eyes widened with surprise. 'Oh fuck, that *is* big news.'

'Yeah.'

'Do you know who it is?'

Conor scoffed. 'I didn't even ask him. Barely said anything when he told me. It threw me completely and I acted like a fecking dick.'

'I'm sure Jim'll understand.'

'I hope so. I feel so bad.'

'Did you not think this was gonna happen at some point?' Matt asked gently.

'It just never occurred to me, didn't cross my mind at all. Like he's just my dad, and not an actual person. Is that fucked up?'

'Nah.' Matt shook his head. 'I think we all look at our parents that way.'

Conor nodded. 'It's funny, isn't it, growing older? You suddenly see your parents in a completely different light. Like, all of a sudden you realise they're just like you. Just people with their own lives that have nothing to do with you, and everything they say and do now takes on a completely different meaning.'

'Like you finally realise they were people before you were born too?'

'Yeah, exactly. But your entire identity is based on them and when they change, it's like you no longer know who you are anymore either. Like it was all based on this idea you had of them, and now the idea doesn't make sense anymore.'

'What's all this, Conor? Are you having an existential crisis? I thought we weren't supposed to have one for another couple of years?'

'Oh, mate, I think I'm on my fifth crisis by now.'

Matt laughed, but Conor wasn't entirely joking. When his mam had died, he didn't so much have an identity crisis as completely lose himself. He didn't even consciously question who he was without her – he just let himself disappear. He'd even stopped writing for a few months. It had taken him so long to find himself again and now, with only a few words from this dad, he could feel the cracks in his foundation begin to reappear.

'Ah, mate, give yourself a break. You're doing alright.'

Conor smiled. 'I hope so.'

More pints flowed as they caught up on each other's lives, and as they said their goodbyes later that night, they made a plan to meet up in Dublin a few weeks later for a concert.

'See ya then, yeah?'

'Grand. And, Matt, don't worry too much about Orla, alright? She'll come round, I know she will.'

'I hope you're right, Conor.'

His dad had fallen asleep on the sofa with the TV on when Conor arrived home. The sound of the sliding door startled him and he jumped up, a dazed look in his eyes. It took him a few moments to realise who was there, but when the fog cleared, he smiled.

'How was Matt?' he asked.

'Good, yeah. He says hello. I'm off to bed now, but, uhm, Da…'

'Yeah?'

'I am really happy for you. Honestly.'

If there was anyone in the world who deserved love and happiness, it was his dad, and Conor couldn't be anything but content knowing he'd found both.

'Thanks, son. Sleep tight.'

'Night, Da.'

Before he turned off the light, he grabbed his phone and opened his contact list. Every part of him wanted to call Ava and tell her what had happened. For a long time he stared at her name, debating the pros and cons. In the end, he didn't call. Emailing was one thing – hearing her voice would open up an entirely different can of worms, and he was not sure he was ready for those consequences.

Wild Waves
Chapter 21

Ava woke to the soft strumming of a guitar coming from the living room. She checked the time and hardly believed her eyes when she saw it was only eight a.m. For as long as they'd been living together, Orla had never been up before eight unless she was still up from the night before. Ava tied her hair into a top bun and, rubbing the sleep from her eyes, made her way towards the music. She found Orla sitting on the sofa, guitar in hand, pen in mouth and several sheets of paper strewn around her.

'Who are you, and what have you done to my friend?' Ava asked.

'I've decided to call Matt today,' Orla replied, impervious to Ava's humour.

'Oh.' Ava pointed at the papers on the sofa. 'I get this now. Should I ask how you're feeling?'

'Don't bother. I don't even know myself. But I should be fine, no? I mean, it's not like I've never talked to him before – he's been my best friend since I was five, like.'

'True, but it's different now, isn't it?'

Orla nodded. 'I hate that it's different.'

Ava gave her a compassionate smile. 'I know. Coffee?'

With a nod from Orla, Ava got a brown paper filter from the cupboard and added coffee grounds to it. 'Do you wish he'd never told you?'

Carefully putting her guitar to the side, Orla gathered her notes from the sofa to make space for Ava. 'I just wish life was less complicated, like. I see people around me being in relationships and it all looks so effortless. They meet someone, they like them, the other likes them back, and *boom*! They're in a relationship.'

'I know, but you'll get there, I promise. And look at it this way: you'll get so many songs out of it, you'll be the new Lily Allen in no time.' Ava handed Orla a cinnamon roll from the IKEA box she'd pulled out of the fridge.

'I do love Lily Allen.'

'We all do.'

Orla finished the roll in two bites, even before the coffee was ready. 'Thanks, Ave. I never understood people who say they can't eat when they're stressed. It has the exact opposite effect on me. I can and will eat anything.'

'You and me both!' Ava exclaimed. To reinforce their statement, they both grabbed another cinnamon roll and wolfed it down.

'Do you know what you're going to say to him?'

Orla shrugged. 'Not exactly, no. I want to explain what happened, but I'm not sure how to do that.'

'Just tell him what you told me. Be honest about it – it's Matt, he'll understand.'

'I hope so. I don't want to lose him, like.'

'You won't.' Ava reassuringly squeezed Orla's thigh. 'Do you think you're ready to meet up with him?'

'Maybe. I've discussed it with my therapist and she thinks it would be a good idea. I just have to be clear with him that it doesn't mean I'm ready to take it a step further.'

'Baby steps.'

'Exactly. I just don't want to get his hopes up.'

Ava nodded. 'When are you going to call him?'

'In about an hour.'

'Do you want me to keep your mind off it until then?'

'You can try.'

Ava grabbed her laptop from the kitchen counter and turned the screen to Orla. 'Do you remember me telling you about the community centre I discovered around the corner?'

'The one with all the female artists?'

'Yeah, that one. I'm going there today to ask if they want to exhibit some of my photos.'

'Oh, that's fantastic!'

'Yeah? I really need a creative outlet again, and I've seen some of the other women's work there, and it's absolutely stunning. I just want to be a part of that.'

'You should. They're going to love your pictures.'

'Want to help me choose which ones to show them?'

'Hit me!'

The distraction worked instantaneously. They browsed through Ava's photos for a while until they came upon the ones Ava shot on their camping trip the year before.

'This one,' Orla said immediately when Conor popped up on the screen.

Ava smiled. 'Do you think he would mind?'

'No, definitely not. And anyway, if you don't know him, you can't tell who it is.'

She hadn't looked at this picture in a while, knowing full well the emotions it brought up in her. She felt the hairs on her arms rise and a warm glow spread through her body, her longing for Conor intensifying. But Orla was right. In the picture, Conor was running towards the water, his back turned to the camera. Ava knew those freckled shoulders and that wavy dark brown hair so well, but anyone else seeing the exhibition would not.

The next photo was one of Orla and Matt, sitting side by side in the back of the van – Matt laughing at something Orla had said, Orla's forehead leaning against his shoulder.

'This is one of my favourites,' Ava said.

'So much for distracting me, huh?'

'Sorry.'

'No worries.' She took a deep breath and nodded. 'It's time,' she said as she got up and grabbed her phone.

'It's time,' Ava agreed.

With a flash drive in her bag, Ava headed for the community centre. She'd been there a few times to admire the artwork, and imagining her own photos on the wall gave her a buzz of excitement.

The building looked a little dishevelled from the outside, and the heavy door creaked as Ava stepped inside. The woman behind the bar looked up at the sound of it, and Ava smiled apologetically.

She walked through the café to the back, where most of the works were exhibited. There were bean bags scattered around the room, a long table in the middle with outlets to charge laptops, a few smaller tables with chairs, a white board on the right-hand wall, and a projector hanging from the ceiling in the middle of the space. Two women, both seemingly in their early thirties, were working side by side.

'Excuse me,' Ava said as she approached them.

The women looked up.

'Do you know who I can speak to about showing some of my photos here?'

'That would be me,' the shorter one of the two said. Her black curls were twisted up in a bun and the many bracelets on her arm jingled as she raised her hand in greeting.

'Oh hi, I'm Ava.' She smiled a big, nervous smile. 'I live around the corner from here, I'm an aspiring photographer and—'

Before she could continue, the woman shook her head and cut her off. 'Stop.'

Completely taken aback, Ava frowned. 'Sorry?'

'Don't say that.'

'Don't say what?'

'Aspiring.'

'Oh… but I am, I mean, I'm not a professional.' Ava adjusted her shoulder bag nervously.

'Do you love taking photographs?'

'Yes, but…'

'Is it something you're passionate about?'

'Well yeah…'

'Is it something you do and think about every day?'

Ava nodded.

'Well, my dear Ava, that makes you a photographer. Period. Don't sell yourself short ever again, please. That's something a man would never do, and I need women to stop doing it too.'

'Okay…' Ava's shoulders relaxed again. She liked this woman, a lot.

'Now, start again.'

'Uhm, so, I'm Ava and I'm a photographer and I was wondering if I could show some of my work here?' Her voice went up at the end of the sentence, as though she still wasn't sure she was doing it right.

'Much better! It's nice to meet you, Ava. I'm Iman and this is Lin.' She gestured at the woman sitting to her right, wearing a bright orange jumpsuit. Lin smiled and wiggled her fingers in a very minimal wave.

'Did you bring some of your work?' Iman asked.

'I did, yeah.' With trembling hands, Ava got out the flash drive from her bag and handed it to her.

'I'm not sure what you're looking for, so I put a little bit of everything on there.'

'Alright, let's have a look.' She tapped the chair next to her, inviting Ava to sit down and connected the flash drive to her laptop.

Ava held her breath, studying Iman's expression for a reaction. This was the first time she'd shown strangers her work, and she desperately needed them to like it. A rejection of her photos would mean a rejection of her as a photographer. Not only that – she felt such a strong emotional connection to the photos, it would feel like a rejection of her as a person.

After what seemed like an hour but was probably more like five minutes, Iman turned to her. 'Can you deliver us the prints by Friday?'

'Really?' Ava's eyebrows shot up and her jaw dropped.

'Yes. Really. These are great, girl. Stop doubting yourself.'

Ava's heart was going a million miles an hour. Even though she'd been hopeful, a part of her had not expected it to go this well. *What a feeling!*

'Oh my God, thank you. And yes, I'll go and get them printed right away.'

'Great. We only have room for three pictures at the moment, though.'

Iman chose the one of Conor running towards the ocean, one of Anna trying to comfort Charlie during a tantrum, and the one of Matt and Orla in the back of the van.

'Thank you so much for this opportunity,' Ava said.

'They're really good, Ava. We'll get them up on Friday. Every first Friday of the month we have an event to showcase our new artists to the wider public. This time there's going to be a poetry reading, a short film, a few other photographers and a painter. It's a wonderful opportunity to meet some of our current artists, and if our visitors want to know more about you, you'll be around to talk to them.'

'That sounds amazing. Count me in,' Ava said. This kept getting better and better.

'Bring a portfolio of your other work,' Lin interjected, 'in case anyone wants to see more.'

'I will. Thank you.'

Ava said goodbye and, fuelled by adrenaline, ran straight to the printer's to get her order in. She was still buzzing when she got home and desperately wanted to share the news with Orla, but she wasn't there. Eager to talk to someone, she grabbed her phone and without thinking it through, rang the one person she wanted to tell most of all.

They hadn't really spoken since her last day in Ireland, and when she heard the sound of the phone ringing on the other end, the consequences suddenly dawned on her. Her palms became sweaty and her heartbeat so loud it was probably audible through the phone. She was about to hang up when he answered, the sound of his deep, grainy voice bringing back so much she wasn't prepared for.

'Ava?' There was a hint of worry in his tone.

She swallowed before answering. 'Hi.'

'Hi,' he replied.

Silence. *This is weird*, she thought. What had she done? Remaining silent was obviously even weirder and so she spoke again: 'Is this weird? Me calling you?'

'A bit,' he said.

'I know. I don't know what I was thinking. Well, I do, I mean, something amazing just happened and I guess I just wanted to tell you. But as per usual, I didn't really think this through. I'm so sorry. When the phone was ringing I realised we haven't really talked in a long time, I mean, emailing is one thing, but this is proper talking, and I also realise now I'm doing a lot of it.' She gave a nervous giggle.

'Tell me, then. What happened?' He was calm and yet she thought she could hear the smile in his voice.

'Okay, well, have I ever mentioned the arts centre around the corner from my flat?'

'No, I don't think so.'

'Well, it's this amazing place for female creatives to get together. There's a little café and then a huge working-slash-exhibition space in the back. It's open every day and run mostly by volunteers, and you can just go there and meet people and collaborate. They do exhibitions, and every first Friday of the month there's, like, a public opening… It's just wonderful.'

'It sounds amazing.'

'Well, today I went in and I talked to Iman. I think she's the one who started the whole project. She's so cool, and I asked her if I could exhibit some of my photos there and I'd brought a few examples, and I still can't really believe it, but she said yes!' Ava took a deep breath. It was quiet on the other end of the line.

'Conor?'

'Yeah, I'm still here. I guess I was just smiling.'

'Oh,' she said, her entire body flooding with love for him.

'It's fantastic news.'

'It is, isn't it? My photos, on show for everyone in London to see. Well, at least the few people who'll visit the centre, but still. I just can't believe it, Conor.'

'I can,' he said, and Ava wanted to pull him through the phone and kiss him.

'It's because of you, you know. You're the one who encouraged me to do this.'

'Yeah, but you went and did it. You made this happen.'

'Thank you.'

'Anytime, Bruce.'

The effect the use of her old nickname had on her internal organs made it clearer than ever how much she'd been longing to be with him. Suddenly the need felt urgent.

'Do you want to come for a visit sometime? To see the photos?' she blurted.

Conor was quiet and her heart sank. It was too soon. Now she'd ruined everything they'd built again. 'You're probably busy with classes and everything. Forget what I said.' She tried to sound casual, but her anguish seeped through.

'Uhm, no, actually, I think I have some time at the end of the month. I'd have to check my schedule, but I could let you know when I get home tonight.'

'Oh okay, yeah. That's great.' She was at a loss for words.

'Alright, I'll text you then.'

'Right. Bye, Conor.'

'Bye.'

Ava was standing by the window, looking out onto the busy street below, when she ended the call. She stood there for a while, her enthusiasm about the arts centre now completely overshadowed by the prospect of seeing Conor again. She walked over to the sofa and closed her eyes. His fair, freckled skin, his wavy thick brown hair, his soft lips and the deep dark blue of his eyes appeared. Her entire body ached for him. She longed to feel his skin against hers, the way she had in the ocean when the world around them had disappeared.

She was glad she'd phoned him. Everything seemed possible again now. It could all still happen.

The sound of the keys in the door shook her from her daydream. Orla walked in, carrying a bottle of red wine in one hand, a cardboard box in the other. She kicked the door shut behind her, walked over to the kitchen and grabbed two wine glasses from the cupboard.

'We're drinking and eating cheesecake!' she shouted from the kitchen.

Ava sat up and looked over to assess the mood.

'Are we happy or sad?' she shouted back.

'Something in between. Give me a sec, I'll be right back.'

Orla stalked into her bedroom and emerged again seconds later, wearing leggings. She sat down opposite Ava on the sofa, placed the cheesecake in between them and handed her a fork.

Ava stared at her questioningly. 'So? How did it go?' she asked.

'Good. I think. I don't know. It's complicated.'

'Okay, I want all the tea. Start from the beginning.'

Orla took a big swig from her merlot and walked Ava through the entire conversation she'd had with Matt earlier that day. She told Ava how, at first, she'd rambled on about insignificant things and Matt had just listened. But then, she'd fallen silent and again he'd let her. She told Ava how she'd finally apologised for running away, and how he'd asked her if there was any chance of her coming back, and she'd told him *no*, but they arranged to meet over Christmas, and in the meantime they would call each other, as friends, like they always used to.

When she finally stopped talking, Ava gave her a hug.

'You did great, Orla, honestly.'

'Thanks. I'm just thrilled I got to talk to him again.'

'Yeah, I think I know how you feel,' Ava smiled. She would tell Orla about her call the next day. This was a big moment for her friend, and she deserved all the attention.

'Do you think boys do this too?' Orla asked.

'What? Drink wine, eat cake and overanalyse every sentence from their conversations with women?'

'Yeah.'

'I hope so, for their sake,' Ava said, and raised her glass in a toast.

Wild Waves
Chapter 22

The morning of Conor's arrival, Ava had trouble focusing on even the simplest of tasks. As she waited for the coffee to run through, Orla pointed out there was nothing but water in the pot. She gently pushed Ava aside and took over.

'Thanks,' Ava said.

'How are you feeling?'

'Big day.'

'Yeah, big day.' Orla pulled Ava close for a hug. 'You'll be fine,' she added.

Ava wasn't so sure. They'd been emailing a lot, but seeing him in real life again was a completely different ball game.

While they drank their coffee, Orla talked about her upcoming gig, but she might as well have been talking to a wall. In her mind, Ava was already at the airport.

When she finished her coffee, she retreated to her bedroom and stared at her wardrobe for a long time, trying to decide what to wear. She wanted to look great, but not like she'd tried too hard. 'Effortlessly stunning' was the look she was going for. After trying on almost everything she had, she ended up wearing the one outfit she'd laid out the night before: a dark green jumpsuit, mustard-yellow cardigan and brown leather boots.

Conor's plane was scheduled to arrive at Stansted around two p.m. and Ava had taken the day off work to meet him at the airport. When he'd confirmed his visit, she'd been beyond excited, but now he was nearly there, all she felt was nausea. What if he didn't like her anymore? What if they had nothing to talk about? What if she had romanticised him in her mind, and in reality he was not as clever, and warm, and lovely, as the image she had of him in her head? After all, she hadn't seen him in over a year.

To try and keep her mind from spiralling, Ava ordered a coffee at the airport Pret and got out her worn copy of *One Day*. On any other day, Emma and Dexter would have been the perfect distraction from whatever was going on in Ava's life, but ten minutes later she was still on the same page, having to reread most sentences not once, but several times.

When she looked up at the arrivals board for the umpteenth time, his flight from Dublin suddenly appeared. Her stomach somersaulted. This was it. All or nothing. She took a deep breath, gave her fringe a little tousle and made her way towards the arrivals hall.

A number of taxi drivers, holding up signs with long and foreign names they probably didn't know how to pronounce, waited patiently for their clients. When the first passengers appeared, Ava held her breath. Her heart skipped a beat every time someone pushed through the doors. Conor needed to be next, because Ava wasn't sure she'd be able to cope much longer.

And then, after what seemed like the longest wait in the history of mankind, there he was. Ava had expected to feel unsettled when she saw him, but this was next level. His dark blue eyes scanned the room for her, and she was overcome with the visceral feeling of what it was like to love someone, wholly and entirely. Every cell in her body lit up as though struck with a match and when his eyes finally found hers, there was no more stopping the raging fire in her heart.

'Hi.'

'Hiya.'

They stood, facing each other awkwardly for a second, until he leaned in to kiss her on the cheek. The familiarity of him was so overwhelming, Ava couldn't help but sling her arms around his neck. As his hands closed around her waist, his soft cheek grazed hers, making the hairs on her arms stand, but just as she felt ready to tell him how much she loved him, Conor abruptly took a step back. As though burnt by the fire raging through her, he cleared his throat, zipped up his jacket and pointed at the sign behind Ava. 'That way to the train?'

What was that? Ava scanned his face for clues, but he averted his gaze and started walking. As she followed close behind him, it dawned on her that he might think she was still with James. She hadn't told him in her emails, because she'd wanted to do it in person. Especially after the way things had ended the last time they were together. So of course he pulled away. He didn't trust her. Yet. She'd tell him soon, though, but not there, not at the airport.

'How was your flight?'

'Good, yeah, short.'

'No traffic, huh?' Ava flinched at her own dumb joke but when she turned sideways, Conor was smiling.

'Off peak,' he said.

The anxious knot in her stomach loosened.

'Orla should be home by now. She was looking forward to seeing you again.'

'Right. Is she still looking for a place? I haven't spoken to her in ages.'

'Uhm, no, she moved into my spare bedroom actually.'

'Oh.' His brow furrowed. Was he putting two and two together? Or was he never even aware that she and James had been living together?

If Orla hadn't told him about moving in with Ava, she probably hadn't told him about her breakup with James either. A kernel of hope burrowed in Ava's chest. She'd tell him over dinner and then maybe, maybe, she wouldn't have to sleep alone tonight.

On the train, the heat of his body radiated against hers. To distract herself from the urge to grab his hand, she asked him if there were things he wanted to see while he was in town.

'I was thinking about going to the Tate Modern,' he said.

'Oh, good idea. We could do that today, actually, and then we could get a bite to eat somewhere along the Southbank.'

'Sound.'

'Anything else?'

'Well, obviously I want to see your photos.'

'That's on the menu for tonight,' Ava beamed.

'I can't wait to see them.'

'Yeah, me neither. Well, for you to see them. I've clearly seen them already.'

When was this verbal diarrhoea going to end?

Probably not until he'd seen the photos. She hadn't told Conor anything about them. Not knowing how he would react when he saw himself framed on the wall of the arts centre made her insanely insecure but still, she decided not to tell him yet. Seeing his reaction in the moment would provide her with invaluable information on the status of their relationship.

When they arrived home, Orla was waiting by the door. She jumped into Conor's arms, screaming with joy. Conor nearly lost his balance and steadied himself by grabbing onto Ava's arm. She closed her eyes for a split second.

'It's so good to see you, Con. I barely recognised ya.'

Conor rolled his eyes at her. 'Eejit.'

'Do you want to come to the Tate with us?' Ava asked Orla.

'Yeah, I'd love to. I have band practice later today, though, so can't stay too long.'

'Are you gearing up for tomorrow night?' Conor asked.

'You won't know what hit you, my friend,' Orla replied. Her band was playing a few gigs in a pub in Camden that month, and this was the first one. Ava had seen them play before, but according to Orla, their setlist was now in much better shape, and she definitely needed to see them play again. With Conor there, it seemed like perfect timing.

The three of them took the tube to Waterloo Station and then walked the rest of the way along the Southbank until they reached the museum. It was a cold day, but the sun was out and there was hardly any wind. At first Orla did most of the talking, telling Conor about her new job and the band she'd joined, and then Conor opened up about his life in Dublin. Ava listened intently to everything he was saying, hoping to decipher any coded messages about a possible girlfriend. Nothing so far. She wanted to ask him, get it over with, but she hesitated, not sure she was ready for the answer.

By the time they left the Tate again it was dark outside. Orla said goodbye and promised to meet them for breakfast in the morning. Before she left, she lightly squeezed Ava's arm and grinned.

'Have fun, kids.'

Ava suggested a burger place not too far from the arts centre. She desperately needed to eat something to drown out the raging nerves for what was coming.

They were seated at a small table for two against the wall, his knees touching hers as she faced him. Seeing him like that, in the dimly lit café, she couldn't believe she'd let him go. He looked beautiful just sitting there, studying his menu, the soft yellow lighting warming his complexion. There was something familiar about him beyond the time they'd known each other, like she'd known him for years – lifetimes, even. If he'd let her, she'd watch him for lifetimes to come.

Just when she was about to tell him about James, the waiter appeared by their side, ready to take their order. They both opted for the special – a portobello burger with guacamole and spinach – but when the waiter left, the moment was gone.

'So how was the exhibition?' Conor asked.

'Oh, it was brilliant. Seeing my own work there and talking to all these other creatives was unlike anything I've ever done before. I talked to so many women and I don't know, it felt like there was this invisible thing that bound us together, you know? It's hard to explain what I felt exactly, but I was buzzing for a long time after it was over.'

'You found your people.'

'Yeah, that's exactly what it was!' she exclaimed, amazed at how he summed it up in four simple words. 'Always the wordsmith, you.'

'Comes with the education,' he said, brushing off her compliment but unable to hide his blushing cheeks.

Their burgers arrived and without breaking conversation, they clinked their glasses in a silent toast.

'Is the centre open every day?'

'Yeah, but on regular days it's mostly just the artists there. I've been a couple of times myself, and I've had so many ideas for things I want to do.'

'Like what?'

'I think I want to photograph them – the women there, when they're working and then in their daily lives as well. How different they all are, but how they still all experience the same things, have to face the same challenges. Even though they take on different shapes, at their core, they're all the same.'

Conor looked at her with a knowing smile on his face.

'What?' she asked. 'Are you going to say *I told you so*?'

He shook his head and took a bite. 'I would never,' he mumbled through a mouth full of food.

'Fine, you were right. Is that what you want to hear?'

Conor gave a smug shrug and laughed. 'I just can't wait to see it,' he said then, holding her gaze, genuine pride in his eyes.

Her stomach lurched at the thought. Soon he would see himself the way she saw him. Soon they would no longer be able to dance around the topic of their relationship. Soon she would know where she stood.

All of the awkwardness between them had dissipated and as they walked, side by side, she noticed the change in his posture too. His hands were buried deep inside his jacket pockets, his arms bent at the elbow. She wanted to link her arm through his, but didn't. *Maybe later*, she thought, after he'd seen the photo and she'd told him about James.

The café of the arts centre was open late on Fridays. Ava greeted a few people she'd seen before who were drinking by the bar, all the while feeling Conor's eyes on her, observing her closely.

'Okay,' she said before entering the exhibition area, 'close your eyes.'

'What?'

'Close your eyes.'

'Are you serious, Bruce?'

A shiver ran down her back at the sound of her nickname.

'Dead serious.'

He sighed but closed his eyes anyway. Ava grabbed his hand and, as her fingers wrapped around his, she took a moment to take it all in. How long she'd waited to be holding his hand again.

Her photos were on display in the far-left corner of the room, and she guided him to the spot in front of his own picture. Before she told him to look, she positioned herself so she could see the reaction on his face and took a deep breath to steady her nerves. 'Open your eyes.'

Conor blinked to adapt to the light before his eyes landed on the image in front of him. For a while his face remained expressionless. He took a step back and studied the other photos – the one with Matt and Orla and the one of Kate holding George – walking from one photo to the next in silence. Ava was about to explode when Conor returned to where she was standing, waiting for his verdict.

When he spoke, it was barely a whisper, but the words reached her heart anyway. 'You're class, Ava.'

A lump formed in her throat. She swallowed it down. 'Fuck, Conor, you sure know how to make a girl panic. I was afraid you hated it.'

He smiled. 'I know. That's why I made you wait so long.'

She punched him on the shoulder. 'Twat.'

'Oi, is that how you treat the star of the show?' he asked.

A deep belly laugh escaped her. They were Conor and Ava again. As they should be.

When his gaze turned back to the images, she wondered what he was thinking. Did he also want to travel back in time and just stay there, on that beach, forever?

'Do you miss it sometimes?' she asked.

Conor didn't speak, but wrapped his arm around her shoulder and pulled her close, letting his cheek rest against her forehead. She had her answer, and it was the one she'd been hoping for.

'We're closing the bar in half an hour. If you want a drink, better get one now,' Iman's voice sounded from across the room.

Ava looked up at Conor. 'Do you want to have another drink here?'

'We could.'

'But you'd rather not?' Her heart sank.

'It's been a long day.'

'Yeah, no, that's fine. We'll go home.' Ava said goodbye to Iman and promised to be back soon. Walking back to the flat, their fingers brushed up against each other occasionally, sending shivers down Ava's spine each time. They talked plans for the next day, and decided on brunch in Hampstead followed by a walk on the Heath, and finishing the day in Camden for Orla's gig.

Back at the flat, there was still no sign of Orla. Ava switched on the small lamp in the corner next to the sofa.

'This, unfortunately, is not a pull-out bed, but I have it on good authority that it's not too bad for a good night's rest.' She smiled apologetically.

'I'm sure I'll be fine.'

There was a long pause, both of them seemingly unsure how to proceed. Being alone with him in a public place was fine, but being alone with him in an empty apartment was something way more fragile. Ava wanted to say so much, but her fear of messing things up trumped her desire for answers in that moment. They had another full day together – there was no rush, she reminded herself.

'Alright then, good night.' She took a step towards the bedroom, but before she could go any further, he grabbed her arm and pulled her back in for a hug.

'Your pictures are amazing, Bruce… You are amazing,' he breathed into her hair while squeezing her tightly.

Ava melted into his embrace. She knew, the moment he'd let go, she would not be able to stand on her own.

The sound of the keys in the door startled them and Conor pulled back faster than he would've, had he just been electrocuted. As expected, Ava's weak knees buckled and she had to steady herself by grabbing onto the sofa.

'Hiya lads, what's the craic?' Orla asked, entering the room, seemingly unaware of the tension in the air.

'Nothing much. Just got back from the centre and ready to call it a night, actually,' Ava said while Conor gave a sheepish smile from the other side of the living room. How had he ended up there so fast?

'Alright. Had a good time, then? What did you think, Conor?'

'Yeah, good, she's done well.'

He said it in such a matter-of-fact way, it almost made Ava question what he'd said to her moments before.

Orla shifted her gaze from Conor to Ava, eyebrows raised.

'You guys are still coming to the gig tomorrow, right?'

'Yeah, definitely – looking forward to that!' Ava exclaimed a little too eagerly, in an obvious attempt to diffuse all the tension with a single exclamation.

'Good.' Orla nodded. 'Anyone want a cup of tea?' As she made her way to the kettle, Ava looked at Conor. He was by the window, hands deep in his pockets. Her eyes found his, but she wasn't sure what she saw in them this time. She should've told him about James when she had the chance. Now things were weird again.

'No thanks. Long day,' he said to Orla.

'Yeah, I'm signing off too.'

'Alright, night, lads.'

'Night,' they said simultaneously, before Ava closed the bedroom door behind her, cursing herself for her cowardice.

Wild Waves
Chapter 23

Conor could blame his discomfort on the sofa, but unfortunately he knew it had nothing to do with his temporary bed. It was dark outside and the girls were still sleeping. He picked up his phone to check the time: 7.07 a.m. He closed his eyes again, but all he could see was Ava. Her golden-brown eyes, the dimple in her chin, and the freckles on her nose and cheeks haunted him. Even when he squeezed his eyes shut tightly, the images were still there, burnt on his corneas. Trying to go back to sleep was not an option either, as she followed him into his dreams, and he had even less control over what happened there. With a deep sigh, he got up from the sofa and headed towards the kitchen, where he made himself a cup of tea. Waiting for the click of the kettle, he stared out the window onto the empty street below. His thoughts ping-ponged from Ava to Niamh and back to Ava. At what point had he decided coming to London was a good idea? Nothing good could come of this. He was making things harder for everyone, and he knew it.

Orla was the first to wake up and join him in the kitchen. She said nothing at first, but wrapped her arm around his waist and leaned against him, following his gaze out the window.

'Anything interesting going on out there?'

He shook his head. 'Not that I've noticed.'

'Anything interesting going on in here?' She poked his temple with her index finger.

This time he shrugged. 'Don't think *interesting* is the right word.'

'Want to talk about it?'

Another shrug. 'I don't have the words, Orla.'

She looked up at him and pulled him in for a hug. 'Let me know once you've found them, yeah?'

He nodded and leaned into it. Ever since he moved to Dublin and she to London, they'd had very little contact. And with things between Matt and Orla being so complicated, he knew even less of what was going on in her life, and she in his. 'I miss you back home,' he said.

'Yeah, me too.'

'You miss you too?'

She chuckled and shook her head. 'Eejit.'

Ava's bedroom door opened and Orla gave his arm one last squeeze before letting go of him. The moment he saw Ava, face creased with pillow marks but still as beautiful as the day he first met her, Conor was completely powerless.

'Morning,' she yawned, stretching her arms behind her back.

'Morning, love,' Orla replied. 'Had a good sleep?'

'Yeah, not too bad. How about you, Conor? Sofa okay?'

Conor nodded. 'Better than expected.'

'How about some breakfast before brunch, eh?' Orla stepped into her shoes, threw on her coat and grabbed her keys from the counter. 'I'll run down to the café. Back in a bit.' She slammed the door on her way out, leaving behind a deafening silence.

Fortunately, Ava was still Ava, and she managed to fill the silence by rambling on about her dickhead of a boss, who also happened to be her uncle. By the time Orla got back with croissants from the bakery down the street, the events of the night before had been pushed to the back of Conor's mind –

not entirely gone, but far enough to allow him to act like a normal human being. *Act* being the operative word.

Obviously, he would have to face the facts at some point, but for now he just wanted to spend the day with two of his best friends.

As they set out for brunch, the combination of Orla and Ava proved to be a great source of entertainment once again, especially when they decided to order a bottle of prosecco with their pancakes. For a few hours, it was as if they were back to their old dynamics, back to simpler times, and as he watched them get tipsy, he was flooded with love for both of them.

At one point, Ava went off on another rant about her uncle, and Conor noticed how much she'd changed. It was like a spark had been lit inside her and something was burning. She was sticking up for herself more and going after the things she wanted. It frightened him somewhat, not because he was opposed to it, but because he feared his last attempts at resistance might be in vain.

'I swear, if that tosser asks me to do his filing one more time, I'm going to file his paperwork so deep up his arse, the paper cuts will have him thinking he's on his period.' She finished this statement with a huge swig of her drink, slamming the empty glass back down with a forceful thud.

Orla, who'd also just taken a sip, burst out laughing, sending prosecco flying everywhere, but mostly in Conor's face. In a reflex, he squeezed his eyes shut. Before he could lift his arm to wipe the spit off, he felt someone else's hands on his cheeks, and when he opened his eyes, Ava's thumb was so close to his bottom lip it was hard to remain still. Their eyes locked. The air around them seemed to thicken and breathing was almost impossible.

'Fecking hell, Ava, you sure know how to paint a picture.' Orla snorted, wiping her chin.

Ava dropped her hand, and leaned so far back in her chair Conor feared it might topple over. His cheeks flushed.

'Here, I think I'll just go to the loo quickly,' he said, jumping up and wiping at some drops that had caught in his brow.

In the men's room he leaned on the basin with both hands for support, trying to steady his breathing. When he looked up in the mirror, the reflection of a lost man stared back at him. The powerlessness he'd felt that morning was back with a vengeance. He opened the tap and splashed the ice-cold water in his face, hoping it would miraculously clear his head and offer him a solution. It didn't. Of course it didn't. He just needed to stop being such a coward.

When he got back to the table, Ava was nowhere to be seen. Orla anticipated his question. 'She had to take a work call.' She gestured to a pacing Ava just outside the café.

'Oh, right.'

Orla waved the waiter over and asked for the bill. 'We're doing a final run-through before the gig tonight, and I want to get there early to set up,' she explained.

'How are you feeling about it?' Conor asked.

'Excited, yeah. I just really want to go over all the songs one more time, you know – sort out the details.'

'Can't wait to see it. I'm sure it'll be great.'

When they joined Ava outside, she finished her call with a grunt.

'What was that?' Orla asked. 'Nothing to do with filing, I hope?'

'Unfortunately not. The bastard's travelling at the moment and something went wrong with his booking – a booking he made himself, I'll have you know – and now I'm supposed to sort it out, on a Saturday, like I have nothing better to do, like I was waiting for him at home with my laptop, hoping he would call! For fuck's sake... I can't believe this guy.'

'Fecking sociopath is what he is!' Orla interjected and Ava nodded fiercely in agreement.

'I'm so sorry Conor, but I have to get back to the flat and fix this.'

Conor suppressed a sigh of relief. This couldn't have come at a better time. It gave him a couple of hours to think about his next steps.

'I don't mind. I'm sure I'll find something to do in London.' He gave her a reassuring smile.

'I'll make it up to you tonight. Drinks on me,' she said.

'It's fine. Really.'

'Yeah, and anyways, drinks are on me tonight,' Orla said. 'We're not getting paid for this gig. We just get free pints.'

'Well then…' Ava shrugged.

They hugged goodbye and each went their way.

Now that Conor had a whole afternoon to himself and a lot of processing to do, he desperately wished there was an ocean nearby. Unfortunately, it would take him too long to get anywhere near the coast, so he went for the second-best option: the bathing ponds on Hampstead Heath. He popped into the nearest shop to buy a pair of swim trunks and a towel. As he walked through the aisles, he found himself in the stationery section and figured a notebook and pen might come in handy as well, just in case the cold water wasn't enough to help him figure things out.

As he'd expected, the pond offered some relief, but it wasn't the same. There was no current to fight and the boundaries made him feel trapped. He realised once again how much the freedom of the boundless ocean meant to him. It was endless and unlimited. It made him feel small, yet part of a bigger whole. He knew who he was in the ocean. He was aware of his body and its senses each time he surrendered to the great unknown that was the deep, dark sea.

When he got out of the water and found the nearest café to warm up with a cup of tea, he couldn't bring himself to write either. Staring at the blank page, he knew if he were to write down what he really felt, it would make it all too real. He loved

Niamh, but he wasn't sure it was the right kind. It was a comfortable kind of love. Nothing world-shattering, or life-altering – just nice and easy. Was that what it was supposed to be? But whether he loved her the right way or not, what he was doing now was not okay. Even though he'd told Niamh he was going to see Orla's gig and Ava would be there too, he felt like a traitor. He'd explained how they met, but not how they parted. And yes, he was going to see Orla's band play, but that was not why he was in London. This had to end. He had to tell Ava about Niamh before the situation got even more out of hand.

'This next song I wrote last summer after a road trip with my best friends. It's about feeling at home no matter where you are, and about the people who make that possible. Two of my people are here tonight and this is for them. This is "The Road to Us",' Orla announced through the microphone.

The crowd cheered as Orla turned to her band for the countdown. Ava smiled but the glint in her eyes told a different story. Conor couldn't help but wrap his arm around her and pull her close. She leaned into it and rested her head against his chest. Could she hear the beating of his reckless heart?

When he went to pick her up at home before the gig, he tried to tell her about Niamh, but she was still fuming about her boss, threatening to quit before realising she needed a backup plan first. As she didn't have one, she decided the next best thing was to get drunk and party. Conor quickly came to the conclusion this was not the best time to tell her. He didn't want to ruin her night, or anyone else's for that matter. They would be alone in the flat after the gig, as Orla was staying with one of the girls from the band. If she wasn't too drunk by the time they got home, he could tell her then. Worst case scenario, he still had the next morning to come clean.

The band picked up the pace after a couple of slower songs. Ava, who was now a few pints in, swayed to the music. Soon everyone was dancing and Ava was in the middle, spinning around like she didn't have a single care in the world.

Watching her twirl, the knot in his stomach tightened. He was reminded of that first night they all spent together in the pub in Ballybridge. He hadn't fully grasped it at the time, but looking back now, he realised he'd already fallen in love with her then. And clearly things hadn't changed much since.

By the time Orla strummed the last chord of the set, Conor and Ava were equally intoxicated.

'Orla, you're an absolute star!' Conor half-shouted.

'Listen to him, Orla, this man knows what he's talking about!' Ava joined in, poking a finger into Conor's chest. They proceeded to name their favourite songs one by one, ending up going over the entire setlist. Orla's face glowed as Ava found superlative after superlative to describe her appreciation of the performance. Suddenly she disappeared, leaving Orla and Conor behind, slightly stunned. When she returned, she was holding a beer mat and a sharpie.

'Sign, please.' she giggled.

'Jayzus, Ava.'

'I mean it. This is going to be worth thousands one day.'

'Ah here, you're going to sell it, are you?'

'How dare you accuse me of that?' Ava tried to throw Orla a nasty look but failed.

'Did you just fart?' Orla asked.

'Orla, God, who do you take me for?'

'Ava Kingston, I live with you, I know exactly who you are,' Orla said. She took the beer mat and the sharpie from Ava and used Conor's back for support.

'Here,' she said, handing it back to Ava.

Ava jumped into her arms. 'I know I'm drunk, but it was bloody amazing, Orla. I mean it. You rocked my world tonight.'

'Thanks, Ave. That means a lot.'

Conor pulled Orla in for a hug too. 'I can't believe my best friend is a rock star,' he said again and kissed her on the forehead. Apart from the band and the pub staff, they were the only ones left.

'Go on, get out of here, you drunk fucks,' Orla said, pushing them out the door.

Right before she left, Ava turned to Orla and whispered something in her ear, after which they both burst out laughing.

'What was that all about?' Conor asked.

'I'll tell you one day.' She squeezed both her eyes shut, attempting a wink, and Conor's heart cracked.

Wild Waves
Chapter 24

'Here, damage control,' Ava said, handing Conor a glass of water, a fizzing tablet dancing around in it.

'Good idea.'

They clinked their glasses and Ava slouched down on the sofa, her head hanging over the armrest. Dizziness hit almost immediately, prompting her to sit back up. Conor was still standing and had moved over to the bookcase. He was studying it, his head tilted to the right, examining the titles. The tension in Ava's body built as she watched him pick one of the books up to read the blurb. Did he feel it too? Was he really interested in that book, or was he trying to find a distraction?

'You can borrow that if you like,' she said.

'Thanks.' He placed it on the coffee table and sat down opposite her, at the other end of the sofa.

Since he arrived, his behaviour had been unpredictable, going from incredibly sweet to standoffish in a matter of seconds. The distance he was keeping now fell into the latter category. Perhaps this was the time to tell him about James.

'Conor?'

He met her eyes but said nothing.

'I miss you,' she said. She had to say it. Her entire body demanded her to.

'I'm right here.' He turned his gaze away and stared at his empty glass on the coffee table.

'You know what I mean,' Ava said.

Conor folded his hands at the back of his neck and bent his head. 'Yeah... I know what you mean.'

They were silent for a long time. Every rational thought vanished from Ava's mind. She shuffled closer, until they were side by side, thighs touching.

'I miss you too,' he finally said, turning towards her again.

Those four words changed everything. With a sigh of relief, Ava leaned forwards, until their foreheads touched. His warm breath was soft on her skin when he opened his mouth.

'Ava...'

But before he could say anything else, she softly pressed her lips against his. At first he remained still, not resisting but not reciprocating either. Her chest tightened with dread and she pulled back. Had she misinterpreted the situation? Did he not want to kiss her? Her eyes were still closed when, suddenly, his thumb grazed her cheek and his lips landed on hers, pulling her in again. Love and longing erupted inside Ava's chest, a pressure so intense it was as though her ribcage was too small to contain it all. She'd been waiting for this moment for so long, it had almost become abstract in her mind, and now it was finally happening, the release was overwhelming, almost painful. The taste of him was familiar, the rhythm of their lips in sync with her heartbeat. Everything around her melted away and she opened her mouth to let him in. His kiss intensified, the urgency building as though he'd been left parched in the desert and she was a freshwater spring. Ava went to stand and pulled her blouse over her head. Intuitively, Conor's hands moved to her hips as he kissed the soft bulge of her belly. His kisses burned her skin, setting her entire body alight.

With hungry hands, she grabbed the hem of his shirt and lifted it over his head before pulling him along to her bedroom. When they connected, skin to skin, the hairs on her arms stood and her stomach muscles clenched in anticipation. Conor reclined on the bed and pulled her on top of him, his arms wrapping around her, as they continued to swallow each other whole. The fiery heat of his touch spread to the rest of her body and she softly pushed him back so she could unbutton his jeans. He watched her intently, his eyes never breaking the tidal pull between them.

They'd never gone further than kissing, but when he unhooked her bra and she felt his thumb stroking her nipple, it felt familiar – it felt right. She let out a gasp when his hands moved down her sides to the elastic band of her knickers. Within seconds they were both completely naked and Ava grabbed a condom from the drawer of her bedside table.

Everything they did had an urgency to it, as though they couldn't allow for the space to reconsider. Without breaking eye contact, he moved inside her, the rhythmic pulse of his body fusing with hers. Ava moaned and he kissed her, swallowing the sound, his lips pressed against hers, not letting go until they both collapsed into one another minutes later, drenched in sweat and love.

Ava tried to stay awake afterwards as he stroked her arm with his thumb, afraid to wake the next day and discover it had only been a dream. She cradled her head in the nook of his armpit, her face resting against his warm skin. As his chest rose and fell in waves of breath, she finally fell asleep, realising for the first time in her life how terrifying it was to love.

Conor was sitting on the side of the bed, his back turned towards her, when Ava woke the next morning. For a while she just looked at him, afraid to stir, wanting this moment to last just a little longer. The freckles on his shoulders made her ache for him. When she finally sat up, she rested her head against his bare back and took a deep breath, hoping to inhale his scent, his essence, his entire being.

'Morning,' she said, her voice hoarse from the night before. She kissed his bare shoulder but there was no reply. Instead, he cradled his head in his hands, resting his elbows on his knees.

Perhaps the alcohol was taking its toll. She got up, grabbed the first shirt she could find and pulled it over her head before she went into the kitchen. Orla would probably not be home yet, but just in case she was, Ava did not feel like running into her completely naked. It would bring up a lot of questions – questions she herself still had no answers to.

She filled two more glasses with water and dropped another painkiller in each one. With the fizzing drinks in hand, she re-entered the bedroom. Conor was still sitting in the same position, his face hidden in the palms of his hands.

Ava handed him one of the glasses but he didn't take it, so she put them both on the bedside table beside him. The bliss Ava had felt that morning suddenly dropped into her stomach and turned into dizzying nausea.

'What's wrong?' she asked.

Finally, when Conor looked up to face her, she could see he'd been crying.

What an idiot she had been. She still hadn't told him about James. Desire and alcohol had taken over the night before, and all her resolutions for open communication had gone right out the window.

'I broke up with James. It's okay, we did nothing wrong.'

Conor shook his head. 'I'm so sorry.'

What was he saying? Ava's legs wobbled and panic gripped her heart.

'Why are you sorry?'

All he did was shake his head, another tear rolling down his cheek. And then she understood. It was like the whole world had been pulled from under her, and in order not to fall into the dark void looming below, she crawled onto the bed and propped her back up against the wall. Pulling the duvet up to her chin was all she could do to protect herself from what was to come.

'Conor, talk to me,' she pleaded, unable to keep her voice from cracking.

Conor pushed the heels of his palms into his eyes and took a deep shuddering breath, making Ava brace herself. But nothing happened. He remained silent.

'You have a girlfriend, don't you?' she whispered, her throat closing up at the thought.

Slowly, his head moved. A nod. 'Ava, I'm….'

He didn't need to finish his sentence. She knew the words he was about to say. He would tell her how sorry he was and how it shouldn't have happened and how he should have told her before. She knew, because those were the things she'd told him the year before when she'd been the one with the heartbreaking secret. It was disorienting being on the other end of this, watching him search for words, feeling her own heart shatter on impact.

Ava wanted to run, the way he had, but there was no ocean, no miles of sandy beach where she could escape this nightmare.

Instead, with tears running down her cheeks, she walked out of the room and into the kitchen, where she switched the kettle on. She rinsed out the mug she'd used the day before and added a tea bag, knowing full well she wasn't going to drink it. She just needed something to do other than falling apart. By the time she slumped onto the sofa, her hands wrapped around the steaming mug, she heard the bedroom door open. Ava didn't turn to look when she confronted him with the one question that was burning a hole in her mind.

'Is this some sort of payback for Ireland?' she asked.

'What the fuck?' He walked over to where she was sitting, crouched down in front of her and cradled her face in his hands, shock and disappointment seeping from his eyes. 'Is that who you think I am?' he asked.

'I wouldn't blame you, you know. I suppose I deserve it.' She pulled away, wiping her nose with the back of her hand.

'Ava,' he said firmly. 'Look at me.' He took the mug from her hands and put it on the coffee table beside him.

'Listen very carefully now, okay? I would never do that to you. I have no excuse for what I did so I'm not going to try and apologise. But I need you to know that I would never do anything intentionally to hurt you. Of all the people in my world, Ava, you are the one person…' His voice broke and he closed his eyes. Even closed, they were swollen, his cheeks flushed red and shiny with tears.

Ava pulled her legs to her chest, wrapped her arms around them and rested her head on her knees, unable to face him anymore.

They sat quietly for a long time, with only the sounds of traffic outside and the hum of the fridge breaking the silence.

'Who is she?' Ava asked after some time.

'Ava…'

'No, tell me. I want to know.'

Conor sighed. 'Niamh. Her name's Niamh.'

'How did you meet her?'

'Ave, come on…'

Ava didn't speak but waited for his answer. He owed her that much.

'She was my girlfriend years ago, when I was at uni. She came into the bookshop a few months back…'

Processing the information, Ava nodded. 'Do you love her?'

'Please, don't.'

Fine, maybe she didn't want to hear this.

'Why didn't you tell me?'

A long pause followed, with Conor's eyes closed, as though he could make it all go away if he just didn't look at her. 'Because I didn't want anything to change.'

'Everything has changed, Conor!' She jumped up and made her way to the other side of the room.

'What about James?' she heard Conor mumble. 'You didn't tell me about him.'

In a fury she turned around. 'Are you joking? I broke up with James – that's a very different story, Conor. I didn't have to tell you that.'

Conor buried his face in his hands. 'Feck, I know, you're right. I'm sorry. I shouldn't have said that.'

For a long time they were both silent. Every part of Ava's body ached. The drinks from the night before, mixed with the realisation they always ended up hurting each other, made for an excruciating cocktail.

'Now what?' Conor asked after some time.

'I think we need to stop.'

'Stop what?'

'All of it. We're not good together, Conor. I hurt you, you hurt me… It's not supposed to be like that. I think we need to go our own ways. At least for the foreseeable future.'

'Please, Ava. I don't want to lose you again.'

She shrugged. 'It's too late for that. You have your life in Dublin, I have mine here. Go home, Conor.'

He reached out a hand, but when she didn't take it, he grabbed the few things he'd brought for his stay and put on his shoes. 'What about the pact?' he asked, his voice fragile, desperate.

There were four years between them and the pact, and no way of knowing how she would feel by then.

'No matter what?' His eyes were pleading as he repeated her own words to her.

This time around, she was the one questioning the agreement.

'We'll see.'

18

Standing in front of the bathroom mirror, Olivia wipes the rivulets of mascara from her cheeks. The moment she got home, she grabbed the book from her bedside table and continued to read. Eager to get it over with. For now, nothing unexpected has popped up yet, but it's getting harder and harder to go on. Reliving that fight is something she'd hoped never to have to do. If she'd known back then it would be the last time she'd see Eamonn, she might not have kicked him out. After all, he didn't do anything she hadn't done to him before. Is that why he didn't show?

It can't possibly explain Graham's need for her to find out the truth. This is still very much in line with her recollection of the events. With a defeated sigh, she splashes cold water into her face and then the buzz of her phone in the adjacent bedroom alerts her to an incoming WhatsApp message. She grabs a towel, dips two fingers into a tub of Nivea Soft and, rubbing cream into her cheeks, she returns to bed to check the message.

Made it to the warehouse. You still up?

Olivia hits the camera button next to his name, and gets under the covers. Almost instantly, Graham's tired eyes appear on the screen.

'Hey.' His voice echoes in the nearly empty room.

'How was the flight?'

He rubs at his eyes and yawns. 'Not great. And the party?'

'Fine. Anna and I went for a walk.'

An awkward silence passes between them.

'What time is it there?' he asks.

'Midnight.'

Graham nods as though he just received a crucial piece of information, and then there's more silence. They both know where the conversation inevitably has to go, but neither seems to be willing to tip the equilibrium just yet.

'How's the flat?' Olivia asks, stalling for time.

'Still mostly empty.' Graham turns his camera and shows her the room. It's as she remembers it when they last visited, except now there's an old, cream-coloured sofa and an ancient dining set standing awkwardly in the middle of the open space, courtesy of Graham's mum. When she found out he was arriving a week earlier, she made sure he had at least a few things to make it through the week.

'Is there a bed, too?' Olivia asks.

'Something like that.'

With the camera still facing forwards, he walks Olivia to a corner of the open space. 'Look at this beauty.' On the floor there's a single mattress, a duvet with an image of a headless dinosaur draped over it, giving the impression that the person lying under the covers has the body of a T-rex.

Olivia can't help but giggle. 'Please get under the covers.'

Graham turns the camera again to show his surprised face. 'Are you into dinosaurs?'

'Only those with the face of a middle-aged man who's just been on a nine-hour flight.'

'Niche. I like it. You won't be able to see though – I can't reach that far.'

Olivia juts out her lower lip. 'Sad. Will you keep it until I get there?'

His eyebrows rise ever so slightly at the mention of her arrival and a loaded pause fills the digital space between them. After a beat he clears his throat. 'Have you finished the book?'

Olivia shakes her head. 'Almost.'

'Are you going to?'

'Why do you want me to? Are you trying to push me away?'

A sad frown. 'You really think I want that?'

'I don't know? I just really don't understand it.'

'Look, Livvie, I don't want you to read it. Trust me, if I could, I'd make the damn book disappear. But I can't. It's out there and one way or another, you'll find out, and it might change everything. I'd rather have you read it now and make your decision before I build an entire life with you here.'

'Graham…' Tears burn behind her eyes, making her nose sting.

'I don't want to upset you, Livvie. I want you to be as happy as you can be.'

'I *am* happy with you.'

His smile is soft, hopeful. 'Okay. Then we have nothing to worry about, do we?'

They end the call with promises to ring again the next day. Olivia wipes at her cheeks as salty tears roll down them. Her chest aches with fear of doing the wrong thing. It seems impossible she could ever question her love for Graham, but when she saw Eamonn the other day, her bleeding heart spilled over with love for him too. There's no way around it. She loves them both and maybe she always will. With a heavy heart, she picks up the book again. Five more chapters. And then what?

Wild Waves
Chapter 25 - May 2011

Conor was studying for his upcoming exam on contemporary Irish literature with Niamh at the other end of the table proofreading a manuscript, her highlighter scratching across the pages. Ever since Jack had started his own IT company and set up his office at home, Conor had been doing the bulk of his studying at Niamh's. Her roommates were rarely in and if they were, you'd have to try your best to catch a glimpse of them. It was a peaceful place to work, and Niamh's work ethic tended to rub off on him.

Six months had gone by since his trip to London and each one of those days, Conor had debated the merit of telling Niamh what happened. Obviously, she deserved to know, but telling her would hurt her so much, it seemed like another selfish thing to do. He'd promised not to break her heart, and yet that's exactly what he'd be doing if he confessed. It wouldn't fix anything, only relieve some of his guilt, and frankly he didn't deserve to be relieved of that.

And they were doing well – they had found a comfortable rhythm that worked for both of them. As long as he didn't think about Ava, everything was just fine. With enough time and distance, his feelings for her would fade anyway. Until they were nothing but a bittersweet memory.

The afternoon sunlight warmed Conor's face. He put down his book and stretched his arms over his head. 'How much work do you have left to do?' he asked.

'A bit. Why?'

'I could eat.'

'Ooh me too, actually. Can you order us something?'

'Sure, yeah. Pizza okay?'

'Mmmm,' she agreed, without looking up. When Niamh was working it was hard to distract her, even with food. Conor had rarely seen anyone work with the same dedication as her. He smiled and got up to grab his phone from the kitchen counter. When he came back after placing the orders, Niamh put down her highlighter and looked him in the eye.

'I think we should get a place together,' she said. 'You're here most of the time anyway. And then at least we wouldn't have to share with other people anymore.'

Conor's stomach flipped. As per usual, this was not an impulse decision. Niamh had thought things through. And although, theoretically, her arguments were valid, Conor was still taken aback. Having a key to her place and living together full-time were two very different commitments.

'Okay...' he said, pulling back the chair opposite her, softly nodding his head. 'You know I still have some time left at uni, right?'

'Yeah, I know, but that doesn't really matter now, does it? You have to pay rent either way.'

She was right, but this was such a sudden proposal, Conor needed more time to think about it. If he was being honest, it hadn't really crossed his mind yet.

His silence didn't go unnoticed.

'Conor, we've been together over a year now, for the second time, so technically two years, and we're twenty-seven. If we're not ready now, I don't think we'll ever be.' Niamh leaned back in her chair, awaiting his answer. 'Well?'

'Sorry, you're right,' he said, reaching out to take hold of her hand. 'You just caught me off guard there. I hadn't really thought about it yet, but yeah, I'd like to not have to share a shower with your roommates anymore.'

Niamh smiled but Conor wasn't sure he'd convinced her of his intentions.

'Really,' he added. 'Let's do it. It'll be grand.'

'Yeah?'

'Definitely.'

This time her smile was more convincing. 'When the food gets here, I want to show you a few places I've come across.'

Of course she'd gone through rent.ie already. Conor couldn't suppress a laugh. 'Oh, so you've already found some places?'

'Sure, look, I figured it would be a good time now. With the new academic year coming up in a couple of months, it'll be easier to rent out our own rooms.'

'Right. Good thinking.'

'Are you mocking me?'

'I would never.'

Niamh threw one of her markers at his head, hitting him right on the nose.

'Ouch!'

She shrugged and returned to her work, a satisfactory grin on her face.

Conor turned his attention back to his notes, but his mind quickly became overcrowded with conflicting thoughts. He glanced over his book at Niamh, her eyes swiftly scanning the pages in front of her, now and then putting the highlighter to use. What would it be like to live together, to share the same space every day? In a way he knew it would be okay – of all the people close to him, he was certain Niamh was herself, always. There would be no discoveries of off-putting character traits, no disgusting little habits he hadn't found out about yet. Niamh never hid from the world, – she was who she was. But what about her expectations? Did she not deserve to know the real man she was moving in with?

The doorbell rang, announcing the delivery of the pizzas and momentarily snapping Conor from his thoughts. Later that night, however, when Niamh showed him the viewings she'd booked for the upcoming weekend, the unease settled in the pit of his stomach, begging for attention. This was going to be a lot more complicated than he'd hoped for.

Niamh being Niamh, she'd managed to find three places, all within a thirty-minute commute to her office and the university. Not only that, she'd scheduled the visits back-to-back in the same afternoon in order for them to compare the pros and cons more effectively afterwards. The first flat had seemed quite spacious on the website. The ad boasted about a recently renovated bathroom, a fully equipped kitchen, a large master bedroom and a smaller guest room.

When they arrived in front of the building and looked up, they turned to each other with questioning looks. The pouring rain however didn't allow them to linger and worry about what lay behind its dilapidated exterior. Fortunately the door was left ajar, and so they stepped inside, joining the estate agent in the hallway, his white shirt stained with specks of rain. There was so much Brylcreem in the man's hair, a few raindrops glided off it, catching Conor's eye. The man bared his recently bleached teeth in an attempt at a welcoming smile, introduced himself as John, shook their hands and invited them to follow him down the stairs.

The basement flat was nothing like they'd imagined. It smelled musty – the air was so damp, Conor wondered if someone had just had a shower. There was old carpeting on the floors, and the tiny windows in the living area barely let any daylight in. The estate agent told them it might need a splash of paint here and there, but that it was an excellent flat for a young couple starting out. Behind his back, Conor and Niamh rolled their eyes at each other.

'Thanks for the tour,' Niamh said. 'We have a couple more places to see today, but we'll be in touch.' She reached out her hand to shake his. Always the professional.

The man gave them his business card and warned them to act fast, as a place like that would not stay on the market for long.

They closed the door behind them and Niamh let out a loud laugh. 'Not on the market for long… Yeah, if the health inspection comes around, it won't.'

'So, not this one?' Conor asked.

The other two viewings were a lot nicer. The second place even had hardwood floors and a small but newly installed kitchen. It wasn't big, but there were loads of windows letting in a ton of light and they both instantly fell in love with it. By the end of the day they'd made another appointment, this time to sign the lease for their new home.

'Are you excited?'

Conor nodded. 'I am.'

Perhaps this was his chance at a fresh start.

'We should celebrate,' Niamh said.

Conor checked his watch.

'Not now, though,' she continued before he could say anything. 'I have a couple of things I need to do for work. But later tonight?'

'Grand, yeah. I think I might head back to my place then, catch up on some reading.'

'Good. Come over to mine when you're ready.'

She wrapped her arms around his neck and kissed him. 'I'm really glad we're doing this.'

'Me too,' he said.

Even though Conor was looking forward to their move in a way, it was all happening really fast and a slight panic was building in his chest. Instead of taking the bus back to Jack's, he decided to walk it off, hoping that would do the trick.

The rain had stopped and the smell of spring was all around him. As he passed the red brick houses with their colourful doors, he tried to picture him and Niamh living together. There were so many wonderful things about her: her ambition, her discipline, her courage. She was incredibly intelligent and someone he could depend on. And yet, something gnawed at him. He loved being with her, but did he love *her*? And was it enough to spend the rest of his life with her? Some would say a great friendship is enough for a lifelong relationship, but Conor wasn't so sure. Perhaps he'd been reading too many novels, watching too many films. Those stories always stop when things get real. When the star-crossed lovers move in together and have to go to work, pay the bills and put the bins out. When they see each other every day, when they run out of things to say, when the romance is gone and the rose-coloured glasses come off.

But what if the glasses have never been rose-coloured enough to begin with? What happens then?

Conor's mind travelled back to London, standing in front of the photo Ava had taken of him. When he'd opened his eyes, he'd been flooded with this warmth, this knowing. There he had seen the love he wanted to feel now, portrayed in a photograph. He'd been at a complete loss for words, looking at himself and his image seen through her eyes.

Ava.

No matter how much he tried to put her out of his thoughts, he still remembered that night after the gig as though it'd only just happened. For a long time he'd tried to keep the memory down, but it was like pushing a ball under water: it required all of his energy and focus, and now, as he considered his life with Niamh, that ball popped back up with an undeniable force, proving the endeavour impossible.

This had to stop. There was no future for him and Ava. She had her life in London, he had his in Dublin.

And now he was moving in with Niamh.

The complexity of it all pressed down on his chest, panic swelling more and more. He picked up speed until sweat dripped from his temples. By the time he arrived home, his light blue T-shirt had turned into a dark one.

'Have you been running?' Jack asked incredulously as Conor swung open the door. Jack was putting on his coat and studied Conor as he kicked off his shoes. Still out of breath and unable to speak, Conor nodded.

'I thought you and Niamh were checking out flats together?'

'We were,' he panted.

'That bad, huh?' he said jokingly, unaware of how accurate his joke was.

Conor didn't respond, hoping his shortness of breath would be interpreted as the reason.

'So, did you find anything?' Jack continued.

'Uh-huh.'

'Good for you. Tell us about it later when I get back, will ya? I'm just meeting some people for a drink now.'

Conor promised he would and released a sigh of relief when Jack closed the door behind him.

With Jack gone, he considered getting the bus to Seapoint for some clarity, but there wasn't enough time.

Then for his other coping mechanism: writing. He grabbed a notepad from his desk, moved to his bed, and with his pillow propped up between him and the wall, he began to write.

When his mam had died, he had so many things he wanted to tell her but no way of doing so. Journalling seemed pointless at the time and so instead, he started writing her letters. 'Void letters' he would call them, the ones he would never send but that helped him process things, get things off his chest, like screaming into the void. When he learned how well they worked, he started addressing them to other people as well, like Ava, for example. He'd started the night she told him about James and hadn't really stopped since. All the pain he'd felt then, raw and unedited, he'd put down on paper. As time went by, the hurt faded and his letters to her changed, but they were always real and honest. It felt somewhat comforting telling her what it was like being the oldest guy in class and yet feeling inferior to his fellow students. How he was struggling with his dad dating this other woman who wasn't his mother. How he missed his mother, but also how he sometimes forgot about her and how guilty that made him feel. How terrified he was of his father dying, the inevitability of it creeping up on him in the middle of the night sometimes, robbing the air from his lungs.

Sometimes his letters were nothing more than him telling her how much he missed her, how he longed to see her and feel the touch of her skin on his. They were short letters, but just the act of writing it down would relieve some of the pressure building inside. Like the tension in his chest now. It needed to go somewhere, before it could do any real damage. Best put it to paper.

> *Bruce,*
> *I'm struggling. For a long time I've tried to forget about you and at times I've succeeded. Or at least succeeded at tricking myself into believing it. But today, all of that, all of us, caught up with me. No matter if I close my eyes or keep them wide open, it's you I see. You're everywhere and still completely out of my reach. I feel restless with the urge to be with you and I hate myself for it. I hate you for it. But you know I don't, really.*
> *Today, Niamh and I signed a lease. We're moving in together…*
> *We're moving in together…*
> *Fuck, we're moving in together…*
> *Why aren't WE moving in together, Bruce?*
> *Would you?*

He chewed on the back of his pen and stared at the wall, his notepad resting in his lap. If he had asked her to move in with him, would she have? Would she have come to Dublin with him until he finished uni? There was no way of knowing. It was too late.

Right?

A thought formed in his mind and his heart rate quickened. But it was insane. He couldn't possibly.

Right?

As though entirely involuntary, his hand moved across the page.

Ava, I'm sorry for hurting you when I came to London but I'm not sorry for what happened. And I know I said I would leave you alone, but I can't. I need to know if you'll give me one last chance. I'm not sure there's much of a point to life without you in it.
If you feel the same, please give me a call when you get this. If not, I will respect that and you won't hear from me again.
C x

He folded the sheet of paper, slid it in an envelope and licked the sides of the flap. Before he could change his mind he wrote down her address, added a stamp and put on his jacket. The postbox was only a five-minute walk down the road – two if he ran. And he did.

19

'What the fuck?'

The book falls from her hands and tumbles to the floor, but it hardly registers.

'What the fuck!'

He sent her a letter? Dazed, she picks up the book and turns back to the last page to read it again. And one more time. And then another time. But the longer she sits with it, the more confused she becomes. The thought of him having written that letter and her never receiving it makes the bile rise in her throat. Could this be a fictional part of the book? It almost has to be. There's no other logical explanation for this. She would've known by now if it had really happened. Right? Even if it had got lost in the post? Someone would've told her by now.

Olivia closes her eyes and focuses on her breath. In and out. In and out. In and out. But to no avail. Her heart is still racing, her mind running a million miles an hour, trying to explain this inexplicable thing.

Why would he write a book about the pact if he's the one who left me stranded?

And then, just like that, the truth presents itself like the moon and sun parting ways after an eclipse – slowly, leaving dark shadows in its wake.

He didn't leave me stranded. None of this is fiction. I'm the one who broke his heart.

To think everything could have been different, everything could *be* different, is overwhelmingly dizzying. A life that could've been flashes before her eyes.

If she'd got that letter, she would've called him. She would've said *don't move in with her*, she would've said *I don't remember why we're not together*, and he would've said *okay* and *I don't remember either*, and they would've figured something out so he could finish uni and she could continue exhibiting her work at the arts centre, and they would've been in love and then he would've graduated and they would've found a place to live together, and they would've been so happy, and years later, on the day of the pact, they would've gone to Ballybridge, just for the hell of it, just to honour their word, even though they knew they never needed a pact to be together in the first place, because they were in love, and they would still be in love five years later, and another five, and another five.

If she had got that letter.

But she never did.

And the obvious reason why is more painful to observe than the blinding sun itself.

Wild Waves
Chapter 26

'Are you excited?' Ava, dressed and ready for work, was leaning in the doorway, observing Orla's frantic hair styling endeavours.

'If by excited, you mean, do I want to boke and scream and run very far away from all of this, like? then yes, I am very excited,' Orla replied matter-of-factly.

Ava laughed and wrapped her arm around Orla's shoulder.

'Oh come on, you can do this. It's just you and Matt, like it's always been just you and Matt. Nothing's changed there.'

'I suppose.' Orla untied her thick curly hair, shook it loose and then tied it up again in a bun.

'What time's he getting here?'

'Around twelve.'

'Are you picking him up at the airport?'

Orla shook her head. 'No, he's meeting me at the zoo.'

'The zoo? Why on earth are you going to the zoo?'

'Because I figured if we go there, we'll always have something to talk about.'

'Because…?'

'Because animals are funny and they have the power to save me from awkward silences. Also, we'd be in public and walking side by side. That means I won't have to look him in the eye when we're talking.'

'And here I was thinking romance was dead.'

'Don't mock me. This is the best I can do at the moment.' Orla's desperate eyes found Ava's through the mirror.

'Sorry, I'm not mocking, I just think you might be overthinking this a bit. You two have been friends for over twenty years and you saw him over Christmas. I think you'll be fine. Matt loves you.'

'First of all, Christmas was in the pub with loads of people, and secondly, ugh, don't say that.'

'Sorry. He doesn't love you. He hates you. You're his worst nightmare.'

Orla turned to look at her. 'Seriously, woman.'

Ava laughed. 'Sorry, babes. Do you want me to come with you?'

'No, you're grand. I think I've tortured him enough now, poor fella.' She cocked her head in the mirror, growled and untied her hair once again.

'Oh, so spending time with me is torture, is it?'

'Well...' Orla started.

Ava put a hand up to silence her. 'Hush, woman. I don't need this abuse. I have plenty of that at work. Speaking of...' She checked the time on her phone and put it back in her handbag.

'I'm off. Good luck, have fun, call me if you need me to leave work urgently.'

'Thanks, love. I doubt that'll be necessary, like.'

'No, seriously, please call me to leave work. Please Orla, please, I don't think I can do it,' Ava pleaded desperately into Orla's ear, squeezing her tightly.

'You're messing up my hair.'

'Wow... so much for friendship,' she said, walking backwards out of the room, shaking her head incredulously. Right before she left the flat, she shouted: 'You'd better hope this thing with Matt works out, because you'll be looking for a place to live real soon.'

Something heavy hit the door just as Ava closed it behind her.

'Feck off!' Orla shouted after her.

'Love you too!'

Ava's reluctance to go into the office turned out to be well-founded. Uncle Richard was on another power trip and she was once again his victim of choice. She'd known it the moment she approached him. He was leaning back in his chair, chest puffed, hands folded behind his head, elbows spread out as widely as possible. Had he taken some kind of class in power poses, or had he seen one too many documentaries on gorillas? It wasn't clear, but either way, he looked ridiculous.

Ava immediately regretted going in there, but she had a question about an upcoming company event, and he was the only one with the answer.

By the time she'd sat back down behind her own desk a mere five minutes later, he'd not only given her an answer but also three new tasks, a headache and the last push she needed to make a decision.

On her lunch break Ava grabbed her phone and went for a walk. When she was far enough away from the building and not likely to run into any of her colleagues, she dialled Iman's number. On the third ring, she picked up. 'Hello?'

'Iman, hi, it's me, Ava.'

'Ava, to what do I owe the pleasure?'

She could hear Iman's smile through the phone. 'I was wondering if your offer still stands?'

There was a beat of silence on the other end.

'Uhm… Yes, it does, but why the sudden change of heart?'

'Because you're right. I've waited too long. I'm done with all of this. Something needs to change.'

'Ah, the magic words. You're a hundred per cent sure? 'Cause other people are interested. I'd rather it be you, but then I need to know now.'

'Yes, two hundred per cent. It's going to be me.'
'Fantastic. I'll draw up the paperwork.'
Ava let out a deep sigh. 'Thanks, Iman. You won't regret it.'
'I know I won't.'
'I have to go now. I'll pop in tonight to sign the contract.'
'Great. Bye, babes.'
'Bye!' Ava hung up and crouched down for a second to regain composure. Step one was done. Now for step two.

She returned to her desk with a clear head and a newfound sense of purpose. From her drawer she retrieved a notepad and pen and began writing. After two badly written drafts, she finally finished the perfect letter, made a copy and headed for Uncle Dickhead's office.

'What's this?' he asked, looking at the sheet of paper as if she'd just served him with anthrax.

'My letter of resignation. I'm leaving,' Ava said, with a steadiness to her voice she hadn't known she was capable of. The old Ava would've been shaking in her boots, but perhaps she'd been pushed so far – her fear of confrontation had become irrelevant. Torture will do that to people.

'Excuse me?' Uncle Richard said, looking bewildered.

'I've found another job. This is my resignation letter,' she repeated. Maybe in a different order, the words would make sense to him. He gave her a baffled look as if he still hadn't heard her properly.

'I know I need to give two weeks' notice, but I still have about five weeks' worth of overtime, so I suggest we make a deal: I won't ask you to pay me for the three extra weeks if you'll agree this is my last day in the office.'

His expression turned from bewilderment to shock at her audaciousness.

'Excuse me?' he said again, clearly at a loss for words. Ava wondered when he'd last been put on the spot like that. Judging by the look on his face, probably never. She wanted this conversation to be over as soon as possible and so she continued: 'I'll finish the things I was working on this afternoon and I'll leave a detailed list of instructions for the next person.'

He stared at her for a while in silence, his mouth slightly agape. She could see he was trying to think of ways to object, but he knew full well she was within her rights and he had no legal way of stopping her.

'What are you going to do, then?' he finally asked, his voice shaky with hostility.

'I'm going to run an arts centre with a friend of mine.'

He scoffed and rolled his eyes. 'You're giving up a well-paid, reputable job to go and play around, are you?'

When he put it like that, she couldn't help but smile.

'I suppose I am.'

Uncle Richard laughed an unhappy laugh, signed her resignation papers and tossed a copy in her direction.

'Don't bother finishing anything. You can pack your things and leave.'

Now it was Ava's turn to be surprised. She'd known him to be a petty man, but she'd at least thought he would make her finish the things she was working on.

'Oh okay, well, goodbye then,' she said.

He didn't reply, nor did he look at her. Ava's face flushed as she closed the door behind her, still not completely immune to the stress of a hostile confrontation. With slightly shaky hands, she gathered the few personal items she had lying around, stuffed them in a tote bag and got in the lift for the very last time.

Once outside, Ava wanted to scream and dance – do something to release the overdose of adrenaline rushing through her veins. She'd never done anything this impulsive and impactful before. The first person she wanted to tell was Orla, but she didn't want to interrupt her date with Matt, so calling her was out of the question. At some point in the very near future she would have to tell her dad, if he hadn't already heard. Even though he wasn't a massive fan of Uncle Richard's either, she imagined his reaction would not be a particularly pleasant one. And so, that conversation would have to wait. There were only so many uncomfortable confrontations she could have in one day.

For a split second Conor came to mind, but she slammed that thought down with the force of a hammer hitting a carnival bell. Her life was finally going in the direction she wanted; she did not need more complications from Conor.

Instead, she bounded towards the tube and rang the one person who'd rooted for her from the start.

'I quit!' she squealed, the moment Kate picked up the phone. A group of tourists walking by glanced at her, one woman giving her an encouraging smile. She clearly understood how Ava felt.

'You what?'

Ava told her the whole story and when Kate squealed with joy, the final kernels of doubt dissipated.

'I'm so proud of you, sis. I knew you'd get there in the end.'

'Thanks. Do you think Dad's going to kill me?'

'If he finds the time in between being important and making money.'

'So no, then.'

'We need to celebrate! Do you want to come over? You have some time now, don't you?'

Ava stopped at the entrance of the underground station. 'Well, I could come up, but, uhm…'

She didn't have to say his name. Kate understood immediately what she was talking about.

'Right. Let me see if I can arrange something at work, and I'll come and see you, okay?'

Ava's heart flooded with love for her big sister. Even though Conor was probably in Dublin, Kate understood the emotional ramifications of Ava coming to Ballybridge.

'Thanks for putting up with me all these years,' Ava said.

'I'm just glad you're finding your way, love.'

When she returned to the flat after signing the contract, she heard voices coming from the living room. Cautious not to break up a private moment between Matt and Orla, she announced her arrival by making an extensive amount of noise, rattling her keys and slamming the door like a drunk trying very hard to be quiet.

'Hello, hello, hello!' she added for safety.

'Hiya Ave, we're in here.'

Ava made her way to the living room, where Matt and Orla were on the sofa, Matt sat upright, Orla sprawled out, her feet in his lap, his hand around her ankle. Ava's heart melted when she saw them.

'Hey Matt! Long time no see.' She went to give him a hug, leaning over the sofa so he wouldn't have to get up. 'How's it going?'

'Pretty good, yeah.' His smile was wide. Ava could barely contain her enthusiasm and gave the two of them a big grin. 'This is great, guys. I mean. It really, really is!'

'Ava…' Orla warned.

'It just is. That's all,' she said, shrugging and holding her hands up in the air as if it was all out of her control.

Matt laughed. 'How was work? Orla tells me you want to murder your uncle?'

She was so excited about the two of them, it wasn't until Matt's comment that she remembered the massive day she'd just had.

'Oh, it was great!'

Orla's eyebrows shot up and so Ava continued. 'Guess what I did today?'

'I don't know. You made a spreadsheet?' Orla said.

The satisfaction she was getting from this guessing game was almost as good as the quitting had been. She shook her head.

'You actually killed your uncle?' Orla continued, going off Ava's silence.

'Something like that.' Ava's grin hurt her cheeks.

'For fuck's sake, Ava, can you just tell us.'

She waited another second for dramatic effect and then screamed: 'I QUIT MY JOB!'

Orla jumped up from the sofa, accidentally kicking Matt in the gut.

'Ouch!'

Orla waved his complaint away, and turned her focus to Ava. 'What in the actual fuck?! You didn't?'

'I did!'

'No way!'

'Yes way!'

'OH MY GOD Ava, that's amazing! How, when, whaaaat?' Orla grabbed hold of Ava's hands as they jumped around like two toddlers on a trampoline, all while Matt just watched them calmly from the sofa, smiling.

'Congrats, Ave. Well done,' he said. 'I've heard some stories about your uncle and I'm pretty sure you made the right decision there. How did he react?'

Out of breath from all the jumping up and down, Ava let go of Orla's hands and planted herself in the armchair opposite the sofa, resting her legs on the coffee table.

'Well, this was obviously not the plan when I went into work this morning. Did I want to go to work? No. Does anyone really ever want to go to work?'

Matt opened his mouth to say something, but Orla nudged him in the ribs. Boy, were they adorable together.

'Anyway, I was working on the company's 50th anniversary event and I needed to get the list of approved hotels, because God forbid they would have to stay in a hotel that doesn't serve venison, and so I went into his office and he was sitting there again, doing absolutely fuck all except for practising his favourite power poses and so, I tried not to roll my eyes at him and I asked him for the list…'

Ava paused to take a deep breath in order to continue her rant. Across from her, Orla had settled down on the sofa again, this time leaning into Matt as he wrapped his arm around her shoulder.

'And then,' Ava continued, 'he asked me how I was managing, with the event and all. Ha, I can't believe I actually fell for it again. You'd think I would have learned by now… I told him I was struggling a bit because I had plenty of other things to do as well, you know?'

Matt and Orla nodded.

'And then…' Ava paused, breaking into laughter, unable to finish her sentence.

'And then?' Orla asked.

'Then…' She started again as soon as her laughing fit had died down. 'He gave me three new jobs, on top of everything else I was already doing.' The laughter returned, a lot more hysterical this time. Orla joined in but Matt arched his eyebrows.

'This fella must be joking, no?' he said, shaking his head incredulously.

'You'd think that, wouldn't you?' Ava said. 'I went back to my office then, my head pounding, my stomach churning. I looked at my stack of paperwork and I knew I was done.'

Ava's laughter died down as the sadness of her old life dawned on her.

'I'm twenty-five and I wake up every morning feeling more exhausted than the night before. I long for Fridays but every time I make it to the end of the week, I'm already dreading the next Monday. This is no way of living my life.'

'No, it's not,' Orla agreed.

'So on my lunch break I called Iman.' Ava noticed the questioning look on Matt's face. 'She's the woman who runs the centre around the corner, where I have some of my photos on display.'

Matt nodded.

'So, I called her…'

Now the look on Orla's face demanded an explanation. She opened her mouth but before she could speak, Ava put her hand up.

'Calm down, Orla. I called her, and not you, because a couple of weeks ago she'd offered me a job.'

Orla's jaw dropped. 'What? You never told me about this.'

'No, I didn't because I knew you would've told me to take it.'

'I…' she started but Matt shot her a look and she went quiet again.

'And you would have been right, Orla, but I wasn't ready then.'

Orla turned to Matt now with a smug smile on her face. He shook his head but gave her a gentle nudge.

'Today, however, I was so fed up with it all that I called her and asked if the job was still available. The centre's been doing really well lately and it's no longer possible to just have volunteers run it. I'll be Iman's second and mostly handle the day-to-day operations.' Ava's stomach twirled at the prospect of her future plans.

'Oh my God, you rock my world!' Orla exclaimed, eyes wide with amazement.

'That's one hell of a day,' Matt said. 'Congrats though. You did well.'

'Yeah,' Ava sighed, now feeling the reality of it all sink in properly. For a couple of seconds they were all silent, processing the information.

'We should celebrate!' Orla jumped up again and went straight for the kitchen. 'Who wants red?'

'Not me,' Matt said. 'I have to get going – the play starts at half eight but we're going for burgers first.'

Ava had suggested Matt could spend the night on the sofa when Orla had told her about their plan to meet up, but Orla had been hesitant. It was their first time spending proper time alone together since they met briefly around Christmas in the pub, and Orla had decided to play it safe for the time being. So Matt was staying with his cousin and apparently also seeing a play with him.

'No worries,' Ava said. 'Have a good night and I'll see you tomorrow.'

She gave Matt a hug and, right before she let go, whispered in his ear: 'I'm so happy for you.' The smile on his face when she let go was louder than words.

He walked off into the kitchen, where he said goodbye to Orla. Ava could hear them making arrangements for the next day and then there was silence. Her heart flooded with warmth for the two of them. She waited patiently until she finally heard the last goodbye and the sound of the door closing behind Matt. Orla reappeared in the sitting room, trying to keep a straight face but at seeing Ava's enormous grin, burst out laughing.

'You look like you're having a fit.'

'Can I be really excited now?' Ava asked.

Orla nodded vigorously, prompting Ava to pull her in for an intense bear hug.

'Oh Orla, I'm so happy for you. I want to hear everything.'

'There's not all that much to tell, though.'

'I don't care. Just make it up then!'

Orla uncorked the bottle of wine and generously poured its contents into two big glasses.

'Soooo…' Orla began, taking a sip and making Ava wait just a few seconds longer. 'I was waiting for him at Regent's Park, just by the entrance to the zoo, and I thought my whole body was going to crumble with anxiety. It was completely overwhelming and I had no idea how I would ever survive the entire afternoon. I kept trying to reason with myself, muttering encouraging and less encouraging things under my breath, looking like a drunk, probably, but it wasn't working at all, like.'

Ava nodded, not completely sure if she understood the intensity of Orla's anxiety, but sympathetic to the nerves of a first date nonetheless.

'I was about to run again, but then he was suddenly there and as soon as I saw him, my body relaxed. It was weird, all the anxiety just melted away. He was just Matt and I was just Orla and we were just us. Exactly like you said. And like… I don't know. Nothing else really mattered.' She shrugged like she had nothing to add to that, like she couldn't even explain it properly. Ava took a big gulp of wine just so she wouldn't audibly swoon.

'We walked around the zoo for a bit and then I don't know, all of a sudden I felt the need to hold his hand and so I did. I could tell he was happy but he was so calm. I think he did that for me, to be fair. Like he didn't want me to feel pressured or anything.'

'Oh God, this is so beautiful, Orla.' Ava let out a deep sigh, pulled her legs up to her chest and rested her chin on her knees. 'What happened next?' she asked.

'We talked a lot and about basically everything and then we walked back to the flat. I asked him up and we had coffee and some pastries we bought along the way.'

Ava's eyes widened in anticipation, making Orla laugh.

'And then?'

'Then he asked me to play him "The Road to Us", so I got my guitar out and played it for him. You should've seen him, Ave. He was so beautiful in that moment, I immediately wanted to write another song just about his face.'

Ava clasped her hand to her heart and made an *ooooob* sound.

'And then he asked if he could kiss me. He said he didn't want to push me and if I wasn't ready I could just say so and he would wait …'

'Jezus, Orla… I can't.' Ava sighed. 'What did you say?'

'Nothing. I put my guitar to the side and leaned in and then I kissed him and I wondered why it had taken me so long to do it, because it was the most beautiful feeling ever. Jayzus, I can't believe how many times I've used the word beautiful now. What have I become?'

The love on Orla's face was undeniable, and Ava's chest swelled with a joy she had rarely felt before. To see your best friend this happy was nothing short of exhilarating.

'Oh Orla, I'm so intensely proud of you. You deserve this so much and it's just *beautiful* seeing you like this,' Ava smiled.

'What a day, eh?' Orla emptied her glass with one big gulp.

'Fucking hell, yeah.'

Two more glasses of wine and endless questions about one another's milestones later, they called it a night.

'Goodnight, love. I'm proud of you,' Orla said, hugging Ava tightly.

'And I, you.'

Wild Waves
Chapter 27

The morning of the housewarming party, Matt helped Conor move his last things from Jack's while Niamh got the place ready for their guests. When Matt picked him up in his old Volvo, he was met with the sound of The Beatles coming through the speakers. As a massive fan, his CD collection in the car never changed. For as long as Conor could remember, the same five albums had been playing on rotation, and this time *Revolver* sounded through the speakers.

'If it isn't Mr McCartney,' Conor said as he got in the passenger seat.

'Absolute legend.' Matt waited for Conor to secure his seatbelt before he took off.

'Would you mind stopping at Dunnes for some more drinks and snacks on our way back?' Conor asked.

'Yeah, sure, no worries. First over to Jack's, right?'

Conor nodded. 'Yeah, last couple of boxes.'

'It's finally happening, is it? How are you feeling?' Matt asked, turning to Conor to study his facial expression. They were stopped in front of a red light, somewhere at the tail end of a long queue, the rhythmic swoosh of the windshield wipers mixing perfectly with the strings on 'Eleanor Rigby'.

'Good, yeah,' Conor said.

Matt just stared and said nothing as they moved up a few cars in the queue. Two more red lights later, they were driving again and the rain had stopped somewhere along the way.

'Can I ask something?' Matt said.

'If you have to.' Conor sensed where this conversation was going. He'd hoped Matt would not broach the subject, but he should've known it was inevitable.

'Do you think it's a good idea, you moving in with Niamh?'

Conor was looking out the window at the oncoming traffic. He closed his eyes for a split second. 'I do. It's a logical next step.'

'Logic. Sure. That's a starting point, I suppose,' Matt replied, running his hand through his hair.

'What do you want me to say?'

'I'm sorry, Conor, but you and logic are two things I wouldn't usually put together.'

There was a long pause but then Matt continued: 'Have you heard anything from Ava?'

Conor had told Matt about his visit to London. He knew he'd had no other option but to tell him everything. Matt and Orla were now officially together, and he was sure the news would find him either way. But he really regretted that decision now. Did Matt know about the letter? Conor couldn't be sure. He wasn't even sure the letter had reached its destination. Orla hadn't spoken to him since he'd left Ava broken-hearted in London, and Ava had never replied, never even acknowledged the existence of the letter. It had been nine weeks since he sent it, and not a word. She was probably living her best life without him, and he couldn't blame her.

'No. That's in the past,' he said.

'Who'd you rather move in with, Ava or Niamh?' Matt traded his good cop routine for a more direct approach.

Conor scoffed, frustration building. 'Can we talk about something else?' he asked.

They had arrived at Jack's and Matt pulled over. He switched off the ignition and turned to Conor. 'Look, I know I'm being an absolute dick, but I honestly think you're making a mistake and I wouldn't be your friend if I didn't tell you. You can't be moving in with Niamh and then changing your mind. I mean, you can, but Niamh deserves better than that. If you have feelings for someone else, you shouldn't be doing this. It's not fair, Conor.'

How could he make him stop talking?

'I haven't spoken to Ava in months – you probably know more about her than I do. Moving in with her is not an option, so why would I even think about that? Ava and I are done. It's in the past. I'm done living in the past, Matt. Niamh is fab, she's clever, she's funny and she knows what she wants. We have a good thing going here and to be fair, we've practically been living together anyway, so I don't see what the big deal here is,' he let out in one long breath.

Matt looked at him, the lack of conviction clear from his gaze. 'Do you love her?'

'Oh, will you lay off?' Conor released his seatbelt from the clasp and threw open the car door, leaving Matt behind softly shaking his head.

With the exception of Matt, Jack, Sadie and Julia, everyone else at the housewarming party was either a colleague or a friend of Niamh's. Conor watched her chatting away, laughing and dancing and getting slightly tipsy, her enthusiasm infecting everyone around her. Every so often she came to find him, slung her arm around his neck and asked him if he was having a good time. He would reassure her and she'd kiss him, leaving behind her sweet perfume as she returned to her friends.

As Conor had expected, Julia and Sadie were the last to leave. When they finally closed the door behind them, Conor and Niamh collapsed onto the sofa, Niamh resting her head on Conor's shoulder. The living room was a mess, with empty glasses and bottles, half-eaten bags of crisps and pizza boxes everywhere. A forgotten coat was draped over the mustard-coloured IKEA chair, waiting for its owner to return. Niamh scanned the room, assessing the damage. She wouldn't be able to go to bed like this, no matter how wrecked she was.

'You want to clean this up now, don't you?' he asked.

She turned to him and gave him a sweet smile. 'Do you mind?'

Conor shook his head and pushed himself off the sofa. 'Let's get this over with,' he said.

Together they only needed about twenty minutes to get the space looking decent again. Conor offered to load the dishwasher and joined Niamh in the bathroom after. She was brushing her teeth and when she noticed the smile on his face, she spat out her toothpaste.

'Are you happy?' she asked.

Conor cupped her face in his hands and kissed her.

'Uh-huh.'

Niamh wiped the toothpaste from Conor's lips. 'Me too.'

When they got into bed, his conversation with Matt popped into his head again. Was he really happy, now? He thought about it for a while as he felt the rhythm of his breath sync with hers.

Yes. He was. Whatever feelings he had left for Ava would fade over time. It was not as simple as flicking a switch.

'Goodnight, roomie,' Niamh whispered, pulling him from his thoughts.

He kissed her and closed his eyes. 'Night.' Everything would be alright.

Wild Waves
Epilogue - July 6, 2014

Where do you think we'll be five years from now? Do you think we'll still be friends?

Ava's words echoed in his mind as Conor watched the minutes tick by. It was almost nine p.m., almost exactly five years after they'd made their pact. On a different timeline he could've been on the beach in Ballybridge, waiting for Ava. If she had answered his letter, if she had loved him half as much as he loved her, they might've even travelled to Ballybridge together, just for the sake of honouring the pact, even though they knew they would be in each other's lives in another five years, and another and another.

But she hadn't. He hadn't heard from her since the day he'd left her crying on the kitchen floor of her apartment, nearly four years earlier.

And now, he was standing in a half-empty flat. Everything Niamh owned was gone and most of his own things were packed up and ready to be moved.

A few weeks earlier, Niamh had been offered a job as senior commissioning editor in London and broken things off with Conor.

'I don't think you love me,' she had said. 'Not with your whole heart, anyway.'

Conor hadn't fought her on it. She was right. He didn't love her the way he was supposed to, but it made no sense to him as to why. *It's not you, it's me,* seemed to be the one horrible explanation there was, and so instead of saying it out loud, he had simply let her go.

But renting a flat in Dublin on his own was impossible. He'd thought of finding a flatmate, but at thirty, his will to share a space with a stranger was basically non-existent. And if he was completely honest, Dublin wasn't the place he wanted to spend his days anyway. He needed some time to think, process, maybe just write, and there was only one place he wanted to do that.

And so, the following day, Matt was helping him drive everything back to Ballybridge, where he would stay on the farm for a while, until he figured out what to do next. His life had come full circle. He was moving back home, to live with his dad, with no real future prospects. But there was a crucial difference. This time he longed to be back home, near the ocean. Not out of fear, but because his soul needed it.

The moment the digits on the clock changed to 21.00, Conor closed his eyes.

He pictured the beach, the ocean, Ava. Her long plait draped over her shoulder, her brown eyes turned to gold by the setting sun, her deep voice as she sang along to her favourite Arctic Monkeys song.

And even now, after all the time that had passed, and everything that had happened, Conor was still holding on to his heart.

20

Olivia is queuing at the airport Pret in desperate need of coffee. She hasn't slept a wink. After recovering from the shock of the missing letter, she finished the book and spent the rest of the night trying to figure out the consequences. She understands now why Graham wanted her to read it. And she understands why he thinks it could make a difference for their future, even though it's hard to admit. Learning that Eamonn had wanted to be with her all along changes everything. It changes how she looks at Graham, how she looks at Eamonn, and even how she looks at herself. Overnight, everything she thought she knew has evaporated. Eamonn has gone from the one who broke her heart to the one that got away, which is an entirely different category of heartache. And knowing he might not actually have got away has triggered the existential crisis that brought her to the airport four days before her flight to Canada.

When she orders her drink, she wonders if the barista notices her red, puffy eyes. It's impossible not to, but then again, airport baristas probably see a lot of teary faces and make nothing of it. She moves through to the far end of the counter to wait for her order.

'Olivia?' A young woman with bright green eyes waves and when Olivia recognises her, she makes her way over. 'Maggie, hi.'

'It's so good to see you.' Maggie wraps her arms around Olivia and pulls her into a hug.

'And you.' Even though she is happy to see Maggie, she still forces a bright smile, hoping to convey her puffy face is no reason for concern. 'It's been so long. What have you been up to?'

'I've just finished my first solo exhibition.' Maggie is nearly bouncing off her feet with pride when she delivers the news and, through her own muddled feelings about everything, Olivia can't help but feel the joy anyway. 'Oh my God, Maggie, that's amazing! How did it go?'

Just that moment, Olivia's drink is called out and Maggie is up next to order. With only one table available, Olivia is quick to claim it, pulling back a chair while she waits to continue their chat. Even though she was in no mood to talk to anyone today, it's surprisingly wonderful running into her former mentee and learning she's doing so well. She'd won a competition that Amira and Olivia had organised for working-class artists about a year ago. Her black-and-white paintings of women carrying groceries had been stunning.

With a large caramel macchiato, Maggie joins her and fills Olivia in on what happened after the mentoring programme – from her work being exhibited by famous London galleries to one of the paintings even making it to New York.

'I am so happy for you,' Olivia says, meaning it with every fibre of her being.

'Thanks, Olivia. This wouldn't have happened without you, you know?'

Olivia waves the compliment away, but Maggie's sincere eyes home in on her. 'I mean it. You gave me the confidence to show my work to people, to try new things. Not to mention the materials I would've otherwise never had access to. It's an important thing you're doing, there at the centre.'

The combination of physical and mental fatigue and Maggie's words brings tears to Olivia's eyes. She might be questioning a lot of things, but the exhilaration at having been a part of Maggie's journey rushes through her veins, making her emotional torment momentarily dissipate.

Maggie's flight to Istanbul is called and they part ways, leaving Olivia to find an empty chair by the window where she watches the London skies, her legs itching with impatience. Her middle-of-the-night flight search had been lucky. She'd found a last-minute to Shannon that wasn't too expensive, even though she would've paid any amount. This is something she has to do in person and something that can't wait. They've waited long enough.

Her phone rings just as the flight attendant calls over the intercom for some late passengers to Istanbul. The name on the screen is one she'd hoped not to have to deal with just yet. She's been expecting the call, and she's been trying to figure out how she feels about her best friend now that it's become clear she's the reason for all the heartache of the past fifteen years, but the overwhelm of everything coming together all at once has paralysed her. For a moment she debates not answering the call, but the desire to find out her friend's motives is too strong. 'Hello?'

'Hi Livvie.' The hesitance in Erin's voice tells her all she needs to know.

Before she can answer, the flight attendant's voice booms over the speakers again and Olivia presses a finger to her ear.

'Are you at the airport?' Erin asks.

Olivia doesn't owe Erin an explanation, not after what she's put her through, and so she doesn't answer. 'Why are you calling, Erin?'

'I'm guessing you've finished the book, then?'

She's never heard Erin speak so timidly. It's unsettling and hard not to feel sorry for her. But still, Olivia remains silent, and when Erin figures out she's not going to answer that question either, she continues. 'I'm sorry, Livvie. I should've told you.'

A surprising choice of words. 'You're sorry for not telling me?'

'I am. I'm sorry.'

'That's it? That's why you're calling?'

'Uhm—'

'What about getting rid of the letter, Erin? Don't you think that's the part you should be sorry for most of all?' Anger flushes Olivia's cheeks and makes it impossible to stay seated.

'Olivia…'

She paces up and down the row of empty seats, tears burning behind her eyes. 'You took him away from me.' Olivia's voice breaks on the last word.

'I'm not sorry for that, Olivia. He was in a relationship, and you had just quit that god-awful job and were finally creating a life you loved. I'd seen you ruin your own lives and break each other's hearts one too many times, and I was not gonna let that happen again, like.'

Outside a plane speeds up and lifts into the sky, as tears roll down Olivia's cheeks.

'You had no right making that decision for us. We were adults, we were perfectly capable of handling it.'

'So you're not on your way to Ireland, then? What is it, five days until you leave for Canada? Or are you not doing that anymore?'

Olivia sighs. There's a part of her that knows Erin is right, but still the interference aggravates her. She's about to bite back when she notices a young family sitting in the corner by the window, their little boy looking up at her. Olivia feels caught. She releases the tension from her clenched teeth and smiles at him before turning away. 'This is a completely different situation.'

'Is it?'

'Even if it isn't, Erin, none of this is for you to decide. It never was.'

They're both silent for a moment. More and more people settle around Olivia, so she grabs her handbag and goes on the hunt for a quieter location.

'Does he know yet?' Olivia asks as she makes her way to the far end of the boarding hall, where a couple of gates are closed and only a few travellers occupy seats.

'I don't know. We haven't spoken much lately.'

At the other end of the line, Olivia picks up faint sounds of Miles' cries and Ben's soothing voice.

'How come you never told him? You must've realised we'd find out once his book was published.'

'I tried to dissuade him from publishing. We had a big row over it, but I still couldn't tell him why. He would've hated me and I couldn't stand the thought of that.' Erin's voice breaks into a sob and simultaneously, Olivia's tears become unstoppable. She finds an empty corner and settles on the carpeted floor, wiping at her wet cheeks with the back of her hand, her limbs heavy with grief.

'I have to see him, Erin,' she says. 'There's no way around it.'

Erin sniffs her nose. 'I know.'

They fall silent again, both breathing heavily through their tears.

'Do you hate me?' Erin asks then, barely audible.

More tears fall from Olivia's eyes. She doesn't know how she feels about her friend at the moment. This is not something that can be fixed in a two-minute phone call. But she doesn't hate her. Erin means the world to her. She couldn't if she wanted to. 'I don't. But let's talk about this more when I get back, yeah?'

'I'm sorry, Livvie. I only ever wanted for you to be happy.'
'I know.'

They hang up, but the conversation lingers in Olivia's heart, heavy and sad. It might be a while before they find a way forwards again.

'Ladies and gentlemen, we are about to board flight FR3897 to Shannon from gate 12. Please proceed to the gate.'

Olivia wipes her eyes and nose with an old tissue she finds in the side pocket of her handbag, and makes her way to the gate. To Ireland. To Eamonn.

21

Catherine Farrelly
19.06.1958 - 16.10.2004

Wild like the waves, soft as the sea
In the air around us
Forever you'll be

Eamonn sits on the bench by his mother's grave at the cliff's edge, looking out onto the ocean below. It's a little separate from all the other graves, the oak tree they planted the day of her burial having grown so much it now offers shelter from the too-bright sun. It took him years to find the courage to come here. It's one thing knowing your mam is gone, but staring at a stone with her name engraved on it forces you to come to terms with the fact she's never going to come back into your life.

The concept was so absurd, Eamonn was overcome with grief the first times he tried, tears coming so fast it became impossible to breathe. In those first months after her death, he had maybe visited three times and each time it had drained him completely. The final time, he'd left before he'd even made it to the far corner of the graveyard. He had turned around but instead of going home, descended to the beach and waded into the ocean, where his tears had blended with the saltwater until they became indistinguishable. It was that day he found solace in the sea, learned it could help carry some of his sorrows, and he's been turning to the ocean ever since.

Twenty years have passed since his mam died. Half his life has gone by without her in it. Time has certainly not healed his wounds, but it's made it easier to come here. He visits a few times a week now, depending on the weather. Sometimes he only waters the flowers, sometimes he sits and reads to her, sometimes he just sits.

Today, he tells her about Olivia. He tells her how, last night, he figured out a painful truth. After his chat with Ruby, he entertained the idea of Olivia never having received his letter. Sure, the postal services weren't the most trustworthy, neither in Ireland nor in the UK, but if it had been a case of getting lost in the mail, Erin would've told him when she read his book. And that's when he saw it. Erin.

Initially, he'd refused to believe she could've got rid of his letter. She's his best friend, has been since they were kids. She rooted for him when Olivia first came to town. How could she be the one to have prevented them from being together? But the more he thought about it, the more the signs pointed in her direction. That's when anger had taken over, rage at the thought he'd lost so many years at the hand of his best friend, making him reach for his phone, ready to shout at her for the first time in his life. But right before he hit the call button, he wondered if it could have been an accident – perhaps she'd meant to give the letter to Olivia but a strong wind had snagged it out of her hands. Perhaps...

But then why hadn't she told him already?

Once again, Eamonn's heart cracked at the thought that his whole adult life could've looked entirely different. Olivia could've called him when she'd got the letter, they could've made it work, he could've loved her the way he was always meant to, with his whole being, his entire soul.

Shoulda, woulda, coulda...

There's something about hearing himself saying the words out loud in this deserted graveyard that is giving him pause for thought. Is all of it Erin's fault? Or was the simple act of sending a letter a mistake in and of itself? If he'd wanted to know Olivia's answer, he could've called her. He could've gone to London and asked her in person. He could have told her he loved her. But he never did.

He's always been afraid of loving Olivia, of losing her. It's something he was certain he wouldn't be able to handle. And yes, losing his mother was the worst thing that ever happened to him, but loving her... loving her was the absolute best.

He sees it now, that one can't happen without the other. That you have to be willing to grieve if you want to be able to experience that soul-shaking kind of love.

And he does. So much.

He can blame everything on Erin, but in all those years he could have contacted Olivia and asked her why she never got back to him. His life has always been in his own hands. It's about time he takes hold of the reins again. There are a few days left before she leaves for Canada. And one day is all he needs. He places his hand on the tombstone and utters the words he hasn't spoken in over two decades, finally ready to let them out again. 'I love you, Mam.'

22

The moment Eamonn gets home, he opens his laptop and finds the first flight to London. There's one departing from Shannon Airport at seven p.m. Some quick maths tells him he still has time to go for a swim and then drop Elvis off at his dad's. There's an anxious energy to him that he wants to try and shed before he gets in the car. He puts on his swim trunks, grabs a towel just in case, and follows Elvis into the ocean. Usually, the cold is shocking enough to distract him from whatever it is he's dealing with, but today the water is too warm. He'll have to rely on exhaustion to ease his nerves, and so he picks up speed. After some time, Elvis leaves him to it and returns to the beach, where he lies down but keeps an eye on Eamonn. The longer he swims, the heavier Eamonn's arms become, until finally he's confident he won't crash his car anymore on the way to the airport from sheer anxiousness. When he turns to swim back to shore, he notices Elvis is not alone anymore. There's someone sitting on Eamonn's towel and for the second time in less than a week, he's certain it's her, even though it's entirely impossible. Memories from a lifetime ago flash before his eyes. Olivia and Charlie on a quilt in nearly the exact same spot. If only he could start over from that moment.

Slowly, he makes his way towards her, wondering why she's here, why she didn't just call him if she had something to say. Knowing full well he was going to do the exact same thing.

'If it isn't Mr Kaczynski himself,' she says as he makes his way towards her. Elvis is by her feet but doesn't jump up to get attention from Eamonn, like he usually would. Even the dog is powerless around her.

'Hiya, Bruce.' He stops right in front of her and wipes at the drops of ocean water on his brow. The urge to bend over and kiss her is nearly overwhelming. Thankfully, she pulls the towel from under her and hands it over to him, giving him something to do.

'No sharks today?'

The corner of his mouth lifts involuntarily. 'Just the one on the beach.' He wraps the warm towel around his shoulders and settles down beside her.

Why is she here?

'I assume this gorgeous guy is yours?' Her eyes are on Elvis' head in her lap as she scratches him behind the ears.

'Yeah, this is Elvis.'

'Elvis?'

The dog wags his tail in excitement at the sound of his name.

'Before he got fat.'

'You're not supposed to say that anymore.'

'Before he struggled to maintain a balanced diet, then.'

Olivia laughs that deep belly laugh of hers, raising the hairs on his arms.

Why is she here?

They fall silent. Eamonn thinks of the plane ticket he just booked, the urgency with which he booked it. No more procrastinating – he has to ask her why she's here. Taking a deep breath, he turns to face her.

'Why are you h—?'

23

'I read your b—' Olivia says at the exact same time he asks her why she's here.

They both laugh an uncomfortable laugh.

'Did you like it?' Eamonn asks, his brow furrowed in anticipation of her review.

Grabbing a handful of sand and facing away from him, she shakes her head. 'No.'

'Yeah, okay,' he says. 'And you came all the way out here to tell me that in person?'

'A StoryGraph review seemed inappropriate.' She knows joking isn't going to make this conversation easier, but she can't seem to stop herself.

'Okay, I'll take the live review then.'

She takes a breath, preparing for honesty. 'Well, for one, the main characters in this book are ridiculous,' she starts. 'If they'd only been open with each other from the beginning, they could've had a wonderful life together. I mean, this Ava girl, what was she thinking, living two lives and not telling Conor about James? Or James about Conor. I don't like her a single bit.'

'She never meant to hurt anyone,' Eamonn says. 'She was just a little lost.' He looks her in the eye and nods, as though forgiving her for their false start. But Olivia shakes her head softly, not accepting it. 'She's a fool.'

A shrug from Eamonn. 'So is Conor.'

'I won't argue with that. Please explain to me why on earth someone would write a bloody letter, in this day and age, and then never follow up when there's no answer? What kind of a twat does that? I've been trying to figure it out for hours, but I can't, for the life of me, understand. What the hell, Eamonn?' Exasperated, she throws her arms up.

Eamonn smiles a sad smile. 'I just assumed you were upset because of what happened when I came to visit you in London, because that would've been fair, you know. I fucked up then. So when I never heard back, I figured you wanted me to stay out of your life and I understood.'

It physically hurts to hear him say these words. Her shoulders ache with tension and her chest feels tight. 'Even if that were the case, I would still have told you. I don't understand how you think I could've just stopped talking to you.'

'Yeah, well, if I could go back, I'd opt for registered post.'

Frustration builds. She pushes herself up and takes a few steps away from him, throwing her arms in the air and shouting at the ocean. 'Or, I don't know, a phone call? E-mail? Who sends a bloody letter? You're an idiot!' Her sudden movement has alerted Elvis, making him jump up too and follow closely. She wades into the water, sandals and all, kicking at the white foam. Elvis runs circles around her, thinking it's a game, but it's definitely not. It's years of cropped up frustration finally finding a release. When, after some passionate kicking, she turns around again, Eamonn is behind her, taking hold of her hand. 'I know,' he says.

The sight of him standing there, half-naked and looking so forlorn, makes all the anger seep from her body directly into the ocean water.

'I should've told you,' he continues. They're only a few inches apart, her hand still in his. He looks her straight in the eye and takes a breath. 'Instead of writing you a letter, I should've told you I loved you.'

And just like that, Olivia's heart cracks and tears spill from her eyes. She's been longing to hear those words for such a long time that the actual sound of them takes away her breath.

He goes on. 'I'm sorry, Bruce. I was afraid to love you as much as I did. It hurt, overwhelmingly so. Saying it out loud would've made it even more painful. Because in my mind, loving you meant eventually losing you and I knew I wouldn't survive that.' He releases her hand and wipes at the tears on her cheeks before pulling her close so that their foreheads touch.

In between sobs, Olivia whispers: 'I was here. On the day of our pact.'

He closes his eyes but still, his pain is obvious.

'I sat here until it got dark and Anna came looking for me.'

'I'm so sorry.' The pressure of his forehead against hers intensifies as he curls his fingers at the back of her neck.

Olivia shakes her head. 'That's not what I'm trying to say. It's not your fault. I just... I want you to know I loved you too.' She swallows, but the lump in her throat remains. 'I would never have cut you out of my life without a word.'

Before her, Eamonn squeezes his eyes tight, and tears fall from his dark eyelashes. For a long time neither of them speaks – they just stand there, their feet in the water, the dog by their side confused as to what's happening. She takes it all in. He loved her, and she loved him. It's always been as simple as that. They just never saw it before. But love *is* simple, when you think of it. It requires very little effort. Those who say you have to work at it are wrong. Love, in all its forms, is there. Always. No matter what. It's there when you forget about it. It's there when you pretend it's not. It's there when you're angry, or hurt, or don't believe in its existence. The only thing love requires of us is that we accept it. That we see ourselves for who we are, and accept the things that make us *us*.

Yes, she loves Eamonn. Still. He will always be the one who reminded her of who she was, the one who fought her on her stuck thinking patterns, and refused to let her go down a path that wasn't meant for her. Without him, she might never have remembered her love of photography – she might never have realised what she was capable of, and how life could be a joyous thing.

He opens his eyes and gives her a sorrowful smile. 'You're going to Canada, aren't you?'

Olivia nods and so does he. They both know it's the right decision. She figured it out on the plane. Her run-in with Maggie had opened her eyes. The thought of helping even more young girls exhilarated her, even through all the distress. And that was exactly the life that was right for her. Would there be times where she'd wonder what her life would be like as a mum? Maybe. Possibly. But knowing she was living a full life, doing what she loved, taking risks to find out what else was out there, would balance that out. There are so many ways of living a life, and there's no one right path – it's just a matter of finding the one that's right for you.

On the flight over, Olivia had composed an email to Graham, to explain to him where she was headed. She wants to be completely honest with him. Going to see Eamonn was something she needed to do, but telling Graham was equally important. She wants to start her life with him and even though, on some level, she's always known that, she needed to say goodbye to Eamonn first.

Her mouth is dry when she asks, 'What about you?'

Eamonn shrugs, looks around. 'I think I like it here.'

They both nod again, this time knowing it's the right decision for him. His hand reaches for hers again, fingers lacing. 'When do you fly back?'

'Tonight.'

With a cock of his head towards his house, he asks her if she wants to see it, and when she says yes, they make their way inside, still holding hands.

The house is as Olivia had imagined it. So achingly Eamonn, it makes her cry again. He pulls her in for a hug and when she tells him it's fine, he runs up the stairs to change his clothes.

On the wall in the living room, there's a framed picture of the four of them on their road trip, taken by a tourist. Erin, Ben, Olivia and Eamonn. All baby-faced, freckled, and wild, having the time of their lives. God, how she loves them all.

They have lunch in the pub and then head to the grocery shop for a Calippo. Orange for Eamonn, cola for her. They take them back to the stretch of beach behind his house, Eamonn taking hers into his palms to loosen the popsicle and then handing it back when there's enough movement to work with. She smiles and then he does the same with his own.

The minutes tick by and they are both silent, tipping the melted juice into their mouths as they finish their dessert. Olivia's hands are sticky, but the ocean has retreated too far for a quick rinse. It doesn't matter anyway. In a few minutes she has to leave.

'Do you know what day it is today?' Eamonn asks.
'Saturday.'
'The 6th of July.'
Olivia smiles. 'What are the odds.'
She leans into him, her head on his shoulder. 'Do you think we'll still be friends five years from now?'
Eamonn wraps his arm around her and kisses her temple. 'I'm always going to love you,' he says.
'No matter what?'
'No matter what.'

Acknowledgements

First of all, I want to thank my buoys: Sophie Hamilton and Elaine Hastings. I honestly don't know where I'd be without you. You are the best writing friends a girl could wish for and without you I would've given up on this book ages ago. You rock!

Secondly, I want to thank my early readers: Lynn, Fien, Joke VA, Maya, Marnie, Kate, Kelly: thank you for not making fun of me.

A massive thanks to my ARC readers, you are the best!

My family: thanks for housing me, for always picking me up from airports and putting up with my highly impulsive lifestyle. I am forever in your debt.

A special thanks to Haroen, Zina, Inès & Farah. You are always the lights in my life. I love you.

To my friend Joke Verschueren, I want to say a special thanks. Without you, the past year would have sucked. I'm lucky to have you in my life.

My wonderful editor, Daisy Watts, you are a star. You lifted this novel to the next level at record time.

Elaine and Adrian Hastings, thanks for helping with my cover design.

My eternal love to the cities of London & Dublin & all the friends & family I made there. You changed my life for the better.

And finally, thank you to my readers. I hope Eamonn and Olivia mean as much to you, as they do to me. And if there's anything I'd like you to take away from this, it's to follow your heart and live a life that's true to you.

Also, thank you Andrew Garfield and Emma Stone. IYKYK

About the author

Malika is a Belgian-Algerian author with a deep love of the sea. Unfortunately, she lives nowhere near the coast so she uses her writing as a coping mechanism. Other than her obsession with the ocean, she can't stop talking about musical theatre, astrology, Emma Stone and Andrew Garfield.

Like the characters in her first novel, *Hold on to Your Heart*, Malika has struggled with societal expectations and loss, but if it has taught her anything, it's that you should always stay true to yourself and follow your dreams.

Malika has lived in Dublin and London and always has a bag at the ready in case they rethink Brexit.

Sign up to the newsletter to be the first to know about new releases: www.malikanekhla.com

If you liked this book, please leave a review on the platform of your choice. Thank you!

Printed in Dunstable, United Kingdom